W

...for me?

by
Rosie B. Davies

First published in March 2015
Second Edition: May 2015

For Neil and Freddie who never stop believing in my magic.

Acknowledgements:

To Naomi for pushing me out of my comfort zone and towards my dreams. To Maggie, Lesley and Ali for their support and for wanting it just as much as I do! Thanks to my rock, my anchor, my immovable snoring monster. And finally to my little gift from the angels – thank-you, Baggins.

"You have your way. I have my way. As for the right way, the correct way and the only way, it does not exist."

Friedrich Nietzsche

Preface

Have you ever felt as though you were living the wrong life? That somewhere in the world there was a place for you but you were not in it? Have you ever waited day after day, year after year for that moment when everything would slot into place and you would finally *be*, be the person you were always meant to be? Could you imagine that life, the feeling that the life would bring you, but have absolutely no idea how to achieve it? Well you are not alone. Elizabeth felt exactly the same way. But Elizabeth didn't know she felt that way, could not put the feelings into words, the only thing she knew was she was angry and she needed someone to blame.

Chapter One

Elizabeth limped along the alleyway at the back of the tube station, aware she was being followed. She saw the men the moment she stepped out of the train and they had clearly noticed her. It was night time and the lights of the tube station faded behind her. Elizabeth knew she should be afraid. The five minute walk through the dark lane usually made her nervous, but today she didn't feel like giving in to that fear. Today she was too angry to cower like a victim. On the way home she sat and seethed about her rotten day. It had been a disastrous day at the office and her foul mood was exacerbated by a catalogue of calamities she had faced since moving to London.

"What was I thinking," she muttered under her breath.

Elizabeth had lived in London for a little under two years. She moved with naïve ideas of opportunities and excitement given to her by her sister who had made the move from their small, sleepy town five years before. But the way was not paved with gold, there were not opportunities around every corner and Elizabeth's behaviour was becoming more self-destructive as the months ticked by. Life was not quite as she expected it to be and today's office debacle was just more fuel for her self-loathing fire.

"Hey! You!" The voice came from behind her. The group of youths were trying to intimidate her. Trying to make her fear for her safety. She stopped dead in her tracks. She could see the streetlights beyond the alleyway. She was close to civilisation. Close enough that if she broke into a run she would be at the street before the men could reach her. A rumble of thunder grumbled through the night sky. It was a starless summer evening and there was electricity in the atmosphere.

Elizabeth could not tell if the sparks in the air were the threat of an impending thunderstorm or the sizzle of her abject anger. Instead of running away she slowly turned to face her pursuers.

"What?" She said and smiled to see the look of surprise on their faces. *They didn't expect that*, she thought. She wanted to see their reaction, wanted them to know she was not afraid. A deep, dark calmness had settled on her. It was a feeling she had never known. She always assumed rage would be uncontrollable but there was something about this new emotion that made her feel more powerful than ever.

She spent day after day, month after month getting people's coffees, taking their phone calls, doing almost everything a willing secretary should do. Her intelligence was belittled, her abilities were sneered at and her talents were wasted. All these little incidents had come to a head today when she stayed behind at work to go to a disability access meeting at the firm of architects she worked for. This was an issue that was close to her heart and she was keen to be involved in the debate. As everyone knocked off for the day Elizabeth was left alone with her boss. "At least I don't have to make any more coffees," she said expecting to get a laugh. Her boss looked at her incredulously, "who else do you expect to get them?" Elizabeth stared in disbelief as her boss walked away.

She had been cajoled and coerced into staying, without pay, by her boss who knew she was interested in disability issues. She felt completely betrayed but was powerless to do anything about it. For the rest of the evening she served coffees, teas and nibbles and was shouted at by another colleague when he pushed his chair backwards just as Elizabeth was walking behind him. The coffee went all over the floor and the chair scraped some skin off her leg.

"Apparently it was my job to let him know where I was in the room, not his job to check if anyone was behind him! I'm such an idiot!"

"What did you call me?" The voice brought Elizabeth back to the moment and she shook away the memory. She watched as the men in the alleyway took up position. They had been huddled together but now they peeled off and started to move towards her. There were three of them. They were all dressed in dark clothes. One wore a baseball cap and the others wore hoods making it impossible for her to distinguish their faces. Elizabeth allowed them to circle her, barely aware of what was happening. She turned her face skywards to feel the breath of tempestuous air and took comfort in her cold, calm rage. She was vaguely aware that the men were jeering at her but their insults seemed so far away.

Any moment, she thought, *any moment I'll realise I'm in danger and I'll be afraid.* But the fear didn't come and the men's taunts were not getting the reaction they were hoping for. Clearly frustrated by Elizabeth's apathy they began to shout louder. Suddenly their aggression turned physical and they started to prod and poke her. Their physical intimidation gathered momentum as they shoved her towards each other. She barely knew what was happening, she felt strangely detached from her physical self being buffeted from one man to the next, when all of a sudden one of them shouted, "you stupid bitch!"

Elizabeth drew in a sharp, hate-filled breath. At that moment, two years of being made to feel inferior exploded in her mind. She watched as the men circling her became symbols of her oppression. Her boss's face swam into view; then the man who had scraped her shin with his chair; the third was a colleague who made constant patronising references to her lack of intelligence. Something inside Elizabeth snapped.

Just as a thunder clap ripped through the night sky and startled the men, Elizabeth's anger reached its apex and suddenly she felt calmer and more in control than ever. A vengeful clarity settled over her and Elizabeth's body began to shake as an unknown energy took hold of her. All at once a searing bolt of electricity burst from Elizabeth like a supernova.

As the power sizzled through her veins Elizabeth instinctively turned her head towards the sky and stretched out her arms. Agonising light poured from her body. She was like a star; bright, powerful and burning. The men, who were momentarily distracted by the storm, had no chance against Elizabeth's power. They screamed in horror and pain and were immediately silenced.

The surge of power was over in an instant, the sky went black and so did the alleyway. Elizabeth closed her eyes. All she could hear was the sound of her own breath. It was laboured and heavy. Elizabeth began to feel like her old, nervy self again. Fear, insecurity and doubt crept back into her mind. The calmness of her wrathful state had gone. She was exhausted from the explosion. She had no idea what had happened or how. A clap of thunder startled Elizabeth and she opened her eyes. There was no sign of the three men in the dark alleyway. Elizabeth squinted trying to catch sight of them in the gloom when suddenly another lightning bolt flashed through the sky illuminating the scene.

Elizabeth stared in horror. She saw a quick flash of a sickening image scorched into the wall when the sky blackened once more and the alleyway was plunged into darkness. Elizabeth's stomach churned. She forced her hand to her mouth but couldn't stop herself from throwing up. Even in the darkness she could see the horrific image in her mind's eye, the smell of it filled her nostrils. She knew she was surrounded by a nightmare. She let out a cry and scrambled around in the dark looking for her bag. That was when the rain came. Quickly and heavily the downpour fell from the sky. Elizabeth could feel it washing away the vomit and the blood.

Finally she found her bag, picked it up and started to run. She did not dare look back. All she could think about was getting away, leaving the devastation behind her. She reached the end of the alleyway, turned onto the street and ran towards her flat.

***

Elizabeth fumbled for her keys at the bottom of her bag. Her hands were shaking as she let herself into the maisonette she shared with her sister and her brother-in-law. She was safe for now, but she was definitely not home. She had moved in with an old friend when she moved to London, but it had not worked out. After a few months of a lot of laughs, too much alcohol and far too many take-aways, James, the friend in question, resumed a relationship with a neurotic ex-girlfriend. Elizabeth watched as the woman systematically poisoned his friends against him and then turned her attention to Elizabeth. James was keen to give the relationship another go and Elizabeth did not want to make the situation worse for him. So she left that house and moved in with her sister. It was only supposed to be for a few weeks but another flat share had fallen through. Four months later she was still at her sister's house and tempers were beginning to fray.

Elizabeth had a strained relationship with her sister at the best of times but they always managed a show of civility towards one another. In the months that had passed the civility had long gone and they had settled on a discourteous silence. Elizabeth was usually home before her sister and brother-in-law so she would eat, wash up and spend the rest of the evening alone in her room.

But tonight was different. Slamming the door shut behind her and taking deep, shaky breaths Elizabeth saw the mass of jackets on the coat rack and let out a whimper. They were home.

"Why, God, why?" Elizabeth whispered. "Why do they have to be in – tonight!"

But she wasn't quiet enough.

"Is that you Elizabeth?" The call came from the front room, it was Jessie.

Sighing Elizabeth knew she only had a short walk through the hallway to compose herself before she met her sister's barrage of complaints. Whatever Jessie found to berate Elizabeth about, whether it was the lack of milk in the fridge, the mess in the flat or the broken lines of communication, the underlying problem was always unspoken. Jessie purely and simply wanted Elizabeth out. Elizabeth knew it and desperately tried to find another flat share but nothing had come up. Like all the other situations in her life Elizabeth felt like a helpless victim riding the tumbling waters of a violent sea. She felt as though nothing was under her control, that destiny had chosen a miserable journey for her and she had no way of changing course.

"What are you doing?" Jessie called again. Elizabeth didn't know how long she had been standing at the door, contemplating her unfortunate life, but it was clearly long enough to annoy Jessie. She walked slowly into the room.

The maisonette was open plan downstairs. In the small living area there was another door which led to the bedrooms. Even if Elizabeth had just wanted to head straight to her room she couldn't have. She had no choice but to walk through the minefield of her sister's inquisition before she could find sanctuary.

"Hello," she said softly from the doorway.

"Pete wants to know how the flat hunting's going," Jessie said.

Poor old Pete, thought Elizabeth, whenever Jessie has something difficult to say she always used Pete as a shield. Elizabeth looked at

Pete who was sat quietly, as always, with his head in a broadsheet and a coffee in his hand. He looked up at Jessie, clearly confused.

"Where did that come from?" he asked.

"Don't pretend you haven't been thinking it," Jessie said.

"That's not what you said though is it Jess," Pete replied, "you said it like that's what I've been going on about. Anyway I'm sure Elizabeth has been thinking it too. This isn't an ideal situation we all know that." Pete looked at Elizabeth before looking pointedly at Jessie. Pete was a good man and absolutely adored Jessie, but he was not so blinded by love that he couldn't see Jessie's faults. He knew she was giving Elizabeth a hard time and did his best to stay neutral, which didn't always help Elizabeth's cause.

"Why are you always taking her side?" Jessie rounded on Pete. "You know as well as I do that she's a nightmare to live with."

Here come the insults, Elizabeth thought.

"She's selfish and unsociable. She's like a teenager skulking up there in her bedroom all night!"

"Believe it or not Jessie, I'm trying to keep out of your way." Elizabeth said.

"Oh don't do me any favours........." Jessie continued this way for some time. Elizabeth could hear the shouting even though she couldn't make out the words. She found it difficult to think about anything other than the alleyway. As Jessie carried on scolding her, Elizabeth played out the horrific scene in her head, right up to the stomach-churning end. Elizabeth heaved.

"Shut up a minute Jessie," Pete said, walking towards Elizabeth with his arms out. "Are you alright Elizabeth? You're as white as a sheet, has anything happened?"

"It's nothing, I'm just....." but Elizabeth couldn't finish. Her head began to swim and she no longer had the strength to stay upright. Pete caught her just before she fell and lowered her gently to the floor.

Elizabeth was only vaguely aware that Jessie and Pete were trying to carry her upstairs. She felt dazed and overwhelmed and welcomed their concern. Jessie became almost hysterical, "Oh my God, what's happened! Should we call an ambulance? Pete. Pete! Should we call an ambulance?"

"Do you need to go to the hospital," Pete said softly to Elizabeth.

"No," Elizabeth managed, "just want to sleep." They laid her on her bed and Elizabeth could hear Pete's voice soothing her and asking her questions but she didn't reply.

"Come on Jessie love," Pete said "we can talk to Lizzie in the morning".

"She hates being called that," Jessie said through her sobs as Pete led her away. Elizabeth knew that she would have some questions to answer in the morning with terrible revelations for her already unhinged sister. But for now all she wanted to do was sleep, to slip out of consciousness and not think or feel anymore.

But the rest she was longing for did not come. Disturbing visions plagued her restless sleep that night and Elizabeth did not know where reality stopped and dreams began. The image from the alleyway haunted her. She could not bear to remember but found it impossible to forget. During one particularly vivid dream Elizabeth relived the whole episode as though watching a film. She watched as the angry Elizabeth stepped from the tube onto the platform; saw the air around her fizzle with years of pent up aggression; watched helplessly as she walked down the stairs at the tube station and stepped into the alleyway. Elizabeth could feel her unconscious body asleep in her sister's flat, desperately trying to wake up before having to watch that horrific moment again. She flailed in bed, trying to regain consciousness. Desperate not to witness the end of the encounter and miraculously she awoke.

She sat up in bed, breathing deeply and sweating. The relief she felt at not having to witness the destruction was short lived. Elizabeth quickly remembered that the dream was not a nightmare; it was a reality, a memory.

"How could I do that," she said quietly, "how could I take another person's life?"

Elizabeth sobbed uncontrollably into her pillow.

Chapter Two

Tap, tap, tap. Elizabeth woke with a start to hear the tentative knock on the door. It was morning.

"I've phoned work for you Elizabeth, I don't think you should go in today." Jessie called through the closed door.

"Thanks," Elizabeth said groggily.

"I've told them you've got a stomach bug OK?"

"Ok."

"But if you don't start getting any better you should probably think about going to the doctors at the very least. Pete says I'm probably overreacting a bit about the hospital."

"I'm OK, just need to sleep," Elizabeth called, shocked to hear genuine concern in her sister's voice.

"I'm off to work now, I'll see you later." There was a pause. Elizabeth knew Jessie was still there. "You should probably phone Mum. She's worried. Bye."

Elizabeth groaned and flopped back down on her pillow. *What am I supposed to say*, Elizabeth thought, "Hi Mum I'm OK but I murdered three men last night!"

"What did you say?" Pete called from the landing.

"Oh nothing! Nothing!"

"I'm off Lizzie, phone if you need anything."

"Thanks Pete but I'm fine. By the way I don't like being called......"

"I know," Pete laughed, "just checking you're still with us!"

Elizabeth heard the door close. Jessie and Pete were on their way to work. *How wonderful it must be for them*, Elizabeth thought, *going about their daily routine in blissful ignorance.* Elizabeth remembered fondly her usual morning routine. Get up, get washed, get on tube, get toast and Marmite from deli on the corner, get to work. She also remembered how much she hated it, but today she would have given anything to have that little bit of normality back.

She grabbed a red fleecy blanket from the bottom of her bed and pulling it around her she wandered downstairs. She was still feeling dizzy but she had to know, had to find out if the world knew about her crime. She switched on her brother-in-law's television and watched as much news as she could find. She was sure she would see the image of devastation from the alleyway emblazoned across the screen as reporters from every channel flocked to tell the story. She imagined the sounds of sirens rushing down the street as police came to investigate the murder. She knew they would find something, even if it was the smallest thing, an item from her bag or a footprint that would lead them to her. She knew that any minute she could be arrested in her home.

She spent hour after hour scanning the television for reports and checking the internet for breaking news but there was nothing.

RING RING. RING RING

The sound of the phone startled her and dragged her away from the telly.

"Hello?"

"Elizabeth it's me, how are you sweetheart? Jessie said you were really ill. She was really worried about you. Why didn't you call? Jessie said you would call in the morning. I've been so worried."

"It's OK Mum, I'm OK." Elizabeth said when her mother paused for breath.

"Jessie said you collapsed?"

"Yeah but....."

"What's going on there?" Gladys continued. Elizabeth took a seat knowing she was in for a one of her mother's kindly lectures. "You girls move all the way to London and I know you're both miserable. I know why Jessie is, but what about you?"

"Jessie's miserable because of me Mum so as soon as I move out we'll both be much happier."

"You've both got your own problems. Maybe if the two of you sat down and talked once in a while you could be a much needed friend for each other, rather than making matters worse all the time."

"Mum we've been through this......."

"What's going on with you Elizabeth?" Gladys said earnestly, "why are you so unhappy? If it hasn't worked out for you there you can always come home. There's no shame in that. There's no shame in admitting it didn't work, at least you tried."

"Please Mum, you just don't know what's going on. Now I need to lie down. I've got a stonking headache and I feel sick. I'll call you when I know something."

"What does that mean – *when you know something…?*"

"Please Mum, I have to go. Bye." Elizabeth put the phone down without waiting for an answer and sat back heavily in the chair. She knew she would have to tell Gladys. She knew that everything would come to light sooner or later. She just wanted to wait. Wait until the police came knocking before she had to reveal her hideous secret.

Elizabeth spent the rest of the day scouring news bulletins but there was nothing. Not one reference to the incident in the alleyway. It was nearly evening and Jessie and Pete would soon be home. Then she would know something. Jessie and Pete had to pass the alleyway, it was the only way home from work.

"Hang on a minute," Elizabeth said picking up the phone, "they walked that way this morning, they would have seen the police then!"

She dialled her sister's work number. No answer. She hung up and tried her mobile. It went straight to her answering machine, no signal. Elizabeth looked at the clock in the kitchen it was almost 6:30. *Surely they would have put two and two together*, she thought. They would have tried to get on the tube, would have been redirected around the alleyway and would have realised Elizabeth must have witnessed something, at the very least, even if they didn't know she was the cause.

Elizabeth paced up and down watching the clock. They were due in at 7pm. The minutes ticked by and as it neared 7pm Elizabeth became more and more agitated. Suddenly she heard a key turn in the lock, "Elizabeth we're back," Jessie called. "Are you OK?"

Elizabeth rushed into the hallway and grabbed her sister by the shoulders, "what did you see? What's happened? Is anyone coming?"

"What's the matter?" Jessie said shocked at Elizabeth's behaviour. She looked towards Pete for support.

"It's OK Elizabeth," Pete said taking Elizabeth's hands from Jessie. "We're OK and we're home now."

"Pete please, did you see anything at the tube station? I have to know if anything is wrong!" Elizabeth shouted. The anticipation she had been feeling all day, the fear, the inevitability of her arrest and her subsequent branding as a murderer was suddenly too much. She broke down in tears and Pete once again stopped her from falling. He led her towards the sofa and sat her down. "I'm going to make a cup of tea Elizabeth, why don't you have a chat with Jess."

Pete walked into the kitchen as Jessie sat next to her sister. "Are you alright Elizabeth?"

"No I'm not. I think I had a dream, a hideous dream, maybe even a hallucination, I don't know." She turned to face Jessie, "I just need you to answer one question please Jessie."

"Alright Elizabeth, I can do that."

"Did anything happen at the tube station?"

"Like what?"

"Like anything at all out of the ordinary. Please Jessie this is really important."

Jessie took her time to think for a moment, "I really can't say I noticed anything unusual anywhere today. What about you Pete?"

"Nothing," Pete called.

"OK Jessie, look at me, this is really, really important. What about the alleyway?"

"What alleyway? You mean the one down there?" Jessie pointed towards the front door.

"Yes, that one."

"Nothing Elizabeth. There was absolutely nothing except the faint smell of piss that's usually there. What on earth's the matter with you?"

Elizabeth gave into another fit of sobs. She told Jessie and Pete in as little detail as possible that she thought she was being followed but the men disappeared. She left out the small matter of an explosive power emanating from her body.

"Maybe Mum's right," Elizabeth said finally, "maybe I should go home."

"I think it would do some good," Jessie said. "Take the rest of the week off and spend some time with Mum and Dad".

16

The next morning Elizabeth phoned work. She told her boss that she was suffering with a stomach bug.

"Oh really," was her boss's sarcastic reaction. "So you're not annoyed because of that meeting?"

"It's nothing like that. I've been violently sick and I'm not going to be back until Monday."

"Fine but when you do come back I want to see you first thing. First thing, do you hear me?"

"Yes that's fine," Elizabeth said and hung up. She sighed.

Her sister had been on at her again to go to the doctors, "there has got to be something wrong if you're seeing things Elizabeth." But Elizabeth wasn't ready to accept that she might be losing her mind.

"Please don't tell Mum," Elizabeth said in response.

"I won't – but maybe *you* should."

"I know. I'll have a talk with her when I see her. I promise."

Elizabeth arrived at Paddington station on Thursday morning and took the 10 o'clock train home. Her mother was waiting for her at the other end and after a perfunctory greeting they took the short journey back to their family home in silence.

As they walked through the front door Elizabeth felt immense relief to be home. Her father greeted her warmly, "hello Little One. How are you feeling?"

"OK," she said and offered no further explanation. Elizabeth could sense that her mother wanted to talk. "Can I just go up to my room and have a sleep? I'm so tired, I just need to get my head down for a bit."

Elizabeth's short nap turned into blissful catatonia. She slept for a whole day and night and the next morning she was finally able to answer her mother's questions.

"I don't really want to talk about what made me ill Mum, 'cos in all honesty I don't know." As happy as she was to be home Elizabeth still couldn't bring herself to tell her mother that either she was going mad or she was capable of murder. "But I do know I'm really unhappy."

Sitting at the dinner table with cups of tea in their hands and biscuits on a plate in front of them Elizabeth and her mother talked for hours. At first Elizabeth moaned and Gladys listened. As always Gladys told

Elizabeth that she had her full support no matter what.

"But I do feel it would be for the best if you moved home love." Gladys said and suddenly a strange look flashed across Gladys' face.

Elizabeth looked away feeling anxious. *Oh God she knows I'm keeping something from her*, Elizabeth thought. She glanced back as soon as she dared and the look on Gladys's face was gone, replaced by her usual motherly affection and concern.

Every now and then Bertie, Elizabeth's Dad, would pop his head around the door and ask if the women wanted anything but he would soon make himself scarce when he saw tears streaming down Elizabeth's face, or the stern *keep away* looks from Gladys. He was aware that his particular parenting skills would be of no use during the girly heart to heart chats. But they came in very handy later when he whipped up one of his famous banana and chocolate milkshakes with cinnamon toast to nibble on.

The weekend passed quickly and first thing on Monday morning, with a final cuddle from her Mum, Elizabeth boarded the train to London. She knew the time had come to face the music at work. Elizabeth arrived back in London early, too early to go to work. The deli she visited regularly was not open so she wandered to a coffee shop that was happily clean but miserably characterless. As usual Elizabeth received an incredulous look from the barista when she asked for a cup of tea. With all the cappuccinos and mochas being ordered Elizabeth felt like a dinosaur ordering only a cup of earl grey tea and an apple and cinnamon muffin.

She looked around at the other punters in the coffee shop and although she was dressed the same as most of the young women there she still felt very out of place. There were men and women in their 20s, talking on their mobile phones, emailing from their laptops and reading books on their Kindles. *Kindles*, she thought, *surely it was cheaper and much more fulfilling to actually buy a book!* This was just another example of how out of place Elizabeth felt in the modern world epitomised by the heart of London's trend setting city.

Sighing, Elizabeth nibbled at the cake in front of her. It was still early but the anticipation was killing her so she left her half drunken cup of tea and barely touched muffin and walked slowly towards the office. She felt as though she was taking the long walk to the hangman's noose.

Not because of the inevitable dressing down from her boss, but because she felt trapped by the job and the life she had chosen. After spending almost a week away from the place she realised she was starting to enjoy the freedom.

She walked into the reception. "Oh my God," the receptionist said unable to disguise her surprise, "Are you actually better?" Elizabeth nodded and remembered that she hadn't eaten properly for days and the weight was dropping off her. Not that she minded, being a voluptuous size 12 was just another way she didn't fit in with the young trendsetters. She had the figure of a woman not a pubescent boy.

"You're really early," the receptionist continued, "nobody's in yet."

"That's OK." Elizabeth smiled, "I knew I would be the first one in, but I thought it might look good for me."

Elizabeth waited for her boss for over an hour. When the woman finally blustered up to the third floor, she looked furtively around for Elizabeth and nodded angrily when she saw her. She held her index finger and shouted, "one minute!" and stormed into her office.

Elizabeth sighed. Being early was not having the desired effect on Lexy. Her boss was clearly flustered. She probably wanted to get herself settled and ready for a fight before Elizabeth's arrival. Elizabeth knew Lexy hated feeling unprepared.

The following 60 seconds were the longest of Elizabeth's life. She watched the second hand tick painfully slowly around the old school clock on the office wall. She felt every *tick-tock* pulse through her body as each moment passed. When the second hand finally completed one cycle Elizabeth took a deep breath and got up. Not for the first time that morning Elizabeth felt as though she was taking a condemned woman's walk of doom. Elizabeth knocked on her boss's door.

"COME!" she barked.

In that instant Elizabeth suddenly felt incredibly sorry for her. Lexy was unbelievably talented and excellent at her job but she really was not a people person. It dawned on Elizabeth that to achieve such an important position in a predominantly male profession Lexy felt as though she had to act like a man. She saw kindness as weakness and expected everyone to be as obsessed with the job as she was. But, Elizabeth wondered, was she truly happy?

"Hello," Elizabeth said quietly as she opened the door. She walked into the cramped office filled with files and papers, and, as always, a dying plant. It was amazing to Elizabeth that this woman, who could juggle so much, was totally incapable of splashing a little water over a decaying flower. Elizabeth first saw the withered flower at her interview, and kicked herself for not noticing the warning sign. Part of her wanted to pick up the poor potted primrose and run but instead she ambled silently through the door awaiting her punishment.

"Oh.....oh!" Lexy exclaimed, shocked to see the change in Elizabeth's appearance. "Well you have been ill! But that doesn't excuse the fact that you left us in a very awkward position. We've had nobody to type our letters, sort the post or answer the phone! I've even had to sort a temp and who's going to pay......."

All of a sudden Elizabeth held up her hand and Lexy fell into a stunned silence.

"I just wanted to tell you," Elizabeth said with uncharacteristic confidence, "that my *illness* has given me a chance to rethink my priorities and as of this moment I'll be leaving this company. Good luck to you and your team for all your future endeavours and I hope there are no hard feelings."

Elizabeth turned to leave then added as an afterthought, "oh by the way, I really hope that *you* find happiness in particular Lexy because it must be miserable being such a hard-faced bitch all the time". With that Elizabeth waved at her dumbfounded boss and walked away from a life and a world that she never really belonged in.

Chapter Three

"My God Elizabeth, you're wired!" Jessie said.

Jessie worked in the City, and Elizabeth had walked the 5 miles across London to her sister's office in a euphoric haze.

"I know, I know!" Elizabeth replied. "You won't believe what I've just done!"

"I'm taking a break Jan," Jessie said to the receptionist, "tell Edgar I'm in the cafeteria if he wants me." Jessie led Elizabeth to the basement of the building. The cafeteria in question was a modern bistro café with a well-known chef made famous for his many TV appearances.

"Look at this," Elizabeth said in awe as she took in the room.

"Well, they can afford it," Jessie said flatly, "they're making a fortune."

Jessie sat in silence as Elizabeth went over the conversation she had with Lexy that morning. "I couldn't believe I had it in me! I just made the decision to leave there and then and I let her have it – with both barrels!"

"Well that's the easy part over," Jessie said. "Now what are you going to do with the rest of your life? There are still bills to be paid Elizabeth, you can't live on thin air."

"I know. I know," Elizabeth said feeling deflated by her sister's practicality. "Don't worry I'm not gonna take the piss out of you and Pete. I think I'll head home for a bit. Take stock and come up with a plan."

"Alright but be careful not to take the piss out of Mum and Dad either."

"Alright. Alright!" Elizabeth said. She was beginning to regret opening up to her sister. Their relationship seemed to change over the last few days but now Jessie was reverting back to her usual superior self.

"Are you gonna nip back to the flat?" Jessie asked.

"No. No I don't think so." Almost a week after the incident Elizabeth had come to the conclusion that stress had induced a hallucination but even in the cold light of day she did not want to venture along that alleyway. Dream or no dream, the memories were just too vivid.

"Point me in the right direction for Paddington then," Elizabeth said as she kissed her sister goodbye.

"You're mad! Why don't you just get on a tube?"

"No." Elizabeth said forcefully and noticed Jessie wince. "I need the fresh air," she added trying to lighten the mood.

Their goodbyes said, Elizabeth was happy to get on her way. She gazed at the sights as she tried to find her way to the station and suddenly London did not seem so soulless. Elizabeth felt more generous about the city now she had made the decision to leave it. All she took with her were the clothes from the weekend. She knew that one day she would have to return and collect her things from her sister's flat but she couldn't think about that now. The familiar welcoming security of her old home was calling to her and she was finally listening.

After a few wrong twists and turns Elizabeth finally made it to Paddington. Her stomach was starting to rumble but there was no time to think about being hungry. The train home was due to leave in 5 minutes and Elizabeth was desperate to get on it. After a fight with the ticket machine Elizabeth made it to the platform and jumped on the train just as it was about to pull out. The carriage was quiet and she had no trouble getting a seat. She sent Gladys a text message explaining what had happened and telling her that she was on her way home. GLD 2 HEAR IT ☺ TXT @ CHPNHM WILL PICK U UP – Gladys replied. Elizabeth settled down for the journey home feeling happier than she had for months.

Good to her word Gladys was waiting at the station. "Now you can get on with your life," she said giving Elizabeth a long, loving cuddle.

"You always knew I was chasing the wrong dream didn't you Mum," Elizabeth said smiling.

"Most Mothers seem to have a sixth sense about these kinds of things my love." Gladys said linking arms with Elizabeth and leading her to the car park. "Anyway I think I might have an idea."

"What's that?" Elizabeth asked getting into her mother's white Vauxhall Astra.

"I'll show you when we get home."

***

Elizabeth's jaw dropped as she scanned the pages and papers displayed on dining room table. "What the f....."

"Elizabeth!" Bertie warned.

"But *Scotland* Dad! What the hell is she thinking?"

"*She* is standing right here Elizabeth," Gladys said indignantly.

Elizabeth stared dumbfounded at the literature her mother had compiled whilst she had been in London.

"You certainly wasted no time," Elizabeth said, "what if I didn't leave my job? What would you have done with all this stuff then?"

"I didn't know what you were going to do did I? I'm not psychic," she added under her breath. "Look I've known these women for years and a couple of weeks ago they told me they had a vacancy and when you came home I just put two and two together...."

"And came up with – not a snowball's chance in hell!"

"Calm down love," Bertie said. "I think your mother was only trying to help."

"I haven't been here 5 minutes and she's already trying to ship me off to the other side of the world!"

"Don't be ridiculous Elizabeth. It's not the other side of the world. And it's not as though I'm expecting you to slum it in misery. The shop they work in is lovely," Gladys said searching for a picture amongst the paperwork. "Look, it's just up your street."

Gladys handed Elizabeth a photograph of two women standing outside a shop called *Nature's Remedies*. There were old fashioned pharmaceutical jars and bottles in the windows next to pictures of plants and herbs. The shop front gave a traditional and welcoming feel but the women were another story. One was tall and broad and wore an elongated grin that gave her an air of a crazy woman, the other was

23

shorter with a petit frame wearing a long skirt and a frown.

"How is this *up my street*? I don't even know what my street is, or *where* it is but I'm sure it's not in bloody Scotland!"

"Elizabeth listen," Gladys ploughed on, "they own a cottage that they will rent out to you. It's little but beautiful. It's set in a small garden with a white picket fence. It's only a two up, two down affair, but it's got a log fire in the downstairs living room and comes completely furnished. And I think, from the look of the pictures, all the furniture is brand new."

Gladys handed Elizabeth the photo and even she had to admit it looked quite inviting. "Alright Mum, it's very pretty. But I am NOT moving to Scotland. Now thanks very much for your concern but I'll sort this out in my own way. I know I've been a miserable bugger recently but I'm pretty sure working in a shop a million miles from home isn't going to help with that." Elizabeth put the photo back on the table and stormed off.

For the rest of the week Elizabeth stomped around the house, slamming doors and sulking. She was adamant she was not moving to Scotland no matter how often her mother left photos or papers lying around the house. It even motivated her to start looking for a job locally. She searched papers and websites and updated her CV, but the harder she looked the more she had to admit that a complete change of scenery was starting to appeal to her.

"Are you going to catch up with any of your old school friends?" Gladys asked nervously one evening when the three of them were sitting in silence.

"Oh my God, are you serious!" Elizabeth snapped, "What the hell would I say to them? Yeah, I'm back from London, it didn't work out after all. Oh by the way I totally screwed up my life whilst I was there and made myself so ill that I started having hallucinations! I've still got some pride left Mother."

"Oh for goodness sake Elizabeth....." Gladys paused, "hallucinations? What do you mean hallucinations? You never said anything about......."

"Oh I can't handle this," Elizabeth said getting out of the chair she was slumped in. "I'm going out."

"Elizabeth! Will you stop acting like a child," Bertie said taking both Elizabeth and her mother by surprise. "All your mother is doing, has ever done, is try to help you. We both love having you here when you're not behaving like a brat but when you are, well quite frankly, I would drive you up to Scotland myself tonight and be done with you."

"Bertie!" Gladys said, stunned at his outburst.

"I'm sorry to have to say it, love," Bertie continued, "goodness knows I wanted you to snap out of this mood by yourself but it's gone on for too long. You're not a child anymore so stop acting like one."

Elizabeth fought back the tears as she listened to her father. She stumbled slightly, shocked at his words, and had to hold onto the sofa for support. "You're right Dad, I'm sorry. I'm really sorry Mum," she said as the tears came freely. "I just thought you wanted to get rid of me like Jessie did. I saw that Scotland stuff and I just thought, why the hell were you so keen for me to come home if all you wanted me to do was bugger off again."

"It wasn't like that Little One," Gladys said.

"Then what was it Mum? I really don't understand. You wanted me to come home, practically insisted on it. Why do you want me to go again now?"

"Elizabeth," Gladys said calmly, "you can't go on living in other people's shadows. You could have carried on at Jessie's but you would have spent all of your time longing to be free of it. The same will happen here after a while. Moving home, moving in with your sister, these are just interim steps. I was desperate for you not to hate being at home as much as you hated being in London. I just thought it might be a chance for you to step out and start having some experiences of your own. Start to live your own life."

"In Scotland?!" Elizabeth asked incredulously.

"Why not?" Gladys smiled. "It's a good a place to start as any. Some people move to Australia or America to start a new life. Look love," Gladys said tenderly, "it was just the opportunity I was keen to run past you, not the geography!"

"I'm sorry I've been such a bitch Mum," Elizabeth said softening. "And I should have let you explain everything. I appreciate the gesture but if I'm going to start *living my own life* then I have to do it myself. It's very kind of you to look out for me and it's very kind of your friends to offer me the job, but please let me do this my own way."

Gladys nodded and Bertie walked over to Elizabeth and kissed her on the forehead. "Now that we've sorted that out, should I make one of my famous hot chocolates?" he said.

"Not for me thanks Dad. I think I'll still just take a walk, get some fresh air."

Elizabeth left her parent's house and wandered into town. She did not really know where she was going but she needed time to think. Her parents' actions and concerns were beginning to suffocate her and she knew she was starting to act like a petulant teenager. She was annoyed with herself that her father was the one who had to point it out. A young couple wandered past her and giggled snapping her out of her reverie. Bright lights caught her attention and she realised she was standing next to the cinema. She had a look at the films on offer and walked inside.

There was a time when she would not have contemplated going to the cinema alone. She always thought of it as something that sad middle-aged men or women did but she was surprised at how liberating the experience was. She chose a film and bought a ticket. She even decided to treat herself to popcorn and a slushy when she heard a voice behind her.

"Elizabeth? Oh my God that is you, hello!"

She turned towards the voice and came face to face with her ex-boyfriend.

"Oh my goodness Steve," she said trying to keep the tone of embarrassment from her voice. "How are you?"

"Really good. I'm here with Jenny," he said pointing to a figure queuing for tickets and waving madly at them.

"Oh right," Elizabeth said awkwardly and waved back. "Are you two friends now?"

"Well a little bit more than friends," Steve said shuffling his feet, looking awkward.

"Oh, you're an item are you?" Elizabeth asked incredulously.

"Yeah."

"It's just that you hated her when we were together."

"I know but after you dumped me and went to London, she was really kind..."

"I didn't dump you......"

"Well you know what I mean. When you had to go and *experience life*, I was pretty gutted and she was a really good friend."

"Was she now," Elizabeth said bristling, "*I* never bloody heard from her again."

"Please Elizabeth, don't be angry....." Steve started but he was interrupted by the arrival of Jenny.

"Oh my goodness, Elizabeth! This is a blast from the past!" Jenny said with a little too much enthusiasm.

"Hi Jenny. Good to see you. You look well." Elizabeth couldn't help but give Jenny the once over. When they were friends Jenny was the tall, thin blonde and Elizabeth was the smaller, plumper brunette. Elizabeth was so used to Jenny getting all the attention that when Steve came along he was like a breath of fresh air. Not only did he just have eyes for Elizabeth but he really disliked Jenny. The two of them were very close and spent two years together, but Elizabeth always felt as though she should be blazing some kind of trail. Jessie moved to London and sung its praises and against every instinct, Elizabeth followed.

An awkward silence fell upon the trio. Elizabeth was just about to make her excuses and leave when Jenny asked the question Elizabeth was dreading, "so who are you here with Elizabeth?"

"Um..." Elizabeth said uneasily.

"Is it one of our old friends from school?" Jenny said looking furtively around the entrance hall.

"Jenny I think...." Steve said sensing Elizabeth's embarrassment.

"Is it Olivia or Lacey?" Jenny said ploughing on regardless. "Or is it one of your old flames like Seth?"

"No," Elizabeth said finally silencing Jenny, "I'm not...."
"Oh my God!" Jenny said realising. "Are you here alone? Oh, how stupid of me, I'm such an idiot."

Jenny grinned inanely as Elizabeth searched for something to say. Once again it was Jenny who broke the silence, "why don't you come and sit with us?"

"Oh I don't think so," Elizabeth said hurriedly.

"That might not be the best idea," Steve added quickly.

"No of course," Jenny said oblivious of the tension, "we're going to be sitting in the back row," she winked at Elizabeth, "if you know what I mean!"

"Oh right, like teenagers all over again," Elizabeth said but the sarcasm was lost on Jenny.

"That's right! You're only young once! Come on then." With that Jenny dragged a mortified looking Steve away and they headed for the stairs that led to the corridor of cinema screens.

Elizabeth turned away feeling humiliated and took up her place in the refreshments queue again.

She felt a tap on her shoulder, "Elizabeth?"

"What do you want Steve," she said unable to hide her frustration.

"I just wanted to say sorry. That was so embarrassing." He signalled towards Jenny who was watching them from half way up the stairs.

"It's OK, just go. Jenny looks like she's about to shoot laser beams out of her eyes, no matter how much she's trying to disguise it with a sickly sweet grin!"

"I know, she's kind of jealous."

"Right, whatever," Elizabeth said turning away.

"You know what Lizzie, you were the one who went away. I didn't want you to go."

"I know that Steve. It was my idea I get it. And you get back at me by going out with the one woman who made finding a boyfriend impossible for me – thanks very much! Oh and by the way, my name is Elizabeth!"

"I wasn't trying to get back at you *Elizabeth*, I like her OK. I know she can be a bitch, but I really like her."

"Fine, whatever. It was nice to see you. Now you'd better go or you'll miss your film."

"Maybe we'll see you afterwards for a drink?"

Elizabeth sighed, "maybe."

Steve left Elizabeth to pay for her popcorn and drink. She watched the couple walk up the stairs and made her way to the pubescent boy collecting tickets. She stood for a while staring at the place where Jenny had been standing wearing a fake smile.

"The movie's about to start madam," the teenage boy said. "Are you staying?"

Elizabeth took a moment to consider his question. "No," she said finally, "I'm not staying. I'm definitely *not* staying."

Elizabeth walked away from the glaring lights of the movie theatre and wandered back home still clutching hold of her cinema snacks. She got into the house with some difficulty after balancing the popcorn on top of her slushy to find her key. She got into the house and closed the door with her bottom.

"MUM!" She called from the hallway. "Where's that stuff about Scotland?"

Chapter Four

After her disastrous experience at the cinema Elizabeth stayed up all night going through the pros and cons of a move to Scotland and ultimately had to admit there were more reasons to go than to stay. When Gladys got up the next morning mother and daughter had another heart to heart and Gladys felt sure Elizabeth had made the right decision.

"Just try it love," Gladys said and Elizabeth thought she saw that strange look in her Mum's eyes again, "you can always come home if it's awful".

"Come home – again," Elizabeth said but that look on Gladys' face made her feel uneasy and she did not have the heart to give her too much of a hard time. "You alright Mum?"

"Fine, fine my love," Gladys said and once again that unfamiliar look was gone. She gave Elizabeth a hug, "just going to miss you that's all."

"Yeah, I've been such a pleasure!"

***

Two days later Bertie dropped Gladys and Elizabeth at Euston Train Station in London and went to find a parking space.

"Well this is exciting," Gladys said.

"This is ridiculous," Elizabeth said under her breath. "You don't have to wait with me you know. I'll be fine on my own."

"I know you will," Gladys replied, "but let us at least get you sorted with your bags and settled somewhere. You've got ages before the train."

"Let's not drag this out OK?" Elizabeth said and held up her hand as her mother was about to protest. "You've got a long drive home and you might as well get going."

It took Elizabeth a while but she finally managed to convince her Mum and Dad to let her wait alone at the station and just as they were leaving Bertie gave Elizabeth a kiss on the cheek.

"It's good to see that twinkle back in your eye," he whispered. And with a wink he left Elizabeth alone and jogged to catch up with an emotional Gladys.

Parked at the nearest café with all her bags Elizabeth waved a fond farewell to her parents and watched them until they were out of sight. This was a massive change for Elizabeth but one she had to make. She knew it. Something had gone seriously wrong in London. Why else would she have had that strange *experience*? The one she now put down to exhaustion and hallucinations. Shaking the image of the bodies scorched onto the wall of the tunnel out of her head with a shudder Elizabeth opened the folder of information her Mum had left with her.

She looked once again at the photo of the two women, one grinning inanely and the other frowning like she was about to pierce the photographer with her x-ray vision. Apparently these two would be taking care of the "remedies" part of the shop but Elizabeth would be organising the books. *Nature's Remedies* had recently expanded their concern and were now selling self-help, new-age and spiritual books and that was why they needed the help. Elizabeth sighed. She was the first to admit that she was not at home in the materialistic, analytical, dog-eat-dog capital of England, but she couldn't say she was much of a hippy either.

Oh well, Elizabeth thought, *there's no going back now*. And for the next few hours she read all the free newspapers on offer at the café, watched the comings and goings of the trains and the travellers and read through the Scotland blurb from her mother numerous times. Finally it was 11pm and she was ready to board the Pandemonium Sleeper to take her to Edinburgh.

This was part of the journey she had been really looking forward to. She had a berth all to herself but it did not take her long to realise that the train wasn't exactly the Orient Express. It was cramped and clinical, more like a prison transport. She bundled herself into the small berth with luggage and boxes but despite her surroundings she drifted off to sleep quickly, rocked by the *clickety-clack* of the moving train. She had a deep and dreamless night's sleep, arriving in Edinburgh just after 7am. To her surprise there was a taxi waiting for her. Apparently organised and paid for by her mother's friends.

The taxi trundled along the stunning city streets of Edinburgh for a while and Elizabeth was amazed by how beautiful it was in the early morning sunrise. It was quiet and full of character, so unlike the harsh soullessness that Elizabeth had come to associate with London. The taxi turned away from the town and into the suburbs then out into the bleak, beautiful countryside. After an hour or so the taxi arrived at the cottage. The sight of it took Elizabeth's breath away. Now she had made up her mind to accept this new turn of events as her fate, she was overwhelmed by the beauty of the little home. Quaint and picture perfect, the cottage stood in the golden morning sun beckoning her to step inside and embrace her new life.

"It's meant to be," she said quietly and the taxi driver smiled and drove off leaving her to gaze in awe at her new life. She was finally home and something deep down inside her knew it.

She dug out the information from her Mum and found a note scribbled on the back of one of the emails saying: *key under right hand plant pot.* Elizabeth looked – no key. She looked inside the plant – no key. She even looked at the plant pot on the left, no sign of it there either. With growing impatience she suddenly realised that she had not taken any contact numbers for the two women from her mother.

She phoned home, Bertie answered, "Mum's out, she'll be gone for ages."

"Can you please call her and find out where this bloody key is?!" Elizabeth said, her mood getting worse.

After 10 minutes and a few phone calls back and forth Elizabeth finally found the key taped to an envelope inside the letter box. And with it Elizabeth found her sense of humour and sighed with relief at the minor hiccough.

Once inside the cottage Elizabeth was just as pleased as she was with the outside. It was cosy and compact and open plan, there was a small kitchen to the right of the front door with pale, sea-green units and a clean, white butler sink. To the left was a living area with an open fire, a two-seater sofa with matching chair opposite that felt soft as a cloud as Elizabeth sat her weary body down. Opposite the front door was a staircase leading to a bedroom and a bathroom. When Elizabeth explored the upstairs she was thrilled to see that the bedroom was just as welcoming as the front room with a big wrought iron bed and a massive Victorian wardrobe. Even the bathroom had a freestanding bath with claw feet. The whole place looked plucked from a Victorian postcard but Elizabeth could tell all the furniture, fixtures and fittings were brand new.

"Ah yes, a modern day take on a traditional vision," she said pompously, "how perfect for me."

It wasn't until Elizabeth had wallowed in the beauty of her new home for a few hours that she realised she had no supplies. Once again she hunted through the papers her mother had given her with instructions to the local shop. She stepped outside of the cottage and took the first turning on her left, as the note said. She walked for 20 minutes expecting to see the village shops at any moment but as she carried on she went further and further into the countryside. Almost an hour later she was so far into the country that she thought she might never see civilisation again. She had no other option but to turn around and find her way back to the cottage. Once she was back at her new home she started again, and this time she turned right. Within 10 minutes she was chatting casually to the lady who ran the corner shop.

"I'm sure they told me to turn left," Elizabeth laughed with the kindly old lady but deep down she was beginning to have some serious doubts.

The shop bell jingled as she left with a week's worth of supplies and a frown. *That's the second piece of spurious information from Mum's "friends" today*, she thought. And suddenly it dawned on her that she had never heard of these two women who were so close to her mother that they would happily offer Elizabeth a job without even meeting her.

The worry began to fade when she was back in the pretty little cottage and had made herself something to eat. She decided to get settled as soon as possible and started to unpack her things.

It was Saturday and there was nothing for her to do until Monday morning when her job officially started so she took out her laptop and started writing. She had always enjoyed writing ever since she was a child, even written numerous adventures about *Saffy* - just a normal little girl that also happened to be a witch. In the comfort of her new surroundings Elizabeth even let herself think about the events of that cataclysmic night but instead of the usual feeling of horror she thought that she must have an amazing imagination. She had never met anybody who had lived through an object of their own imaginings so vividly before. She began writing on her laptop:

Maybe this is it! Maybe this is what I'm meant to be! I love books. Always have and now I'm going to be surrounded by them at work. OK, so they'll be self-help type books but that's OK. I could do with a bit of insight and motivation! I will have all of this amazing insight right at my fingertips and I'm going to write a book! At last I can hold my head up high knowing I have a skill, a talent that might, finally, help me make my mark on the...

KNOCK - KNOCK KNOCK!

Elizabeth looked up from her computer startled by the sudden interruption. It took her a moment to remember that people knocking on doors usually require entry when the unexpected visitor knocked again, this time with a little more urgency.

KNOCK KNOCK KNOCK KNOCK!

She pushed her chair back and picked her way through the unopened suitcases and boxes and made her way, rather clumsily, to the unopened door.

Chapter Five

Once at the front door it dawned on Elizabeth that she was a woman on her own, new to the village and did not know a soul. Why would someone be knocking on *her* door? Cautiously she pressed her ear up against the unopened door.

"Who's there?" she asked.

"Oh for goodness sake!" came the exasperated reply in a heavy Scottish accent.

There was some murmuring from behind the door and Elizabeth realised her visitor was not alone.

"Can I help you?" she asked, getting nervous.

The mumbling became more animated as Elizabeth listened. The voices were all female and they were having quite a heated discussion. They were clearly trying not to be heard so their whispers sounded like growls which did little to allay Elizabeth's fears.

Finally, a second voice attempted to gain access to the cottage, a voice that Elizabeth recognised.

"Hello my love. It's me!"

"MUM!" Elizabeth shouted in utter disbelief through the closed door.

"Do you want to open the door darling? It's a little bit chilly out here." Gladys said.

"What the hell are you doing here?" Elizabeth asked, unbolting the door.

It was dark outside and the stars peppered the early evening sky and the faces now staring at her were illuminated by the security light on her front porch. There were three women standing in front of her. Of course, there was her Mum smiling with her usual warm, welcoming charm. Elizabeth was pleased to see her *little Mum*. Gladys had a petit frame at only 5 foot 3 inches tall, she had light brown, long hair which was usually tied up in a loose bun at the back. She wore very sensible, middle-aged clothes but Elizabeth knew there was a touch of the inner rebel about her mother because try as she might she just could not manage to look tidy.

The other women were complete strangers. The first, who must have been the exasperated knocker, was equally as small, if not a little bit shorter than her mother. This woman was probably in her late 50s with blond hair streaked with grey and she had the ferocious look of a terrier about to chew through its own leg. The final visitor was completely different from the first two. She was over 6ft tall and on the plump side. She was the youngest of the three and wore ancient NHS spectacles. She looked as though she was about to burst into fits of giggles at any moment.

Drinking in the image of these three unexpected visitors, it suddenly dawned on Elizabeth who the other two women were.

"So *you're* my Mum's friends?" she said looking from one to another. "I just can't thank you enough for everything you've done for me!"

Gladys embraced her fondly and Elizabeth watched the other women enter from within her mother's hug. The terrier stomped straight past the cuddling pair and looked derisively at Elizabeth's belongings strewn around the tiny cottage, tutting as she picked her way through. The jolly giant stooped into the cottage and had to remain crunched until Elizabeth signalled them both to sit down. The terrier perched on the arm of a chair as the giant plopped down into the very soft furniture practically bending in half as she sat.

"I want to introduce you to my friends. This is...." Gladys began but was interrupted by the terrier.

"I'm Shiona," she said and practically jumping off the chair she held out her hand to Elizabeth.

Elizabeth took it and was *not* surprised by the ferocity of Shiona's grip.

"And I'm Daphne." The jolly giant said struggling to extricate herself from the chair. Her voice was surprisingly gentle with a soft Scottish twang.

"Hi," Elizabeth said, slightly bewildered and the four women stood or stooped in silence for a moment. Elizabeth looked from face to face. There were a lot of things that concerned her about this sudden visitation but one thing in particular had been niggling at her since she had heard her mother's voice.

"Mum?" she asked. "How did you get here so quickly? When I called about the keys Dad said you'd only just gone out."

"Oh!" Gladys exclaimed looking cautiously at the other two.

Elizabeth glanced in the same direction, the terrier just shook her head and raised her eyes and the jolly giant just smiled.

"I .....flew," Gladys finally answered.

"You flew?" Elizabeth said stunned. "How is that possible? You could barely raise the train fare to get *me* up here, how on earth could you afford a plane ticket?"

"I had some savings........that I totally forgot about........I just wanted to make sure you were OK! Anyway, that doesn't matter now," Gladys said clearly eager to change the subject, "there's some things we need to tell you about your new job."

"I'm going to work in their shop," Elizabeth said gesturing to the other women, "what else is there to tell?"

"That's only a part-time job," Shiona said, with the air of a Sergeant Major. "There's another job we were hoping you could help us with."

"Oh yes?" Elizabeth asked with interest.

"There's some training we need to do with you," Shiona continued, "and as it took you so long to get here we need to start as soon as possible......"

"BUT", Gladys cut in quickly, "we don't really need to go into all that right now. I just thought I would introduce you to the girls and we can start training tomorrow."

"Training?" Elizabeth was mystified at the turn of events. "But when do I start working at the shop?"

"You worry too much." Daphne said smiling. "Try to have a good night's sleep and we'll go through everything you need to know at the training ground."

"Training ground?"

"Why don't we just say goodnight to Shiona and Daphne," Gladys said, dismissing her friends, "and it'll all be clear tomorrow my love.

You don't mind if I bunk in with you tonight do you?"

Elizabeth smiled. She was surprisingly relieved to have company on her first evening so far away from home. "As long as you don't snore," she said, giving her mother a wink.

Daphne and Shiona said their rather uncomfortable goodbyes. "Did you like my little joke with the keys?" Daphne asked as she pulled Elizabeth into her ample bosom and hugged her like a long lost friend.

"What?" Elizabeth asked.

"And the direction to the shops?" Daphne laughed.

"WHAT? You did that on purpose?" Elizabeth said beginning to bristle.

"Call it lesson number one Betty," Daphne giggled, "you need to lighten up a bit!"

Before she had time to protest Shiona said a dismissive farewell and they both turned and walked away, shattering Elizabeth's illusion of her idyllic new life.

"What just happened?" Elizabeth asked her mother as they closed out the night.

"Don't worry about Daphne," Gladys replied, "she's got a funny sense of humour. You'll get used to it."

"Not that Mum, although that was bizarre enough, I mean, this new job and the *training ground*."

"Oh, my lovely," Gladys said rubbing her face and for the first time in months Elizabeth noticed that her Mum looked tired, really tired. "Don't worry about that now. We'll figure all that out tomorrow."

Elizabeth was so pleased to see her Mum that she didn't say another word about the strange women for the rest of the evening. Instead, Elizabeth and Gladys unpacked some of Elizabeth's belongings and made the cottage feel a lot more homely. They talked about Elizabeth's journey and her reaction when she saw the cottage and Gladys even tried to talk about Jessie, but Elizabeth rolled her eyes. Gladys laughed when she noticed Elizabeth's reaction, "you girls are so different aren't you!"

"We are!" Elizabeth laughed, "she's so bloody neurotic!"

Gladys looked at Elizabeth and smiled.

"Ok, I know, I've been neurotic too recently but nothing like Jessie – what is her problem?!"

"Who knows my lovely," Gladys replied. "But something I do know is that just because you're related to someone doesn't mean you have to be *anything* like them – trust me."

Elizabeth watched her Mum fussing through her things. Gladys talked rarely about her own family. Elizabeth had only ever met her Grandmother once and that was a scary enough experience. Gladys was an only child whose father had died when she was very young. *No wonder*, Elizabeth thought, *that she wants me and Jessie to have a decent relationship.*

"Don't worry Mum. Jessie and I will be fine – when we grow up," Elizabeth joked. Laughing the pair of them carried on tidying late into the night when they both decided it was time to go to bed.

Elizabeth was in a reflective mood as she climbed into bed. Her Mum fell quickly into a restful sleep in the double bed they were sharing, but Elizabeth lay awake for a while, thoughts whirling around her head. She thought about the moment when she saw the cottage for the first time. She believed that she had "come home". Now she wasn't so sure. For one thing her Mum had turned up with her strange friends and suddenly Elizabeth's life felt beyond her control - again.

But tomorrow was another day and as she tried to sleep Elizabeth thought about what kind of *job* it was that Shiona, Daphne and her Mum needed her for. When she finally did sleep she dreamt she was splashing through tumbling water, the clouds were grey and sea was violent. She was trying to steer a course to quieter waters, but with each falling wave and spray of sea mist, Elizabeth felt as though she were drowning. Tossing and turning in bed she was vaguely aware of Gladys' calming voice and her dreams changed to bank heists and robberies. To Shiona and Daphne as gangsters, menacing her to do *the job* "or else!" But in all her wildest dreams she could never have imagined what kind of adventure these three women had in store for her.

Chapter Six

The early evening sky crackled with the expectation of a thunder storm as Elizabeth stepped out of the train. She buzzed with a fury that she had never known fuelled by the bitter comments of colleagues now fizzing through her thoughts. It was an all-consuming feeling spreading through every pore, every sinew, every muscle and cell of her body. It made her feel powerful in the most malevolent way.

She walked away from the train and down the steps of the station every footfall booming as her power turned her into something non-human. She grew into a giantess of a woman making each and every person quake with fear where they stood. She had been shamed and ridiculed for the last time. Someone would have to pay. She would make them pay.

She lumbered into the alleyway. Anger and loathing pouring into her, through her, out of her, she embraced it. It was magnificent. Like no other feeling she had ever known and she would not reject it. At the end of the alley she turned. Waiting for the moment, she knew it was coming, she was prepared and she wanted it.

As the men entered the lane she was already facing them, and this time it was their turn to look shocked. She smiled a humourless grin, watching their reactions. This time they were frozen with fear, no longer taunting her but terrified of her. Once again their unknown faces turned into three people she recognised, her boss, her *friend*, her colleague. All people who had humiliated her and now they wouldn't even get the chance to scream.

A bursting flame of rage poured from her outstretched arms and she laughed to see their astonished faces moments before they were incinerated by her power.

Then a voice, tiny at first, became audible amongst the crackle of her spell. Instantly, Elizabeth began to shrink as doubts crept into her heart. The smaller her frame, the clearer the voice, and it was saying, *"stop"*

A whisper at first, but as doubt overwhelmed her and she slowly became human again, the voice grew louder and louder. By the time she had reached her normal size it was a scream, **"STOP!"**

She woke up, stunned to find that the shout was coming from her, from a place inside her that refused to succumb to the enveloping anger. She sat bolt upright in bed, breathing heavily for a moment. The dark of the room was oppressive, she longed for light. Disturbed by the vivid dream, she kicked off her covers and fell out of bed. She kept on falling, much longer than she expected and thumped heavily onto her left arm as she landed. As her eyes adjusted to the gloom, she saw that she was on the sleeper train, travelling to Scotland. She had been asleep in the top bunk. She pulled herself to her feet and scrabbled around the walls searching for the light switch.

She found it, flicked it and the modest cabin was instantly illuminated. She rested her head against the wall, trying to calm herself. Taking a moment she wondered why, after all this time, she had dreamt of that night again. She had put it all behind her and written it off as a synaptic brain malfunction. But now, on the precipice of a massive life change, the images came back to haunt her.

"Maybe, I'm subconsciously *self-sabotaging*, or whatever they call it," she said to the empty compartment.

Breathing more easily, the nightmare finally a dim recollection she turned back to her bunk. She froze. Elizabeth took a sharp breath and stared in horror at the scene in front of her. There in the top bunk lay the scorched and singed body of her boss, her eyes open, frozen in terror. Lying beneath her boss, on the bottom bunk, were the distorted, rotting bodies of her friend and her colleague lying hideously entwined.

She screamed, but the only sound that came from her mouth was "squawk squawk, squawk!"

SQUAWK SQUAWK SQUAWK.

"Can't you hear that alarm," Gladys said, shaking her awake. "It's been going off for ages. I hate this old alarm clock, why ever did you

41

bring it with you!" Gladys disappeared from the room, leaving Elizabeth, a stunned and shocked gibbering mess, sitting up in bed.

Elizabeth scanned the room. She was in the cosy little cottage in Scotland. At least she hoped she was, this time she took no chances. She gave herself a vicious pinch. She winced, thankfully she was awake. Just to be sure she punched herself in the arm, "Ouch!" She was definitely awake. The SQUAWK SQUAWK SQUAWK carried on until Elizabeth thumped the plastic bird on the head. She had acquired the hideous alarm clock macaw from London Zoo when she was 12 years old. She had instantly fallen in love with it when they passed through the gift shop and was not prepared to leave until she had purchased the thing. Her Dad had bought it for her and she had thoroughly annoyed her family by waking the entire household up every morning with the melodious melody. The most infuriating thing for Jessie was that Elizabeth could sleep through the noise. Many a morning she was awoken by a swift punch from her seething sibling.

The dream, so vivid just moments before, was now happily disappearing back to the place where it belonged, deep in her subconscious. And the hideous images that had caused her to wake covered in sweat were now barely even a memory. She flopped back down into bed. It was soft and welcoming and the eiderdown covering her was just too soothing and warm for her to contemplate leaving it behind yet.

As she lay there allowing real memories to come back, she remembered how lucky she was to be the proud occupier of this beautiful home. She could happily hide away from nightmares and disapproving family for the rest of her life. Just as she considered spending an eternity in bed, the smell of freshly toasted bread wafted through the doorway. Mum was doing the breakfast and there was nothing like toast and tea when you were truly hungry. Elizabeth realised that she had not eaten since lunchtime the previous day. She was ravenous.

In no time at all she was up, dressed and tucking into her third slice of toast and second cup of tea. Gladys smiled to see her daughter scoffing up the breakfast.

"I see you've got your appetite back!" she laughed. "You should have a good breakfast, we've got a busy day today."

"Oh yeah," Elizabeth garbled, her mouth full of toast, "the *training ground*! Where exactly is that?"

"It's not quite what you're thinking." Gladys smirked, "I warned you about Daphne's sense of humour! Anyway, finish up, wash up and let's go."

Elizabeth washed the dishes in her tiny little kitchen. She caught her Mum smiling at her newly acquired fastidiousness but she did not care. She was actually beginning to feel like a responsible adult for the first time in her life.

Before they left Elizabeth and Gladys wrapped themselves in warm clothes. Gladys insisted that Elizabeth bring her Wellies on the trip to Scotland and now Elizabeth knew why. They were heading out into the forest, not far from Elizabeth's ill-advised journey the previous day. It was still summer, albeit late summer, but it was a very chilly, early morning start for the pair. The leggings underneath her trousers and the skiing jacket were welcome relief from the pricking of frosty air.

They plodded through the fields and Elizabeth was surprised to notice that her mother knew exactly which route to take.

"My goodness Mum," she giggled, "it's as if you know this place like the back of your hand."

Gladys just laughed along with her daughter and carried on leading the way. Elizabeth noticed a change in her mother, a rejuvenation. It was almost as though she could see her getting younger right in front of her eyes. They laughed, and messed around and tried to push each other into ditches for the best part of an hour before Gladys looked up.

"We're here!" She said.

As far as Elizabeth could tell, "here" was not a particularly exceptional place. In fact, directly ahead of them was nothing more than a fence separating the field behind them and the forest ahead.

"I think we're in the wrong spot, there should have been a stile here." Gladys said distractedly.

Not for the first time Elizabeth wondered at her mother's knowledge of the area, "Mum how do you know.....?"

But Gladys was already out of ear shot by the time the words left Elizabeth's mouth.

"Mum!" Elizabeth called and traipsed after her mother.

"This is it!" Gladys said, scaring Elizabeth as she jumped out from a low hanging tree.

"What?" Elizabeth asked, catching her breath.

"The stile, I knew it was here somewhere."

"*How* do you know that, Mum? When was the last time you were ever up in Scotland?" Elizabeth quizzed as she clambered over the steps in the fence. "Is this a secret part of your life that you've never told any of us about?"

Elizabeth's last question was meant as a joke but Gladys grinned mysteriously at her daughter. Suddenly Elizabeth thought that maybe it was not such a ridiculous notion after all. She was beginning to sense something in that grin, something in her mother that she didn't immediately recognise, but somehow always knew was there.

They walked a little bit further until they reached a clearing in the woods.

"TA-DA!" Gladys said, and presented what must have been the *training ground* to Elizabeth.

They had been walking away from the rising sun, to the west, and they were now standing on the edge of a woodland glen. The sun was just high enough to give the glade a golden sheen. The light danced and sparkled from moisture that had settled on the ground. Some of the dew drops were so enormous that they looked like diamonds. The entire floor of the clearing was peppered with them. The plants and flowers that grew there were some of the most exquisite Elizabeth had ever seen. Hyacinths and forget-me-nots, daffodils and tulips, roses and pansies, their delicate petals created a rainbow hue in the deep green grass. Even the trees that encircled the glade had a hearty, bronze glow.

Elizabeth stood in silence, drinking in the view. It was breath-taking. It was like nothing she had ever seen before. It was a magnificent, artistic representation of how a perfect woodland glen should be. Elizabeth stood rooted to the spot, wondering at Mother Nature and how majestic she was. She had rarely taken the time to care about the countryside but she defied anyone, even the most hard-nosed city type, to be unmoved by this place. She was utterly spellbound.

"What's wrong with this picture," said a cold voice behind her, breaking the spell.

Elizabeth turned to see the stern face of Shiona staring back at her. Elizabeth was amazed to see that Shiona was totally unimpressed by the view.

44

"Surely that's a trick question," she replied, "this place is perfect."

"It's beautiful, aye, I'll give you that. But there is definitely something not quite right here." Shiona insisted, "If you know what it is, that's the most important lesson learned."

"Oh for goodness sake," it was Elizabeth's turn to feel exasperated. "Maybe it's you!"

"Elizabeth!" Gladys chastised.

"I'm sorry Mum, but if Shiona can't see the perfection here, then maybe she's the one with something wrong."

"Ha, ha, ha, ha!" They all turned to see Daphne at the edge of glade, clearly enjoying herself. "You tell her Betty!" She laughed, causing her friend to turn a vicious shade of red, making Daphne snigger even more.

"Daphne, you're not helping." Gladys said, stepping in diplomatically. "She's right," Gladys continued, turning to Elizabeth, "a mistake *has* been made here. Do you think you could tell us what that is?"

Elizabeth took a breath, trying to calm down. She had taken an instant dislike to Shiona from the moment she walked into the cottage. Elizabeth found her patronising, rude and very unfriendly. On the other hand, despite sending her on a wild goose chase and insisting on calling her "Betty", Elizabeth did like Daphne and she absolutely loved her mother, so for the sake of these two amenable women she decided to swallow her pride and attempted to answer the question.

"Ok," she said, taking another look around, trying to be a little more critical about the exquisite glen. She walked through the trees, tiptoed over the flowers, gazed at the petals and noticed the beads of moisture glistening like jewels. Try as she might, she just could not find anything wrong with the place. She even found the mud on the ground beautiful, it was a healthy, chocolate brown colour filled with soft, spongy moss and cascading ivy.

"I give up," she said eventually. "I can't see *anything* wrong here." Gladys sagged, Shiona looked smug, and Daphne smiled sympathetically. "It's perfect," she added, "almost too perfect."

"Ah-ha!" Daphne exclaimed, just as Gladys said, "That's it!" and Shiona said "Humph!" sulkily.

"What?" Elizabeth was shocked by their reactions. "What did I say?"

This time it was Shiona's turn to swallow her pride. "What do you mean by *too perfect*? Think about it and explain it to us."

"Well..." Elizabeth hesitated.

"It's OK Betty. There's no right or wrong answer. Just give it a go." Daphne encouraged.

"Ok, OK. Well...the flowers are the healthiest I've ever seen. Look at those snow drops over there," she said pointing at the edge of the glade, "they're amazing. They are so white it's almost blinding. The snowdrops I've seen before have a kind of greyness about them. The same with those daffodils, and those incredible pansies! Their faces are so clear, you can almost hear them laughing."

They followed her around the glen as she made her explanations with Daphne and Gladys shooting each other various looks of agreement and excitement as she talked. Even Shiona was starting to look impressed.

"And look at this beautiful holly tree," she said finally, "the berries look so bulbous and satisfying, even I would risk eating one!"

She had finished. She was thoroughly pleased with herself. She knew she was right. Never had there been such a collection of unblemished flora and *that* was why it was all so wrong.

"I know what you are!" she said, realisation suddenly dawning, "you're horticulturists! Gardeners! Aren't you? Is that what you need help with? Will that be my second job? Do you need another *hardy perennial* to join the gang?"

She laughed at her feeble attempt to make a joke and looked towards Daphne whose fixed smile was now looking like a grimace. She looked from one face to another and all satisfaction began to fade. Gladys looked shocked, Shiona looked livid and even Daphne's perpetual smile was fading.

"Oh my goodness!" It was Shiona who broke the silence. "Are you serious?"

"No. Wait!" Gladys said stepping in. "*What* we do is not important at the moment." She rubbed her face, feeling slightly beaten. "The question was: *what's wrong with this picture?*"

"I thought I told you that," Elizabeth started to get annoyed. "It's too perfect!"

"Yes but there's something else," Gladys said. "You've practically told us what it is, now all you have to do is put the clues together."

"I've told you as much as I can!" Elizabeth said starting to get angry.

"Think girl!" shouted Shiona.

"That's enough." Daphne said, her usual mirth-filled manner gone. Using her full height she stepped between Shiona and Elizabeth, putting a protective arm around the girl.

"You're right," she said encouragingly, "we're very good at growing plants. You've named so many of them. Now think about the ones you know, where have you seen them grow, *when* have you seen them grow?"

It took Elizabeth just a few seconds to finally understand. "Oh!" She said, "they're ALL here! Not every flower, but every season!" She started pointing out plants once again. "The snowdrops are an early spring, practically a winter flower, they shouldn't be in bloom at the same time as those roses. And the holly tree, you don't see the berries on a holly tree until the winter!"

"I think she's got it," said Daphne quietly, nudging Shiona.

"Yeah alright, alright very good," Shiona said begrudgingly, "took you long enough."

And that was the first lesson – learnt. After that the ladies began to relax a little. Gladys and Daphne took Elizabeth on a guided tour around the glen. They pointed out the various plants and the seasons in which they belonged and bragged at how faultless each variety was. Elizabeth was surprised to find herself having fun learning about the different species and although they must have talked for hours the glade did not lose its lustre of sunrise. It was an incredible place. Not quite made by Mother Nature as Elizabeth had first thought but woman-made which, she supposed, was the next best thing. "So *this* is where you get your ingredients for *Nature's Remedies*," Elizabeth said, suddenly feeling excited at the prospect of being trained in the art of natural healing.

They talked well into the afternoon until Daphne pointed out that they hadn't eaten a thing all day and she produced a well-stocked picnic basket. Elizabeth watched the strange group of friends as they ate their sandwiches. How on earth Daphne and Shiona could be so close was utterly perplexing. They were worlds apart in mannerisms, humour and physical appearance. Daphne was so funny, but it was too much at times. It was difficult to have any kind of conversation with her without her finding something to joke about. Except for the moment when she stepped between Shiona and Elizabeth, she could not take anything seriously. Shiona on the other hand took *everything* seriously. She was boorish and unkind and when she was not opening her mouth to be derisive, insulting or bossy, then she would sit quietly not engaging with any of them. And then there was Gladys, a consummate nurturer. Supportive and kind she was always attentive to everyone and what they had to say. She laughed at Daphne's jokes, showed proper gravity to Shiona's instructions and encouraged Elizabeth. She treated everyone individually but still retained her ability to just be herself. She was truly an inspiration. And happy as she was to be experiencing this fascinating new way of life, there was something about the whole situation that just kept niggling away at Elizabeth. As she took a huge bite of a chicken sandwich it dawned on her what it was.

"Mum, how do *you* know about all this? What's it all got to do with you?"

Chapter Seven

Gladys froze. Her sandwich hung in mid-air, halfway to her mouth as she regarded Elizabeth. Then, with a sad smile she stood up and walked away, dropping her sandwich towards Daphne who plucked it out of the air and gobbled it up greedily.

"Mum!" Elizabeth called after her.

Shiona put her hand on Elizabeth's arm to stop her following. The touch was firm but soft. "Just give her a minute," Shiona said, her usual coldness gone.

She patted Elizabeth on the arm she was holding, gave her a sympathetic nod then took her hand away.

The three women sat in silence for a while. Elizabeth's quizzical gaze darted from Shiona to Daphne as the older women furtively searched around for anywhere to look other than at Elizabeth. Realising it was pointless expecting an explanation from them and knowing that Shiona would only stop her again if she tried to follow her mother, she stared ahead of her, at the spot that her mother had once occupied.

They seemed to sit for an eternity until,

PAAAARP!

Shiona and Elizabeth both turned towards Daphne.

"That was me," she said, completely unashamedly, "thought it would break the tension!"

"Now's not the time, Daphne!" Shiona barked and got up to follow Gladys.

Elizabeth shook her head at Daphne's entirely inappropriate sense of humour and resumed her silent vigil.

"I didn't actually fart," Daphne said sulkily, "I made the noise with my mouth. *PAAARP*," She managed again, "you see!"

"Enough Daphne! OK?" Elizabeth pleaded. She just wanted to sit quietly and wait, she certainly was not in the mood for Daphne's attempts at humour.

Moments later Shiona and Gladys walked back into the clearing. Gladys had been crying and Shiona was holding her by the arm.

"Will you walk with me?" Gladys asked.

Elizabeth got up and noticed that Daphne had also risen, smiling expectantly.

"Not you!" Shiona barked at Daphne. "You already know this story!"

"Story...?" Elizabeth began as her mother took her gently by the arm.

"Come on," she said. "There's something I need to tell you." They walked away leaving behind them the bickering pair and the beautiful glen.

Elizabeth wanted to demand to be told what on earth was going on. She was suddenly desperate for Gladys to behave like her mother again and get back into the convenient little box that Elizabeth had filed her away in. But there was something in her mother's mood that stopped Elizabeth's recriminations dead in their tracks. She had to admit it had been a wonderful day and the *new* Gladys was pretty amazing and unbelievably talented. Her mother was practically a stranger to her now, she was getting younger by the hour, and not just emotionally, but physically too. The life that she had with these two *friends* was something that Elizabeth had never known about and the entire situation was fascinating – and frightening.

Gladys stopped as they reached the edge of the forest. Ahead of them was nothing but a vast field stretching towards the horizon melting with the late afternoon sky as it turning a dazzling shade of pink. Elizabeth remarked on the view but as she looked at her mother she saw the weight of a major burden lying heavily on her heart. She saw an exhausted, almost broken woman, gazing into the distance. In that moment there was a small, almost imperceptible shift in Elizabeth's attitude. What was this new emotion? Could she possibly be feeling empathy? That one emotion that was practically extinct in 21st Century life. She reached out and touched her mother's hand. Gladys grasped it like a lifeline holding back tears. The bond between the two secured, Elizabeth waited patiently staring at her mother until Gladys took a deep breath and began to tell her story.

"This is something I hoped I would never have to tell you, I thought it wouldn't be necessary and I promised your father it would never come up. But we are in a bit of a pickle, Little One, and I have to ask you a huge favour."

It had been a long time since anyone had called Elizabeth *Little One*. The name instantly made her feel comforted. A smile spread across her face as she remembered the terms of endearment that Gladys had given to her and Jessie in childhood, "Little One" and "Princess". Elizabeth had felt cheated out of the more lavish title but standing here with her *little* Mum she relished the title.

"These women are my ... friends," she continued, "friends I have known for many years now. I lived here once, in all this beauty, and for a long time Shiona, Daphne and I worked together righting wrongs, overthrowing corruption and cowardice - all from the comfort of our own homes and our glorious glen."

"What!" Elizabeth said, "*Overthrowing Corruption*? What the hell does that........"

"Please Little One! Just let me finish before you start firing questions at me!" Elizabeth nodded quietly and Gladys paused for a moment, considering how to continue. "One day, I met a man. A wonderful man and although I tried I couldn't stop myself from falling in love with him. Even though they knew I would have to leave, Shiona and Daphne didn't judge me. They wished me nothing but happiness and only asked that I make a promise to return one day, if necessary, to carry on our work. But days, turned to years, years turned to decades and to be honest, they didn't really need me anymore. And my life as a wife turned to one as a mother and I immersed myself in it and I loved it! I was utterly fulfilled by it and I knew that Albert was the love of my lifetimes and we were all strong together, as a family."

"Mum, why haven't you ever told me.........?"

"When you and Jessie were quite young," Gladys continued ignoring Elizabeth, "I got a message from Daphne. Shiona was too proud to ask but they needed my help. When I arrived, the problem was worse than I thought. Another...," Gladys paused for a moment and eyed Elizabeth cautiously searching for the right words, ".....*fascist dictator* had been causing problems and Shiona and Daphne had been fighting him alone, he'd gone into hiding but was still powerful..."

"My God Mum, what are you guys?! Spies?"

"No questions Elizabeth!"

"Sorry."

"Together," Gladys continued shooting Elizabeth a warning look, "Shiona, Daphne and I are a pretty incredible team. But Shiona and Daphne had begun to notice..... *leaks*.....and where we found and treated these um.......*leaks*......we also found evidence of the....um...um...."

"*Fascist dictator*," Elizabeth offered.

"That's right! Fascist dictator!"

"I'm sorry Mum," Elizabeth said, trying to decipher her mother's rather cryptic story. "I'm just not getting it. What "leaks" are you talking about? Do you mean like government secrets? Are you trying to tell me that you, Shiona and Daphne, (of all people)" she muttered under her breath, "are the only people who can stop this dictator?"

"*Fascist* dictator," Gladys corrected.

"*Fascist* dictator," Elizabeth replied. "Really Mum, what do they need you for, why don't you go to MI5 or 6, whichever one that deals with *fascist dictators* and be done with it. You can't honestly tell me that the three of you can cope with that kind of thing now. After all, you're not getting any young....."

The last words were barely out of her mouth when something knocked her off her feet and she landed heavily on her backside in a muddy ditch splattering her hair, face and clothes.

"What the hell was that?" She yelled sitting in the middle of a cold, damp, muddy puddle. She tried to get up, lost her footing, and fell flat on her face in the dirty water.

"Plagh! Plagh!" She cried spitting out mud.

"HA! HA HA HA!"

She heard a familiar laugh behind her and wiped dirt out of her eyes in time to see Daphne and Shiona approaching.

"I'm not sure you've quite got it have you Betty!" Daphne laughed, helping Elizabeth to her feet.

"Who did that?" Gladys asked, suddenly angry, glaring at Shiona.

"It wasn't me!" Shiona said defensively.

They both turned to look at Daphne who was trying to look completely innocent, "just a little nudge in the right direction," she said.

"Who did what, Mum?"

"Nothing," Gladys replied crossly, "it doesn't matter!"

Elizabeth knew her mother well enough to know when not to push a matter, but Shiona had no such understanding.

"But it *does* matter Gladys," she said, "this is what you've been trying to tell her, what you've been skirting around."

"I was getting to it!" Gladys shouted.

"What?" Elizabeth said, getting very confused.

"*Fascist dictator*!" Daphne scoffed and they all looked at her.

There was a palpable friction in the air between the three women, most of it aimed at Daphne. After a few moments of silence Daphne finally piped up.

"I knocked you on your arse," she said happily.

"What?" Elizabeth asked.

"Just then," Daphne continued, pointing at the ditch. "I did that."

"I fell!" Elizabeth said, becoming more and more agitated by Daphne's attempts at humour.

"HA! HA......AARRGH!"

Then, right in front of her eyes, Elizabeth saw Daphne, mid-laugh, rise from the ground, hover in the air and begin to spin around. Slowly at first and then faster and faster, until Elizabeth's stomach churned at the sight.

"I'm gonna be sick!" Elizabeth said.

"SO AM I," screamed the revolving Daphne, "PUT ME DOWN!"

"NO!" Came the reply and as Elizabeth slowly turned she saw that Gladys' face was contorted with rage and concentration. She was holding a stick in her right hand and twirling it around and around. "Not until you say sorry!" Gladys called up to the pathetic spinning figure.

"I'm bloody sorry!" Daphne called down, sounding far from apologetic.

"Oh this is ridiculous," Shiona said and she grabbed something out of her coat that Elizabeth could barely see. She flicked her wrist and Gladys fell to her knees. As she did Daphne came crashing to earth with a thud and landed in the same ditch Elizabeth had been in only moments before.

"You two are acting like children," Shiona said stepping between the pair.

Gladys rose quickly to her feet aiming the stick at Daphne.

"You say sorry to Elizabeth now," she said rounding on Daphne holding the stick firmly under Daphne's chin.

"Or what?" came Daphne's reply as she ferreted around in her own jacket pocket trying to find something.

"Or I'll ..."

But Gladys didn't get a chance to reveal exactly what she would do to Daphne because her hands involuntarily jumped behind her back and stayed firmly in place, no matter how much she struggled.

"Shiona!" Gladys shouted, "Let me go!"

"I won't!" Shiona said and Elizabeth could see that she too had a stick in her hand that she was now pointing at Gladys. "This is ridiculous. You stop this nonsense now!" Suddenly Shiona turned her attention to Daphne, "and you apologise properly or believe me I can be a whole lot more creative than Gladys!"

Gladys stopped struggling and Daphne sulked for a moment or two.

"I'm sorry," she said finally managing to sound sincere.

Shiona released her invisible hold over Gladys. "Satisfied?" she asked.

"I suppose," came Gladys' sulky reply and the three women turned towards Elizabeth.

Elizabeth was watching them in horrified silence. She had just witnessed one woman after another being thrown around by a seemingly invisible force only to realise that the force was actually coming from the women themselves. She had turned her arm blue from pinching herself, believing, hoping, she was actually asleep. Now they looked towards Elizabeth and she cowered away from them.

"What... are... you?" She managed, in a tiny, croaky voice.

"I thought that might be obvious by now my girl," Shiona replied, "we're witches."

Chapter Eight

The next few minutes passed in a blur for Elizabeth. Her knees began to buckle and she sat with a thud on the ground. Her mother was there instantly, sitting beside her, supporting her. Elizabeth clasped her head in her hands in the vain hope she could stop her brain from imploding. She was vaguely aware of a conversation going on between them. Shiona was saying something about Gladys being "too protective" and Gladys' temper was threatening to flare again, but Elizabeth wasn't taking it in.

Witches! She thought and the word hit her squarely in the face. What did that mean exactly? Her childhood notion of witches was cauldrons, broomsticks and warty noses. The three women standing around her bickering were just normal women. And yet when was the last time she saw "normal women" control each other with a magical force. She had observed some women physically weaken each other with hard stares and bitchy remarks but this was a little bit more than preying on someone's insecurities.

Witches! She thought as she clutched her head. She wanted to ask, "What do you mean? What the hell do you mean?" She wanted to shout, "Don't be ridiculous! You're just teasing me!" but the words would not come. Above all else she just did not want to believe that her mother could harm someone with the ferocity of her anger. And then all at once the memory of the fateful night in the train station came flooding back. The rage within, the power, the memory of it hit her and she suddenly knew where it all came from.

She looked slowly towards her mother. She felt her mother's warm, comforting touch but she could not shake the image of Gladys's enraged face from her mind. Every notion that Elizabeth once believed to be true about her mother was fast disappearing like grains of sand running through fingers. And knowing what her mother was capable of suddenly made the destruction Elizabeth had caused just outside of the train station, very possible and plausible. For a long time now Elizabeth had put that episode down to a figment of her imagination. Now she knew it could have been real. And it was all her mother's fault.

Elizabeth managed to stagger to her feet. Daphne and Shiona, who had carried on bickering with one another, fell silent as they watched her rise. Elizabeth forced herself to look at their faces. A horrible, unbelievable truth now sat between them simultaneously separating them and joining them. They were locked together in a world of indescribable and inexcusable power. All Elizabeth could do was turn and run.

She ran. She ran as fast as she could and kept on running even with the shouts from the others behind her telling her to "please stay" and "not be so naïve" and on and on. Their shouts continued on but she knew she had to run. At first she was directionless and scared but then she thought she recognised some of the passing countryside. Suddenly she was grateful to Daphne for sending her on a fool's errand. She knew the fields she was running through, knew where she was going – she was heading back to the cottage.

She carried on running. She had absolutely no idea if she was being followed or if she would suddenly feel her feet being lifted from under her. She knew she was powerless to stop the women controlling her or hurting her, but she did not stop running. She was no athlete but that did not seem to matter now. Physical fitness was unnecessary, she was being carried along on a wave of adrenaline. *Fight* or *flight* and she had chosen the latter.

Her heart was throbbing in her chest as she rounded the corner and approached the little cottage at high speed. She thought an attack would come at any moment. It didn't matter to her that one of those women was her mother. She saw what they were able to do to one another, more than that, she knew what she was capable of too. The image of the scorched corpses in the tunnel swam back into view.

There was no sign of the three witches as she darted up the path and jumped over her picket fence towards the cottage. She fumbled with her keys, looking around wildly as she found them, dropped them and found them again.

With shaking hands she finally managed to unlock the door and let herself in. She slammed it shut behind her, bolted it and leant heavily against it. With her back to the door her eyes darted around the little cottage. She did not even know if they had magically appeared in her home making her manic dash for escape utterly pointless.

Breathing heavily, her back to the door, she waited. She was dizzy and light-headed from the run. Her vision was impaired by her efforts and the room looked hazy. She took some deep breaths desperately trying to get her breathing under control and her vision back to 20/20 so that she was prepared for an oncoming attack.

After a few minutes she was breathing normally but not easily. She was too frightened to move away from the closed door. *What the hell is going on*, she thought, *I mean what the bloody hell is going on? Is that really my mother out there? How the hell can that be my mother out there?!* Then another thought struck her, maybe it wasn't Gladys after all. Maybe the reason she seemed so different since they'd been in this little Scottish village was because she *was* different. She was a completely different woman. Maybe it was magic that had made her look like Gladys. That woman was not her mother, could not be her mother.

KNOCK KNOCK.

Elizabeth jumped. The knocking came from behind her and was uncomfortably close. She swung around and grabbed the nearest weapon she could find, her butterfly covered umbrella. Her breathing became heavy again but she said nothing.

Knock knock.

The last knock was much more tentative, but still Elizabeth did not say a word. Maybe if she stayed quiet they would think she had not come home. Maybe they would believe that she had run straight to the station, hopped on the first train to anywhere and they would never see her again. The fact that the nearest train station was miles away, and they could have easily caught up with her didn't occur to Elizabeth in her terrified state.

"Hello Betty!"

She turned quickly to see where the voice was coming from. There in the window looking in, spotting Elizabeth easily was the grinning face of Daphne, waving inanely.

"GO AWAY!" Elizabeth shouted.

"Oh dear," Daphne said turning toward the other two, "I think she's in a bit of a state."

"Honestly Daphne," Gladys said pushing the enormous woman to one side and looking through the window.

"Let us in love, we can sort all this out."

Elizabeth looked straight at the woman that she had been sharing tea and toast with that morning, "who are you?" she said quietly.

"Little One, don't do this."

"*I* haven't done anything!" Elizabeth screamed, "WHAT HAVE *YOU* DONE WITH MY MOTHER!"

"Oh Elizabeth, it's me," Gladys said sadly and sagged.

Shiona came into view putting a comforting arm on Gladys' shoulder that was instantly shaken off.

"I told you this would happen," Gladys hissed at Shiona.

Shiona looked in through the window, "You come out here now and talk to us!" She shouted.

"Get away from me!" Elizabeth cried, "get her away from me! ALL OF YOU – get away from me NOW!" She was breathing heavily again and getting dizzy.

Gladys could see her daughter turn a disturbing shade of red and tried to calm her. "It's OK, it's OK," she said soothingly. "We're not coming in. We're going to stay out here until you're ready to talk."

"But we *could* get in if we wanted to," Daphne said matter-of-factly.

"NOT NOW DAPHNE!" Gladys screamed pushing the woman back out of the window frame.

"This is ridiculous!" Shiona said and with that the front door blew violently into the cottage missing Elizabeth by inches. As she looked to where the door had once been she saw the tiny shape of Shiona standing there with outstretched arms, with her stick in her hand.

The stick that even in her shocked state, Elizabeth realised was a witches' tool of power – her magic wand.

"There you go." Shiona said to Gladys, gesturing for her to go inside.

"No Shiona," Gladys shouted, "not like this!"

And with that the door hovered in the air, flew back to where it had come from and reattached itself to the distorted frame. Within seconds the frame had been perfectly repaired with no sign of a disturbance.

Elizabeth watched in open-mouthed disbelief. She slumped to the floor.

"Go away," Elizabeth said quietly.

"Come on," Gladys said. "She's had enough." She gestured for her friends to follow and they turned away from the cottage leaving Elizabeth alone lost in her thoughts and fears.

***

For a few days Daphne, Shiona and Gladys would come over to the little house and coerce, goad, or chide Elizabeth through the unopened door. Daphne came on her own on one occasion and told Elizabeth joke after joke with a magical flavour, clearly trying to make light of the situation but to no avail. After three days Shiona and Daphne stopped bothering all together, leaving Gladys as the only contact.

Elizabeth did very little with the time except for feel sorry for herself and she was becoming something of an expert at that. Her mother would sit next to the door apologising, chatting and sometimes reminiscing but none of her attempts worked. The only thing that Elizabeth did come to realise was that this woman was indeed her mother. The woman she had looked towards to feel safe and connected to her whole life was now a complete stranger to her. Gladys was not so different though, she was still nurturing, still caring. She always left a food package so Elizabeth could wallow in well fed misery and didn't even have to leave the house.

Elizabeth spent most of her time in bed. She was numb and exhausted and sleeping was the only respite she had from the misery which was now much less about her mother's betrayal and much more about Elizabeth's own experience with the men in the tunnel. When she did wake up she rarely dressed, preferring to spend the day in her pyjamas. The unkempt laziness of her attire matched her mood perfectly and she was extremely adept at giving every situation its full drama. She would listen to her mother's ramblings in silence not knowing how to reply and not really caring whether she did or not.

When Shiona and Daphne stopped coming, Elizabeth really wanted to speak to her mother but as time passed she found it more and more difficult to mutter a sound. Her mother's musings were comforting and Elizabeth began to look forward to her visits, but she still refused to let her in. Although she was unable to comprehend or admit it, Elizabeth had reached her lowest ebb and was in the grip of a full blown depression.

On the sixth day Gladys popped over for her morning chat, as usual, leaving Elizabeth supplies for the day. When she came back for her second visit that evening Gladys had something very particular to say.

"I can't keep coming back here every day my love, and you certainly can't stay locked up in there for the rest of your life. Now I've been thinking about it and I think you have two options, you can come home and I can do my best to make sure you forget all about the past week and you can start a new life back home utterly unaware of the fact that your mother is a witch," Elizabeth flinched at the word, "or, you can open this door, get over yourself and help the three of us with a problem that could ultimately affect the whole of mankind.

"Now I know that's a daunting thought but surely it's better than sitting in that house all day and all night worrying yourself into an early grave. I'm offering you a chance to make a bit of a difference in the world. *I* know you're capable of it, do you?"

Elizabeth was slumped against the door on the inside, Gladys was sat cross-legged outside. The two women were sitting on opposing sides, one in exhaustion and confusion the other in hope and resolution.

Elizabeth knew her mother was right. She knew that this self-imposed imprisonment could not last forever and deep down she did not want it to last forever. But as weak and as vulnerable as she felt two months ago when she ran back to her sister's flat in London believing she had murdered 3 young men was nothing compared to the fragility she felt now. Her mother was her rock, the one person she could turn to when the whole world seemed to be losing its appeal and was becoming a lost and lonely place. Gladys was always there with Albert to offer stable and comforting advice. Over the past few days Elizabeth had come to realise how much she depended on them for security but they were different people now and the world, *her* world, had gone mad.

"I don't expect you to be able to decide right now," Gladys continued, "but just read this." Gladys passed an old piece of paper under the door to Elizabeth. "It might help you realise that I didn't reveal my other life to you just to make you miserable, I did it because I need your help. We all do."

Elizabeth could hear her mother readying herself to leave. She heard her get up on the other side of the door, not easily, Gladys was not a young woman anymore. Sadly Elizabeth listened to the slow retreat of fading footsteps. She sat with glazed eyes staring, not focussing on anything in particular and not wanting to look at the piece of parchment that Gladys had passed to her.

She sat there for nearly an hour before the call of nature interrupted her contemplations. She got up to answer it and as she did her hand touched the paper and her eyes briefly and involuntarily scanned the sheet. She stopped as she was rising. A word had caught her eye. Just one word but it was enough to spark Elizabeth's interest. Somewhere in the depths of her self-pity she was still interested in a good ole fairy tale. The word was "gypsy".

She picked up the paper and took it to the bathroom with her. She ran herself a bath and read it. She got into the bath and read it again. She put on some clean pyjamas, got into bed and read it for the third time. Before she was ready to turn off the light that evening she had read the parchment 12 times. It was only one sheet of paper but it was all the story she needed. For the first time in a week she set her bird alarm clock and fell to sleep.

She got up the next morning and dressed herself, ate a big breakfast of toast and porridge oats with warm milk all washed down with a cup of tea. She gave her little house a clean, washed the dishes, dressed in her waterproof boots and a warm coat for protection against the early morning chill and opened the front door.

She took in a deep breath of fresh air and began walking towards the beautiful glade that her mother had taken her to what seemed like a lifetime ago. She left the door to the cottage wide open. She had no idea where her mother was, but she knew that if Gladys wanted to find her it would not take her too long to realise where she had gone. And if the three witches really did need her help then they needed to get cracking and what better place to start than at Daphne's *training ground*.

Chapter Nine

An account of Baron Von Diederich and the gypsy once known as Ryder
by Elias Tomb.

The Baron and Ryder were childhood friends, from wildly different backgrounds. Amused by each other they put their differences aside and were great friends. However, one aspect of their friendship set them apart from other boys of their age and instilled fear in the townsfolk. The Baron and Ryder tapped into the forbidden powers of the earth.

What started as a game soon became an obsession for the pair as they learnt to harness the powers of nature. But the divine power in nature was not enough for the gypsy known as Ryder and his attentions turned to the mighty animal kingdom and ultimately his fellow man. The boy, Erich Von Diederich, grew up to take his place as head of the family and became Baron after his father died. His new duties educated him in the ways of his people in the small village of Branko. He used what power he had to ensure the lives of his people were harmonious and lost contact with the gypsy known as Ryder.

Many years into the Baron's reign a stranger calling himself Lord Darius, accompanied by his family, visited the small village of Branko. He was charming and enigmatic and although feeling uneasy in his company the Baron welcomed him into his home. But Lord Darius murdered the Baron's men one by one and began to take the villagers hostage. Darius created an army from the vanished villagers who were captured to satisfy his bloodlust. He turned the poor people of Branko into beasts, an echo of his own image, for in his natural state was nothing but a monster. Lord Darius overthrew the Baron and took over Castle von Diederich throwing the Baron to the mercy of his once loyal village folk.

Lost, beaten and left for dead the Baron was found by the villagers who had not yet been turned by Lord Darius, who had hidden away and kept themselves safe. Through the goodness and kindness of these people the Baron began to recall the ancient supernatural powers that had been lost to him, but never forgotten. Using the heart and soul of the village the Baron became strong again and set out to overthrow Lord Darius.

A great battle ensued but Lord Darius was no match for the love and defiance of the Baron and his people. The poor souls that were once lost were returned to the Baron by three sisters in the village who also knew how to call up the mighty supernatural power of the land. His people now returned to him the Baron fought magnificently and with the magical powers that he shared with the 3 sisters he placed a protective dome over the land of Branko. Taking as many souls as they could the Baron and the sisters fled from Branko leaving this small piece of land in the charge of Lord Darius.

Darius' plans to conquer the world were halted at Branko. The Baron and the sisters lived out their days patrolling the Branko dome ensuring the continued imprisonment of Lord Darius.

Lord Darius cannot escape, he is imprisoned by a love of the land that he cannot possibly comprehend as he has no love in his soul. Lord Darius the betrayer, the usurper, the monster, was once the gypsy known as Ryder.

****

Elizabeth sat at the training ground with the parchment in her hand re-reading the story. It was an ancient story of good versus evil but she did not know how relevant it was to her current dilemma, or for that matter, what it had to do with her mother. She had no idea the part she would play in the final chapter of the story of Branko. All she knew was she had a lot of questions to ask and she did not want to do that behind a closed door. Elizabeth had not been in the beautiful glen long when Gladys strode into the clearing. She gulped when she saw the expression on her mother's face. Gladys was livid.

The conversation started coolly, "hello," Elizabeth said.

"Mm-hm," Gladys just about managed and Elizabeth knew her mother well enough to know when she was fighting the urge to shout and scream. Taking a deep breath she carried on, "nothing need be said, as long as we're willing to let bygones be bygones then we can move on from here."

"No," Elizabeth said simply, "there *is* something that needs to be said." She walked over to her mother and although she was still clearly very angry she allowed Elizabeth to take her hands. "I behaved like a brat. I had some stuff going on in London before I left that frightened me, and maybe one day I'll tell you about it but for now I just want to say that I'm sorry. Believe it or not I actually think what you can do is amazing! I'm sorry," she finished in a small voice.

Gladys nodded slowly but said nothing and the tear-filled reconciliatory hug that Elizabeth was expecting did not come.

"My job," Gladys said after what seemed like ages, "is to train you how to make plants grow. Not in a traditional, plant the seed, water the seed way you understand but in a more.........." Gladys carried on like this for a while but Elizabeth was more concerned with the tale of Lord Darius and the Baron. She had read and reread the parchment and she felt like she knew the two men. She was intrigued by the reference to the three sisters and assumed they were also three witches. She was fascinated by the story and longed to find out more. But she felt her time would be better spent building bridges with her mother who had somehow forgotten all about the parchment she pushed under Elizabeth's door.

The tension began to lift between the women and Elizabeth ventured a joke about when she could get her own magic wand only to be met by a stony look from her mother. Clearly, Gladys was not ready to joke about the incident.

"I don't understand why you're still so cross Mum," Elizabeth said petulantly, "I've said sorry."

"Don't get me started Elizabeth, whatever you do. You've made my life hell for the last week now let's just try to put it behind us."

"But Mum........."

The look on Gladys' face made Elizabeth clam up quickly and she decided to be an obedient student until she had regained her mother's trust.

The two women worked together bringing perfection to the plants within the glade. It was hard at first because all species were so well formed that they needed little work. But after a while Gladys showed Elizabeth how it was possible to use too much power on a plant, making them grow too fast and quickly into old age, one step away from death. That's when Gladys taught Elizabeth to rescue them.

Under the tuition of her mother, Elizabeth began very slowly to encourage the plants to grow. Her first success was a blade of grass.

"It's all about the intention," Gladys explained, "as long as you are crystal clear in your thoughts you can do anything."

Elizabeth cupped the grass and willed it to grow. She watched as the grass grew from 1 inch to 2 inches in her hand. She was thrilled, it had taken her hours to perfect the spell.

After they had been working solidly for three days Elizabeth was starting to find her own abilities and was slowly beginning to manipulate nature. Every time she fixed a broken leaf or mended a bent stem she was exhilarated by the power. But her excitement always gleaned another lecture from her mother about always using her gifts for the greater good.

"After all," her mother said time and time again, "with great power comes great responsibility."

After hearing this particular phrase for the umpteenth time Elizabeth spoke out. "*You* didn't say that."

"Yes I did," Gladys said looking confused, "didn't you just hear me say it?"

"No I don't mean you didn't *just* say it, I mean you didn't say it originally."

"Oh I don't know who said it. I remembered it and thought it was very apt. Anyway, the point is, be careful how you use this power and don't get cocky!" Gladys paused for a moment deep in thought. Suddenly she said, "Oh, I *do* know who said it! It was Spiderman's uncle," and with a chuckle she carried on encouraging a tree sapling to grow.

At the end of another busy day Elizabeth and Gladys started the long walk back to the cottage. They had been getting on very well but as the darkening sky encouraged them to quicken their step Gladys became quiet.

"You OK Mum?" Elizabeth asked.

"I've told Daphne and Shiona how well you're getting on and they think it's time we went to phase two."

"Phase two?"

"The next step in your training."

"Ok," Elizabeth said feeling a little crestfallen. She had enjoyed the time with her mother and had forgotten all about watching the women fight. The thought of having to face Shiona's cold stares and Daphne's irrepressible mirth filled her with dread.

"It is important my love," Gladys said noticing Elizabeth's reluctance. "I don't want you to go to Branko without being completely prepared."

Elizabeth's ears pricked up at the first mention of the Baron and his story.

"Mum, will you please tell me what this is all about. Was there really a Baron who placed a protective dome over an entire village? Is that even possible?"

"It really is a long story Elizabeth," Gladys said.

"I can imagine!" Elizabeth said. "But I have to know Mum, it's only fair."

Gladys sighed heavily. "Where do I start," she said.

"At the beginning," Elizabeth offered with a sarcastic grin.

"The story of the Baron and his childhood friend *is* true," Gladys began as they started the long walk back to the cottage. "The two boys found ancient writings within the caves that Castle von Diederich itself stood on. They were already naturally talented within these arts but the writings helped them grow stronger. Their experiments took them deeper into ancient and mystical powers and Ryder uncovered a terrible manuscript buried deep within the walls of the caverns. This manuscript had been hidden and walled up for good reason, within it was the way to harness darker powers. But the Baron was frightened of the more malevolent forces and the friendship between the two soured and eventually broke down altogether. Without the Baron to keep him in check and left to his own devices Ryder became power hungry and sought out ways to control things other than the elements. He started with birds and beasts in the fields before turning his attention on his fellow man. It was said that the two of them had an almighty row and Ryder ran away clutching this evil manuscript. He disappeared for years. In that time he harnessed the worst power of all, he exposed his soul to pure evil changing him forever and forcing him to live as a beast for eternity."

As the sun began to set Gladys went on to say that the gypsy Ryder died and in his place a monster remained. But that monster evolved and regained some of its forgotten consciousness. "When Ryder finally tamed the beast within and found his way out of the woods he had reinvented himself," Gladys continued. "He now went by the name of Lord Darius and was utterly powerful. He was no longer a man but no longer a creature. He adopted a respectable exterior but the beast within needed to satisfy an all-consuming bloodlust. He fed on the blood of people he found. He would kill them entirely or leave them in a half-life, neither human nor beast, and they acquired a bloodlust of their own. In no time Lord Darius had a following of these creatures. Some he would allow to reach their full consciousness again by casting spells over them. There was one story that he fell in love with one of his victims, brought her back to consciousness and called her his wife."

"My God!" Elizabeth exclaimed, "They sound like vampires."

"The rest happened as it says in Elias' account," Gladys continued. "Lord Darius came looking for reconciliation with the Baron, but the Baron barely recognised his old friend. He would not sit and serve Lord Darius, no matter how powerful he seemed.

"They fought, Darius won. The Baron was left for dead but he summoned the ancient power of the land once again and this time three sisters were listening. The witches revived him and the townsfolk loved him and this gave the Baron such power that nobody was a match for him.

"The fear that Darius found within people he thrived on, it fed him almost as much as the souls that were drained of their blood. But the Baron was a brave and mighty leader and with him the villagers felt stronger. The people were no longer afraid of Darius."

As they reached the cottage Gladys went on to explain that the final deal that the Baron struck with Darius was that, in memory of their childhood friendship, the Baron would allow Darius to live. But it was to be an existence between worlds. Darius could no longer stray from the lands, acquiring power and preying on the souls of the miserable and fearful. He was confined to stay in the land of Branko with his *wife* and children. A few villagers stayed as a point of contact for the Baron, but only those with a particular strength of character – that did not scare easily.

"Everyone else left," Gladys continued sipping the cup of tea Elizabeth handed to her, "the Baron and the three sisters and most of the villagers. They lived out their lives in the real world, affected by time as we all are. So the Baron and the sisters grew old and died and Darius was all but forgotten. Until Daphne and Shiona uncovered his story and linked it to some strange occurrences they were investigating in the real world."

"Oh!" Elizabeth said sitting at the table, "the leaks!"

"That's right, the leaks. As the centuries passed Darius became very clever and started to look for ways into our world, a world he wanted to consume with his evil. He had manipulated some of the villagers that stayed behind, had turned them into his puppets.

"These poor souls would be sent through weak spots in our reality. These weak spots weren't hard to find for Darius. He only had to search for places where anger and resentment bred swathes of negativity. All he had to do was to look to the cities! Wherever he found these leaks, Daphne and Shiona would find these poor souls that had been stripped of their humanity, shadow souls, barely recognisable as humans."

"Zombies?"

"No, nothing as scary as zombies! In fact these poor creatures weren't scary at all. They were merely experiments thrown through the leaks that Darius found to see if the rift would ever be big enough to carry the evil that he brought with him. Shiona and Daphne found the souls and revived them."

"Weren't they evil?"

"No Elizabeth they were just abused souls. And where there is a soul there is always a spark of good. Daphne and Shiona would find that spark and try to bring these creatures back to something resembling humanity. But they could only do so much. Each human being is made of 3 vital components, mind, body and spirit. Shiona's skills are to cure the body, Daphne's the mind...."

Elizabeth scoffed.

"It's true! She has the healing power of laughter and believe me there is nothing better for curing a troubled mind. But they weren't complete without their souls. That's why witches are most effective in threes, why we always have been. Some people have called us the maiden, the mother and the crone, although don't let Shiona hear you call her a crone!"

They both laughed.

"But it all amounts to the same thing, mind, body and spirit. What is one without the other two? All three need to be in harmony for a person to exist in peace. That's why Daphne called me again. We revived these poor souls, brought them back into existence and they gave us the key to finding Darius. We found him, fought him and once again took his power. But without the Baron there was only so much we could do.

"So we take a yearly trip on 31st October when the expectation of magic is at its highest and therefore Darius's opportunity is at its best. We strip him of as much power as we can, weaken him and by the next year – he is strong again."

"This is mind-blowing Mum," Elizabeth said putting some food on the table. "Can things like this actually happen?"

"They can and they do. But most people need never know. And that's how we would like to keep it. If, for one year only, the girls *didn't* take that trip, Darius would become too powerful. He has to be contained and the only way to do it is to send *three* witches."

"Then why don't you go?"

"I can't Elizabeth, I wish I could," Gladys sighed heavily, "I'm too old now."

"That's rubbish Mum, you're no older than Shiona."

"No, you're right. In fact, she's older than me, and Daphne a little younger. But they stayed here and kept practicing magic. I moved to the West Country with your Dad a long time ago and I've got too much to lose. Standing up to Darius is more than about having supernatural powers, it's about having confidence, and bravado. He's very clever you see, and very manipulative. If I were to face him he could read in me that I have more love for you and your father and your sister than I do for myself and he would see that as a weakness and use it against me.

The fear of something happening to my family would be too much for me. I would be a weak link in this chain of power and that's the last thing humanity needs."

"*You* a weak link, what about me? I jump at my own shadow. I go on and on about how I want an exciting life, but could I actually live with that excitement? If anything crazy happened to me Mum, I know I would......I would......" she trailed off not wanting to relive that moment in the alleyway.

"You would what love?"

"I wouldn't be any use to you there Mum, I know it. Look at how I reacted when I found out about you. It completely did me in."

"That's why I didn't tell you. I didn't want you to be part of this. I wanted a normal life for you and your sister. These troubles were mine and Daphne's and Shiona's. No-one else's."

"So why are you telling me now then?"

"Because you're not happy Elizabeth. You never have been. I've watched you living different lives, trying on different roles and I've always hoped you'd find something that fit but you never did. Then I thought to myself, what if *this* is what you are meant to do. What if I'm stopping you finding your path?"

Mother and daughter sat in silence eating their supper for a while. Of course Gladys was right. Elizabeth was 25, nearly 26 years old and she watched her friends take their chosen paths, gain their qualifications and work in the industries they loved, while she was still struggling to find out what the hell she wanted to do.

"And don't forget we're starting phase two tomorrow," Gladys said getting up from the table and putting on her coat.

"Oh yes, phase two." Elizabeth smirked.

"I'll pick you up in the morning and we'll drive there together."

"Where?" Elizabeth asked, surprised to hear they would be going somewhere other than the training ground.

"Just you wait and see," Gladys said with a wry smile, "and don't worry, you're going to LOVE it!"

Chapter Ten

Early the next morning Gladys knocked on the door of the cottage. Elizabeth was ready. She had barely slept all night, excited about the next stage of training especially after seeing the glint in her mother's eye. Gladys had hardly finished knocking when Elizabeth burst through the door, dressed head to foot in her warm clothes, ready for another outdoor adventure.

She thought about Lord Darius for most of the night and her natural instinct was to be terrified. He sounded like a monster the likes of which she had never encountered, but by the end of the evening she had become more and more thrilled at the prospect of meeting him. She did not even wait for the light of the early morning before dressing and readying herself for the day's events. She ate well and sat waiting for her mother already dressed in her boots and waterproof coat.

Two hours later her mother finally rapped on the door and Elizabeth jumped up practically knocking her mother over as she bowled passed her. Gladys smiled and closed the door behind her watching Elizabeth as she ran down the path to the picket fence and the gateway to the driveway beyond. Just as she reached the garden gate Elizabeth froze. There parked in her narrow driveway was an image that sent shivers through her very soul.

"You did *not* come in that death trap did you?" She shouted at her mother.

The contraption in question was a Citroen 2cv. It had a faded red body and the sunroof was white. It looked more like a pram on wheels than anything resembling a safe mode of transportation to Elizabeth.

"Don't worry," said Gladys laughing at Elizabeth's reaction. "I know how to drive it!"

"That's not what I'm worrying about!"

But Gladys was already in the car and Elizabeth realised her protestations were pointless.

"Whose car is this?" She asked as she carefully lowered herself into the passenger seat.

"Shiona's. But she doesn't drive it that often which is why it's a little bit neglected."

"A *little bit* neglected!"

Gladys started up the engine and reached up to the dashboard for the gear stick, grinding the gears until she found one she was happy with. She looked across at Elizabeth who was scrabbling around over her left shoulder desperately trying to detach the thread bare seatbelt from its holster. Gladys couldn't help but laugh at her daughter's nervousness. Elizabeth glared at her mother.

"Just when I thought there was nothing else you could do to scare me!" Elizabeth cried.

"Where's your sense of adventure," Gladys replied revving the engine twice and raising her eyebrows in perfect unison. Gladys reversed the car at unnerving speed and stopped just before crashing into a gatepost. She ground the dashboard gear stick mercilessly once again and kangaroo hopped out of the driveway.

Once they were on the open road the car found its rhythm and chugged along happily. Gladys hummed as they continued their journey, Elizabeth carried on fighting with the seatbelt over her shoulder, still unable to detach it, believing it was the only thing between her and certain death.

"Don't worry about the seatbelt my love." Gladys said. "If we do get hit by anything this thing will crumble like a biscuit. The seatbelt would be useless anyway!"

"Honestly Mum, that's not funny!"

But Gladys was clearly enjoying herself.

"I think you've been spending a bit too much time with Daphne," Elizabeth chastised. "You might have to move back in with me before you get any worse!"

That particularly tickled Gladys and she dissolved into another fit of giggles. Elizabeth tried really hard not to laugh but her mother's mirth was becoming contagious.

"Seriously though Mum," she said stifling a smile, "concentrate!"

Gladys saluted at her daughter and tried to curb her merriment. Laughter was indeed a great healer and after Elizabeth's initial fears for her life, she began to relax. For the first time in a long time Gladys and Elizabeth forgot about their problems and enjoyed the time together as any normal mother and daughter.

After 25 minutes Gladys and Elizabeth reached their destination. Elizabeth was surprised as they turned the corner and entered a disused airfield. The dirty grey tarmac was old and broken and weeds were growing up through the cracks. At the end of the runway was a dilapidated building that must have once been an aircraft hangar.

Elizabeth looked around in wonder as they climbed out of the car. Gladys took the lead and walked towards the hanger.

"Are we not working outside today?" She asked her mother.

"Not today," Gladys replied, "training is going to be a little bit different today."

The old aircraft hangar had seen better days. It was timber built and the wood was now a rampant breeding ground for woodworm. The whole building looked as though it would topple at any moment. Gladys and Elizabeth walked inside.

The inner building told a different story. It had been cleaned up and made safe. Although there were still holes in the roof where the wooden beams had rotted allowing the sun above to stream through, casting shafts of light on the ground, but what plaster there was left had been painted white and there had been attempts at structural renovation. Externally the building screamed DO NOT ENTER but internally it was fresh and slightly more inviting.

Just as she was about to ask her mother what they were doing there she heard a familiar voice behind her.

"Hello Betty." It was Daphne.

Taking a deep breath and stealing herself for the inevitable onslaught of snide comments and inappropriate humour, Elizabeth turned to face Daphne. Standing next to her with her usual expression of disdain was Shiona.

"Let's just get this straight," Shiona started with no attempt to soften the blow, "as you're here I suppose you've decided to come with us to Branko and if that is the case I want no more histrionics, crying, recriminations and terror of any kind. What we have shown you already or will show you today is nothing compared to what you will face in Branko and you need to start toughening up!

"Daphne's going to show you something now," she gestured to Daphne that she should take up position, "and you will probably want to scream and run away. But I'm warning you this is your last chance. If you get hysterical, I'm done with you, got it?"

Elizabeth sighed, she was never any good at taking a lecture, least of all from someone like Shiona.

"Ok," Elizabeth said flatly.

"I want more than that," Shiona said, "you've got to promise to control yourself."

"Ok, OK!" Elizabeth repeated, "I promise."

"Alright," Shiona said as satisfied as she could be. "Come on out Daphne."

Elizabeth looked towards the door that Daphne had walked through. The three women watched and waited. As the moments passed the air between them began to sizzle with expectation. A few moments more and the tension began to fade.

"Daphne, what are you doing?" Shouted Shiona.

"I'm maximising effect!" Daphne shouted back.

"Not really working," Elizabeth called, "going off the boil here!"

With that a blurred figure crashed through the window from the room at the top of the building, that must have once been the office, and zoomed past them.

Elizabeth barely had time to take in what she was seeing. She looked at Shiona and was surprised to see Daphne standing next to her with a satisfied look on her face. Shiona rolled her eyes.

"What are you doing?" Shiona asked Daphne. "How on earth is she going to learn if you go at that speed?"

"You wanted me to teach her," Daphne answered back, "so let me do it my way."

"Ok fine," Shiona said backing off, "but don't blame me if she doesn't learn a thing."

Elizabeth stared at the pair utterly bemused. "Um...just what are you supposed to be teaching me?"

"I'm in charge of teaching you how witches get around Betty. And I'm the best one to show you how because I'm particularly fantastic at it."

With that she pulled out a rather innocuous looking long-handled brush from behind her back.

"Are you trying to tell me that you actually fly on broomsticks?" Elizabeth scoffed.

"That's exactly what I'm trying to tell you." Daphne said.

She climbed onto the broomstick with ease placing her foot on the cluster of twigs at the bottom and holding onto the neck at the top. With effortless grace she glided elegantly into the air and hovered just above Elizabeth's head.

Daphne gazed down at the three women, Elizabeth stared back at the hovering giant, Shiona and Gladys shot glances at each other waiting for the usual terrified reaction from Elizabeth.

Elizabeth just carried on gawping at Daphne her mouth open in a fixed "O". Suddenly and almost imperceptibly a smile began to spread across Elizabeth's face. It started small and grew into a fixed, demented grin.

"Gimme, gimme, gimme!" She said reaching above her head to Daphne's broom.

Gladys sighed in relief, Shiona raised her eyebrows in surprise and Daphne floated towards Elizabeth mirroring her enormous grin.

Daphne handed the broomstick to Elizabeth. It was not quite the magnificent specimen that she had seen in films about witches. It was worn and grubby and the bristles at the bottom were bent in odd directions but to Elizabeth it was the most amazing thing she had ever seen. She tentatively reached out her hand to take it from Daphne. Once she was in possession of the mighty stick she copied exactly what she had seen Daphne do just moments before. She held it parallel to her body, placed one foot on the bristles at the bottom keeping the other foot on the floor. Then she grasped the broomstick at the top almost in line with her face.

"What do I do now?" She asked, gazing at the broomstick in awe.

"Fly!" Daphne said.

"Fly?" Elizabeth asked and with that the broomstick began to wobble.

"That's it Elizabeth," Gladys said, "it's all about intention. Concentrate."

"Fly." Elizabeth said again. This time the broomstick began to shake.

"Keep your mind focussed girl!" Shiona chipped in.

"Fly!" Elizabeth shouted.

The broom shot through her loose grip, scratching her hand and flew straight up into the air knocking Elizabeth to the floor.

"Ha, ha-ha!" Daphne laughed.

Shiona just tutted and Gladys tried to stifle a giggle as she helped Elizabeth to her feet.

"Why do you ride it like that?" Elizabeth asked, brushing her mother away angrily, trying to hide her embarrassment. "Why don't you get on it properly and ride it like a horse."

"Try it." Daphne offered, passing her the broomstick.

"I will," Elizabeth said defiantly taking the broomstick from Daphne and this time got on it like a cowboy mounting a bull.

Although her right hand was sore from the previous attempt she held on tightly and told the broomstick to, "Fly."

This time the broomstick didn't shake or wobble. Instead it began to rise very slowly from the ground. For 3 seconds the broomstick and Elizabeth hovered in mid-air an inch from the ground.

"That's it," cried Gladys, "you've got it."

Just at that moment Elizabeth said, "down" to the broomstick in a very strained voice.

She dismounted the broom and leaning over held on to the tops of her thighs with both hands. "I can see why you don't ride it that way now," she said breathlessly.

"Hurt your thighs have you Betty?" Daphne asked gleefully.

"You know very well it's not my thighs that are hurting Daphne." Elizabeth said catching her breath. "Ok. You win. Show me what to do."

For the rest of the morning Daphne trained Elizabeth in the delicate art of broomstick flying. Elizabeth spent most of the time falling to the floor on conveniently placed mats that kept magically appearing courtesy of Gladys and Shiona but she did not care. If she had known this was going to be part of the deal she would never have had any concerns about following in her mother's footsteps.

Shiona and Gladys looked on in amazement as Elizabeth relentlessly got back in the saddle. On one occasion she fell close to the pair almost knocking them off the bench they were sat on. She got up and grinned at the two witches, with a mouth full of blood. Up close they could clearly see the bruises and scratches Elizabeth had sustained and watched in disbelief as she limped back towards Daphne.

"I love flying!" She called over her shoulder as she walked away.

After another hour Gladys stepped in and told Daphne and Elizabeth it was probably time to have a break.

"There's something else we need to tell you," she said as Daphne and Elizabeth joined her and Shiona.

"We need to send you to Branko as prepared as we possibly can so you need to know all of the facts," Gladys said, "you aren't the first trainee witch to take on Lord Darius."

"What?" asked Elizabeth.

"And we've never had a witch that was up to the task." Shiona added.

"What do you mean," Elizabeth asked, "surely you've done what was needed by the time you come home."

"Of course," Shiona said, "but they get the fright of their life in Branko and once back home never want to come again. It's important for you to know that this isn't going to be a holiday."

With that Shiona left Elizabeth with a head full of unanswered questions and beckoned Gladys to follow. Elizabeth kept her eye on the pair for a while. They were clearly talking about her. She could not quite hear them but judging by the gestures Shiona was questioning Elizabeth's abilities and Gladys was defending her.

Elizabeth sighed, she was never going to be anything other than a moody teenager in Shiona's eyes and she only had herself to blame.

"Don't worry about her Betty," Daphne said from behind making Elizabeth jump. "She was born with the skin of her arse on her forehead."

Elizabeth burst into laughter. She didn't know exactly what Daphne meant but it was hilarious hearing her talk about Shiona like that.

"Come and sit down Betty," she said gesturing to the now vacant bench.

"What are the girls like that go with you?" Elizabeth asked as she sat.

"Oh they're usually very nice. Very nice indeed." She paused for a moment. "But Shiona's right. It all gets a bit too much for them up there. We give them as much warning as we can but there are some......." she searched for the word, "issues we can't prepare them for. They all come home elevated by the battle but once they're back in the comfort of their old, safe lives we never hear from them again. There was one time," she went on conspiratorially, "that a *man* wanted to come with us! I have no idea how he found out about it but there he was one day on the front step of our shop asking us if he could accompany us on our *annual quest*. Well you know me I just laughed. Shiona raised her eyebrows and ignored him, but I took the time to get to know him and he was a very nice little man indeed. His name was George and just between you and me I had a soft spot for wee George!"

They laughed together. Elizabeth was warming to Daphne. It was difficult *not* to like her. They had spent most of the day falling out of the sky together, it was a necessary part of the training for Elizabeth but Daphne was falling for the sheer fun of it. And through it all they laughed and teased one another and Daphne was thrilled to see Elizabeth take on the challenge with such enthusiasm.

"She's not moaning about George again is she," said Shiona from behind.

"He was a nice man and you were awful to him," Daphne chastised. "Just because you're jealous of my feminine charms." With that she winked at Elizabeth and swaggered back to the abandoned broomstick.

Elizabeth chuckled at the retreating figure and turned her attention back to the two other women. "Why don't you go anymore Mum?"

"Because you and Jessie were growing up and it was getting harder and harder to explain why I was away for a long time."

"Can't you go now that Jessie and I have left home?"

"No I can't. It's like I said yesterday. I'm not quite the girl I used to be!"

"Would you come if *I* asked you to?" Elizabeth asked quietly.

At this question Shiona walked away and left the matter for mother and daughter to discuss. For a moment Gladys said nothing but gazed sadly at her daughter.

"You don't need me," she said finally, "you've got these two old birds and you're going to get the best training. We've still got a whole month before you make the journey. You'll be fine without me." She squeezed Elizabeth's shoulder reassuringly.

"What do you think is going to happen when we get back Mum?" Elizabeth asked, "Do you think I'll lose contact with those two like all the other girls?"

"I really hope not," Gladys replied. "Anyway, I'll always know them and you had better not lose contact with me! Maybe you'll work in their shop after all. I don't know Little One, I can't tell you who you should be or what you should do my lovely. I can only equip you with the tools to find out for yourself."

"Hey Mum," Elizabeth asked remembering a question that she had been meaning to ask her mother all day, "that first night in the cottage, when you said you *flew* up here to meet me........."

She didn't even get a chance to finish the question before Gladys, with a click of her fingers, produced her own broom from nowhere. Elizabeth stared at her mother in utter disbelief as Gladys mounted the broom and zoomed into the air showcasing her own particular flying style.

Chapter Eleven

Elizabeth took every opportunity to practice flying. Every day she encouraged her Mum to borrow Shiona's beaten up old Citroen and mother and daughter took the 25 minute drive to the aircraft hangar. Daphne was often on hand for advice and even Shiona would show up from time to time just to be amazed at the transformation in Elizabeth's attitude from frightened rabbit to daredevil flying ace.

After nearly two weeks Elizabeth had all but mastered the delicate art of the broomstick. One day Shiona explained to Elizabeth that each one of the girls that accompanied them to Branko had undergone broomstick training, as it was the only way to get there, and there were varying results. From the proficient to the awkward, from the show off to the cautious, but neither Shiona nor Daphne had seen anyone take to the broomstick quite like Elizabeth. She was not as good as some of the girls, but her enthusiasm was incomparable. She was even attempting stunts.

There was one particular stunt that Elizabeth had been trying to master for days. She had recently formed rather a close relationship with her very own broomstick and she had even created a way to transport it without looking too conspicuous. She used her mother's skill for growing with one particular twig that had fallen to the ground. She found that if she strengthened the spell and concentrated hard enough the twig would actually grow in her hand. Initially the broken branch did not have enough life in it to grow at all, later on it grew too much. Finally she found the perfect kind of sticks, that were neither too brittle or too new, and once she had mastered growing them she considered reversing the technique to shrink them.

Elizabeth told her mother what she was attempting. Gladys said that she had never tried it before but it should work, in theory. So together, after flying practice had ended, they stayed up most of the night trying to get a broomstick to shrink back down to the size of a twig. Night after night this nocturnal practice would go on usually ending with Gladys insisting that Elizabeth go to bed.

One night they finally did it and the walls of the cottage nearly collapsed with their screams. After that Elizabeth found it easier and easier to get a twig to grow and then shrink it again. But as they were already close to the end of their life when she found them on the ground, they barely had one good grow and one good shrink left in them. Elizabeth got through a lot of twigs. Until one night, after flying practice, she had an idea to plant the shrunken branch in the garden. Under her mother's expert tutelage she offered it a gentle growing spell like she did with the flowers in the glade. When she pulled up the branch the next morning it had sprouted some tiny roots and it was healthier and stronger than all the prototypes that went before it.

Using the planting and pulling method with the stick meant that she could always use the same one. Because of this, she had grown quite attached to her new flying aid and she gave it a name – Sonny.

She brought Sonny back to the hanger with her mother one early autumn morning and carried on with the stunt.

It was a particularly complex feat and it called for some rather advanced spell casting. Considering she was still a novice witch this was no simple matter. She would stand on one side of the hanger and Sonny in his twig-like state would be at the other. She would then call him to her and en route from one end of the building to the other she would remotely cast the growing spell and Sonny would grow in mid-air. Then, Elizabeth would raise her hands above her head, by the time Sonny had reached her he had grown to full size, she would then grab hold of him as he pulled her straight up into the air. Once they were high enough Elizabeth would let go and instruct Sonny to circle beneath her, she would catch him quickly as she fell hoping to have enough time to get on and fly before hitting the ground.

The success rate of this particular stunt was touch and go. Sometimes the remote growing spell would fail, sometimes Sonny would grow but not move from the far end of the hanger. On one occasion Sonny was at full size and zooming across to Elizabeth nicely, only to smack her squarely in the nose. But as with all things that Elizabeth was learning lately, practice made perfect and it was not long before the basics of the stunt were there, it just needed a little fine-tuning.

It was during one of these fine-tuning sessions that she heard her mother call across the hanger.

"I'm just nipping out to run a couple of errands," Gladys said but Elizabeth did not pay much attention. She merely waved distractedly and got on with the stunt she was attempting, when the light in the hanger suddenly grew dim.

Natural light was the only source of illumination in the hanger. Elizabeth looked above her at the sky through the roof and saw that there was barely a cloud in the sky to block out the sun.

"It must be getting late," Elizabeth said aloud in the gloom.

She had become so lost in her new found love of flying these days that the hours literally flew by. Elizabeth stole a glance at her watch when suddenly the hanger grew darker and darker until barely a shaft of light remained.

Clinging on to her broomstick, Elizabeth tried to stay calm. In the unnatural gloom of the vast hanger Shiona's words about Elizabeth's hysteria were thrown into sharp relief. Elizabeth could feel the panic rising.

"Stay calm. Stay calm." She told herself in the pitch black.

Holding Sonny out in front of her she stumbled through the darkness trying to reach the door of the hanger. Just then, the atmosphere began to change. Suddenly she felt the chill of a passing breeze, smelt the vague hint of car fumes and heard the rumble of a train behind her.

Elizabeth froze, but there was a simple fact that she could not ignore, she was no longer in the aircraft hangar, and she was no longer in the Scottish countryside. Somehow Elizabeth had been transported to the city. And this city was very familiar to her, one she had lived in for a long time, too long.

She began to breathe deeply and felt another familiar sensation, a thunderstorm brewing in the sky above. The thick blackness that enveloped her sight began to disperse and with a sharp intake of breath Elizabeth noticed familiar surroundings. Still frozen to the spot she watched in horror as the scene she hoped was lost to her forever began to unfold once again.

She was standing in the alleyway at the back of the train station. Her heart was pounding in her chest when all at once she began to move, involuntarily, and with a slight limp. She walked towards the open street ahead of her. She tried to stop herself, desperately wanting to gain some control of events, but it was no use, she was trapped inside the scene like an echo forced to repeat itself. Tears of fear and frustration rolled down her cheeks as she heard a shout from behind her. Unable to stop herself, she turned.

There in front of her were the faces of the three men she had longed to forget. Here they were shouting at her from no more than 3 metres away. She could not make out what they were saying because of a low hum inside her head. A soft buzz that Elizabeth recognised as the sound of her anger. Only a few words penetrated that noise.

"Give us........money."

"Whatever you have."

"Useless bitch!"

That was the turning point, she remembered it vividly, and her echo-self reacted. She felt her body respond. She was moving without choice. She was reliving the moment and she could not scream or cry out or make herself stop. Her arms moved outwards as the three people staring at her transformed into her old boss, the woman she had once called "friend" and the colleague who had given her the limp.

Now that she was not living the emotion Elizabeth felt where the power was coming from. It rose from her diaphragm up through her chest and out towards her arms. The inner strength coursing into her hands now sought fusion with the atmosphere itself and drawing power from the electricity in the sky Elizabeth's hands shot out a bolt of lightning to the figures whose faces were now contorted in fear.

"NO!" Elizabeth screamed, and suddenly she was in control of her body again.

But it was too late. The damage had been done. She slumped to the ground weeping where another input for her senses awaited her – the stench of burning flesh. She could barely breathe the smell was so putrid, and she did not dare imagine the sight that went with it. But fighting the desire to look was futile. She knew the vision. She had seen it over and over again in her nightmares since that day. Forcing herself to face up to what she had done, she slowly raised her head.

She heaved at the sight. Witnessing it in dreams was completely different from living it in reality with the added horror of smell and sound. At the side of the alleyway, etched into the wall was the terrible motif of a killer. The bodies were burned into the concrete and covered in moist ash, the residue of burning flesh. Where the bodies had been forced backwards and then fallen to the floor there was a smudge of clean wall leaving a black outline of corpse. The faces of the bodies now piled together on the ground were grotesque. The scream of terror had been scorched onto their mouths forever but the most disturbing sight was the fusion of limbs. It was impossible to tell where one body stopped and the next one began.

Forcing herself to look more closely at the distorted figures horrified her beyond comprehension. The three men that had confronted her in the alleyway were not the only faces she saw. Visible amongst them, giving each body the look of a two-headed monster, were the equally grotesque and distorted faces of her work colleagues. Unable to stop herself, Elizabeth threw up.

Weeping uncontrollably, saliva and sick dripping from her chin Elizabeth tried to get up. She no longer knew what to do but she knew one thing with absolute certainty, she had to get out of there. After a few attempts her legs found the strength to take her weight and she stood up. She was upright for no more than a few seconds when the scene before her started to look fuzzy. Elizabeth sat down quickly fearing that she might faint and fall amongst the bodies as her sight continued to blur. She closed her eyes but the shift in atmosphere was again noticeable and within minutes Elizabeth knew she was sat on the floor of the aircraft hangar.

This time she cried with utter relief but as she opened her eyes the sickening sight of the bodies was still in front of her. She may have returned from the alleyway but she had brought them back with her. She stared in disbelief at the fallen bodies but there was something different about them. As she looked closer she noticed that the flesh was not quite as charred, that there were not as many heads and that the bodies were markedly more feminine.

Elizabeth's hand shot to her mouth stifling a scream of terror as the bodies began to move. Staring in horrified amazement Elizabeth heard the figures groan with exertion and feebly try to get to their feet. Head spinning, a faint threatening to overwhelm her, Elizabeth forced herself to stay conscious through the horror. She watched as the blackened figures got to their feet and she heard something that chilled her heart.

"Blimey Betty, ever tried anger management classes?"

There in front of her, extricating themselves from the black, dusty mess were Daphne, Shiona and Gladys.

***

Elizabeth stared at the three women as they got to their feet. Daphne was the first to get up and she held her hand out to Shiona who was hanging onto the crouching figure of Gladys who was also trying to rise. They were groaning and moaning and grabbing aching limbs as they stood. Gladys rubbed her neck, Shiona stretched out her back and Daphne rubbed her bottom.

"We're not as young as we used to be," Shiona said simply.

Elizabeth tore her gaze away from the whimpering trio. "I'm so sorry," she managed in a very small voice.

"What?" Gladys asked.

Elizabeth burst into tears. "I'm...so.... sorry Mum!" she managed through her hysteria. She was gulping in breaths and trying to calm herself but now that her hideous secret was out she needed to tell the whole story. "I...was.......so angry that night. I...had....enough! They were awful to me at work, just awful and I was so angry with them. But I was more angry with myself for not having the balls to say "no, I won't be your skivvy" or at least ask for some kind of payment. I stayed behind on my own time, to pour coffee for *those* people! I always thought, or hoped I was worth more than that. You and Dad always made me feel so special, and the world just thought I was a nobody, and I let the world make me feel like that. I didn't know what to do, I've never known what to do – and that night I snapped!"

Elizabeth took a hysterical breath before carrying on. "These three men followed me home and they shouted abuse at me and I was sick of feeling humiliated so I just...I just...I just let the anger take control. I don't know how I did it, I didn't even know I was capable of it. But that night I killed three men and I ran home and hid in Jessie's flat waiting to be arrested but nobody came and as time went on I thought it was all in my imagination, I let myself believe that I didn't do it. I didn't kill those men." Elizabeth buried her head in her hands.

"You didn't," Shiona said simply.

"Please, Shiona you don't have to be kind," Elizabeth sobbed. "It's time I faced up to this."

"Believe me I'm not being kind." Shiona replied kneeling beside her. "But you are right about one thing, we do need to discuss that evening."

Elizabeth just stared at Shiona wiping away tears.

"Let's just call it," Shiona paused for effect, "phase three."

"What?" Elizabeth asked quietly.

"*Phase three*," Shiona said rising decisively, "the next part of the training."

"What?" Elizabeth asked again, feeling a familiar sensation of anger rising.

"Elemental Control. And we'd better get cracking." Shiona said clapping her hands together. "It was beginners luck back in that alleyway with the various elements combining to make you perfectly susceptible. It's a very different matter when you have to start from scratch."

"Will you please tell me what the hell you are talking about?" Elizabeth said standing to face Shiona.

Gladys and Daphne sensed Elizabeth's blossoming anger. They took a step towards her trying to calm her, trying to explain. Shiona, however, was completely unaware and ploughed on regardless.

"As witches we are able to control the elements," she said relishing the chance to explain her particular area of expertise. "Earth, fire, water and air. You had a fantastic opportunity that night because of the thunderstorm, there was literally fire in the air and you used it!"

"How could you know about that?" Elizabeth asked suspiciously.

"We were there! I know you didn't kill those three men, because they weren't three men at all. They were three women! Me, your mother and Daphne."

"WHAT!" Elizabeth cried.

"It was a test," Shiona went on oblivious to Elizabeth's dangerous mood, "and you passed it rather well. Although we were lucky with the kind of day you had, you really were angry weren't you! And the thunderstorm was such a gift."

Shiona was almost gleeful but Elizabeth's rage was rising just as it had that very night.

"Let me get this straight," she said seething, "you made me believe that I had murdered those three men as part of my *training*?"

"Not strictly as part of the training, more as a test to see if you had it in you." Shiona said simply.

"HAD IT IN ME!"

There was no mistaking Elizabeth's anger now. Even Shiona had the good sense to back away, joining Daphne and Gladys who were already cowering.

"Listen love........." Gladys began but Elizabeth wasn't finished yet.

"I never in a million years thought I *had it in me* to kill a man! You made me feel like a monster, like a devil! And when I didn't hear anything about it on the news I felt worse. I felt like I was going mad and all of that just because you wanted to *test me*?!"

"Calm down love."

"And, you!" Elizabeth rounded on her mother, "you knew how desperately miserable I was after that. I couldn't talk to a soul. I thought I was going to be sent to prison or the funny farm, and you knew all along what you had done when you were comforting me!"

"Come on Betty," Daphne said trying to put an arm around her.

"Don't you touch me," she said, "don't you ever come near me again."

Elizabeth backed away from the threesome. Not out of fear of what they might do to her this time, she was afraid of what *she* might do to them.

"That's right little girl," Shiona said closing in on her, "run away. We all thought you would. But your mother said you were better than that. I tried to tell her........."

SMACK

Elizabeth never found out what Shiona tried to tell her mother because just at that moment she punched her straight in the face.

"Elizabeth!" Gladys shouted rushing to Shiona's side.

Tears of anger and frustration stung Elizabeth's cheek. She grabbed Sonny and flew out of the aircraft hangar.

"Elizabeth! You can't....." Gladys called out to her but it was too late. "Go after her Daphne! Make sure she lands.....quickly!"

87

Daphne was already on her broomstick. She knew she could not let Elizabeth go too far, if only for the simple reason that she had never flown outside of the hanger before.

Daphne soon caught up with Elizabeth. As skilful as Elizabeth had become she was no match for the more seasoned flyer. Daphne circled in front of Elizabeth blocking her way making her stop quickly. Elizabeth struggled to stay in control of the broom.

"Get out of my way Daphne or I'll just fly over you!"

"You can't Betty, I'm quicker and better than you are. You know I am."

In her rage Elizabeth tried to fly above the hovering witch. But Daphne was indeed too quick for her and she shot straight up stopping inches in front of the novice.

"Alright Betty, I understand that you're angry," Daphne said, "but what about all those people down there." Daphne pointed out towards the horizon and Elizabeth saw that she was gesturing towards the city. "Do you really want little children coming home from school looking up at you and saying, "Mummy you told me there was no such thing as witches" do you? I know this has been hard for you but do those people deserve to go through this as well? You'll give them the fright of their lives!"

Elizabeth just stared at Daphne for a while, thinking that the woman might wither under her gaze, but Daphne was made of sterner stuff. She met Elizabeth's steely gaze and refused to back down. Taking a deep breath, knowing that Daphne was right, Elizabeth let herself float slowly to the ground.

They floated down into a forest, the fading light of day cast long shadows on the ground. The setting sun was beaming through the trees turning the ground a vibrant shade of orange. Elizabeth slumped down where she landed and wept. She was bemused and scared once again, but this time she was utterly devastated by the betrayal. She understood the need for secrecy when it came to her mother's powers, she had come to terms with that particular revelation, but that day in the alleyway was the most horrific of her life and knowing her mother was involved was a terrible blow.

Daphne was sitting quietly next to Elizabeth, watching her cautiously. "Your Mum didn't want a part of that you know Betty," she said as if she knew what Elizabeth was thinking, "it was Shiona's idea. And to be honest, I had a little bit of input too."

Elizabeth's head snapped up at this admission.

"It's OK Betty," Daphne said raising her hands, "before you go punching me in the face, just let me explain." Daphne took Elizabeth's silence as permission to carry on. "We've been in trouble this year. We seemed to have exhausted our supply of eager young women happy to come with us to Branko. Your Mum mentioned how worried she was about you in London, that you had been having a miserable time. And to top it off you were changing. You had gone from being full of vitality, a social butterfly, to a hermit. She said you even changed your appearance. After seeing you leave home with your own quirky style, it was hard for your Mum to watch you become a clone. It was your Mum that suggested you might be the next one to come with us, it was Shiona that suggested that we give you a test and it was me that thought up the muggers."

Elizabeth was staggered at this revelation, "You!"

"Before you judge me Betty, answer me one question and answer it honestly."

Elizabeth eyed Daphne suspiciously for a moment then nodded.

"Have you ever watched the news and seen little old ladies, or children or anyone being attacked by a gang of youths or thugs and thought, *those buggers need stringing up?* Have you ever thought, *I wish I had the kind of strength to give those sods what for*?"

Elizabeth paused already knowing the answer.

"Well, have you?" Daphne pushed.

"Yes," she said flatly

"Of course you have. Who hasn't wanted to see the entrails of those bastards splashed across a dark alleyway? There are a lot of people in this world who make horrible choices every day of their lives and their victims have to live with the consequences of those choices. It is a choice to rob a little old lady and it's a choice to fight back – if you can. You're one of the lucky ones who can fight back. That's nothing to be ashamed of."

"But I thought I had *killed* those people Daphne," Elizabeth said, sagging. "And not the three men who were going to attack me, I think I would have been too scared of them even in that state of anger. But the three people you turned into."

"We turned into?"

"Yes! My boss, my ex-*friend* and that idiot I worked with. They were the people who humiliated me, they were the ones that I wanted to hurt."

"Oh," said Daphne deep in thought, "that's very interesting."

"Interesting!?"

"Well Betty, we didn't do any changing. Once we had picked our person, as far as we knew we stayed that way. You must have projected a different image onto us!" She looked at Elizabeth in awe, "that's pretty advanced stuff for a newbie."

Elizabeth snorted a half-laugh.

"You've every right to be angry with us Betty. But think about this, if you weren't as capable as you were none of that would have happened. You might have met us in the alleyway but if you had nothing to throw at us we were going to pretend to be disturbed by a noise and run off. But you certainly had something there Little One, just like your Mum always knew you would."

Elizabeth suddenly clapped her hands over her face and began to giggle.

"I thought I had an epiphany!" she laughed hysterically.

"What?"

"When I heard nothing about the murders on the news I thought I was going mad to begin with. But then I suddenly thought, what an amazing imagination! I thought, OK if I am hallucinating then, what a fantastic story. I was going to be a writer!"

"Oh Betty," Daphne said sounding slightly ashamed, "you might be a writer yet. You never know."

"Yes but it wasn't my story was it, it was *yours*!" She shouted on the verge of tears again. "Maybe *you* should be the writer."

"Well at least we made sure you got out of that job that was making you miserable."

"Yeah, I couldn't have stayed in London after all that."

"Oh, I don't actually mean that Betty." Daphne said awkwardly.

Elizabeth looked quizzically at Daphne.

"We kind of forced your hand when you were in your boss's office. We thought you might chicken out, take your punishment and wander back to your desk with your tail between your legs." Daphne stared cautiously at Elizabeth fearing another explosion.

Elizabeth just scoffed, "I thought I wasn't quite myself!"

She paused for a moment watching the fading light of day, feeling exhausted by yet another revelation.

"You're right you know, I probably wouldn't have done it myself. Another bit of advice from my mother?" Elizabeth asked.

Daphne nodded.

"She's always had an uncanny knack of just knowing things."

"Don't I know it Betty!"

The sun had nearly set on another day of surprises for Elizabeth. As hard as she found it to be bombarded with one shock after another in the safety of this world, she knew it would be infinitely worse once they reached Branko.

"When I came around to the idea of Mum being a witch, I decided there and then I was going to see this through to the bitter end." Elizabeth told Daphne.

"And how do you feel now?"

"I'm really not sure to be honest with you, but I'm willing to give it another go. Anyway, controlling the elements could be cool, I suppose."

"Atta girl!" Daphne said.

They both mounted their broomsticks and in the dark made a much less conspicuous twosome in the sky.

They flew straight back to the little cottage with Daphne coaching Elizabeth about flying techniques all the way. As the cottage came into view they noticed a couple of figures standing on the doorstep. They drew closer and saw that one of the figures held a bottle of wine in each hand and the other held two bags. Closer still and they recognised the faces of Shiona and Gladys. Shiona's was a little more swollen.

"A peace offering," Gladys said holding up the bags of takeaway food.

Daphne and Elizabeth landed.

"Are you OK?" Gladys asked.

"I think so," Elizabeth answered simply and opened the front door. Daphne and Gladys walked in but Shiona remained on the doorstep.

"You can come in too if you want," Elizabeth said flatly.

"I know I can be a little .... difficult," Shiona said, attempting an awkward reconciliation, "but I want you to know that I do what I think is for the best."

Elizabeth took a deep breath. "Look Shiona, we clearly don't get on," she said, "but my Mum cares a lot about you which is enough for me."

Shiona looked up and nodded at Elizabeth the bruise on her jaw clearly visible.

"Plus," Elizabeth added, "you've got the wine."

Shiona smiled and pushed passed Elizabeth into the little house. "Let's get this open," she said.

"There's a corkscrew........" Elizabeth began.

"That's alright," Shiona said with a wink, "I don't need one." Shiona took out her wand, pointed it at the wine and the bottle dutifully opened – all by itself.

Chapter Twelve

Elemental control was the hardest training yet for Elizabeth. It seemed that without an emotionally fuelled rage she could not even muster a spark. Try as they might the other three witches found it impossible to provoke a reaction.

"You've got rubbish hair and you smell like poo!" Daphne tried during the training session. Elizabeth snorted a laugh.

"You'll never amount to anything, you're a useless article," Shiona offered.

"Be careful Shiona or she'll match up that bruise on the other side of your face," Daphne said and Elizabeth could barely stifle a giggle.

They had opted to try elemental control training outside the aircraft hangar. They had started inside but there was really no point. The only element they could easily use was air, but Elizabeth's attempts had been so useless they decided to head outside where the elements were at their most vibrant.

"This is awful," was Gladys' input. "I'm not even sure that I want Elizabeth learning a power that she can only use if she's in the grip of a ferocious temper. There's got to be another way."

Daphne slumped next to Gladys. After seven long hours of training with nothing to show for their efforts the witches were at a loss.

"Maybe it's not just anger, maybe it's any extreme emotion," Daphne said, "what about being very happy?"

Elizabeth shook her head, "you've known me for a couple of months now Daphne, do you really think I've got it in me to be *that* happy?"

"That's a good point," Shiona said. "How about we work on cultivating fear instead?"

"Absolutely not!" Gladys shouted getting quickly to her feet and almost knocking Daphne to the ground. "There is no way you are going to teach Elizabeth how to capitalise on her fear, that's exactly how Darius wants her to be – afraid. He grows from people's fear!"

"*That* is also a good point," Daphne chipped in.

"The last thing we need is him using the fear of a witch. That's a ridiculous idea," Gladys concluded.

"Alright then!" Shiona said petulantly. "What do you suggest we do, she hasn't shown even a flicker of talent in this area."

"Maybe she never will," Daphne said.

"That's not funny Daphne," said Shiona.

"And I'm not joking," protested Daphne. "This particular skill might be something we haven't got time to teach her, after all it's taken *us* a lifetime to master it."

"What about the other girls?" Elizabeth asked. "Surely some of them knew how to do it?"

"We had varying results with their powers," replied Shiona, "at least *they* could muster a cool breeze."

"Thanks," Elizabeth said flatly. "Anyway, I must be good at this. Have you all forgotten what happened in the alleyway?"

"No we haven't and neither have you," Gladys said, "and I think that's the problem. You might be suppressing your abilities because of how awful you found the whole experience."

"But what about the other day?" Elizabeth protested. "I repeated the whole thing in the aircraft hangar."

"You didn't repeat it Elizabeth," said Shiona, "you just remembered it. That was just a memory echo we were all living through so that you could feel where the inner power was coming from."

"Yes, and it was coming from beneath my navel and that's what I've been focussing on all morning."

"And it's still not working Little One," said Gladys. "Maybe we should call it a day on this one and get back to it when you all return from Branko."

Even with the fresh Scottish breezes whipping around and the sultry earth beneath her feet, Elizabeth was no closer to mastering this particular skill. She was about ready to give up herself.

Suddenly Daphne piped up, "I've got a cracking idea! Everyone follow me."

Daphne stomped off towards the forest leaving the others in shocked silence.

"Come on then!" She said reappearing for a moment. The others reluctantly followed.

Daphne carried on for about a quarter of a mile sniffing the air like a bloodhound as she went. She changed directions twice but finally seemed sure of where she was going. After walking for ten minutes she stopped abruptly.

"There," she said and pointed ahead of her.

She was gesturing towards a small loch, barely more than a large pond, flanked by bracken on one side and gorse grass on another.

"What are you thinking about?" Elizabeth asked cautiously.

"Isn't it obvious Betty?" Daphne said smiling. "I'm thinking you should get in."

"NO WAY!" Elizabeth cried. The late afternoon sun was beginning to set, autumn had finally gripped the country and *this* was Scotland. Elizabeth knew that the loch was going to be freezing!

"Well we're running out of options and we're going in less than two weeks," Daphne said. "What do you suggest?"

Elizabeth looked from Daphne to her mother to Shiona in stunned amazement. From the look on their faces, *all* of their faces, they seemed to think it was a good idea for her to plunge into the muddy, cold water.

"How on earth is me catching double pneumonia going to help us? You're right – we *do* have to go in two weeks you don't need me spending the best part of that time in bed recovering from the rotten cold I'm gonna get if I put one foot in there!" Elizabeth gestured toward the water.

"Pah!" Shiona said derisively. "A little bit of cold never hurt anyone. Anyway, I can cure a common cold."

"Really, *Medicine Woman*?" Elizabeth said sarcastically.

"What about seeing things through to the bitter end Betty," Daphne said.

Elizabeth eyed her carefully, contemplating the suggestion.

"Sod it!" She said finally and started taking off some clothes.

"I don't expect you to do it in the nude, Betty!"

"I want *some* dry clothes to put on when I've finished." She said to

95

Daphne as she strutted past her heading towards the loch.

Daphne, Shiona and Gladys were stunned to see Elizabeth splash straight into the loch only stopping once she had reached the middle. The freezing cold water came up to her waist and she held on tightly to her arms in a teddy bear embrace.

"W...wh...what should I d...do now?" She asked, as the cold took hold and she started shivering.

Shiona and Gladys looked towards Daphne.

"Don't look at me!" Daphne said. "I'm not the expert here."

Gladys and Daphne looked at Shiona.

"Um..." was all that Shiona could say.

"Well, ssssome..one tell me wh...what I sh...should do!" Shouted Elizabeth from the loch, "I better n...not have w....walked in h..here for n..n..nothing!"

"Um, um..." Shiona said with a little more urgency.

"I'mmmm g..gonna kill y..you d..d..d..Daphne!" Elizabeth yelled and started wading out of the loch.

"No!" shouted Shiona, "stay there!"

Everyone jumped at Shiona's sudden reaction and froze. Elizabeth stopped in mid-stride and Gladys and Daphne watched the older witch begin her magic. It was very rare to see Shiona lost for words or for a solution and now, her steely determination was back. She knew exactly what to do.

"Don't fight the sensation Elizabeth," she said, "don't try to block out the cold. Feel every needle prick of pain on your skin. Let your senses describe to you what they are experiencing. Consider the smell of the cold air as it stings your nasal hairs. What about the taste in your mouth as you clench your teeth against the discomfort? What do your muscles feel like as they tighten? Listen to your body Elizabeth. Block out what you perceive to be "pain" and just feel the reactions. Once you've listened to each and every part of your body, find that place of power below your belly button and use it."

Elizabeth closed her eyes and listened to Shiona's soft, slow voice guiding her through the reactions of her body. When she was sure she had successfully fought the desire to flee the cold, she tried to shut off her concept of pain and began to focus on each sensation. The discomfort was intense but she tried to think about it in another way. She focussed on her energy source. Remembering the scene in the aircraft hangar she thought about the area below her navel and she stretched out her arms. The air was cold, so cold. It squeezed at her taking her breath away, but she tried to shut it out.

Suddenly she felt a pin prick of warmth in her energy centre. Shocked at this sudden change she nearly lost all concentration but she forced herself to keep her eyes closed and carry on. She used every agonisingly cold ounce of flesh as a focus for her power. The stab of warmth turned into an ooze of heat and rose up slowly through her navel. A blissfully comforting trickle of inner sunshine glided towards her chest and outwards to her arms. She was doing it. She was utilising the same power as before but this time it was soothing, warming, calming her.

Elizabeth knew something was happening because she could hear gasps from the assembled witches but she forced herself to stay focussed. She was enjoying the relief of the warm energy flowing through her after the torture of the blistering cold. Her hands were held out towards the loch and the warmer she became the further she stretched her arms. She felt as though she was on fire, the heat in her body was unmistakable. She was in a state of bliss. She could have stayed like that forever.

"Um.....Elizabeth?" Gladys said hesitantly.

Elizabeth was shaken from her reverie but her eyes remained closed.

"I think you'd probably better stop now." Gladys finished.

"Why?" Elizabeth asked in her blessed-out state.

"Perhaps you'd better just look for yourself," Gladys replied and there was something about her tone that unnerved Elizabeth. She slowly opened her eyes.

The sight that confronted her nearly knocked her off her feet but something very firm was holding her tightly around the waist stopping her from going anywhere.

"Get me out of here!" She said panicking.

Elizabeth stood in the middle of the loch. The body of water around her had changed but not into the bubbling warm bath that Elizabeth had been experiencing. Elizabeth was encased in ice.

"NOW!"

"Alright, alright! Calm down." Shiona said. "Gladys! Daphne! Go around the other side. Keep enough space between you both. We need to do this together."

Gladys was the first to react, quickly scurrying around the loch. Daphne just stood open-mouthed staring at the helpless figure of Elizabeth in the middle of the frozen water.

"Go Daphne!" Shiona said pushing her.

"HURRY UP!" Elizabeth screamed, becoming more frantic.

"Get closer," Shiona shouted at the other two witches. "You'll have to touch it."

"But it looks freezing," Daphne complained.

"I'm gonna kill you Daphne," Elizabeth shouted, "touch the bloody ice!"

Shiona, Daphne and Gladys all knelt beside the loch. They already had their wands ready in one hand, touching the frozen water. The other hand they placed directly on the ice.

Gladys looked up at Elizabeth, a desperate figure in the middle of the frozen loch, "oh, Little One," she groaned quietly.

"Concentrate!" Shiona shouted across at Gladys.

Gladys closed her eyes and focussed on the task. The experienced witches found it easy to create the warmth. Each pair of hands glowed with a honey radiance that surged through the wands and the ice. They spread the heat as quickly as they dared.

Elizabeth watched as the women slowly defrosted the loch. She had no idea what happened. One minute she was exuding warmth from every inch of her body, the next minute she was standing in the middle of the loch and it was frozen solid.

By the time the loch had liquefied enough for Elizabeth to walk through she was shivering uncontrollably. All trace of inner warmth had gone and her body shook violently. When the heat of the women's spell finally reached her she attempted to move but her legs had seized from the crippling cold.

"Just give us a minute Elizabeth!" Shiona barked at her. Suddenly Elizabeth felt a concentration of heat around her lower limbs. The hot water was massaging life back into her legs.

"Try it now," Shiona called.

After a few failed attempts Elizabeth finally managed to coax her legs to move. Every step she took was an agony of pin pricks as she desperately waded to the bank.

When she finally splashed her way out of the loch she fell to her knees and collapsed in a heap. Her three companions were by her side in seconds, performing the same warming spell as they had used on the loch.

"I d...don't uu..un...understand." She said. "I w...was s...so w...w... warm! What w...w...was I d...doing w....wrong?"

"You were doing everything right my lovely," Gladys said. "You focussed all your energies and you used your internal power source."

"W...why d...d..did I FREEZE the b...bloody l...lake then?"

"You used the most prominent power source at your disposal," Shiona chipped in, "the cold. All your focus was on the cold and how it was making you feel. There was extreme cold in the water and the air whipping around you. You simply made more of it."

"But you *made* me f..f..focus on the cold!" Elizabeth said.

"I know," Shiona said slightly embarrassed, "and what I did was absolutely right. It helped you get in touch with a strong internal, ancient instinct. I just forgot to tell you to reach for an alternative external power source rather than the cold."

"L...like what?" said Elizabeth.

"Like that big flaming gaseous ball in the sky Betty," Daphne said, "the Sun?"

Glancing upwards Elizabeth could see the last rays of the setting sun streaming towards them as the three witches used their own powers to harness its heat and warm Elizabeth where she lay. Sighing heavily Elizabeth closed her eyes and ignoring the panicked cajoling from the others she allowed herself to fall blissfully into unconsciousness.

Chapter Thirteen

After spending two days slipping in and out of consciousness with the three witches casting healing spells over her, Elizabeth finally woke up. She felt revitalised and energised but she was still not willing to undertake any more elemental control training. The witches assured her they were prepared for every eventuality now and nothing like freezing the lake could ever happen again.

"We could do it with heat this time Betty." Daphne offered.

"What so I can set myself on fire," Elizabeth replied "I don't think so!"

Quickly realising that they were wasting their breath Gladys, Daphne and Shiona settled for honing her flying and nature skills instead. Elizabeth had become quite efficient at growing plants. She had even taken to planting seeds in pots at home. She would use the same growing spell that her mother had taught her and after a few hours the seedlings grew into beautiful flowers. She often wondered how this particular skill would help her in Branko but she knew better than to ask. So she continued to re-plant Sonny every night after flying practice. Everything she did was under the watchful eyes of her mother and the other two witches and even Shiona had to admit that she was getting on well. Elizabeth was pleased with the constant supervision, as she still did not feel confident enough to be left alone with her newly acquired powers.

All too quickly the time was fast approaching for Elizabeth to leave the comfort of her cottage and face the adventure that awaited her in Branko. The night before they were due to leave Gladys stayed in the little house with Elizabeth. Elizabeth tossed and turned all night, thinking of the moment she would meet Lord Darius.

On the morning of 31ˢᵗ October Elizabeth sat in silence with her mother and tried to eat breakfast. Both women just pushed the food around on their plates barely a morsel touching their lips until Elizabeth finally spoke.

"Mum," she said quietly, "do you mind if I spend a bit of time on my own today?"

"Oh," Gladys replied a little shocked, "of... of course not."

"I just want to get my head straight. If that's OK?" Elizabeth felt guilty shooing her mother away but she knew Gladys would try to distract her from thinking about the trip. The witches were leaving at dusk and Elizabeth knew it was going to be a long day but she wanted to spend the time preparing herself, not trying to forget about it.

"I understand," Gladys said rising from the table. "I'll see you at the meeting place later." She looked as though she wanted to say more. That she was searching for the right words of encouragement. In the end she merely leant over the table and gave Elizabeth a kiss on the forehead.

"I'll see you soon," she said and walked out of the cottage.

Elizabeth spent the day packing and re-packing the small bag she was allowed to take. The witches would have to fly the whole way on broomstick which was not the most comfortable way to travel even without bags. Shiona suggested she only take a small back pack and Gladys had bought her one. When she was happy with her luggage Elizabeth stood downstairs, in the middle of the cottage, surveying her home.

With nothing more to do and unable to stand the wait a moment longer, Elizabeth said a quick goodbye to the cottage, and closed the door for the last time. She hoped she would be back again one day but she was too filled with fear about the trip to truly believe she could ever have a normal life again. She paused only to pick up Sonny from his usual spot in the garden and then she walked away from her home, not daring to look back.

Elizabeth walked towards her destination. The meeting place was the village park. At the top of a steep hill encircled by trees and grass where people could walk their dogs, never daring to step foot into the hallowed grounds of the fenced off children's play area at the very summit of the hill. It was the topmost point in the village and the witches were due to meet at dusk and wait for dark to start their journey.

Sometimes with company, but often alone Elizabeth explored the area and over the past month had become quite familiar with it. She discovered there were two ways to reach the park, the easiest was to climb the avenues flanked by a few houses to the main entrance or the alternative was to ascend the steps that started in a back alleyway and meandered through the woods on the side of the hill. Elizabeth named this staircase Jacob's Ladder after the steps she had once climbed near Cheddar Gorge in Somerset. She remembered being amazed at how something that was referred to as the stairway to Heaven could be such an unholy nightmare to climb.

Elizabeth set off well before dusk, and she could have easily taken the most commonly used route. However, she decided to search the back alleyways for Jacob's Ladder. For no reason other than to experience it. She wanted to *feel* to ascent and the affect it would have on her body.

Starting the climb and fearing the worst she was relieved that the exertion was not beyond the realms of her physical capabilities. However, 30 steps in and a tightness started creeping across her chest. By the time she had climbed 60 steps a strange thickness was forming on her left side. She mused that she was probably having a heart attack but she did not want to give into the idea that she was in pain. She was breathless and uncomfortable but that really was the extent of the sensation.

She had heard so many philosophies state that physical discomfort was all in the mind. And although she still could not believe that about extreme illness and disease, she was beginning to realise what mind over matter meant in a much smaller way especially after the disaster in the loch. The throbbing she was currently feeling was not an enjoyable sensation but like hunger and coldness, unless in extreme circumstances, she reasoned that she was not about to die from her breathlessness. She registered the way her body was reacting to the physical exertion just like she had noticed the cold in the loch. She took note of it with some interest and then carried on up Jacob's Ladder to her final destination.

When she reached the park she was breathing heavily, sweating profusely and seeing tiny little specks of light in her vision. *I really need to get fit!* She thought as she took a few minutes to catch her breath

102

before she climbed the last part of the hill. She stopped just outside the fenced playground at the place that she was due to meet Gladys, Shiona and Daphne.

Elizabeth closed her eyes in the bright afternoon sunshine. Keeping down out of the wind Elizabeth felt the warmth of the sun's rays on her body even though it was a cold day. Some clouds were already beginning to litter the sky. The weather forecast had not been promising, predicting rain for most of the night. *Just one of the many adversities I'll encounter over the next few weeks*, she thought.

Elizabeth enjoyed her last taste of normality before the Branko adventure began. She listened to the sounds of people going about their normal daily routines and living their lives. She heard the sound of children with their parents in the playground. The children were laughing and one child was shouting, "higher, higher" as he was being pushed on the swing. Elizabeth could sense the enjoyment from the father, relishing this opportunity to relive his own childhood through his son.

Elizabeth opened her eyes for a better look. She watched the father and son on the swings leave as the early evening air became nippy. The father put the boy on his shoulders, and they giggled excitedly about what costume the little boy was going to wear to go trick or treating. Mothers, fathers and children came and went, enjoying the late afternoon sun and a chance to play while the weather was surprisingly mild for the time of year. Slowly, as the sun began to set, the families dispersed and Elizabeth was left alone in the park. She listened to the departing voices talking about apple bobbing and trick or treating.

Elizabeth, at last, was alone. She thought about the last few months and realised how much she had changed. She genuinely cared about these families and the joy they were experiencing. There was a time, not so long ago, when Elizabeth wouldn't have even noticed the mothers and fathers. Preferring to simply categorise them as *middle-class and middle-aged.* She found it so easy to lump people together, that way Elizabeth was the only special one and everyone else had their place. She cringed to think how she would judge herself if the old Elizabeth could see her now.

"Probably think I was a nutter!" She said aloud. She could picture the old Elizabeth seeing her sitting alone in the park for hours, just watching family interactions and getting colder and colder as the sun began to set. Elizabeth shuddered at the thought. She didn't know what was worse, how judgemental she used to be or how crazy she must look now.

She shook her head at the thought and watched the night sky turn from pale blue to pink, the inevitable dusk was not far away and Elizabeth was soon to start out on the most important journey of her life.

She watched and waited. When suddenly the cool autumn air whisked around her sending shivers down her spine. The fallen leaves strewn across the ground in front of her were disturbed by a ripple of wind in the air. The breeze turned into a strong gust and began whipping the leaves into a frenzy. Just then the leaves gathered together around a central column of air that swirled magnificently in front of Elizabeth climaxing in a whirlwind of twigs, leaves and anything that lay helpless on the ground. Then, as quickly as it started, the wind dropped revealing in the centre of the vortex Gladys, Shiona and Daphne.

"WOW!" Elizabeth said, "that was cool!"

The witches brushed themselves off looking very pleased with their dramatic entrance.

"Alright Betty," Daphne said excitedly. "You ready to go?"

"Nearly," the answer came from Gladys. "I just want a moment alone with her if that's OK?"

Shiona and Daphne both nodded their agreement and Gladys caught hold of Elizabeth's arm leading her away from the other women. Once she was sure they were out of earshot Gladys took something from her pocket.

"This is from your father," she said producing a black drawstring pouch. "He wanted you to have something that was important to him. When he heard what we were planning to do he was so angry with me. But when I promised him that you would only go to Branko if it was your own choice, he accepted it. Then he spent a couple of days in the attic searching for this." Gladys pushed the pouch into Elizabeth's hand.

"He was so pleased when he found it. He said his grandfather had given it to him when he had come home from school in tears one day. He had been bullied horribly and was full of bruises. His own father couldn't get out of him what had happened but his grandfather took him off quietly and they went to the old man's allotment. They said nothing for a while just planted and weeded but when Albert scratched his hand on a twig, the tears started to come again and he blurted everything out to his grandfather. Not one for massive displays of affection his grandfather patted him on the back, went into the shed and came out with this in his hand."

Gladys motioned for Elizabeth to open the pouch. Elizabeth undid the string and tipped the contents into her hand.

"He called it a protective amulet, like the Knights of the Round Table wore and said it would make Albert brave. Brave enough to stand up to these bullies."

Elizabeth held the amulet in her hand. In the failing light she could just about make out the bottle green colour of a stone roughly cut into the shape of a circle set in a silver disk and hanging on a piece of old leather cord. It looked more like a pendant than an amulet and when Elizabeth turned it over it had the letters "B u d" inscribed on it.

"Bud?" Elizabeth said thinking for a moment. "Oh Buddy? That's what they used to call Dad's grandfather isn't it?"

Gladys nodded. "Your Dad laughs about it now," she continued, "but the next day at school he felt really courageous and he took on those bullies. It sounds as though he got in a lucky punch with the ring leader and was never bothered again. But he wore that stone for years, apparently. Then he grew up. He realised that it wasn't a protective stone after all but the power of suggestion and his grandfather's love that made him feel strong. And that's why he wants you to have it. He wants you to remember, whenever you look at that stone, that we love you and we want you to come home safely and if anything happens to you, we will move heaven and earth to bring you home."

"And *you* could probably do that too," Elizabeth smiled.

"Don't you forget it," Gladys said with a wink.

Elizabeth slipped the leather cord over her head and tucked the amulet into her clothes. She patted the stone through the layers of cloth, and immediately felt comforted by it. It was a reassuring thought knowing that her Dad was wishing her well and wanting her home safely. She hadn't thought about her father much over the past few months and she assumed he knew nothing about the witches' endeavours, that it was a guilty family secret between her and her mother. It was a relief that Bertie knew Elizabeth was going to Branko, and going with his blessing and his protection.

Gladys put her arm around Elizabeth's shoulders and led her back to the others. The witches said nothing but smiled encouragingly at her.

Elizabeth thought about what a strange sight they must have been - three women gathered together in the early evening to say their final farewells to Gladys. Shiona adopted a traditional approach to her witchy wardrobe. She had a full length black winter coat covering a long black skirt, black blouse and jumper. To top off her look she wore the traditional black pointed witch's hat. Daphne went for more of an ace pilot look. She had a leather hat with goggles, a thick black leather jacket padded with sheepskin, a tight pair of Capri pants (that weren't particularly flattering to her fuller figure) and riding boots. Elizabeth wore her own customised full length, layered black skirt that she had slit at the front to aid broomstick flying. She wore a thick pair of black leggings underneath and found a warm puffy jacket to keep out the cold on their flight. She topped off her outfit with a black and white woollen Peruvian-style hat with plaits falling from the flaps covering her ears and a big plait cascading from the top. She was amazed to see Gladys smile with pride at the mismatched trio.

Elizabeth knew the time had come. She nodded that she was ready and whispered the growing spell over her twig. Sonny sprang into life and Elizabeth kissed her mother one last time. Gladys pulled her into a tight embrace. After a few moments, and with an encouraging hand from Shiona, Gladys let go. Elizabeth gulped down tears as she saw her mother's eyes glistening in the gloom of the early evening. But there was no turning back now, so with a forced smile she nodded to her mother. She climbed on Sonny and rose silently into the air with the other two witches. She watched her mother get smaller and smaller as the three witches flew further and further away.

Chapter Fourteen

Flying away from her mother sent a hot tear down Elizabeth's cold cheek. Even in the company of the other two witches, she had never felt more alone. She pushed the tear away as Daphne looked at her. "The wind," she said by way of a false explanation and raised her eyes in mock exasperation.

Under the watchful eye of the experienced witches Elizabeth did not dare to sneak a look behind her, but part of her was not ready to give up hope. She kept expecting to see her mother behind them, flying expertly, accompanying them on their journey to Branko after all. But as the hours ticked by Elizabeth finally conceded that there would be no chance of a tearful reunion with her mother. Instead, she turned her thoughts to the quest that lay ahead.

Throughout her training she had been given snippets of information regarding Branko and she pieced together all the details. As far as she knew, at midnight on 31st October, every year, Lord Darius would stand on the outskirts of Branko at the protective shield's weakest point and attempt to gain entry to the surrounding world. It was always on this date because, as the witches had explained to Elizabeth, magical expectation was at its highest. In this ever-developing world a massive shift in consciousness, from fear based indoctrinated religions, was changing to a more personal, spiritual and creative connection. The idea that *anything* was possible was growing stronger and stronger. This, in turn, meant that Darius' powers were becoming less and less the thing of fairy tales and more and more plausible. It was this possibility and expectation of a transforming world that gave Darius his chance.

On the stroke of midnight the shield of Branko could be penetrated but at that stroke, every year, instead of passing through to Elizabeth's reality, Darius would be faced by the formidable sight of Shiona and Daphne accompanied by a somewhat less exceptional novice witch. The power of three – mind, body and spirit in full functioning order to keep Darius in his place as per the original spell cast hundreds of years ago by the Baron and the 3 sisters.

The shield to Branko would only regain absolute strength after a tried and tested power struggle between Darius and the women, and the witches always won. It was only ever a display of supremacy by Darius, he could never match the power of the witches. The Baron had cursed Darius to succumb to their might for eternity. It was part of the deal to let him live.

The women had been flying for nearly three hours when the weather took a nasty turn. Elizabeth's muscles were already aching from holding tightly onto Sonny, her broomstick, petrified to shift her footing an inch for fear of falling. Then the rain lashed down stabbing Elizabeth with icy coldness, obstructing her vision, making it difficult to hold onto Sonny as it soaked both her and the broom. Her handhold began to slip, she grasped the broom tightly, but her hands were numb after three hours of holding on. She could not feel the stick beneath her grasp and just as she was trying to pump life back into her fingers her foot slipped and Elizabeth fell from the sky.

Plummeting down terrifyingly earthbound Elizabeth's survival instincts took over, she grabbed out at something, anything, but she only managed to clutch at thin air. She tried to focus on Sonny hoping that wherever the broomstick was it would heed her call but as she continued to fall her heart sank. She felt powerless to save herself and she was sure the witches had not even noticed her fall. She knew she was about to die.

Within an instant Shiona and Daphne were at Elizabeth's side. Daphne had found Sonny and forced him beneath the plummeting Elizabeth. Elizabeth grabbed hold of the stick and pulled up slowly. Even in her desperation she knew that stopping short in mid-air on a broomstick could be just as damaging as hitting the ground. Forcing herself to stay calm she carried on slowly encouraging Sonny to take her weight. *Slowly, slowly,* she thought until she was safe enough to bring Sonny to a halt in mid-air.

Breathing heavily Elizabeth closed her eyes, relieved to finally be in control.

"Uh...Betty?" Daphne said. "Do you want to get off and we'll have a little breather?"

"Get off," Elizabeth said opening her eyes. "Shouldn't we land fi......?" Elizabeth looked down and saw that she was hovering inches from the ground.

"That was a close call," Daphne said.

"Yeah," Elizabeth replied stepping down and shakily handing Sonny to Daphne. She slowly walked away from the other two women.

"Where's she going?" Daphne whispered to Shiona.

"I don't know just give her a minute." Shiona replied quietly.

Elizabeth vaguely realised she was wandering aimlessly and stopped. "Um..?" she said hesitating.

Shiona acted quickly. She picked a nearby spot under a canopy of trees, lit a match and from that spark she created a raging fire. The three women sat close to the blaze and huddled together to stay warm.

They sat in silence. Daphne undid her pack and took out some nibbles to sustain them for the rest of their journey. They tucked into nuts, flapjacks and bananas. They ate in silence until Daphne could take it no longer.

"You OK Betty?" she blurted out.

"Yeah," was all Elizabeth could manage. "I'm OK."

"Bit of a shock, I'll bet?" Daphne continued but Elizabeth was not really listening. "You know, facing sudden death and all that. I suppose you didn't know how close you were to dying? Well, until you saw the ground that is!"

"Thank you Daphne," Shiona said, "that will do."

"Trying not to think about it Daphne if that's OK." Elizabeth said looking over her shoulder at Daphne and trying to give her a hard stare, when she suddenly noticed that something was not quite right with Daphne. She turned her attention to Shiona and felt the same niggling doubt. She quickly looked back at Daphne. Elizabeth could not shake the feeling that they looked wrong. She sneezed and pulled her wet clothes tight around her hoping that the fire would dry her enough to carry on with the journey. Suddenly it dawned on her what it was.

"You're not wet!" She said.

"No." Shiona said.

109

"No we're not Betty," Daphne said and the two witches carried on tucking into their snacks.

"Um........" Elizabeth said impatiently. "Why aren't you wet?"

"It's too hard to fly when you're wet Betty. I think you've just realised that!"

"I can understand why you don't *want* to be wet Daphne," Elizabeth replied, "who the hell does! What I don't understand is *why* you are not wet and I'm bloody soaked to my skin!"

"Oh right," Daphne said. "We just made sure we didn't get wet," she offered by way of meagre explanation and resumed eating.

"What on earth do you mean?" Elizabeth ranted. "What spell did you use? Was it elemental control? Is that why I'm soaking and you're not because I'm no sodding good at elemental control?! And why the bloody hell didn't you at least offer me some advice on staying dry in hideous weather conditions thereby possibly preventing my certain death!"

"Shall we all just calm down a minute please?" Shiona said offering a voice of reason. "This is a complicated one Elizabeth and we weren't sure we had time to explain it to you."

"Why don't you try!" Elizabeth said folding her arms and glaring at Shiona. They were still miles away from Branko's borders and the little pit stop was eating into their precious time, but it was clear that Elizabeth was going nowhere without further explanation.

"It's a little like elemental control but on a much more subtle level," Shiona began, "It's something more akin to atomic manipulation."

"Yeah," Daphne interjected, "we pretty much just convince the air to be a little denser around us so that the rain can't get in."

"What?" Elizabeth said staring at the witches. "Surely if the air is denser around you then you wouldn't be able to breath?"

"That's where the spell becomes a little complicated and not suitable for a novice." Shiona said. "The manipulated atoms form a kind of hollow bubble around you, not a solid sphere that you're trapped inside. As long as you remember to refresh the air supply in the bubble every once in a while, you could go on for hours."

Elizabeth looked at Shiona and for the first time since knowing her, she was awestruck by the accomplished witch. "How do you ever *learn* something like that?"

"It's practically impossible to teach," Shiona explained, "and we've never tried."

"What about the other girls?" Elizabeth asked.

"Well it was never necessary and if I was being perfectly honest, I wouldn't know where to start."

"Then how do *you* know," queried Elizabeth. "Surely someone must have taught you?"

"We've got a long way to go in a short space of time Elizabeth." Shiona said.

"Please Shiona," came Elizabeth's keen response. "I will fly flat out to get to Branko with you two by midnight – I promise! Just please explain it to me."

Shiona sighed. Unable to resist Elizabeth's keen interest, she began to explain. "It's a long lost forgotten power but at some point in our distant past every human being was so attuned to the universe that we all had the ability to manipulate matter. We evolved from creatures that climbed from primordial waters and recreated themselves to easily inhabit the changing world. As part of the process, whilst ancient creatures adapted themselves to fit into their surrounding environment, the surrounding environment shifted to accommodate new life. We all lived in perfect harmony with one another and this harmonious existence carried on until the birth of man.

"For thousands of years the ancient skill of matter manipulation was used by all. We were blissfully unaware of anything other than our immediate surroundings so any power we had benefited us and our families and our communities. But as the evolution of man grew and we became aware of our neighbouring societies the ancient powers were abused. Man wanted to conquer all but within each community there was always a trio of revered or worshipped women. These women were the mind, body and spirit of each colony. Back in those days we knew we needed all three to survive and these women took it upon themselves to deal directly with the natural world. When man became destructive and power-hungry these women asked the universe to make humankind forget their manipulative abilities and fight with their own skills, if fighting was necessary. The deal was done and mankind began to forget.

"It took generations for the skills to disappear altogether and there were always some female elders who retained their talents but as the years went by these women were hunted by men who had nominated

111

themselves as *religious* leaders and the women were executed as witches."

"That's an incredible story Shiona," Elizabeth said. "But is it really true? How can we ever know for certain?"

"We can tell by the state of mankind," Shiona replied. "We only have to watch as men and women everywhere look to various philosophies for the meaning of life. From science to religion and from maths to art, we are all searching for something. That lost thing that is buried deep down in our humanity. That feeling of being whole and connected. We've lost our connection but it's not forgotten. The human race is an amazing animal. We know we're missing something but we'll never know that ultimate connection to the universe for as long as we want to abuse that power for our own ends."

"Surely it can't be that simple?" Elizabeth asked. "The desperate search for the meaning of life that's been going on for centuries comes down to the plain fact that we should live harmoniously with the universe?"

"Why not?" Daphne asked. "Look what happens when we don't. We over-farm, over-populate and over-pollute our poor old planet. And we arrogantly talk about how we will destroy the earth when the simple fact is that the planet will go on without us. It burst into life long before our little species ever set foot on it and it will be here long after we've gone. The only problem we create is for ourselves. We *will* probably make it impossible for the human race to survive but *some* form of life will carry on, and the planet definitely will."

"It's probably a good job that people don't know your simple meaning of life," said Elizabeth. "A lot of physicists would be out of a job!"

"I would hate to see that," Daphne said, "especially as they come up with such hilarious theories."

Shiona scoffed in agreement.

"Have you heard about the physicist who thinks we are projections of a hologram from outer space?" Daphne snorted. "Bless him!"

The three women laughed.

"It's pretty mind-blowing stuff," said Elizabeth. "I can't believe you know all of this."

"And we could go on about it for days," said Shiona, "but we really have to get going if we're going to get to Branko by midnight."

"Oh right." Elizabeth said.

The three women stood up and prepared themselves for flight. Shiona extinguished the fire with a concentrated blast of icy air and Daphne passed Sonny to Elizabeth.

"Maybe we'll manipulate a bit of air around *you* this time." Daphne said to Elizabeth.

"That would be kind." Elizabeth said sarcastically. "Just a shame you didn't think about it before!"

Daphne looked at the bedraggled Elizabeth and nodded in agreement. The three women took to the air once again. This time Elizabeth felt a lot warmer as she rode between Shiona and Daphne staying blissfully free from the pouring rain.

The pitch black of night left Elizabeth blind but Shiona and Daphne, having flown this route countless times, efficiently negotiated the journey. Another two hours of flying and Elizabeth's muscles were beginning to seize again. But this time, as she had in the loch, she made herself think about the aches as sensations rather than pain. She found it worked very well and she was able to fly the final hour in relative comfort.

With twenty minutes to go before the stroke of midnight Shiona, Daphne and Elizabeth landed at the boarders of Branko. Once on the ground the sense of foreboding began to envelope Elizabeth. Daphne squeezed her hand reassuringly.

"It's all about the show Betty," Daphne said, "even if you don't feel confident, just pretend. We'll do the rest. Remember, nothing can hurt you while we're around." Daphne smiled at Elizabeth who attempted to return the sentiment, barely managing a strained grimace.

Just a few minutes before midnight, Shiona looked at the other two women and nodded. This was it.

"It's show time," Daphne said.

Shiona walked in front of the others and took up position. Daphne and Elizabeth stayed a few feet back either side of her. The women adopted a triangular position of power. Elizabeth had to admit they looked imposing even if she did not feel it.

The women stood in silence for what felt like an eternity when suddenly there was a sound like a reverberating gong. Elizabeth jumped at the noise and there in front of her the forest around them began to melt and distort. Within moments it had disappeared altogether revealing the outskirts of Branko.

Ahead of her, being blocked by Shiona, Elizabeth saw a family emerge into view. They were impressively dressed and regal in manner. There were two women and three men and the air of confident disdain surrounding them was terrifying to a nervous Elizabeth. At the head of the family standing inches away from Shiona matching her suspicious expression with one of his own was a tall imposing figure. He was easily over 6 foot tall and dressed from top to toe in purple velvet edged with fur. He had long black hair that cascaded down his back, flashing sparks of silver in the moonlight. He had piercing black eyes and looked no older than 50. The left side of his face sported a scar that led from the top of his ear, across his cheek to the corner of his mouth. He was weather worn and stern and he was everything Elizabeth expected he would be. He was once known as the gypsy, Ryder. The man standing only a few feet away from Elizabeth was Lord Darius himself.

Chapter Fifteen

Shiona and Lord Darius stared at one another in silence. In this supreme battle of wills neither one was going to be the first to look away. This was the beginning, an ancient power of evil battled an ancient power for good and it started with this simple game of eye-balling. Elizabeth stared at the pair, the atmosphere was charged between them. They held one another's gaze, neither one giving an inch or backing down in anyway. This was the show that Daphne talked about and it started now.

The shield was down, and the only thing to stop Darius from striding into her own world was the might of the witches.

Elizabeth looked from Shiona to Darius and back again. They stayed locked this way for 10 minutes or more and it looked as though this could go on for a while.

"Oh come on you two," the words came from the older of the two women flanking Darius. "Are we going to be here all night?" She spoke in a heavy Russian accent and seemed utterly bored by the encounter. Elizabeth found her confidence and unnatural beauty unnerving. She looked like a goddess dressed in a long gown of deep red velvet trimmed with dark fur. Her hair was long and straight and it sparkled like gold dust in the moonlight. She walked away from her family towards Daphne.

"Hello dear," she said kissing the air either side of Daphne's cheeks, "so nice to see you again."

"Lady Ingrid," Daphne replied coolly. "How are you?"

"Well we've been better dear," she said. "After all, we've been planning to get through this blasted shield for a whole year. And here you are – again."

"Sorry to disappoint." Shiona said through gritted teeth still locked on to Darius.

"And I see you've brought us fresh meat," Lady Ingrid said looking at Elizabeth.

At this, Lord Darius smiled mirthlessly at Shiona and turned his attention to Elizabeth.

"Well, well, well. What do we have here?" He said sending terrified chills through Elizabeth's body. Like his wife his voice was heavy with an Eastern European accent but his was more muddled. He was oozing ice cold arrogance and he strode towards Elizabeth.

Every muscle in her body was screaming at her to run away from this approaching monster but Daphne's words kept repeating themselves over and over again in her head, *"It's all about the show, Betty. All about the show."* She forced herself to fight the instinct to cower beneath his glare and engaged in her own game of eye-balling as he advanced on her.

He circled her like a wolf sizing up its prey. He sniffed the air around her and his steely gaze crawled up and down her body. Elizabeth shivered when his breath touched her neck as he circled behind her. He stopped in front of her towering above Elizabeth's tiny frame. The fear of being face to face with this demonic man gripped Elizabeth. She had never been more terrified in her life. And considering what she'd experienced over the last few months, that was certainly saying something. *It's all about the show,* she told herself once more and drew herself up as tall as she could to meet Lord Darius' cruel stare. He snorted a condescending laugh at her and turned away.

"So this is what you have brought with you?" He asked Shiona. "At least the fat one could hurt me if she sat on me, what can this little thing do?"

With that he turned sharply away from the witches, propelled himself through his family and walked back towards the village of Branko.

"I'll show you what the *fat* one can do," Daphne said angrily and started rolling up her sleeves preparing for a fight.

"Don't rise to it Daphne," Shiona said. "There's plenty of time for that."

"Don't pay any attention to him Daphne," Lady Ingrid said, "you know how he likes to rile you. Anyway dear," she said turning to

116

Elizabeth, "who are you?"

Suddenly all eyes were on Elizabeth and she went red with embarrassment. "Elizabeth," she squeaked. She took a deep breath trying to calm herself, "Elizabeth," she repeated, in her normal voice.

"And I'm Lady Ingrid," she said offering Elizabeth the same air kisses that she had subjected Daphne to. "These are my children." Lady Ingrid said signalling for the other three members of Darius' family to step forwards.

"This is Diana." Diana was tall and svelte like. Her hair was blonde like her mother's but sat in curls on her shoulders. She stared at Elizabeth with the same air of disdain as her father then smiled coolly and walked away.

"This is Wilhelm," Lady Ingrid continued. The man that walked forward was also tall like the rest of his family, but his build was markedly different. He was broad and stocky and reminded Elizabeth of a rugby player. His skin was bright like his mother's but his hair was dark and a mass of curls. Unlike his sister he seemed quite pleased to meet Elizabeth, he bowed deeply and kissed her hand.

"Welcome," he whispered as he rose and Elizabeth knew that message was for her ears only.

"And this is my baby," Lady Ingrid said as the last of her children stepped forward. "This is Victor."

Victor was a surprise to Elizabeth. He walked forward with the awkwardness of a gangly youth and looked as though he was more nervous of Elizabeth than she was of him.

"H...h....hello." He stuttered then scratched his head and turned clumsily away.

"I suppose we should take you to the Inn," Lady Ingrid said.

The family seemed resigned to the fact that this would not be their year to conquer the world after all. Instead they led the witches away from the shield at the edge of Branko towards the village itself, following the route that Lord Darius had taken moments before.

Elizabeth looked behind her. The hour was no longer midnight and as they moved away from the meeting point she noticed that the forest around them began to shimmer. This was the shield regaining some of its strength.

Lord Darius's family led the way with Shiona and Daphne following a

117

respectful distance behind. They walked in silence for a while. Elizabeth was at the back of the group trying to make sense of her first meeting with these so-called monsters. It was strange to Elizabeth that she had noticed familial resemblances. After all this *family*, if the stories were to be believed, weren't even related. They were just wandering souls that Darius had decided to claim for his own. Suddenly Elizabeth could feel breath on her neck. She could sense a presence. She knew someone was close – too close. She spun around to see who it was and came face to face with Victor, Lord Darius' youngest son. She took a deep breath remembering what Daphne told her. *It's all about the show.* She tried to adopt an air of confidence as she looked across at him.

"You looked funny," he said smiling at her.

Considering the horrors Elizabeth was bracing herself for she was not expecting that.

"What?" She managed and was suitably aggressive.

"The three of you, when the shield disappeared," he said, "you all looked quite funny."

Victor was not what Elizabeth expected. He had the same Eastern European accent as his mother and he was tall and swarthy looking. His hair was equally as dark as his father's, he did not look like an intimidating supernatural being and there was something in his character made him appear awkward. She was glaring at him, trying to figure him out and he seemed to whither under her gaze.

"I m..m..mean you didn't look "ha-ha" funny," he said trying to recover, "more sort of strange funny but quite impressive actually..."

Elizabeth raised her hand. "Don't you think you should probably stop before you say something you regret?"

"Sorry," he said shyly, "I'm not very good with women."

"Clearly," Elizabeth said flatly.

Victor stepped in line alongside Elizabeth as they made their way to the Inn. Uncomfortable though she was around this strange boy, for a moment she saw the situation from his perspective and had to admit he was right. They must have looked a bizarre trio. There was no uniformity in their appearance except that they were all wearing black, and the only reason for the dark of their clothes was so they could easily blend with the dark of the night during their flight. All Elizabeth had been told was to dress in warm, black clothes and to pack light because

118

there were always supplies waiting for them in Branko.

Elizabeth imagined how they must have looked to the family – Shiona was the only one who really looked like a witch; Daphne looked like a 1940s flying ace and Elizabeth looked about as witch-like and foreboding as a skier. She had to admit they must have looked quite a sight and she stifled a giggle, hoping nobody had heard. But she was too late, Victor had seen her snigger and smiled across at her.

"You know what I mean don't you?" He giggled.

"Yes, I do!" Elizabeth exploded unable to stop the laughter.

Elizabeth felt like a naughty schoolgirl as she and Victor attempted to laugh quietly but not quietly enough. Shiona scowled at Elizabeth and Ingrid glared at Victor, which only made them worse. The relief of feeling such an enjoyable emotion was too much for Elizabeth and she found it impossible not to succumb to it. And Victor simply found Elizabeth's laughter infectious.

By the time they had reached the Inn Victor and Elizabeth were almost hysterical.

"Oh Betty," Daphne said as she gestured for her to go inside the tavern. Daphne and Shiona said polite goodbyes and followed Elizabeth inside.

Elizabeth was already taking in the décor of their new surroundings. The bar was like something out of a fairy-tale – a Grimm fairy-tale. Thick, chunky wooden tables were surrounded by three-legged stools all sitting on a floor of sawdust and hay. The bar itself was as the back of the building and stretched the length of the small tavern.

"Well, that went well." Daphne said looking accusingly at Elizabeth.

"It's not my fault," Elizabeth protested. "Victor made me laugh."

"Oh my God, you sound like a child!" Shiona rounded on her. "You be careful my girl. This lot know what they're doing and they are going to try to break our chain of command one way or another. They might as well aim at our weakest link."

"Oh thank you very much," said Elizabeth. "I suppose you mean *me* when you say that."

"Of course I do. Daphne and I are far too old and experienced for them to bother with us. You better believe they are going to try and get around you. They've already had an excellent start what with you playing silly beggars with that Victor."

"Ok Shiona," Elizabeth said, "you've made your point."

"Hello ladies!" A voice boomed from behind them making them all jump.

"It's good to see some things don't change," the voice said from the shadows. "You still whipping your novice into shape Shiona?"

"Show yourself," Shiona said.

Behind the bar a vast creature stepped from the shadows. He was as tall as Lord Darius but much broader. His face was full of a bushy beard but his head was completely hair free. As he moved further into the light Elizabeth saw that he was as round as he was broad and she wondered how on earth he could fit behind the bar.

"Yorik, you silly old sod," Daphne said. "You frightened the life out of us!"

Swiftly, with agility that belied his size, he jumped over the tall bar and landed within an inch of Daphne.

"Come here beautiful," he said sweeping her into a massive bear hug. She giggled like a schoolgirl as he kissed and tickled her with his beard.

"Get off me you old goat," she laughed.

"Yes get off her Yorik." Another voice came from behind them. This time it was a woman's.

Yorik made a look of mock chastisement and swung back over the bar manhandling the other woman just as he had Daphne.

"Are you a bit jealous Greta?" Yorik said.

"I don't know which is worse," Greta said "you grabbing Daphne or you grabbing me. Put me down you big oaf so I can say hello to the girls!"

Yorik lifted Greta over the bar and once again catapulted his huge frame over to join her.

"Hello dear ladies," Greta said to Daphne and Shiona.

She embraced them tightly and Elizabeth knew that Greta's affection was genuine and heartfelt unlike the display made by Lady Ingrid.

"Oh my goodness," Greta said holding her hands towards Elizabeth, "is this your newcomer?" Elizabeth felt compelled to take the woman's hands. "You are so beautiful," she said making Elizabeth blush. "You have an amazing energy around you."

"Don't mind my wife," Yorik interrupted, "she thinks she is psychic. She believes she has a sense number six."

"That's a *sixth sense* Yorik," said Shiona.

"Ya, ya, whatever. But if she was such a good judge of character how come she didn't warn us about Darius...huh?"

"That is an awful thing for you to bring up now," Greta said. "Even the Baron was fooled by him."

"Come on you two!" Daphne said to the quarrelling pair. "Are you going to keep having the same argument every time we see you?"

"You are right Daphne, it is not important now." Greta looked back towards Elizabeth, "what is important is this lovely lady that you bring with you. A bit different from the others I think - yes?"

"We think so," Shiona said. "She's practically a member of the family."

Elizabeth noticed Daphne shoot a strange look towards Shiona and for the first time since knowing her Shiona looked embarrassed.

"Anyway," Shiona said trying to regain composure, "is it OK if we see our rooms now?"

"Of course, of course. Ya, what were we thinking." Yorik said, "You ladies must be so tired."

"Just a little bit," Elizabeth said suddenly feeling overwhelmed by exhaustion.

"But we have lots to discuss in the morning, ya." Greta said.

"Oh yes, much to discuss," Yorik added gravely.

"Is there a problem?" Asked Shiona her suspicion aroused.

"In the morning," Greta said ushering the trio up the stairs ahead of her, "it can wait until morning."

Shiona and Daphne were led to rooms just at the top of the wooden staircase directly opposite one another. Elizabeth suspected that these must have been their usual rooms because they went to them with ease. Elizabeth was led to the next one along the corridor on the left hand side, next to Daphne. Greta opened the door and smiled expectantly at Elizabeth.

Elizabeth was pleasantly surprised when she saw the room. She was expecting basic accommodation with no home comforts, but this room was warm and inviting. There was a double bed next to the door that was made with a puffy and inviting eiderdown; there was a wardrobe one side of the bed and a fireplace to the other side. Greta had obviously lit the fire for their arrival and it was blazing in the grate. There was a large window facing the bed with a view of the woods that edged Branko. To one side of the window was a dressing table with a mirror, a jug and bowl. On the bed were some linen towels and extra blankets.

Greta walked into the room pleased by Elizabeth's reaction. She went to the wardrobe and opened the door.

"I think we've thought of everything you might need, yes?" She asked Elizabeth.

Elizabeth was surprised to see that the wardrobe was packed full of clothes for her stay in Branko.

"Is that for me?" Elizabeth asked.

"Oh yes," Greta replied. "We do this every year you know. Only this year I got a bit carried away. I really hope I've got your size right. I'm usually quite good a guessing but you are a bit smaller than I thought."

Elizabeth smiled her appreciation at Greta. Greta couldn't resist giving her one last hug before leaving the room.

"Sleep well, ya?" She said as she left.

Elizabeth nodded and as soon as she had closed the door she raced back to the wardrobe and checked through the clothes. There were indeed plenty of supplies just as Shiona said there would be. There were trousers and skirts, shirts and jumpers and even some underwear in the dresser drawers. Elizabeth eventually found what she had been looking for, a nightdress. It was long and white and made of brushed cotton, it was just what she needed.

She unpacked her own modest collection of bits and pieces from her backpack. A toothbrush and some pants. As kind as Greta was Elizabeth just couldn't bring herself to wear another person's underwear. She changed quickly and washed her face in the warm water left by Greta. She was exhausted from the journey but she knew there was no point going to bed just yet. The meeting with Darius's family was terrifying and exciting and the memory of the encounter was buzzing in her head.

She opened the window and was hit by the frosty air. The long white nightgown she was wearing offered little protection against the icy breeze and Elizabeth shivered. The air was so refreshing and she filled her lungs with it, breathing deeply it stung her nose and made her eyes water. Through blurry eyes she looked across at the stunning view that was the land of Branko. The snow-topped mountains in the distance, the wandering stream cutting through the landscape and the ancient trees surrounding the tavern.

There was a huge oak tree directly opposite Elizabeth's window. It was gnarled and imposing, she imagined the lifetime of memories it held, the stories it could tell. She gazed at the oak thinking about all the secrets it could reveal when suddenly she noticed something else amongst the branches. Something was glowing unnaturally in the sparse leaves.

She stared at the spot waiting for her eyes to focus in the dark. She leaned out of the window to take a closer look, she could see the light split, there wasn't just one glowing spot anymore, but two. There was something recognisable in those tiny shimmering spots and in front of Elizabeth's eyes they disappeared for an instant and came back again. All at once Elizabeth knew exactly what she was looking at. Eyes – blinking in the dark.

As her own eyes became more and more accustomed to the dark the rest of the image was revealed to her. It was not long before Elizabeth could make out a face, a body and long gangly arms and legs. Elizabeth backed away from the window. It was Victor. The battle started here and she felt utterly unprepared. She was backing towards the door and was nearly there when Victor spoke.

"Please," he said, "don't be frightened."

He was coming out of his hiding place in the tree and edging along the branch towards the tavern window. Elizabeth was moving backwards, Victor was moving forwards but his footing in the tree wasn't as sure as Elizabeth's in her room. As she reached the door he reached the end of the branch and fell.

Instinctively, Elizabeth ran towards the window and watched the falling figure of Victor. He hit practically every branch on the way down, long arms and legs sprawling outwards trying to save himself. He looked completely ridiculous and Elizabeth could not help but snort with laughter at the descending figure. From the first moment with Victor Elizabeth realised he was not terrifying at all.

He made such a racket that by the time he hit the ground a light was on in the bar and Elizabeth heard Yorik stumbling around downstairs. She watched as Victor hauled himself off the ground and scrambled behind the tree trunk to hide.

Yorik stepped into the night with a lantern and a weapon that looked like a machete. Elizabeth's reactions were slow and before she could pull in her head Yorik had spotted her.

"What's going on here?" He said.

"I don't know." Elizabeth said innocently. "I heard a noise and came out to see what it was."

"As did I," Yorik said satisfied with Elizabeth's answer. "Did you see anything?"

Elizabeth began to shake her head but just then she saw Victor pop up from behind the tree. He started miming something at Elizabeth.

"I saw a..." she began attempting to decipher his actions. "A...bear?"

Victor shook his head, and got down on all fours and raised his head upwards pursing his lips into a grotesque kissing action.

"Not a bear," Elizabeth said recovering, "a dog?"

Victor shook his head but gave her an *almost there* gesture – she was getting close.

"A wolf?!" She said finally and Victor gave her the thumbs up and ducked down behind the tree just as Yorik looked around.

"A wolf?" Yorik repeated but there was something in his tone. He sounded fearful. "Where did it go?"

Victor was back and pointing towards a magnificent building that Elizabeth could just about make out in the gloom.

"That way," she said pointing in the same direction as Victor, "towards the castle."

Yorik was clearly shocked. "Ok, Elizabeth," he said, "you go back to bed now and make sure you bolt that window."

"Ok," she replied as Yorik moved swiftly into the tavern.

Elizabeth waited for the lights to go out downstairs before she stole a look towards Victor.

"Sorry to frighten you," he whispered stepping out from behind the tree.

"What are you doing here," she hissed at him. Victor seemed harmless enough but Elizabeth was careful to keep her guard up.

"I just wanted to talk," he said quietly. "If you'll permit?" He gestured towards the tree and Elizabeth realised he wanted to climb it again. She did not know what to do. She stared at Victor trying to see something evil in him, willing a monstrous appearance to suddenly emerge. But all she could see was a somewhat awkward young man that looked totally ill at ease in his own body. He was like a teenager that had grown a foot overnight and didn't know what to do with his new lanky limbs. She could not help but like him. She nodded, and Victor began to climb.

As he ascended Elizabeth assured herself that there was nothing to fear from him. His climb was laboured and ungainly and on more than one occasion he almost fell back to the ground. Elizabeth's heart was in her mouth as he ascended, how would she explain it to Yorik if he fell again, *I'm not sure he'll buy the wolf story next time* she thought in a panic.

When Victor finally reached Elizabeth's window he took a moment to catch his breath. He was about to speak when Elizabeth held up her hand for him to stay quiet. She reached through her window and grabbed one of the branches of the oak tree that Victor was standing on. She held it tightly and closed her eyes as she spoke her healing intention. Within seconds the entire tree glowed and the branches that Victor had broken during his fall knitted together. Victor looked on in amazement as Elizabeth healed the tree. When she had finished she turned her attention to Victor.

"Ok Victor," she said, "what do you want?"

"I'm so...so...so s...sorry," he stuttered dragging his gaze away from the healed branches. "I really did not want to frighten you. I like you and I just want you to know that I'm not a monster. Really it's important to me that you know."

"Why?" Elizabeth said trying to appear stern.

"I just," Victor struggled to find the words. "I have very few friends. The young people here are frightened of us. It is only the witches who treat us as equals. I spent years trying to find a kindred spirit, but I always alone – you see?"

"Ok." Elizabeth said. "Then why haven't you spoken to Daphne or Shiona. They're witches too and they come every single year."

"Oh, no no no!" He said becoming agitated. "I dare not. Imagine if they knew I was not happy here, was "the weak link" I'm afraid they would use that against my father. Do you understand?"

"Yes I do," and Elizabeth truly did. "How do you know I won't tell them? We *are* all part of the same team after all."

"You won't say anything Elizabeth because you have beauty and compassion in your soul. I can see that very well you know. I have spent so much of my life living with evil and hatred that I can easily recognise a bright shining soul when I see one."

Victor's words shocked Elizabeth. Her ego had taken a battering over the past few months since knowing the witches and she was ready for most things, but she did not expect kindness. She felt tears stinging the back of her eyes.

"Thank you." She said quietly.

KNOCK KNOCK KNOCK.

The noise came from behind startling Elizabeth and nearly sending Victor plummeting earthwards again.

"Elizabeth," it was Shiona. "Get some sleep, we've got lots to do in the morning."

"Yeah OK," Elizabeth replied hastily. "Just getting into bed now."

When she was sure Shiona had gone Elizabeth nodded at Victor, and Victor began his ungraceful climb to the ground. Once on the ground he bowed deeply, gazed at Elizabeth for a moment, then turned and walked away. Elizabeth thought he seemed to have a little more confidence as he strode away. But as she continued to watch him he tripped over the root of a tree. Elizabeth stifled a giggle as Victor picked himself up quickly and rushed away.

She climbed into bed more confused than ever. After months of training for her trip to Branko nothing prepared her for this. Whatever else she was expecting she was not expecting to find a friend.

Chapter Sixteen

Elizabeth woke early the next morning. The fire was still smouldering in the grate but the air in the room had a distinctive chill. Elizabeth however was warm and cosy wrapped in the fluffy eiderdown. Lying in bed with the cool air brushing her cheek Elizabeth listened for signs of life in the tavern. There was nothing. No movement, no voices, no sounds other than her own breathing and the faint rustle of the trees outside. Elizabeth closed her eyes, just for a moment she imagined she was the only person on the planet. She sat up quickly, the thought of being alone terrified her. She got out of bed and hastily got dressed into some of the clothes that Greta had provided. She chose a pair of cotton trousers that were lined with a modern fleece material for warmth and a knitted jumper that was made from acrylic rather than wool. She wondered at the strange mix of old and new, *probably a legacy from the visiting witches*, she thought and put them on with one of her own long sleeve tee-shirts and, of course, her own underwear.

She made her way downstairs to the bar. It was still early but the sun was beginning to rise. The sky was a blanket of clouds giving a murky greyness to the early morning light. Looking through the window at the side of the tavern Elizabeth could see much more of the village. Some of the little houses were stone cottages built in rows, others had a somewhat Tudor feel to them with wooden beams on the outside with white paint between the beams. Some were set at ground level and some were two or more stories high with smoke coming from the chimneys. The dwellings were set closely together, giving a feeling of intimacy and community. To Elizabeth the scene was glorious, like something from a Christmas card. But Elizabeth hurriedly reminded herself that the

127

omnipotent man in power was not Father Christmas but the cruel Lord Darius.

She wrapped the blanket she brought from the room tightly around her and sat at one of the window seats in the bar. Gazing out at the picture postcard village of Branko Elizabeth realised that at another time she would feel like the luckiest woman alive to be visiting such an exquisite place, but not today. There was something to be done here, a battle to be won and she felt completely out of her depth.

"What was I thinking?" She said quietly to herself, her breath fogging up the window.

"What was that liebling?"

Elizabeth jumped and turned to see Greta coming through the bar. She was curiously relieved to see another human being. "I didn't think anyone else was awake," she said.

"Sorry," Greta said busying herself. "I get up to light fires. It is cold, yes? You are not used to this with your very warm houses?"

"I'm OK actually, I've got this." She said pulling the blanket further around her.

"What do you think of our little village?" Greta asked as she worked. "You were having a little look, yes?"

"It's stunning," Elizabeth said.

Greta sighed. "Yes it is a very beautiful place. But such horror has happened here. It is very hard for us to see it with your eyes."

Elizabeth remembered the story her mother told her about most of the villagers escaping with the Baron. "How did you get left behind?" She asked Greta.

"We chose to," said Greta. "The Baron needed volunteers to be a link with the outside world, to keep watch on Darius. And, more importantly, we did not want to leave our home."

Greta walked over to the window and sat next to Elizabeth gazing at the castle.

"We let Darius play Lord of the Castle up there on the hill," she motioned towards the castle. "But it is us, down here that keep our eye on him and the village. We have fought him and won, we are not frightened of him. Darius lives on people's fear, he feeds on it, it makes him so strong. But with that fear gone he cannot touch us. And we thought it was gone forever – but we were wrong."

Elizabeth was about to ask Greta what she meant when Shiona appeared through the bar. "Of course it has," Shiona said defiantly but there was no mistaking the look on Greta's face. "Is there something you're not telling me?"

"Plenty of time for that," Greta said getting up, "we will talk when Yorik gets up, yes?"

"Greta tell me……" Shiona started.

"No Shiona." Greta said firmly. "Not yet. When Yorik gets up."

Shiona sat quietly next to Elizabeth and they both watched Greta work. A few minutes later Daphne appeared closely followed by Yorik. Before Greta allowed Shiona to ask any questions she insisted they all eat breakfast. Elizabeth was glad of it, it was delicious. There were freshly made breads with cheese and thick ham that melted in her mouth and rich, fresh coffee. Elizabeth was amazed at the freshness of the food and the richness of the flavours. Everything she ate at home tasted dull by comparison.

Greta and Yorik spent most of the meal time quizzing the witches about modern life. Daphne and Elizabeth were happy to fill them in but Shiona stayed quiet. Once Yorik had cleared the dishes and brought more coffee Shiona finally spoke up.

"Let's have it then," she said looking across to Yorik and Greta. "You've wanted to tell us something since last night, so out with it. What's been happening?"

"And where are all the other guests," Daphne said looking around the tavern, "This place is usually heaving when we come to visit."

"Why?" Elizabeth asked. "They've all got houses of their own in the village. Why would they need to stay here?"

"They like to talk about the outside world," Daphne laughed. "They love to hear all about it. Some questions are serious like political leaders and the state of the environment which always starts off a heated debate. But others we struggle to answer, like up to date fashions and music. We usually leave that to the young witch that comes with us." She nudged Elizabeth knowingly.

Yorik and Greta fidgeted uncomfortably as Daphne spoke. Shiona eyed them suspiciously. "Where is everyone?" she asked.

"They are afraid Shiona," Yorik replied. "Very afraid."

"Of us?" Daphne asked.

"No, of course not." Greta said.

"Then of who?" asked Shiona. After a moment of silence she added slowly, "not Darius?"

"Ya, of Darius," said Greta. "That is why they are not here. They do not want to leave their houses and risk seeing him. It would be dangerous for him to know he is creating fear amongst the people once again."

"Well we just need to tell them they've got nothing to fear," Daphne said cheerfully, "we're here now, everything will be back to normal in no time."

But Shiona knew there was more to the story, "why now?" she asked simply. "Why after all these years are people *scared*?"

"There is a man," Yorik said, "a *new* man in the village. He appeared shortly after you left the last time and he is a stranger."

Daphne and Shiona gasped.

"What's so bad about that?" Elizabeth asked.

"Oh Betty, surely you're getting it by now," Daphne said, "the shield is up to stop Darius getting out but it also stops anyone else getting in. It's only ever weakened once a year at Halloween and it takes a strong force to get through it, even in that fragile state."

Shiona got up and started pacing the floor. "He must have followed us in last year. That's the only explanation."

"Ya, that is what we thought," said Yorik. "Only we have never had a chance to find out. It was late one night, very late but I had not yet closed for the evening. There were very many locals here making merry a few nights after you left, last year, when the bar door opened and in he walked. He looked exhausted and weak like he'd been through a terrible ordeal. He asked for some food and water. We gave it to him. The tavern was full and we had many questions to ask him, but he pleaded with us to wait until he got his strength back. We let him sleep in one of the rooms upstairs and we waited.

"But rumours of the stranger flew through the village and by the next morning there were so many people in the bar they were spilling out into the street. The crowd demanded that I wake him. I tried to calm everyone down, but it was no use, they wanted answers, and so did I. I went up to his room, the bed had been slept in but the window was open and the room was empty.

"We searched the tavern, even searched the village, but nothing. It was like a dream and if it had only been Greta and I here, I might have said it *was* a dream. But there were at least twenty witnesses." Yorik hung his head but Greta put a reassuring hand on his shoulder urging him to go on.

"After a few weeks the rumours started to die down. The villagers remained alert but the incident was becoming old news. Months later stories began to emerge about a stranger in the castle. We do not usually care about what goes on at the castle," Yorik said throwing a disgusted look up the hill, "but talk of this stranger was very worrying. At last, one of the young people in the village returned with a description of this newcomer – it was the same man that had come into our tavern all those months ago. He was now at the castle and he was working for Lord Darius."

Just as Yorik was finishing the story the door to the tavern slowly creaked open. Yorik and Greta and the three witches all held their breath. As the door slowly swung open it revealed behind it a little old man. Elizabeth was on eggshells but the others breathed a sigh of relief.

"Gerhard, what are you doing?!" Greta asked, "you nearly scared us to death!"

"I am not staying behind closed doors for the rest of my life," Gerhard said waving a stick at them. "Seeing these ladies is the most interesting thing that happens to this village all year!"

Nothing more was said about the stranger after Gerhard's entrance and soon after the old man sat down to join them the door opened once again and a trickle of villagers filed through all morning seeking out the company of the witches. The women were happy to see some familiar Branko faces and dutifully put on a show of confidence and courage. Keen to dispel any rumours that Darius was regaining some of his power.

Elizabeth was fascinated by some of the stories the older villagers told her. In all the time they had lived in Branko as Lord Darius' prison guards, they had not aged or altered. Some of them still remembered the original three witches that left with the Baron. Elizabeth had a long chat with Edith who told her all about Branko in it's heyday in exchange for information about the modern world.

Elizabeth was so deeply involved in conversation with Edith that she jumped when she was tapped on the shoulder. "Come on Betty," Daphne said, "time to show our faces."

Both Daphne and Shiona were next to her beckoning her away from the fascinating conversation. They put on their outdoor clothes and went for their annual walkabout in the village of Branko.

"We have to do this every year," Daphne explained. "We take a stride around the village so that everyone knows we are back and ready for a fight!" Daphne explained that the procession through the village was usually a welcome sight for the villagers but this time even Elizabeth could sense there was something wrong.

"Not quite the roaring welcome you were expecting?" Elizabeth asked as they walked the streets of Branko. There was the odd person who defiantly stood in front of their home waving at the witches, buy mostly the doors were closed and shutters were locked tight.

"This is weird," said Elizabeth. "It's like a ghost town."

"Pssst!"

Elizabeth heard a noise behind her and turned to see. The other witches heard it too. "What was that?" She said.

Daphne and Shiona shook their heads.

"What do you think Daphne?" Shiona asked.

Daphne closed her eyes. "In the shadows to the left, there's a frightened girl. I can't see her face. No....wait a minute, she's turning into the light.....it's...it's ...Gretchen."

"Where?" asked Shiona.

"There." Daphne pointed to a small alleyway behind one of the two-storey houses. There was a wooden walkway above and Daphne was gesturing below it.

Shiona marched straight to the spot.

"What were you doing?" Elizabeth asked Daphne as they fell into step behind Shiona.

"Just having a little look around, Betty."

"But your eyes were closed!"

"I'll explain all that later," Daphne said and for the first time Elizabeth noticed a hint of fear in her tone.

"There's no-one here." Shiona said scanning the alley.

"She's not far," Daphne said.

"Gretchen?" Shiona called quietly. But there was no reply. "I don't

132

like this. I don't like this at all."

"Nor do I," said Elizabeth remembering how her own alleyway encounter had started this whole adventure.

"We're behaving like scared children," Daphne said. "It's not supposed to be like this!"

Just then, they heard a scurrying behind them. They turned to look but there was nothing there.

"I'm not cowering in a corner," Shiona said decisively taking her wand from her robes. "If they've got something special planned for us I want to know what it is – now!" A blast of light shot out of Shiona's wand, "SHOW YOURSELF" she screamed.

The bright light illuminated the whole alleyway and there in a doorway at the far end they found what they were looking for. Cowering from them was a pitiful creature, and as far as Elizabeth could make out, it was a young woman. Her clothes were torn and filthy, hanging from her body like rags. The creature's matted hair hung down covering her face. Her feet were bloodied and filthy tucked into the body for warmth, and the body, all too visible through the rags, was smothered in dirt and covered with cuts and bruises.

"Oh my God," Daphne said softly, "It is Gretchen!"

"You didn't tell me she was in this state!" said Shiona.

"She wasn't," Daphne replied, "in my vision she was just scared, nothing like this!"

Shiona moved slowly towards Gretchen as though approaching an injured animal. Gretchen trembled in the doorway, shivering and moaning quietly.

"Gretchen, it's Shiona. Do you remember me? Are you hurt?"

Gretchen did not seem to notice the witch edging gently towards her. Her head hung down, she carried on groaning. Shiona crouched low as she got closer, careful not to make any sudden movements. Daphne stayed back but Elizabeth was drawn in, fascinated by the creature until she felt a pull on her arm.

"Goodness knows what's happened to her Betty," Daphne said, "best leave this to Shiona."

Inch by inch Shiona got nearer and nearer to Gretchen reassuring her as she went. She spoke softly, trying not to make any loud noises or sudden movements. Daphne and Elizabeth looked on, hardly daring to breath.

"I've got you Gretchen," Shiona said, "nothing can hurt you now."

Suddenly Gretchen jumped to her feet knocking Shiona to the ground as she rose. She scanned the three women a look of pure malevolence in her eye. Her head was low and she stared at them like a tiger waiting to pounce, her low moan was replaced by a deep growl that rumbled through the alleyway.

"GGGRRRRRRR!" she growled and jumped over Shiona aiming for Elizabeth.

Elizabeth was knocked backwards by the force of the blow. In an instant Gretchen was on top of her, mouth wide open, trying to bite her. Elizabeth managed to grab hold of Gretchen's shoulders and with all her might she pushed her away, dodging the vicious attack. But Gretchen was too nimble and every time Elizabeth blocked one blow the woman quickly changed tack and went at her from a different angle. She was at her neck one moment, her shoulder the next and then she went for her arm. Elizabeth had no time to summon any spells, she was too busy fighting for her life. Gretchen was like a crazed animal. *This is how I die*, Elizabeth thought.

"HELP!" she screamed.

Shiona scrambled to her feet as Daphne tried to drag the ferocious Gretchen away from Elizabeth. Gretchen kicked out at Daphne knocking her to the floor and turned her attention back to Elizabeth. Elizabeth was helpless to defend herself against the beast, "aaargghh!" she cried in exertion when suddenly and thankfully she saw Shiona get to her feet and turn that steely gaze on the monster. Shiona knew it would be no use engaging in hand to hand combat so she used her own magnificent power. With a wave of her wand Gretchen was thrown off balance. Unable to stand she crawled back towards Elizabeth – her prey. With a flick of her wrist, Shiona sent Gretchen flying towards the wall. She crashed to the ground with a thump, slightly injured but not finished yet. She slithered towards Elizabeth who was still lying on her back trying to get away from the approaching creature.

Finally, Shiona raised both arms and as she did Gretchen was invisibly lifted into the air. Even in mid-air the monstrous figure twisted and contorted and fought the witch's control, but Shiona was too powerful. She flung her to the far side of the alleyway, away from

134

Elizabeth and away from the heart of Branko's village.

For a moment Gretchen just lay in a heap breathing deeply.

"Help Elizabeth!" Shiona roared at Daphne not daring to take her attention from Gretchen. Tearing her eyes away from the floating, snarling girl Daphne ran over to the fallen Elizabeth.

"I'm OK." Elizabeth said getting to her feet.

Once all three women were standing they formed their usual triangular defence. Now they knew what to expect, they moved cautiously forward to the heaped figure.

They were close to Gretchen when she started to move. They stopped dead in their tracks as they watched her rise. Slowly, as a phoenix rising from the flames Gretchen emerged from the ground. Piece by piece of her crazed body was revealed as she inched up from the floor. The witches saw her feet first, then her legs, her torso, arms and hands until the only thing left was her head. When she finally faced them the witches could see she was smiling viciously.

"What the hell is going on Gretchen?" Shiona hissed.

With that, Gretchen laughed. It was a hideous sound devoid of any mirth. "Too late," she growled and prepared to pounce.

The two witches were ready for her this time and prepared to cast their defensive spells. Gretchen laughed again and slowly retreated. She was clearly aware that she was no match for their power. She turned around and ran away from them.

They watched her flee towards the castle. Every now and again they caught sight of her running through the trees. When she was sure that Gretchen wouldn't return Shiona finally let down her defences.

"Wh...what the hell?" Elizabeth stuttered. "I wish you had warned me about that! Is that normal?"

"NO!" Shiona said storming past her.

Elizabeth stared at the departing creature, watching her retreat through the forest. Daphne and Shiona began talking in hurried whispers. Then Elizabeth saw something that filled her with horror.

"Uh.......you two," she said.

"Not now Elizabeth," Shiona replied curtly.

"Yes NOW!" Elizabeth said. "You really need to see this!"

Sensing the urgency Shiona and Daphne were at her side in seconds. They looked at where she was pointing, still at the disappearing figure

135

of Gretchen but now they could see that Gretchen was not just using her legs to make her escape, she was using her hands as well. Gretchen was running on all fours – like an animal.

Chapter Seventeen

"What the hell is going on?" Daphne said. "Have they turned Gretchen into an animal? She looked like a bloody wolf running up that hill!"

Something suddenly occurred to Elizabeth. "Are there are lot of wolves around here?" she asked.

"What the bloody hell has that got to do with anything Betty? That was a woman!"

"I know, I know!" Elizabeth said. "Just tell me."

"No." Shiona said. "There are no wolves. There are hardly any wild animals left. Their consciousness can't cope with an unnaturally long existence. The only ones left now are the farm animals, the others die out, even though the villagers live on, ageless."

"Oh no," Elizabeth said quietly.

"What?" Shiona asked rounding on her. "What is it Elizabeth?"

Elizabeth started to tell the witches about her late night meeting with Victor. The words were barely out of Elizabeth's mouth before Daphne and Shiona were racing along Branko's streets back to the tavern.

"What the hell were you thinking Betty, having a clandestine meeting with the enemy?"

"Victor's ..... not ...... like that," Elizabeth panted.

The three women had left their broomsticks back at the tavern and were reduced to using a more primitive method of transport, their feet. They were running as fast as they could and Elizabeth was stunned that she was finding the exertion far harder than her much older companions.

"I'm not worried about Elizabeth's stupidity," Shiona said shooting her a look, "I'm more concerned about Yorik. If he didn't think that the idea of you seeing a wolf was ridiculous, then he's hiding something."

They rounded the corner at the end of Branko's main street and saw the tavern looming in front of them. Like a bullet being shot from a gun Shiona stepped up her pace and sped towards the inn leaving Daphne and Elizabeth gasping in her wake.

When they caught up with her Shiona was already in the bar. "YORIK!" she cried. "Where are you? You've got some explaining to do!"

"What on earth is the matter?" Greta said emerging from the bar.

"Where's Yorik?" Shiona asked, "or perhaps *you* can tell us what's going on?"

"Tell you what Shiona?"

"About the *wolves*."

Greta gasped, "how d...did you f...find out?"

"Just a minute Shiona." The three witches turned, Yorik was in the doorway, filling it up with his huge frame. "Do not shout at Greta now," he said. "It is not her fault. It is not the fault of anybody."

"Alright," Shiona said coolly, "why don't *you* tell me why we just saw Gretchen running up the hill on her hands and feet like an animal?"

"Oh Gretchen!" Sobbed Greta.

"Please Shiona," Yorik said "this is incredibly hard for us. It is not a game."

"No this isn't a game – for *us*," Shiona said, "but you can bet your life it is a game for Darius. So tell us what you know so that we can start playing it properly!"

"Come, come," Yorik said gesturing for the sobbing Greta to sit down. He offered a seat to the witches but Shiona blankly refused.

"Are they werewolves?" Elizabeth asked.

"No child," Yorik said, "there are no evil creatures like the ones you read about in your books. There are only lost souls and evil men who want to control them."

Yorik sighed heavily, and Elizabeth could see he was desperately trying to find a way to explain this terrible turn of events. "Once the stranger was seen at the castle," he began, "the villagers started to feel a long forgotten fear. We had a town meeting and it was decided that we stay as far away from Darius as possible. Just until we were sure the stranger was no threat. To make sure Darius could not sense our fear.

"But for months nothing really happened so with our confidence returning some of the young ones turned it into a game."

Shiona snorted derisively.

"We have been here for hundreds of years Shiona," Yorik said defensively, "but we are still the same as we always were. The old folk are still old but no older, and we still have teenagers. They are so bored with this perpetual existence and the thought of a stranger was too enticing for them. They began to dare one another to see who was brave enough to get close to the castle.

"As soon as the elders heard about it we put a stop to it, angry with their irresponsibility. But they carried on anyway, this time they made sure that there was no way we could find out. When one or two of them went missing the ones remaining thought it was just part of the fun and simply carried on, calling out to their friends as if they were playing a game of hide and seek. Then suddenly they were all gone - except Gretchen. She came to us and told us everything. We ordered her back home, told her to stay there and keep safe. She did so for a while but her guilt was unbearable. She slipped away from her mother leaving a note saying she was going to make it better. That was the last we saw of her."

"That was exactly the kind of girl she was," Greta said, "always wanting to help. I know that when the others started to play their stupid game, she would have only gone along with it to talk some sense into them. She was such a good girl."

Greta buried her head in her arms and sobbed uncontrollably.

"I honestly think," Daphne said putting her arm across Greta's shoulders, "she was still trying to help. Even today. Maybe she was trying to get our attention."

"Well she certainly got *my* attention," Elizabeth said rubbing her arm.

"What happened?" Yorik asked noticing Elizabeth's wounds.

"She went for me," Elizabeth replied, "just me. She only attacked Daphne because she was trying to help me."

"Why did she attack only you?" Yorik asked confused.

"The weakest link I suppose," Elizabeth scoffed remembering what Shiona said to her.

Elizabeth expected Shiona to look ashamed, being reminded of her unkind comment, but Shiona only shot Daphne a wary look and started muttering to herself.

"This isn't right," she said, pacing the floor. "It's different this time. But how could it be different? What powers could this stranger have? Surely we would have known about him if he came from our world. Someone so powerful would have easily been spotted."

"What do you mean *it's different this time*?" Elizabeth asked. "We're still going to win, aren't we?" Shiona looked at her and Elizabeth didn't like what she saw in Shiona's eyes. "Shiona," Elizabeth said, "please tell me........" but she didn't get a chance to finish.

BAM!

The front door of the tavern exploded inwards.

Yorik, Greta and the witches were blown backwards by the force of the blast. Elizabeth was knocked clean over the bar, crashed into the liquor wall and fell in a heap on the floor, broken glass and bottles rained down on her.

She had no idea what happened to the others but behind the protection of the bar she heard blast after blast exploding into the tavern the air around her lit up with fireworks and every crash ripped through her body. She could hear parts of the broken building falling around her, the *CRASH* and *THUD* of Yorik's livelihood being transformed into rubble. Then as quickly as it had started – it stopped. The only sounds Elizabeth could hear were the smashes and bangs of tavern debris falling around her.

She lay for a moment listening for movement from the others. She strained to hear, not daring to move or make a sound. Finally she heard footsteps walking slowly over the rubble. She knew it was not any of her companions – the sound was coming from the doorway. Elizabeth was in considerable pain but she put pressure on each limb, resisting the urge to groan in pain. Nothing was broken. She closed her eyes listening to the crunching footsteps moving through the tavern. She could hear nothing of her fallen friends, she felt entirely alone and terrified. Something had to be done, she knew that, that was the reason they were there after all, and if Shiona and Daphne were in no state to do anything then it was all down to her.

As the attackers drew closer Elizabeth desperately tried to think of an appropriate spell and suddenly realised how ill-equipped she actually was. Everything she knew, everything she had been taught had not prepared her for this moment. She suddenly realised how irrelevant *witch number 3* was. The third witch was for show, it was the elder two witches who held the power and it was just starting to dawn on Elizabeth how incapable she was. *What good would a growing or healing spell do now?* she thought.

She heard the low voices of the attackers as they wandered freely around the building. She couldn't understand what they were saying but she knew they were satisfied with themselves. They spoke confidently, arrogantly and they were giggling. Elizabeth pictured the attackers looking at the dead bodies of her fallen friends – laughing. Slowly she started to feel a heat in her stomach. A familiar feeling of rage began to course through her veins. She remembered what Shiona had taught her about that place of power below her navel that it was vital to align with that place if she was to attempt an elemental control spell. And there it was that feeling of power, the corner of Elizabeth's mouth twitched upwards as she began to enjoy the feeling of raging energy as it enveloped every cell in her body. All doubt had gone, the old Elizabeth had gone. This time, as in the alleyway, she did not stop to think about consequences.

She allowed her body to search for that point of power and she found its low grumble once again. This time it was not an uncontrollable animal, there was a calmness to it that reassured Elizabeth, the next thing she had to find was the element. She searched around her trying to find something. Then, at the far end of the bar, she saw what she was looking for.

She crawled along the floor as quietly as she could. But the rubble slipped from under her and the attackers were alerted by the sound. They were on to her. Elizabeth could hear them moving towards her but it did not matter, she had already reached her prize. The bucket of dirty water that Greta used to clean the floors was still standing upright amongst the devastation. The only piece of their old life that was still intact. Elizabeth threw away the mop and stood up defiantly.

She rose from behind the bar and was shocked by what she saw. She was expecting to be confronted by the wolf-teenagers, Gretchen amongst them. She was amazed to see Wilhelm and Diana doing their father's dirty work. But the sight that shocked her the most, the very last person she expected to see, was Victor.

She stared at him and shook her head. Victor spotted her and shuffled uneasily on his feet. *At least he has the grace to look ashamed*, she thought. Not like Wilhelm and Diana who were clearly enjoying themselves.

"You are not going to do much damage with a bucket, little witch." Wilhelm laughed standing at the front of the trio, the self-appointed figurehead.

Elizabeth merely stared at him, any fear she might have felt at being the lone defender vanished as soon as she saw that Victor was amongst the attackers. She had been played for a fool, just as Shiona said she would be, and the idea of listening to her say 'I told you so' only fuelled Elizabeth's rage.

Suddenly she knew exactly what to do with that pit of power in her stomach and the dirty water in her bucket. She looked at the grinning faces of Wilhelm and Diana and offered a cruel grin of her own.

She did not stop to think if the spell was going to work or not. She threw the bucket of water towards the siblings. Wilhelm and Diana smirked as the liquid looked as though it were about to fall short of its target when suddenly Elizabeth seized the power at her navel and threw out her arms. All at once the water shot forward like a cannon, knocking them all to the ground.

The spell was not as powerful as the lightening in the alleyway but it did what Elizabeth wanted. She knocked them off balance buying herself some time to think. But they were getting to their feet, quickly, and this time Diana and Wilhelm looked as though they were out for her blood. Elizabeth gulped and in that moment she felt her fear make an unwelcome return. *No, no!* She said to herself. *Stay angry, please stay angry!* But it was too late, she had seen the look on the faces of the brother and sister and underneath their thin veneer of humanity she felt sure she could see the animal within. Victor kept his distance but Wilhelm and Diana walked slowly and maliciously towards Elizabeth.

"Is there something we can help you with, Wilhelm?"

Elizabeth jumped. The voice came from directly behind her and she had never been so pleased to hear this particular voice laced with rage. Shiona's calmness was unnerving, even for Elizabeth.

"We are not here because of something you can do for us," Wilhelm answered, but his air of confidence had all but disappeared. He was faced with a much more powerful opponent and he knew it. "More something we can do for you. Here…" he said and threw an envelope at Shiona.

It landed at her feet but she did not bend to pick it up. She gripped her wand tightly, keeping her beady eyes on Wilhelm.

"What is it?" Shiona asked gesturing towards the envelope.

"See for yourself," Wilhelm replied.

"I'd much rather you *tell* me."

Wilhelm smirked but it was an empty show of hostility. He knew that the accomplished witch would not be distracted even momentarily.

"It is an invitation," he said, "for all of you." He glanced towards Elizabeth and smiled.

Elizabeth looked Wilhelm straight in the eye, but she was longing to glance over to Victor, to see if he still looked ashamed or if he was feeling the same sadistic coolness as his siblings. She wanted to know what all this meant to him, but she did not dare show any signs of interest in him. She had started to like Victor. She thought he was an ally on this otherwise bizarre journey. She had even concealed him from Yorik, but he was purely and simply the enemy just as Daphne said.

"An invitation for what?" Shiona asked.

"For a masquerade ball to be held in your honour," Wilhelm said and started to wander around the building, like an officer giving orders. "It was my father's idea. He thought your new girl might like to see the castle."

"That's very kind of him," Shiona said through gritted teeth. "Why now?"

"I'm sorry?"

"We've had *new girls* before. Why would your father invite us to the castle now?"

"Maybe this one is a bit special," Wilhelm said shooting a knowing glance at Victor.

Helpless to stop herself, Elizabeth looked at Victor too. He was scowling at his brother and shaking his head. Elizabeth had no idea what the unspoken thought was between the two of them but it was clear Wilhelm was enjoying himself.

"What a mess we seem to have made," Wilhelm continued. He stepped through the rubble arrogantly surveying the scene of devastation.

"Yes," Shiona said, "will you be staying to clean it up?"

"I do not think so," Wilhelm scoffed, "but before we go I have one last message from my father."

Wilhelm was quick but Shiona was quicker he sent an explosive bolt towards her but Shiona blocked it with her own spell. The force of the blow did not connect but was strong enough to send her flying backwards. Shiona fell heavily on the other side of the bar.

Elizabeth was paralysed with fear. She stared open-mouthed at Wilhelm, unable to believe that he could disarm such a powerful witch so easily. She saw Wilhelm and Diana laugh. She looked across at Victor who remained silent. Diana saw Elizabeth glance her brother's way and chastised him in her native tongue for not joining in with the levity. Wilhelm also turned on his brother. While they were momentarily distracted Elizabeth took her chance and launched herself behind the bar where Shiona had landed. Shiona was disorientated but was coming around quickly.

"What are they doing?" Elizabeth asked.

"I have no idea, this has *never* happened before."

"Should we split up? I'll take one you take the other two."

"No, we've got to find Daphne."

Elizabeth was buoyed by her successful elemental spell and was sure she could be put to better use. "Victor's got a soft spot for me, that's obvious. If I can just get him away………"

"No! You can't. We've got to find Daphne!"

"Shiona let me help," she insisted, "if I can get Victor clear of the pub then you only have to deal with Wilhelm and Diana."

"You can't Elizabeth. You just bloody can't. Do I have to spell it out for you, you're useless without us!"

Leaving a devastated Elizabeth gaping on the floor Shiona got to her feet and jumped nimbly over the bar sending out a flash of light as she went, knocking the siblings to the ground. Still in a daze Elizabeth stood up.

"Get to Daphne," Shiona screamed at her and with a flick of her wand she catapulted Elizabeth over the bar.

Elizabeth landed with a thud, groaning as she got up. "I could have just climbed over," she grumbled and scoured the ruins for Daphne.

Daphne was not hard to spot within the rubble. The large lady was visible and audible, groaning on the floor a few feet away. Elizabeth crawled across to her and tried the healing spell she had used on the tree the previous night. But with Shiona's cruel words buzzing around her head she suddenly doubted she was capable of any spell, even a simple one.

"Do you want to play?" She heard Wilhelm say to Shiona.

Elizabeth glanced across at the witch and noticed the same thunderous look she had seen many times before. She had to admire Wilhelm's bravery at taking on such a fearsome foe, or maybe he simply had no idea what he was letting himself in for.

"THIS IS NOT A GAME!" Shiona screamed.

It happened in a split second. As far as Elizabeth could see Shiona summoned every ounce of power she possessed in a bid to teach Darius' children a lesson. Within an instant an explosive light burst from every pore, Shiona looked as though she were on fire as she advanced on them, her wand pointing directly at Wilhelm. Suddenly Shiona sent the spell bursting towards the three enveloping them within the blaze. She lifted Darius' children off the ground and walked towards the blown in doorway forcing them backwards. Enraged, Wilhelm attempted to burst through Shiona's spell but Daphne jumped to her feet, knocking Elizabeth backwards, and grabbing her own wand she added a searing blue flame to the mix. Elizabeth heard the screams of the siblings and watched as their faces contorted in pain as they were forced out of the building. They were encased in the golden sphere of Shiona's spell and the dazzling blue flames of Daphne's, both witches too powerful for the monsters to fight back. The hovering figures looked as though they were trapped in a vicious snow globe and even though Elizabeth knew Wilhelm and Diana had it coming, she could not bear to watch Victor's pitiful face. She turned away from the grotesque sight.

"Do you hear me, people of Branko," Shiona shouted once they were out in the open as she raised the groaning captives above her head. "We are back. And we are here to keep you safe!" With that she dropped the ball of flames to the ground, it crashed and sent the terrible trio tumbling across the ground.

Elizabeth could see Daphne and Shiona standing proudly above their fallen enemies and as hurt as she was by Shiona's comments she did her duty and fell into place completing the trio of witches.

"And you," Shiona hissed crouching next to Wilhelm, "give your father a message from me." She grabbed him by the ear and pressed her face to his, "tell him to be careful."

Shiona threw the man to the floor and took up her place with Elizabeth and Daphne. With a nod of her head she signalled to the siblings to go. Victor, Diana and Wilhelm lurched to their feet. Diana and Wilhelm were beaten in body only, the defiance in their faces was unmistakable. Victor, however, was different. As the three siblings limped and staggered away Victor's injuries looked worse than the others. He hung his head in shame whilst his brother and sister attempted a show of strength as they hobbled away.

Elizabeth watched the departing trio as Daphne and Shiona rushed inside to search for Yorik and Greta. Elizabeth could tell that the injuries the siblings sustained would not last long. They were practically fully recovered even before they were out of sight. Just as they were about to turn the corner to head northwards to the castle, Victor looked back. Elizabeth scowled at him from a distance, too far away to be heard and too confused to say anything of consequence. He mouthed something at her, hung his head and followed his brother and sister up the hill.

When she was sure they were out of sight and away from the village Elizabeth turned back to the Inn. She had been expecting utter destruction, but remarkably most of the tavern was still in-tact. The damage was superficial. The entrance had been blown away and the bottles and plates were in pieces but the tavern itself was still standing strong. Elizabeth searched through the dust for the others and she was relieved to see that Daphne and Shiona had found Yorik and Greta. They were alive, but they were badly hurt and each witch was performing a healing spell on one of their friends.

"Come on Betty, give us a hand," Daphne said, beckoning her over. "Let's see if you can work some of your magic on Yorik."

Daphne was smiling but Elizabeth glanced across at Shiona unable to forget her cutting remark. Shiona looked everywhere but at Elizabeth, concentrating just a little bit harder on Greta's healing.

Elizabeth looked back at Daphne still smiling expectantly. Now the battle was over and the adrenalin was no longer pumping Elizabeth allowed Shiona's cruel words to cut like a knife, she shook her head at Daphne and walked away from them all.

She thought about what she could have done to provoke such hatred from Shiona as she walked upstairs to her little bedroom in the Tavern. She always behaved like a good little witch doing what she was asked when she was asked. She knew she found it hard when they first met as every revelation was like a punch in the ribs, but since then she had embraced the idea whole-heartedly. Even after all she had given of herself, Shiona still did not trust her.

She sat heavily on her bed staring out of the window, remembering the night-time tryst she had with Victor and she was helpless to stop the tears from rolling down her cheeks. Shiona had always been unkind to her, but for a while now they had reached an unspoken understanding. Elizabeth was bewildered and hurt by Shiona's constant resentment.

Through the window Elizabeth saw the oak tree that Victor had sat on the previous night and she thought about the words he had mouthed to her as he rounded the corner with his siblings. The same words that she was sure would never pass Shiona's lips. *I'm sorry.*

Chapter Eighteen

Elizabeth lay in the darkness of her room swaddled in the cotton wool comfort of her thick duvet. Nothing could tempt her from this exquisite place of safety. She stared through the window at the spot where Victor had stood. *Victor, friend of foe? The weakest link, like me, or a clever manipulator?* Was her friendship important to him or was he just using her? She had so many questions but no way of finding out the answers. In the black of the night she wished she could see him again, alone – as equals, one lost soul to another.

Suddenly as she was gazing at the ancient oak tree Elizabeth thought she saw something glowing in the gloom. She sat up for a closer look but there was nothing. She thought perhaps her eyes had deceived her when all at once there was a flash of green light that slowly divided into two luminescent green eyes that stared at her. They felt like tiny searchlights into her soul.

"Victor," she said quietly.

With that, the figure of Victor started to melt into view. Bit by bit, as the light of the tavern gradually illuminated him, he appeared. Elizabeth swung her legs from the bed. Despite everything she was pleased to see him, now she would get some answers. She strode over to the window but as she reached it she saw that Victor was different this time. He did not wear his usual expression of gauche timidity. He did not cower under her stare looking ashamed. He was bolder this time, frighteningly confident. But it was more than just arrogance, his eyes were cold, his grin was evil and he slowly crouched down on all fours. Elizabeth instinctively knew he was ready to pounce.

She backed away from the window and turned towards the door.

She started to run but it was too late. Within seconds Victor had sprung to the tavern, latched onto the side of the building, like a spider, and smashed through the window showering Elizabeth with glass. Elizabeth crashed to the floor and Victor landed inches away. Elizabeth tried to scramble to her feet but Victor was too quick. He leapt into the air and landed on her pinning her to the ground. In the gloom Elizabeth could see he had transformed, like Gretchen he was an animal drooling and snarling on top of her. She was powerless under his weight, his long fingernails dug into her arms and his unnaturally long legs crushed her body. She had nothing to fight with and she started to scream.

Elizabeth woke up in a cold sweat, arms thrashing as she fought with the weight of her duvet. She was wrapped up tight and felt like she was suffocating. It was still dark but Victor was nowhere to be seen. She struggled to catch her breath.

"It was a dream," she reassured herself, "just a dream."

She sat up in bed. The room was cold, dark and unnerving. She tried to convince herself that it was definitely a dream. But she was not sure. She did not know anything with any certainty anymore. She had seen enough of Branko and its inhabitants to realise anything was possible. As her tired eyes adjusted to the gloom, the familiarity of the room swam into place. But it was not the room she expected to be in. Elizabeth gasped. The small fire and antique wardrobe in her bedroom at the tavern had gone. In its place were posters on the wall; a white dresser and matching wardrobe; ornaments and remnants of Elizabeth's life as a teenager. She was back home. The home she had grown up in. The home she had shared with her sister, her Father and her...

"Mum!" She cried noticing Gladys at the end of her bed.

"Hello Little One," Gladys said moving to embrace her daughter.

A wave of utter relief swept over Elizabeth as she dissolved into her mother's embrace. She could not fight the tears any longer.

"Mum," she sobbed, "oh Mum."

"Sssh, Little One. It's OK. I'm here."

"I have no idea what's going on. I could be dreaming, or I could actually be back home. But I don't care." Elizabeth said through her tears, "I'm just so... b.. bloody glad..to.. to see you." Unable to say another word Elizabeth sobbed uncontrollably on her mother's shoulder.

"I know, I know." Gladys said reassuringly, "It's going to be

OK Elizabeth. But you have to listen to me now, OK?" Gladys lifted Elizabeth off her shoulder and held her gently by the arms.

She looked Elizabeth straight in the eye but Elizabeth noticed there was something wispy about the way her mother looked. She was solid enough, Elizabeth could feel the pressure of her grip at the top of her arms but she felt like she was watching her mother through a mist. She could not quite get Gladys into focus.

"I'm dreaming aren't I," she said finally and it was not a question.

"Yes you are. I'm sorry."

"You're not going to turn into a monster are you?" Elizabeth asked.

"No," Gladys smiled, "at least I hope not!"

Suddenly a thought occurred to Elizabeth, "Oh God! You're not dead are you?"

"Oh Elizabeth, you're so morbid!" Gladys said. "No I'm not dead, I'm not dying, I'm just, technically, a figment of your subconscious."

"Oh. I see." Elizabeth said sadly, "not really here at all."

"Or," Gladys whispered leaning towards Elizabeth, "is it *you* that's not really here?"

Elizabeth looked around the room. It *was* her old room. The one she had as a child. The one she stayed in when she visited her parents. The one she had used before moving to Scotland. "Am I......?"

"Listen Elizabeth, there's no time for a million questions." Gladys said. "You're going to wake up in a minute so you have to listen to me."

"Ok," Elizabeth said soberly, readying herself for a gem of advice from the elder witch.

"You *have* to listen to Shiona."

"What! Is that it?" Elizabeth said. "Did you drag my subconscious all the way back home to tell me that?"

"It's important Elizabeth. You may not like what she has to say but it's important you listen to her."

"I'm sick of listening to her," Elizabeth said. "I do nothing *but* listen to her. And she's being such a bitch!"

"Elizabeth! There's no need for that!" Gladys took a deep breath trying to compose herself. "She's only doing what's best for you and there is something very important she has to tell you. And like it or not – you *have* to listen! But she can't tell you everything. There are some things even she doesn't know."

"But......" Elizabeth began to argue petulantly but suddenly the image of her mother swam out of view and she was plunged into darkness once again.

"Elizabeth, Elizabeth."

A warm hand was shaking her gently by the shoulder. Elizabeth opened her eyes. She was back in the tavern.

"Are you alright Elizabeth?" Greta asked. "I think you were having a bad dream."

The sun was streaming through the window making Elizabeth squint as she woke. She had fallen asleep where she sat, at the end of the bed covered by nothing but the cool afternoon air. She shivered and Greta pulled her into a cuddle.

Elizabeth allowed herself to be warmed and comforted by this kindly lady. It was a welcome relief after the abrupt loss of her mother. She watched as Greta rubbed her cold limbs like her mother used to when she was a child. She longed to be back home. Back with her mother and father. Back to a place that made sense to her, a place that was familiar and welcoming not frightening and cruel. She was about to lose herself in this daydream of home when suddenly she noticed Greta's injuries.

"Oh my goodness!" She said, pulling out of the embrace and looking up at Greta's face for the first time "you look terrible, are you OK?"

"Better now thank you. Shiona helped mend a couple of broken fingers."

Elizabeth suddenly remembered walking away from the witches when they were trying to heal Yorik and Greta and a deep feeling of shame washed over her.

"Do not worry about these flesh wounds, Elizabeth" Greta said reassuringly, "I have seen much worse."

Elizabeth could not help but admire Greta. She had been through unimaginable horrors but was still one of the kindest women Elizabeth had ever met and her resilience put Elizabeth's fragile ego to shame. "I'm sorry I didn't ...."

"There is nothing for you to be sorry for Elizabeth," Greta interrupted. "You, like all the other girls, will do the best you can. That is the most important thing."

"Well maybe I can do something about that cut on your arm," Elizabeth said and placed her hands over the wound. As with all her spells, she cleared her mind and set her intention. This spell, however, was different. Elizabeth was desperate for this one to work. She needed Greta to know that despite appearances she was just as capable as those who had come before her.

After a moment, Elizabeth took her hands away and the wound had disappeared.

"Good as new!" Greta said holding up her arm and admiring Elizabeth's handiwork. Smiling at Elizabeth she gazed intently into her eyes. "I do not know about you Elizabeth. You seem different from the other girls."

Elizabeth could feel her pale complexion colouring, she looked away embarrassed.

"Anyway," Greta said, "will you apply some of your gifts downstairs and help me fix my home?"

"Of course," Elizabeth said hurriedly remembering the devastation caused by Darius's children. No matter how she felt about Shiona the least she could do for Yorik and Greta was help them tidy their home because, for some unknown reason, Elizabeth felt responsible for the chaos.

Greta gave her a reassuring tap on the arm and stood up. Elizabeth was about to follow when something flashed in her peripheral vision. She scanned the room and saw a deep green glow coming from the dressing table. She went over to find the source of the light. She reached the table and scrabbled through her belongings. She saw that the glow was coming from underneath one of her gloves. She moved the glove and the glowing stopped, but the light source was clear. Elizabeth picked it up and held it in her hand.

"Are you coming dear," Greta said calling from the doorway.

"I'm coming," Elizabeth said following Greta and she put her father's talisman around her neck.

***

The five friends set about clearing the bar as best they could. Mostly they undertook the task in the spirit of great camaraderie, encouraging each other and slapping each other on the back as they tidied. The atmosphere between Shiona and Elizabeth, however, was decidedly cool. At times Shiona would attempt to engage Elizabeth in conversation, or comment on how well she was doing but Elizabeth would turn her back or simply walk away. She did not even care if she was being rude. As far as Elizabeth was concerned the cold shoulder treatment was exactly what Shiona deserved.

The clean-up operation was a hefty job, even though the witches used the odd spell the real skill required was physical exertion. Every now and then a villager would come and join in with the clearing, but as the day wore on the bar of the tavern still looked like a bomb site. By the end of the afternoon Yorik disappeared into the kitchen behind the bar. When he reappeared he brought a pot of piping hot tea, with warmed sweet pastries to keep the workers going.

"Come," he said, "let us eat before we drop."

Elizabeth managed to find one table that had not been smashed into pieces and turned it upright. The others found stools and chairs that were mostly intact and Yorik carefully arranged himself on top of a pile of rubble.

They ate in silence. Relishing the food provided by Yorik. Elizabeth tucked into a warm, plaited pastry that oozed sticky sweetness. The delicacy was like nectar to her starved tummy. When they were finished Greta poured them all a strong, sweet cup of tea and they began to talk.

The conversation was a blur to Elizabeth. Nobody said anything of any consequence, just niceties and small talk. Every now and then Elizabeth would smile as someone looked across at her for a reaction but all she could hear were Shiona's derisive words ringing in her ears *you're useless without us.* Anytime the conversation turned to Shiona and politeness dictated she should look in her direction, Elizabeth could not help but scowl at the witch.

Useless. Useless.

Daphne noticed Elizabeth's anger. "What's the matter with you Betty?"

But Elizabeth just shook her head and looked down at the tea cup she was stirring viciously.

"You're going to take the pattern right off that cup if you're not careful," Shiona smiled attempting to break the ice but Elizabeth only glared at her.

"Anyway," Shiona said, "what are we going to do about this?" And she produced the invitation that Wilhelm had thrown at her.

"We have to go," Daphne said.

"You cannot go," Greta said. "They will tear you apart."

"What does it say exactly," Yorik said looking at the envelope in Shiona's hand.

Shiona opened it and read aloud. "It says, 'this is an invitation for the *unbeatable witches* to join Lord Darius and his family at a Masquerade Ball to be held at Diederich castle'." She scoffed as she looked at the invitation, "There's a post script, 'a last chance to see our world before we step into yours'."

"You know it is a trap," Yorik said, "you have never been invited there before. Why now? Why this year? I'll tell you why. Because they have the stranger up there and he has done something terrible to the children, turned them into animals. They are planning something Shiona."

"I know," Shiona said simply.

"How do you know it was the stranger that turned Gretchen and her friends into animals?" Elizabeth asked.

"We do not know for sure, but it is all too much of a coincidence." Yorik replied.

"Are *all* the missing teenagers like Gretchen now?" asked Elizabeth.

"I do not know child," Greta replied, "we have only seen one or two, stealing food and bounding away from the village. We were horrified at first but then we tried to catch them, to get them back, to bring them home."

"*Did* you ever catch one Greta?" Daphne asked.

"Yes," Greta paused, "Gretchen. Even though she is like an animal there is something in her that is drawn to the village."

"But she escaped," Yorik continued, "and we did not have the heart to hunt down another. It was so desperately upsetting holding one of our children captive, and to see what they have become. We had no stomach for it after that. We just waited and hoped that when the three sisters appeared they would finally be able to defeat Darius once and for all."

"Sisters," Elizabeth scoffed looking daggers at Shiona, "we're hardly that."

"Not you child," Gretchen laughed, "but these two are."

Greta gestured towards Daphne and Shiona. Elizabeth turned slowly towards them. "Something else you didn't bother to tell me........." Elizabeth said in an audible whisper.

".........It didn't crop up, Betty...."

".........There wasn't the time......."

They spoke hurriedly both at once.

"Oh ya, ya," Greta continued, oblivious of the discomfort she had caused. "There is another sister as well. A lovely lady she was but she had a family she did not want to leave. What was her name?"

Elizabeth's heart sank and suddenly she realised why she was there and who these women were to her mother. "Gladys?" Elizabeth asked through gritted teeth.

"Of course," Greta said, "Gladys."

Elizabeth was just about to open her mouth to speak, to rant and rave, when her mouth involuntarily pursed into a gruesome pout. She stared at Daphne and Shiona in disbelief. Daphne was holding her wand and pointing it at Elizabeth's face. Yorik and Greta could see something was not right with the trio, but before they could ask any questions Shiona and Daphne grabbed Elizabeth, dragged her out of the chair and started manhandling towards the door that led upstairs.

"Let's not do this here," Shiona said, throwing a false smile at Yorik and Greta.

Landlord and Landlady just looked on in confusion as they watched the great bulk of Daphne practically lift Elizabeth off her feet and carry her away.

The sisters quickly ushered Elizabeth into Daphne's room and closed the door firmly behind them. When they were sure they were alone Daphne lifted her gagging spell and the two witches turned warily to their young niece.

"I don't even bloody well know what to say anymore!" Elizabeth said and started to pace the room, "Firstly, I find out my Mum is a witch, then I find out all about this crazy-arsed Branko business and now, just when I've got my head around all this nonsense, I find out that I'm related to the Jolly Lean Giant and Bitchy the Kid! AND if I hadn't been brought up to respect my elders – fists would be flying!

"Is there even any point asking why you didn't bother telling me?"

155

She continued, "Why you have never bothered visiting me or my sister? Or even send a bloody Christmas card once a sodding year!"

"Now calm down Betty...."

"And why the bloody hell didn't Mum tell me about you two? Is she ashamed of you? God knows you're not the easiest people to get along with but we all know you can't choose your bloody FAMILY!"

"Is everything OK?" Greta called from behind the door.

"Yes it's all bloody marvellous thank you Greta," Elizabeth continued to rant, "I've just found out....."

But Daphne quickly cast the gagging spell once again and Elizabeth was left mute. Daphne nodded to Shiona to see what Greta wanted. Shiona left the room quickly, careful to shut the door behind her.

Elizabeth could hear a muffled conversation. Greta seemed concerned but Shiona's tone was reassuring. Elizabeth noticed that Daphne was also distracted by the mumbling on the other side of the door and took the opportunity to grab Daphne's wand breaking the spell.

Daphne grabbed at the wand but it was too late, Elizabeth scuttled across to the other side of the room. Daphne mimed to Elizabeth to come back. Elizabeth shook her head violently and pointed towards the door. But Daphne was too quick for Elizabeth, she jumped over the bed and blocked her way. Elizabeth scooted back towards the window, again Daphne heaved her bulk across the room and barred Elizabeth's alternative exit. The two were engaged in a silent game of cat and mouse when Shiona came back in.

Daphne sighed, and Elizabeth could see she was relieved that the game was over. Then suddenly her face dropped again.

"Oh no," Daphne said.

Elizabeth followed the direction of her gaze and saw that Shiona was holding some kind of material.

"What's that?" Elizabeth asked.

"Dresses," Shiona said simply.

"Oh no, no way Shiona," Daphne said backing away from her sister. "You are not putting me in a dress."

"Well you can't go to a ball in your trousers Daphne," Shiona replied.

"Hee, hee!" Elizabeth giggled, "I cannot wait to see you frock up Daphne. I bet you'll look great!"

"I don't know what you're laughing about," Shiona said, "this one's yours." And she threw Elizabeth an armful of grey material.

"Oh you've got to be kidding," Elizabeth said pulling at the bundle of rags, "this thing is hideous!"

"Just put them on."

"But Shiona......" Daphne argued.

"Both of you."

"I'm not......." Elizabeth started.

"NOW!"

Elizabeth and Daphne scowled at one another. Suddenly their argument was over and they turned their anger on Shiona.

"I don't care," Shiona said flatly not at all fazed by their fury. "Don't forget you two, this is *all about the show*." And with that she smiled sweetly, took out her wand and pointed it at Daphne and Elizabeth. "Now get changed!"

Chapter Nineteen

They dressed in silence and readied themselves for the ball. There was a palpable tension in the air. Elizabeth glared viciously at the sisters who were engaged in a battle of dirty looks of their own. Daphne was angry with Shiona, Shiona was angry with Elizabeth and Elizabeth was absolutely livid with them both.

"I can't believe you're making me wear this Shiona," Daphne sulked.

"Oh stop whining! Until we know what we're up against we have to play Darius at his own game."

"I'm just wondering whose *game* this actually is," Elizabeth sneered, "it seems all we've done so far is follow Shiona's rules."

"Come on Betty, that's not fair."

"Isn't it *Aunty* Daphne? Because I don't really see what difference it would make if we turned up at this party in our birthday suits."

"It's about the show, Betty. You know that."

"Oh yes, it's all about the show. As long as it's *Shiona's* show."

"What does that mean?" Shiona said bristling.

"Well as long as we do what we're told like good little witches, isn't that right *Aunty* Shiona."

"Betty, you don't know what you're......"

"Let me ask you this then *Aunty* Daphne...."

"Stop calling us 'Aunty' like that!" Shiona cried.

Elizabeth ignored her and resumed her taunts, "*AUNTY* Daphne have you ever offered any tactics, ever ventured any opinions about how *you* could help?"

"It hasn't been necessary....." Daphne fumbled, "there was never a need......Shiona has always...,"

"A-HA!" Elizabeth cried, "She's never let you have a mind of your own has she? She's always forcing *her* way on you isn't she?"

"Stop it Betty!"

"It's always got to be *Aunty* Shiona's way otherwise....."

"That's enough!" Shiona said.

"Or what Shiona," Elizabeth said calmly, "what are you going to do?"

Elizabeth was pleased to see Shiona's cool façade slip. She took great satisfaction knowing Shiona could feel pain just like anyone else.

"Are you going to throw me to the ground like you did poor old Gretchen...."

"She would have killed you if I hadn't........"

"Or cast a sphere of agony around me?"

"Elizabeth they were......"

"Or are you just going to insult me again. Tell me over and over how utterly useless I am," Elizabeth's show of strength faded as she started to cry, "make me doubt myself and be of absolutely no use to either of you because I don't know what you expect of me!"

Suddenly Elizabeth felt the weight of the situation fall heavily on her shoulders and sobbing she fell to her knees in a puddle of grey taffeta.

"Is there something you want to share with the group, Betty," Daphne said and sat awkwardly next to her, her own muddy grey dress straining at the seams.

"Ask her." Elizabeth said through her tears and pointed at Shiona.

"Would *you* like to tell me what's going on *Aunty* Shiona?"

"It's nothing......I just," Shiona started. "She's just overreacting."

"Overreacting," Elizabeth said and got to her feet. "Time and time again you have made me feel totally inadequate. You laugh at me, you mock me, you're openly critical of me to in front of my own Mother, and then when I'm finally trying my hardest, trying to help in any way I can, you tell me I'm nothing! You tell me that I'm utterly useless to you. That I will never be able to help you so there's no point trying!"

"You didn't actually say that did you Shiona?" Daphne said staring at her sister.

"She did! She was horrible to me." Elizabeth answered for her. "And I was the one who stood up to those... those... monsters! While the rest of you were lying unconscious on the floor!"

"Shiona, why did you.......?"

Shiona lowered her head. "She wanted to split up the group. She wanted to try to take on Victor – on her own. Away from the tavern. Without us." She said added quietly.

"Oh," Daphne said flatly.

"So," Elizabeth said. "So what? I could have done it! I could have tried. I was only trying to even out the playing field."

"Oh Betty, Betty, Betty," Daphne said as she got up and sat heavily on the bed. "So what exactly did Shiona say to you?"

"I've just been telling you!"

"No Betty, you've just given me your interpretation. Probably with a bit of VAT."

"What?"

"*Value Added Trauma.* What were her actual words?"

"I don't know," Elizabeth said sulkily.

Shiona remained quiet while the other two talked and Elizabeth saw that far from her usual air of superiority she looked exhausted, beaten.

"Was it something along the lines of you needing *us*, and your powers being useless without *us*?" Daphne asked.

"Something like that."

Shiona wandered across to the window and gazed out at the early evening. Elizabeth could not be absolutely sure but she thought she saw a sparkle of water glistening on Shiona's cheek, the setting sun revealing a tear.

"There were so many things your mother and father didn't want you to know," Shiona began. "They didn't want you to know that Gladys was a witch, and when you did find out, they didn't want you to know that we were your aunties. They thought if Darius knew you were Gladys's daughter he might try to get you out of the way, to hurt you somehow. And the one thing they made us promise not to tell you was this," she looked directly at Elizabeth and the sorrow in her eyes was unmistakable, "they didn't want you to know that you are *powerless* Elizabeth."

"That's so unfair, you've always been....."

"She's right Betty."

For a moment Elizabeth just stared at the pair in stunned silence.

"I'm sorry," Shiona said choking, "you're not a witch."

"What?....What are you talking about Shiona?"

"The only powers that you have are the ones you get from us," Shiona said. "If you left us, ran out to the forest with Victor, like you suggested, you would be helpless."

"That's rubbish!" Elizabeth said. "What about everything I did at home, the healing, the flying, freezing the lake?"

"We were *always* there with you Elizabeth, every time. At least one of us was by your side each time you performed a successful spell. Even when you thought you were alone in that alleyway back in London, we were the ones feeding the power to you."

"I don't believe it!"

"It's true Betty," Daphne said gravely.

"How is it possible? How is that even possible?"

"Think of us as gravity Betty. It is a very important force that keeps us all rooted to the planet. But within this force human beings can do extraordinary things. They can walk, dance, glide and even defy it, but they are still governed by it. What you have achieved is amazing Betty. Your spells are fantastic and it's like watching poetry in motion seeing you on the broom. But the best ballet dancer in the world would be nothing without gravity pulling her down to the sprung dance floor. She would just float away, into the air, along with all the others who went before her – nothing without gravity."

"But my mother's a witch. What I can do is because of *her*, it's in my genes. I've inherited these skills from Mum!" Elizabeth could feel the warmth of the green talisman around her neck and snatched it off angrily.

"It doesn't always work like that Elizabeth," Shiona said, "you could have a parent who's a doctor but that doesn't necessarily make you genetically predisposed to heal the sick! You may have an interest, but you still have to learn. Still have to study for years."

"Well what have I been doing then? All the time I spent with you before we came here. Those months when I was doing nothing but casting spells, and flying and nearly freezing to death in that loch. Wasn't I learning then?"

"Yes, of course you were, and you were learning very well Elizabeth. But you were only learning to cast spells with borrowed magic. Every single time you did anything extraordinary one of us was there sending you a bolt of power, to see what you did with it. After a while we didn't have to consciously *send* you anything, you instinctively found our

161

energy source whenever you cast a spell. You really were quite brilliant Elizabeth."

"Then how do you know I *can't* do this on my own? If I'm that *brilliant* why didn't you just let me try? I am Gladys's daughter after all, your niece, maybe there's something inside me that even you don't know about."

"There's not, I'm sorry." Shiona said simply.

"How can you know that? You didn't even let me try!"

"I did."

"That's not strictly true Shiona," Daphne said, "we never actually tested her."

"No *you* didn't Daphne," Shiona replied, "but I did."

Shiona sighed heavily and pulled out a chair from underneath Daphne's dressing table. She sat and rubbed her face.

"What are you talking about Shiona?" Elizabeth said.

"Your mother panicked the moment you moved to London. She was fine when Jessica left, because she had Peter and she knew Jessica was following the right path. When you left, you were swimming upstream Elizabeth, making life unbearable for yourself, but Gladys knew you had to get it out of your system. She came to see me and asked for my advice."

"You didn't tell me this Shiona," Daphne looked astonished at the admission.

"Gladys didn't want me to, she couldn't bear the thought that she was going behind Elizabeth's back. Or Albert's for that matter."

"What advice could *you* give my Mum," Elizabeth snarled. "She's the kindest most loving woman I know and you're a complete bitch!"

"Now Betty, there's no need........"

"No!" Elizabeth said shutting Daphne up, "I want to know. How could *you* possibly give her any advice on parenting?"

"Alright Elizabeth," Shiona said, "I know what you're trying to say. 'How could Shiona the old crone possibly have any maternal instincts,' well maybe I haven't. But I love my sister to pieces and believe it or not, I'm actually quite fond of you too!"

"Pah!" Elizabeth exclaimed derisively.

"What I'm curious about though Shiona," Daphne said, "is *how* did you test Betty's powers?"

"When Gladys came to visit we decided to give Elizabeth time to settle into her London life," Shiona explained. "I told Gladys she could be wrong about Elizabeth, that she might surprise her and make a good life for herself in London."

"Gee, thanks," Elizabeth said coldly.

"But you were so miserable Elizabeth, so self-destructive, and Gladys insisted I help. She thought, that maybe you should be the next young witch to come with us to Branko. She thought that you, more so than Jessica, might suit the lifestyle. She wanted something more for you, anything, rather than watch you destroy your spirit."

"So I just get killed in Branko? She thought *that* would be better for me!" Elizabeth asked sarcastically.

"It wasn't like that. The Branko visits have never been like this before. We had no idea things were going to change so radically."

"Can we just stick to one thing at a time Shiona," Daphne interrupted, "Betty's tests?"

"There were just a few things," Shiona continued, "dotted through your life, to see if you had the instinct to cure, or set things straight."

"Like what?" Elizabeth asked.

"Like your boss's plants, always at the brink of death, no matter how much the poor bugger tended them."

"I remember that," Elizabeth said, suddenly alert, "I remember feeling sorry for the plants, wishing I could help them."

"You see, if you were a witch instinctively you *would* have helped them. You couldn't have stopped yourself. You would have reached out and nourished the dying creature."

"I wanted to, I really wanted to."

"There were other things too," Shiona carried on, "harder tests. Noticing the lives of others around you and caring enough to help. Not from a displaced sense of martyrdom but from the true spirit of love. The friend you lived with who had the psycho girlfriend, the lady at work that you once called 'friend' but lost patience with because she 'insulted your intelligence', even Jessica ..."

"How could I have helped Jessie? She was a complete bitch!"

"Like me," Shiona said simply, "everyone's a 'bitch' if they don't live up to your high moralistic standards. You didn't think about anyone but yourself."

163

Elizabeth tried to formulate a counter-argument, tried to find a way to prove her point, to defend herself. To tell the witch that she wasn't like that. But it was no use. Deep down Elizabeth knew that Shiona was right.

"Ahhh. You're not the only one Betty," Daphne said clapping her on the shoulder adding her own philosophical note. "It's just a symptom of 21st Century living I'm afraid. All out for ourselves, bugger the rest of you. But there are still a lot of people out there who care more for the happiness of others than their own individual needs. And that's not a completely selfless ideology. Consider Shiona and I coming to Branko every year to make sure Darius is unable to break the shield and wreak havoc on our world. It's not because we're selfless angels......."

"Far from it," Elizabeth said under her breath.

"It's because if he gets to our world and the people in it, then he gets to us too. We like the way we live and we don't want some evil overlord messing with our existence, do we now Betty?"

"So I'm powerless because I'm selfish, is that what you're telling me?"

"It's a little more complicated than that, but that's basically it Betty. It's about instincts. If your instincts are 'all for me and me for myself' then you're probably not a witch."

"So you two were *born* with healing instincts were you? Caring more about the greater good as babies, than where your next feed was coming from?"

"Of course not," Shiona said, "but we learned everything from a young age. Before we were even old enough to think about our powers being *super*-natural. It was drummed into us like potty training. Something we had to do, no questions, it was part of our lives. But when your Mum met Albert she wanted to be free of it and wanted you and Jessie to find your own paths."

"What about the other witches, the ones that came with you before. Were they all selfless givers who cared more about the universe than they did themselves?"

Daphne and Shiona looked awkwardly at one another.

"In for a penny in for a pound eh Shiona?" Daphne said, looking resigned. "Might as well tell her the whole thing."

"The last time your mother came with us, she faced Darius on her own." Shiona explained, "not for long, but for long enough to scare her. She told us afterwards that she could feel him searching into her very soul for a weakness. Before she could stop herself the image of you and Jessica popped into her head. She was petrified that he might use that against her, she begged us to find a way for her not to go again.

"We knew it wouldn't be easy. Like we've told you before, we come as a trio: mind, body and spirit, incomplete unless we're all together in perfect functioning order. But the power of three isn't just about being a whole unit, it's also about having eyes in the back of your head. When two of you are at the front, it means someone's always covering your back. It's about magical content – yes, but it's also about numbers.

"Luckily enough Daphne had been working on a projection concept. Out of sheer laziness I hastened to add," she said shooting Daphne a look.

"I managed to get the cat to fly to the front door and answer it for me, Betty!"

"Anyway," Shiona continued, "that's where it started. Then it evolved to offering our powers to people, as long as they were willing. Not telling the girls they were powerless was for their own benefit. We couldn't risk Darius looking deep into their souls like he did with your mother, and finding out they were mere mortals."

Elizabeth hung her head and sat heavily on the bed. "How could you do this to me," her voice was barely a whisper, "after everything you've put me through? Why didn't you just tell me?"

"We couldn't risk anyone finding out, even Greta and Yorik." Shiona said. "If Darius or his family were ever to find out that the third witch has no powers, that would be it for us, for the people of Branko and ultimately that could be it for the rest of the world."

After a moment Elizabeth got up slowly and walked away from the sisters, out of the door and onto the landing, silently seething all the way.

"What are you going to do now Elizabeth?" Shiona asked following her.

Elizabeth said nothing. She walked into her own room and slammed the door behind her. She leant against it breathing heavily, her head a thunderstorm of anger and confusion. She still held Albert's talisman in her hand. She threw it to the floor. She stared around the little room, she had cast spells in here, she healed the tree that Victor had damaged and cured Greta's wound. But it was not her. None of it was her. She was stealing power from the other witches. That's all she was – a parasite.

She reached a decision and crossed to her wardrobe flinging open the doors. She found her little backpack and started to grab her belongings. She packed quickly. It did not take long because very little in the room actually belonged to her. A few pieces of clothing, a toothbrush, toothpaste and Sonny, stuffed at the bottom of the wardrobe. He looked a little like Elizabeth felt, a useless twig that could be great but was nothing without the power of the witches.

She bent down to pick Sonny up and caught sight of herself in the wardrobe mirror and the reflection only fuelled her fury. She was dressed in the grey taffeta gown Shiona had flung at her. She looked like a Victorian school mistress as the dressed skimmed the floor covering her ankles, threatening to trip her every time she took a step and the buttoned up collar almost choked her. Her hair was scraped up into a bun but some strands were escaping from the tight coil and whispered around her cheeks, tickling her nose.

Elizabeth was about to hurl Sonny at the stranger in the mirror when Shiona stormed into the room and slammed the door shut behind her.

"I knew you would do this, I knew it! Run away as usual Elizabeth, go and hide your head in the sand and pretend none of this is happening, pretend people don't need you.

"I told your Mother that you should know; that we should trust you to do the right thing; that you would come with us even if you felt powerless. But Gladys was worried about you. Thought your fear would show through. She was afraid that Darius would get to you. But I told her, I said 'we've drummed it into her, it's all about the show, she'll understand' I said." Shiona flopped down onto Elizabeth's bed. "But maybe your mother was right to doubt you. Maybe your mother knew you'd act like a scared little girl. Maybe I was wrong to give you the benefit of the doubt."

"I know what you're trying to do Shiona but it won't work. If I've got nothing to offer you, then you won't miss me when I've gone will you," she said and carried on packing.

"So you're *not* special Elizabeth. You haven't got any powers, you're

166

just the same as anyone else. Is that such a bad thing? You're no more special than anyone else, but then again you're no *less* special either." Shiona held onto Elizabeth's hand stopping her packing, "But you *are* important Elizabeth, whether you like it or not. You're important to your Mum and Dad, they adore you. You're important to Daphne, she thinks you're hilarious, since you came to Scotland she's been acting like a giddy schoolgirl. And, I know you won't believe this, but you're important to me. You keep me on my toes Elizabeth, put a fire back in my belly. And I can tell you something – I've never been so frightened to reach the border of Branko. Not because I thought you were less capable than the other girls, but because I knew I felt differently about you. I love you, you silly sod. You're my niece. I've always loved you!

Life isn't easy, Elizabeth, no-one ever told you it was. Sometimes we feel as though we fit, as though we're *meant* to be somewhere, or *meant* to do something and along comes yet another disappointment. That doesn't mean our life has gone to pot, that we've taken a wrong turn somewhere and we're lost again. The measure of who we are as a person is not taken by what challenges we face, but *how* we face them."

Releasing Elizabeth's hand Shiona rose from the bed and walked towards the door.

"You could choose to be cold, like me," she said as she made to leave the room, "you could joke about everything, like Daphne, you could be graceful, like your mother. *Or* you could choose to act like a child. And I'm afraid, Elizabeth, you will always choose to be that child until you grow up."

She closed the door softly behind her leaving Elizabeth alone.

Shiona's words stung Elizabeth deeply. But the truth of them was undeniable. Shiona was right and Elizabeth knew it.

She took a deep breath and walked over to the window. The sun had almost set and gave the land of Branko a faint golden hue. Elizabeth expected Branko to be a land of possibilities. Somewhere she could finally shine and be the person she was meant to be. But she did not know who that was anymore. A few hours ago it was all very clear. She was a witch. One of many to make sure that Darius and his family would never cross the threshold into her world. And now, she felt just as useless as when this whole thing started. Once again, she was a nobody.

She caught a glimpse of her reflection in the mirror, done up like 'a dog's dinner', as her mother would say. Well if she was going to be part of the act then she was going to do it her own way.

"And this," she said grabbing at the grey dress, "is not my way!"

Chapter Twenty

Inside her room Elizabeth could hear the sisters in the corridor debating what to do. Daphne was all for trying to talk some sense into Elizabeth. Shiona clearly felt differently. Finally, Shiona said, "Just leave her," and Elizabeth heard the witches walk down the narrow staircase to the tavern.

Elizabeth opened her bedroom door and could just about make out a heated conversation between the witches and Yorik. He mentioned Elizabeth's name a couple of times, clearly nervous that they were leaving without her. The witches were trying their best to allay any fears. Elizabeth heard the unmistakeable sound of Daphne laughing. *Another inappropriate joke* Elizabeth thought. She heard a door slam and suddenly there was silence.

Elizabeth closed the door, looked out of her bedroom window and watched as the witches mounted their broomsticks and rose into the air. With their gowns flowing behind them in the moonlit night the sisters looked magnificent. As they flew towards the castle they looked every inch the confident defenders of Branko. Their argument with Elizabeth and their depletion in numbers was forgotten, for now. *It has to be*, Elizabeth thought, *they can't show any signs fear*. Darius would only use it against them.

"Don't go too far," Elizabeth whispered to the departing witches. She took one final look at herself in the mirror.

"Better," she said and grabbed Sonny.

Hoping she was still close enough to the witches to use their magic, she performed her growing spell on Sonny. He sprang to life in the middle of the small bedroom and Elizabeth jumped through the

169

open window. She fell. As she descended she forced Sonny's bristles beneath her feet and held firmly onto the neck. She felt the broomstick sweep the ground moments before she soared skyward. That was one of her favourite manoeuvres and she practiced it daily back at the old abandoned hanger much to the horror of her mother.

Elizabeth hovered as far behind the witches as she dared. She had made up her mind to stay in Branko, to see this ridiculous charade through to the bitter end, but she was not ready to talk about it. She was still sulking and she wanted to put off the moment of supercilious smugness from Daphne and Shiona for as long as she could.

Elizabeth looped and curled through the air on Sonny, keeping a safe distance from the sisters. The sensation of flying was always exhilarating. Learning that she was powerless without the witches was a devastating blow at first but now she felt free. There was nothing she could do to help unless the sisters were present, and they were infinitely more powerful than Elizabeth anyway. The feeling of uselessness was surprisingly liberating. All she had to do was sit back and enjoy the ride and she was doing exactly that, turning somersaults in the sky, enjoying the freedom of flight.

The witches were at the castle by the time Elizabeth started her descent. She watched them climb the stairs, broomsticks in hand, pointy hats perched on top of their heads, an air of resigned foreboding about them. They were ready to fight. Elizabeth landed at the bottom of the steps, shrunk Sonny back to size and tucked him into her dress. The sisters disappeared through the huge doors of the castle as Elizabeth sprinted up the stairs two at a time.

She could hear the faint murmur of music coming from the castle as she ran. The party was in full swing. Whatever Darius was planning, this *party* was clearly for the benefit of the witches. Nothing was going to plan for the sisters this time and they were worried. After all his years of impotence Darius was finding a way to control the villagers and Elizabeth found that terrifying. But like Alice following the white rabbit Elizabeth was curious. She had to know what he was up to and instinctively she knew that tonight was the night she would get some answers.

She reached the top of the stairs breathing heavily. She looked up at the formidable sight of Castle Diederich. It towered high above her, rising high into the night sky. With the pale moonlight behind it and the faint light of billions of stars the castle looked as though it could go on forever. As Elizabeth gazed at the sight it soon became clear that the castle was not quite the magnificent stately manor she had expected. The walls were crumbling, the doors were cracking and in some places the building was in ruins. In stark contrast to the immaculately kept village, very little of the castle was actually habitable. Elizabeth imagined that Darius had allowed his children to practice their powers there, doing to the castle what they gleefully did to Yorik's pub.

Trying hard not to think of the devastation these creatures were capable of Elizabeth opened the huge wooden doors of the castle and peeked inside. Shiona and Daphne were there, standing in place behind a curtain, clearly waiting to be given instructions by one of Darius's lackeys. Elizabeth was horrified to see that this lackey was Victor. He looked just as Elizabeth remembered him, tall and awkward. He was desperately trying to summon up courage to talk to the witches.

"And Elizabeth?" He asked quietly.

There was no immediate response from the sisters but after a pause, and in perfect unison, they both slowly turned their heads to look at him. There was something unearthly and sinister in that action. Not a direct threat but the robot like uniformity was terrifying. The effect on Victor was immediate, he backed away quickly and started to open the curtains for the witches to make their grand entrance.

"WAIT!" Elizabeth shouted from behind them, and she was pleased to see that she surprised them all.

Shiona and Daphne regained their poise quickly but Victor remained flustered. The witches turned their attention away from Elizabeth and back to the murky red curtains waiting to be announced to Darius. Elizabeth took up her place next to Shiona and felt a surge of energy as she stood next to the witch.

"Uh...Hello Elizabeth," Victor ventured.

"Not now Victor," Elizabeth said.

"I just wanted to apologise....."

"Not NOW Victor," Elizabeth reiterated and shot him an irate look.

"When then?" Victor persisted, "you know that was not me back at the tavern."

Elizabeth was about to answer when Shiona pushed her to one side and stepped towards Victor fixing him with her hard stare. Shiona was more than a foot shorter than Victor, and the sight of the older lady glaring at the gauche schoolboy might have been amusing in another situation but Shiona's calm ferocity was far from funny.

"Do not think for a minute that you and Elizabeth will be friends," she said slowly, enunciating every word. "I suggest you leave her alone unless you want to take another trip in that agonising sphere."

"She'll do it too, Viccy," Daphne interjected, "and I won't stop her. Neither of us are particularly pleased with what you did to our friend's pub."

Victor withered under the glare of the older witches, and Elizabeth could tell he was looking to her for some kind of support. Support she would not give. Shiona was right, he was the enemy and she did not want to give Daphne and Shiona anymore reason to doubt her. Victor gave up his attempts at reconciliation and pulled violently on the rope next to him. The curtains opened.

The witches stood in a row at the top of the stairs that led into a massive room which, Elizabeth guessed, must have been the banqueting hall. The false opulence was apparent here too. The floor that had once clearly been made of the highest quality polished wood was now faded and chipped; the curtains hanging on the windows were thread bear and colourless and the late autumn wind whipped through the broken glass of the windows. From the top of the stairs Elizabeth noticed that below were dozens of people, all masked, dancing to barely audible music coming from an ancient, tuneless harpsichord.

"THE WITCHES," Victor called from behind them.

The music stopped abruptly and so did the revellers, they all turned to stare at the three women. Elizabeth was careful not to show any signs of fear at the unnerving sight. Couples and groups of revellers stopped to glare at them through their facial adornments. Their real eyes were imperceptible through their animal masks. It was like watching rabid creatures waiting to pounce on their prey and after her encounter with Gretchen Elizabeth knew that, in some way, they were.

"Come, come, do not be shy." The voice came from the bottom of the huge staircase. It was Lord Darius.

"Who are all these people," Daphne whispered as she watched the scene in horror.

"The missing villagers," Shiona hissed as they walked slowly down the steps.

"I was only expecting to see Darius and his family," said Daphne.

"I *knew* he was planning something," said Shiona.

"I didn't have a clue," Elizabeth said, her lack of experience showing.

"Betty!" Daphne said taking her first proper look at Elizabeth. "What have you come as?"

The last time either of the witches had seen Elizabeth she was wearing the buttoned up, grey, old, miserable dress that made her look like a repressed governess. Since then, the matronly frock had undergone a drastic transformation.

Underneath all the grey material Elizabeth noticed that the dress had an amazingly vibrant harlot red underskirt. Elizabeth ripped the front of the dress and pinned the edges back to the waist exposing the sumptuous colour and her shapely legs underneath. She wore her own pair of thick black tights with a pair of black lace up boots she found in the supplies left by Greta. She had unbuttoned the high necked collar as far as it would go and folded it down to expose a little bit of her shoulders, some of her cleavage and more of the exquisite red lining.

"Do you like it?" Elizabeth smirked and Daphne nodded her approval.

Shiona just tutted and rolled her eyes, "Get it together you two - it's *show time*."

"I think she's actually enjoying this," Elizabeth said quietly to Daphne.

"I think you might be right Betty," Daphne whispered, "mind you, you look like you're having a bit of fun there yourself."

"Do you know what Daphne, I am. I had two options, slither away and hope to God I could get through that shield, or brazen it out," she grasped the vibrant red collar of the dress, "and I went with the brazen option as you can see."

"Good for you Betty," Daphne said and patted her firmly on the shoulder.

They reached the bottom of the stairs and they were greeted by Lord Darius who waved at the musician. Once again the indistinct music started up and the crowd resumed lurching around the dance floor.

Darius greeted Shiona and Daphne like long lost friends.

"I am so sorry for my dreadful manners the other night," he said showering them with air kisses, "I do not know what I was thinking. And my children! Well I can only say that I am devastated by their behaviour! I told them merely to deliver the invitation to you. But *kids will be kids* as I believe you say in your world."

"So you didn't give Wilhelm *a message* for me then?" Shiona asked seeing through his thin veneer of respectability.

"Of course not," Darius lied unconvincingly and he led Shiona and Daphne to the corner of the room where his wife was waiting for them with her customary air of self-importance. Elizabeth was hot on the heels of her companions when suddenly she was grabbed around the waist and swept onto the dance floor.

It was Wilhelm. And he had clearly noticed Elizabeth's change of appearance. "Well, well, little witch," he said drawing her into his arms, "you look a little different from the last time we met."

"Probably because I'm not picking myself up from under a pile of rubble," she said trying to resist his grasp.

"I have to do as I am told, Elizabeth," Wilhelm said, his mood suddenly serious. "I'm sure you understand this. Darius is head of my family as Shiona is the head of yours. Are there not things she does that you find distasteful?"

Elizabeth remembered the image of Darius's children writhing in agony in Shiona's sphere and was unable to look Wilhelm in the eye.

"Maybe she does," Elizabeth replied, "but you appear to enjoy your *distasteful* tasks much more than she does. Now let me go!" Elizabeth fought against him, but she was no match for his strength.

"Just one dance, Elizabeth," he whispered in her ear, "then you can go back to your people."

Elizabeth looked across the dance floor towards Daphne and Shiona. Daphne was engaged in a forced polite conversation with Darius and Ingrid but Shiona was looking fixedly at Elizabeth. Comforted by the witch's attention Elizabeth allowed herself to be whisked around the dance floor.

Elizabeth stared around wildly at the other dancing couples trying to follow the simple dance steps. After a while, the dancing became easier and Elizabeth was surprised at how quickly she picked up the rather monotonous dance routine. There was no particular skill involved and

Elizabeth had an excellent partner in Wilhelm who twirled her and span her and held her close gazing into her eyes. When she met his gaze she found his attention mesmerising. She forced herself to look away. She tried hard to keep her wits about her. But there was something about the music, the movement and the closeness of the enemy that was starting to make her head spin. She told herself that she would not melt into the shimmering green of Wilhelm's intoxicating eyes. He held her clasped to his body, so close that she felt his heartbeat pounding through her chest, could feel his warm breath on her ear and was utterly unable to free herself from his strong arms.

She was careful to keep some resistance between her and Wilhelm, to maintain some tension in her body, to stop herself from being swept up in the strength and power of this extraordinary man. But something about this moment appealed to Elizabeth's inner romantic. The eternal battle between beauty and the beast, good and evil, love conquers all. Elizabeth was getting caught up in the fairy-tale.

But there was something stronger keeping her pinned to Wilhelm than childlike romance. Elizabeth spent so long using the power of the witches, and when their ancient magic was coursing through her body it was beautiful and pure. Dancing around the ancient hall with Wilhelm holding her closely she could feel another source of power flowing through her. Whatever had been passed from Father to son was now at Elizabeth's disposal and Wilhelm was happily offering it to her. Darius' power was more primitive and vital than the witches' and Elizabeth was beginning to sense an animalistic need to survive at all costs. The sensation was stifling. Her head was spinning.

"I'm a lost soul Elizabeth," Wilhelm said quietly, "we all are."

"What do you mean?" Elizabeth asked shocked by this confidence.

"We're all held captive by Lord Darius," he whispered.

"But he's your father," Elizabeth said.

"Is he?" Wilhelm said stopping abruptly. "Do you know that for sure?"

Wilhelm looked around nervously, suddenly aware they were being watched and for a moment he resembled Victor. Elizabeth was shocked by the similarity and despite herself felt sorry for him.

Wilhelm scooped Elizabeth up once again and they carried on dancing.

"If he *is* my father," he said conspiratorially, "I've no idea if I was once human and he's turned me into this creature or if I was born like this." He held Elizabeth softly by the hands and looked deeply into her eyes. "I envy you, knowing who you are and where you come from. I have no idea. And worse than that – I have no idea what he expects of me. I know that he hates my human tendencies, but it is who I am. How can I be something that I am not?"

Wilhelm looked anxiously away and Elizabeth followed his gaze. She saw Victor and Diana staring at them. Elizabeth tried to smile at Victor but there was something in his look that unsettled her. His usual friendly demeanour was gone and he stared at her with icy coolness.

"Come," Wilhelm said, "we cannot talk here."

Wilhelm led her towards the back of the great hall and Elizabeth lost sight of Victor. She looked through the crowd for him, trying to catch a glimpse of him, when finally she saw him just as Wilhelm paused at a door to light a candle. He was having a heated conversation with his sister, trying to get away, searching the room wildly.

"Come, come," Wilhelm whispered.

Suddenly all thoughts of Victor were gone as Elizabeth heard Wilhelm's hypnotic voice in her ear and felt the strength of his body next to her. They were standing at an open door. It led to an old stone staircase that spiralled upwards. Wilhelm held the candle in one hand and with the other he led Elizabeth through the doorway.

"This way," he said started climbing the stairs.

The warmth of his hand was comforting in the dark and Elizabeth started to believe that maybe she was wrong about Wilhelm.

At the top of the stairs they entered a huge room through a secret door in a wall heavy with tapestries. Elizabeth looked behind her as the door closed, stunned to see it disappear, camouflaged by the material. She felt a chill in the air and noticed a balcony to her right covered by thin curtains. They were in a huge, stately bedroom. As she scanned the dimly lit room her eyes fell on an enormous four-poster bed, antique furniture and dressings that were all gathering dust.

Suddenly she felt Wilhelm's breath on her neck sending shivers down her spine. She turned to face him and he seemed to notice her nervousness.

"There is nothing to fear," he said, and led her towards the balcony.

"I brought you here merely to talk, nothing else." He walked towards the edge of the balcony and leant against the stone balustrade. He sighed heavily and turned towards her. "I have something to tell you," his voice was soft and melancholic, "my father knows about you."

"Knows what?" Elizabeth asked.

"I am so sorry Elizabeth," he said quietly, "he knows you have no powers. That none of the young witches have ever had powers."

Elizabeth went cold. The only power the third witch ever had was Darius' ignorance. And now he knew.

"That's rubbish," Elizabeth said, desperately trying to hide her fear. "Of course we've got powers."

She slowly backed away from Wilhelm.

"You do not have to fear me," Wilhelm said, "I really want no part of this life. Victor is not the only one who has craved friendship over the years."

He sat heavily on the ancient wall of the balcony which crumbled slightly under his weight.

"Be careful," Elizabeth said and instinctively reached her hands out towards him. "That doesn't look safe."

"I sit here to show you that you have nothing to fear. I would sooner fall from this balcony than hurt you, beautiful Elizabeth."

Elizabeth's face coloured and she looked away.

"You do not think you are beautiful?" He asked jumping down from his perch. "Look – I show you."

Once again he held Elizabeth firmly around the waist. This time she did not fight. Instead she allowed him to scoop her close and lead her back into the room towards an iron mirror ornate with floral mouldings. They moved in unison, their bodies once again close. As they reached the mirror Elizabeth stopped and Wilhelm held her from behind, his arm wrapped tightly around her middle, his lips touching her ear as he spoke.

"See how beautiful you are Elizabeth."

Staring into the mirror Elizabeth could not believe her eyes. The reflection was undoubtedly her, but an Elizabeth she had only dreamt of. Gone was the home-made gown of grey and red taffeta and in its place was a floor length midnight blue dress that hugged her closely at the chest and hung from a high waistband just below her breasts. Her hair was swept away from her face and gathered up with a beaded head-band exposing a soft, sweeping, elegant neckline. Thin shoulder straps made of diamonds kept the gown in place and every ounce of skin that was exposed was even-coloured and flawless. Even the excess weight she was carrying was blissfully gone and Elizabeth was amazed to see her radiant reflection glow.

"You look like a goddess," Wilhelm whispered and Elizabeth could feel the heat of his breath on her cold ear.

Suddenly she was very aware of his closeness, of the intimacy between them. She had been awestruck by her own transformation but Wilhelm's words brought her back to reality.

"But it's not really me," she said closing her eyes, losing herself to the sensuality of the moment.

"It is you. It is who I see before me now," Wilhelm said his lips moving from her ear to her cheek, "the *you* that you could be if you were to let go of the trappings of your society"

As Wilhelm's lips found Elizabeth's cheek he kissed her softly. Unable to fight his advances a moment longer Elizabeth turned her head searching for his kiss with her mouth. As his lips brushed the corner of her mouth Elizabeth reached behind her and held his face. She knew that at any moment she would turn and allow Wilhelm to sweep her into an embrace but she had to see the stunning reflection one last time. His lips were still pressing against her skin when she opened her eyes.

Elizabeth froze. Her goddess-like reflection was still there, still perfect but as she reached up with her arm, caressing Wilhelm's face, in the mirror she was holding nothing but a monster. His face was a hideous mixture of creatures: the ears of a wolf, the snout of a bear and the cold manipulative eyes of a wildcat. Wilhelm's arm that held her tightly around the waist was elongated and hairy his nails dug into the beautiful dress. The reflection was grotesque. An enormous beast held a petit woman captive and Elizabeth could see coldness in her own eyes as she stared in horror at her reflection.

Wilhelm felt Elizabeth's body tense beneath his grip and he held on a little tighter. "You could be with me Elizabeth, could stay in Branko and be powerful just like us."

His tone had changed. The breathless urgency had gone and she could hear confidence in his voice. The Wilhelm that tried to destroy

Yorik's tavern was back.

"We know you have nothing," he continued, "the only power you have is what the witches deign to give you. But with us Elizabeth you could be eternally magnificent."

Elizabeth closed her eyes. With the reflection gone, so was her fear and in its place she felt a familiar enveloping rage rising. She was livid. Once again she had been played for a fool. She had allowed her inexperience to make her vulnerable. She had taken Wilhelm at his word and willingly allowed him to separate her from the sisters. He was absolutely right of course, she had nothing to fight him with especially as she was far away from the witches, in a distant part of the castle.

"Are you alright?" Wilhelm said. It was clear that Elizabeth's thoughtful silence was beginning to unsettle him, he loosened his hold on her.

One thought crossed her mind as she turned to face him, *it's show time.*

"Oh Wilhelm," she said summoning as much fake confidence as she dared, "what on earth makes you think I'm not powerful?"

She met his confused glare with an unwavering one of her own.

"Well...uh...we *know* you haven't....," Wilhelm spluttered.

"You '*know* I haven't'," she said walking away starting to get some distance between them. "That's very interesting. How can you 'know I haven't' when I *know* I have."

Caught up in her own bravado Elizabeth was unsure what to do next, but like a gunfighter searching for his weapon of choice, she put her hand into her dress and grasped the only familiar friend she had. Wilhelm backed away.

She pulled Sonny out from beneath her gown.

"What is this," Wilhelm smirked but Elizabeth could tell he was not sure anymore how this game would play out. She knew all she had to do was get some distance between them and find the witches. It seemed simple enough. But if she moved away too quickly then her own spell would be broken and Wilhelm would realise that she was only playing for time.

"This," she said and took a confident step towards him, "is a magic wand. And it is what *I* use to create my *own* magic." She attempted a sarcastic laugh and turned away waving Sonny wildly, "did you think

179

that by dragging me all the way up here, you were taking me away from the source of my power?"

Elizabeth was pleased to see that her performance was working. Wilhelm backed away from her as she carried on raving.

"I know you have nothing," he said, not so certain this time.

"Oh really," she said stopping in her tracks pointing Sonny directly at him, "and how do you know that? Something you've guessed over the years with the other girls? Hm? Noticed something about them have you?"

"No!" Wilhelm said, "it was nothing like that. We did not know."

"HOW THEN!"

"We were told!"

The statement stopped Elizabeth in her tracks. The witches were always so careful not to let anyone know that the novice witches did not have any powers. Even the witch herself was oblivious. Who could have told Darius's family that they were powerless?

Elizabeth's stunned silence gave Wilhelm his chance to act. Whilst she was distracted he bounded towards her and knocked Sonny out of her hand. He grabbed her by the top of her arms and raised her up into the air, his face contorted in rage. He began dragging Elizabeth back to the balcony when suddenly he jumped. Elizabeth screamed. They plummeted towards the ground and Wilhelm began to transform. Elizabeth could see that his eyes now resembled those of the monster in the mirror, his teeth had grown and his body was lengthening and growing in unnatural ways. He had become the man-beast of his reflection and Elizabeth was helpless to get away.

They were inches from the ground when Wilhelm suddenly soared skywards holding Elizabeth firmly in his grasp, laughing like a madman. All she could do was push his snarling face away from her with all her might. He was trying to bite her.

Oh my God! This is how they turn people. Elizabeth thought. *They bite them!* But somehow Elizabeth found the strength to fight this cruel monster. She pushed his face away and managed to raise her legs in mid-air. She pushed against his body with her knees and noticed that, in her own small way, she was controlling the flight path. If she leaned to the right, he would lean that way too. If she pulled backwards, he would have to follow. His animal instincts had taken over, all he wanted was to take a bite out of Elizabeth. She was his prey and like a true predator he was not about to give up until he had squeezed the fight out of her.

Elizabeth searched around her for a way to escape. She managed to draw him away from the castle. Leaning backwards, Elizabeth dragged the flying creature towards the forest. They flew high above the trees, Wilhelm snapped and snarled at Elizabeth, enjoying the fight from his victim.

They were high above the tops of the trees before Elizabeth made her move. *Please be close, please be close* she chanted to herself. Finally they reached what she hoped was the perfect spot. She managed to release one of her knees from Wilhelm's chest and with all the strength she could muster she kicked Wilhelm squarely between the legs.

Wilhelm screamed and the beast was suddenly gone. The instincts of the man took over and he automatically grabbed at his injured genitals releasing Elizabeth from his vice-like grip.

Elizabeth fell.

Chapter Twenty-One

Elizabeth felt the rush of air against her body as she plummeted uncontrollably towards the earth. Wilhelm had dragged her so high into the sky that any chance of surviving the fall seemed impossible. As she neared the tops of the trees Elizabeth held out her hands, hoping the sisters were close. She needed to use their magic.

She fell towards the trees, casting as many spells as she could think of. But it was useless. The witches were not close enough for Elizabeth to use their magic. They may have been concerned by her disappearance, may even have started searching for her but Elizabeth had no idea *where* they would start their search. They may still be in the castle for all she knew. Escaping from the kicking and snarling Wilhelm was suddenly the least of her worries. She was falling through the sky and she had no way of stopping herself.

The trees loomed towards her. Any minute now she would crash into them and feel the searing pain as she landed. All of a sudden she was swept sideways by a fierce blow. Something or someone had crashed into her. Her fall lost some momentum but she was still dropping towards the ground, this time hitting branches as she fell.

Amidst the broken branches and torn leaves, Elizabeth realised she was not alone. A figure was falling with her. As she desperately tried to cling on to one of the trees to stop her fall, the other person was also trying to save himself. Suddenly Elizabeth's foot got a stronghold on a thick branch and she instinctively reached out to her falling companion. Elizabeth knew she would not be able to hold him for long but his reflexes were quick. As she grabbed hold of his arm he used that moment of stillness to get a foothold of his own.

Elizabeth clung onto the tree, not daring to move, fearful she might fall again. They were still high off the ground, saved by the enormous tree they were clinging onto. Elizabeth was bruised and sore and shaken. Elizabeth's companion was equally stunned and stood just underneath her on the other side of the tree.

"Hello Victor," she said breathlessly, "What are you doing......."

"Shhh!" Victor said distracted by a noise above them.

Elizabeth looked up, circling them like a vulture circling its prey was Wilhelm. Elizabeth could not believe her eyes. From somewhere in his monstrous transformation he had sprouted bat like wings that stretched from his wrists to his ankles. But his humanoid face was clearly recognisable. On it Elizabeth could see the determination of a predator.

"Get down!" Elizabeth hissed at Victor and they started their descent.

They slipped and clambered down the trunk of the old tree. Grabbing at branches as they went. Using knotholes as foot holds. They went as fast as they could, sliding all the way. As they reached the ground Elizabeth chanced a look above them. Wilhelm had heard their descent and was scanning the ground.

"What should we do now?" Victor hissed.

"How should I know? He's your brother!"

"Elizabeth do you not know by now......."

"Alright Victor," Elizabeth interrupted, "we can discuss family dynamics when we're not running for our lives!"

With that she grabbed the gangly youth and sprinted away from Wilhelm. He may have lost sight of them, but Elizabeth realised he was not about to give up his prey that easily. He circled the area flying closer and closer to the ground with every pass. Elizabeth pulled Victor behind one of the trees.

"Did you see where my aunties went?" Elizabeth asked.

"Your *aunties*! I did not know......."

"Please Victor, concentrate. Where are the witches?"

"When they realised Wilhelm had taken you they demanded to search the castle but my father would not allow it. They had no option but to leave and search for you themselves."

"Ok, that's good, so they're not in the castle. Now this is very important Victor, which way did they go?"

"To the north I think, I cannot be sure, I was too busy looking for you myself."

"Aren't we north of the castle now?" Elizabeth said looking furtively around.

"Yes," said Victor, "I'm sure the witches came this way."

Suddenly, from high above them, they heard a sickening *CRACK*. The monstrous shadow of Wilhelm directly above them. They had been found and Wilhelm was beating his way to the forest floor.

"This way," Elizabeth said hoping her instincts were right and she led Victor back towards the castle.

"Why are we going this way?" Victor shouted behind her.

"Trust me," she said.

"He is coming Elizabeth," Victor said looking behind him, "you must go on alone. I will try to stop him."

"NO!" Elizabeth said and stopped abruptly. She felt a familiar sensation rise through her body and it was blissfully welcome. She started searching furtively around the forest. Her pattern was erratic. She was looking for something in particular. Suddenly she spotted what she was looking for and sprinted towards it.

She stopped at the foot of a tree, examined it briefly, nodded her approval and started climbing.

"We are going up a tree – again?" Victor said from beneath her looking confused.

"Come on," she urged.

The branches were low and thick, it was easy to climb and it was covered in ivy. Wilhelm was getting closer, he was having some trouble seeing them in the dark but he was listening intently and sniffing the air like a bloodhound.

Halfway up the tree Elizabeth stopped and made sure she had a strong foothold. Satisfied that it was a good spot for what she intended she reached across to Victor and halted his climb. She gestured to him to take a firm stand. They stood opposite one another holding hands, each on a thick branch, the gnarled trunk of the tree between them.

"Do you trust me," she said to Victor, hoping she was right about him.

He looked into her eyes, gulped deeply and said, "Of course. Why?"

But the last word barely had time to leave his mouth before the ivy surrounding the tree jumped to life and began binding them tightly.

"Elizab...!"

Victor was panicking but Elizabeth had to concentrate on the spell. She knew the witches were near when she felt the bolt of their powerful energy course through her body. She also knew that there was no way to outrun Wilhelm, so hiding was their only option. Victor held tightly onto Elizabeth's hand as he was bound to the tree, the ivy covering every inch of him, including his mouth. She could feel his fear surging through his fingertips. Once they were thoroughly covered by the ivy Elizabeth tried a calming spell on Victor which worked instantly. Within moments his grip relaxed in Elizabeth's hand. Watching him relax in the darkness suddenly presented Elizabeth with another problem. Victor's eyes were glowing in the dark just as they had the night he was outside her window.

Elizabeth was gagged by the enveloping ivy, unable to talk. She only hoped her powers stretched to telepathy. *Close your eyes*, she thought, as clearly as she could. Elizabeth watched Victor and from behind her she heard Wilhelm approaching. Now it was her turn to panic. If Wilhelm did find them because of the luminosity of Victor's gaze they were trussed up by the ivy unable to move, prisoners that were already bound. He would have no trouble disposing of them. *Close your eyes, close your eyes! Please Victor close your sodding eyes!* After one last desperate search for his brother Victor closed his eyes.

A moment later Wilhelm appeared, flying haphazardly around their hiding place. Elizabeth could feel him sniffing the air behind her. There was a possibility that her plan would not work. That Wilhelm's animal instincts were too finely tuned to be fooled by her spell. Elizabeth hoped that the new growth of the ivy might confuse his olfactory senses. That he would not be able to pinpoint their presence or smell their fear. He circled around the tree behind Victor. Instantly Victor's hand moistened with fear as his brother sniffed all around him. Now Elizabeth could see exactly what Wilhelm was. He was nothing but an animal. His handsome exterior had vanished. All that remained was a beast, with long teeth and fingernails. His eyes were the same colour as Victor's but they were devoid of Victor's humanity. His body had lengthened and distorted. His legs were longer and the knee joint was bent at sickening angles. Elizabeth felt no fear towards him just revulsion. It made her sick to think that only moments before, this creature was holding her more intimately than she had been held for a very long time. Elizabeth could not bear to look at his monstrous appearance any longer so she, like Victor, closed her eyes.

Wilhelm did not give up his search easily. He knew he was in the right area. He had not been completely deceived by Elizabeth's spell. Suddenly Wilhelm scratched wildly at the tree just above Victor's head. Elizabeth could feel the panic rising in her companion but frozen by her own terror she was unable to offer him comfort. As the moments ticked by Wilhelm still could not find the concealed couple.

"Aargh!" he screamed in rage and frustration and jumped from the tree into the air. He moved slowly away from their hiding place sniffing and listening as he went.

Not daring to move Elizabeth and Victor stayed frozen to the spot until they were sure that Wilhelm had gone. When she was sure they were safe she set her intention and murmured a spell to reverse growth of the ivy. Nothing happened. Elizabeth panicked as it suddenly occurred to her that the witches might have been close when she created the spell but now that she wanted to undo it, they could have wandered further away. She forced herself to calm down, sent her internal power search out a little further than before and tried the reversing spell once again. She could feel the ivy try to contract around them, but her original spell had worked too well. The ivy had burrowed into itself as though it had been there for years and dissolving back into youthful buds was no longer possible.

Victor sensed Elizabeth's panic, had probably sensed the strained movement from the plant now entangling them and his eyes widened in fear. *Think, think.* She said to herself. Then she remembered working with her mother in the glen. How the only way her mother could teach her any rescuing spells on the perfect plant life was to take them to the brink of death. All at once Elizabeth knew what she had to do. The ivy had to carry on growing. This time at such a rate that it would complete its life cycle and die.

She closed her eyes and forced the ivy to grow. And the growth rate had to be even more unnaturally fast than the last time. All of a sudden, the ivy started to grow. They felt it wrapping them up more and more, stifling them, suffocating them. They held onto each other, grabbing tightly until the weight of the plant started to get heavier and more brittle giving them a little room to move. Victor felt a little give in the plant and tried to wriggle free but Elizabeth grabbed his hand urging him to be patient.

As Elizabeth continued to cast her spell the ivy went from green to yellow, from yellow to brown, then from brown to black and became so brittle that they could finally break free of its grip. Ripping the dead vines from around their bodies, Victor and Elizabeth broke free.

"We have to get you back to the others," Victor said and he motioned for Elizabeth to follow him down the tree. When they were safely back on the ground they started to walk north this time Victor led Elizabeth by the hand.

Suddenly Elizabeth froze. Victor stopped quickly and noticed that Elizabeth was staring at the departing figure of Wilhelm.

"What is it?" Victor asked. "Is it Wilhelm? Is it because you love him?"

"Don't be ridiculous, Victor." Elizabeth smirked. "Of course I don't *love* him. Honestly for an immortal beast you really are quite naïve!"

She paused, looking behind her in the direction that Victor wanted to go, then back at the castle. "I just have a feeling that Shiona and Daphne wouldn't have come this far."

Without further discussion she headed towards the castle.

"I am not so sure this is a good idea," Victor said as he obediently followed her. "They will be looking for you Elizabeth, be sure of that. Wilhelm does not like to lose a fight."

"You don't have to tell me that," Elizabeth said rubbing her arms where Wilhelm's claws had left their impression.

Victor went quiet and Elizabeth sensed the change in him. For a moment it unnerved her, remembering the dramatic change in Wilhelm. But there was something about the boy that Elizabeth instinctively liked. No matter what Shiona said, Elizabeth did not fear him.

"Are you OK Victor?" She asked.

"I am just thinking about Wilhelm. I do not know what it is about him. Maybe he is just better with women than I am."

"What are you talking about?" she asked.

"It is just that I would have liked to dance with you at the ball tonight."

"Oh Victor," Elizabeth sighed, "I didn't *want* to dance with Wilhelm. The whole thing was a set-up, you must know that?"

"Yes I did know they were planning something. They asked me to take you away from the other witches. Even though I said I would, I think they must have known I would never betray you."

Elizabeth stopped and turned to face him, "I know you wouldn't Victor. I trust you. Even if Shiona doesn't."

"No," Victor said awkwardly, "Shiona has never liked me. But why should she?" he added as they carried on walking. "As far as she is concerned we are the offspring of an evil man. I cannot blame her for seeing only the evil in us. But I was not always like this Elizabeth. I have vague memories of a mother and a father. People who truly loved me, until Darius turned me into a monster. Wilhelm and Diana have no memories, but I do. Perhaps my soul is not altogether lost after all - yes?"

"No Victor, I don't believe it is...."

Suddenly they heard a sickening howl from the castle stopping them dead in their tracks.

"Quick Elizabeth, we must get to higher ground."

Elizabeth and Victor clambered upwards from the castle climbing the closest hill. Victor stopped at the mouth of a small cave. From their high vantage point they watched the unfolding scene below. Branko's wolf-villagers poured out of the castle battlements. Their gowns and masks gone, like Wilhelm before them they were now merely beasts. Elizabeth felt sure that Gretchen was amongst them.

"What's going on Victor?" Elizabeth asked.

"They are looking for you Elizabeth. Wilhelm wants you for his next victim and he will do whatever it takes to find you."

"That, I kind of gathered," she said, "but what the hell has happened to the villagers? Why are they animals? And how the hell does Darius know about the third witch?"

Elizabeth chose her words carefully, unsure if the family had let Victor in on their dirty little secret.

"Do you mean, that you have no powers?"

"Yeah something like that," Elizabeth sighed.

"My father was told."

"By who?"

"By the stranger. The same man who knew what to do to the villagers."

"Is that the same man that stayed in the tavern?"

"Yes. It must be. He told my father that he took sustenance at the tavern the night he arrived in Branko."

"Who is he?"

"I do not know but he has given my father much information. He told us about your lack of power and he explained to us why the witches always defeat my father."

"And why do they?"

"The villagers have always been the key. They are pure souls. They surround my father and no matter what he does during the year when the witches are away he can never regain the power he once had. The stranger explained to him that it was not just the witches that he had to defeat, but the villagers as well."

"Now you've lost me Victor!"

"You have met Greta and Yorik, you have seen what kind of people they are. They are beautiful people and the goodness in their souls is something my father does not understand. His power is from the beasts in the forest and the fear of the people. But since the Baron bested him the people of Branko do not fear him. They are like angels imprisoning his evil, only the purest of souls stayed. So the stranger explained what he must do to create an army of his own."

"Take away their souls," Elizabeth said, suddenly understanding.

"Yes. These creatures," he said gesturing towards Elizabeth's search party, "are soulless animals. Created from anger and cruelty. My father's army, they are quite simply fighting machines that only he can control. They are no longer a threat to my father, can no longer be the allies of the witches. And he will not stop until he has turned every single one."

"Come on," Elizabeth said rising quickly. "We've got to tell the others."

"I cannot come with you now Elizabeth," Victor said quietly. "I must go back before I am missed. At the moment they trust that I will not forsake them. But if they suspect for a moment that I have helped you, they will turn me into one of those beasts. Then I will be of no use to you. I must keep that little bit of my soul, yes?"

"Yes," Elizabeth said and hugged Victor tightly.

"Go," Victor said when Elizabeth released him, "find your family." Then he added as an afterthought, "trust your instincts." With that he began his climb down the hill back towards the castle.

Elizabeth sat for a moment trying to listen to the language of her soul. Victor was running towards the castle and Elizabeth felt an undeniable pull that way. She could sense that same visceral power that she felt when she was close to Wilhelm. But this was not the power she was looking for. She tried to remember what it was like to feel the infinite purity of the witches' magic.

She sat for a while. Not daring to move. The overwhelming desire was to follow the beast within. To run towards Wilhelm and Victor and everything they could offer her. But she knew she had to block out that instinct and feel the power of the witches. In her mind's eye she could see the red and muddy brown of the animalist survival instinct. It was all-consuming and penetrating, trying to bore into her soul. When suddenly there was a note of purity. The white smoke of beauty that illuminated the dark. A spark of clarity and honesty, and Elizabeth knew who it was coming from. A moment later, she knew where. Quickly she got to her feet to follow the source.

She clambered down the hill feeling the witches' universal power. She knew she was getting closer as the internal animal quietened and she could feel clarity return. As she scrambled through the forest she saw a light flickering ahead of her. Elizabeth was struck by a wave of relief. The knowledge that the witches were close allowed her to relax her aching body and she stumbled towards the warm glow. It came from a circle of trees. As she reached its origin she saw two figures sitting around a camp fire, drinking tea from a flask.

"Got into a bit of a pickle there did you Betty?"

Neither witch looked up as she limped into the clearing and plonked herself close to the fire. Shiona merely handed her a cup of tea and Elizabeth drank it down greedily. The feeling of warmth and familiarity was incredibly welcome.

"So where was the *reflection of perfection* for you then Betty?" Daphne asked amused. "In a lake, or in a window? Oh, don't tell me he got out that tired old mirror again?"

"What!" Elizabeth said spitting out her tea.

190

"Oh, yes," Daphne continued, "we've all had a look at that over the years haven't we Shiona?"

Shiona nodded.

"I was quite pleased with my reflection," Daphne said matter-of-factly, "I was much thinner in my reflection which was nice, but what I liked most was being shorter! What about you Betty?"

Elizabeth could not answer. She sat in stunned silence for a while.

"What about you?" Daphne asked Shiona with a knowing grin.

"Pah!" Shiona said.

"She doesn't really like to talk about that Betty. Shiona was a bit naïve back in the old days and had a bit of a thing for Wilhelm. Came as a bit of a blow when you realised he was having you on didn't it Shiona?"

"That's enough of that thank-you Daphne," Shiona said curtly.

"Well it's good to know I'm not the only gullible idiot in the family!" Elizabeth said wearily.

"Oh yes Betty. You haven't been through anything tonight that *we* haven't gone through before you!"

"Except you two had the power to fight him."

"Oh yeah," Daphne said. "Except for that."

"They know, by the way," Elizabeth said sipping her tea, "they know I haven't got any powers."

"What!"

"What?" Shiona and Daphne said together.

Elizabeth explained the whole encounter. When she finished she looked across at Daphne who was stifling a giggle.

"A *magic wand* Betty!" She exploded, "you didn't tell him that Sonny was a magic wand!"

"I was improvising," Elizabeth said bristling, "anyway, you two have got one! Why shouldn't I? What else was I supposed to do?"

"Not go with Wilhelm in the first place," Shiona offered.

"You're probably right," Elizabeth said, "but it sounds like we've *all* made that particular mistake!"

Shiona looked away embarrassed.

Then Elizabeth told the witches about the soulless villagers.

"So that's what he's planning," Shiona said.

"What I don't understand," Elizabeth said, "is where are their souls?"

"What's that Betty?"

"Well surely they have to go somewhere. They don't just vanish do they?"

"I don't know Elizabeth," Shiona said. "I know Darius has an 'evil' soul that can no longer be touched by goodness, but I had no idea a soul could be absent altogether."

"How did any of this happen?" Daphne said, "None of it makes any sense. How did he know about the villagers and how on earth could he have found out that the young witch doesn't have any powers?"

"*I* told him."

The witches jumped as shadow appeared from behind them. They stood up quickly, wands at the ready. Slowly, a man entered the clearing. As he moved towards them his features were revealed by the firelight.

"Oh my God!" Shiona said.

Daphne gasped and her hand shot to her mouth.

"Hello Daphers," the figure said.

"George!?" Daphne cried.

Chapter Twenty-Two

George wandered slowly into the camp towards the stunned witches. Elizabeth had no idea who this man was but by the reaction of the sisters he was clearly known to them. Daphne watched him with wide eyes and Shiona glared hatefully at him.

"Georgie, how on earth...?" Daphne began.

"Stop Daphne," Shiona said sharply still glaring at George.

"Still the same Shiona," George chuckled, "still bossing Daphers around. Some things never change."

"Who *is* that?" Elizabeth whispered to Daphne.

"So you're the new witch?" George said turning his attention to Elizabeth.

"Uh, yeah." Elizabeth said flatly.

"So what's so special about you then?" He sidled up to Elizabeth. "What's so special about any of them?" Suddenly he rounded on Shiona. "*I* could have been the next one. I could have come with you, then none of this would have happened! It's all your fault Shiona. Remember that. When you and all the people of Branko are breathing your last breaths remember it's ALL YOUR FAULT!"

"Oh!" Elizabeth said, remembering the story Daphne told her about the man who had come knocking at their door; the man who had found out about their yearly pilgrimage to Branko; the only man who had ever wanted to become their next novice witch. *This* was George. And far from being the sweet little man Daphne described, it was clear to Elizabeth that this man was insane.

"What have you done George," Daphne said taking a step towards him.

Suddenly George sagged, all sign of anger gone. He gazed up into Daphne's face and there was genuine affection in that look. He was older than Daphne, his hair greying at the temples, in no particular style, just a mass of forgotten curls. Daphne towered over him. He was a small and stout man. His tummy protruded through the dark, tweed suit he wore that had patches on the elbows. He looked to Elizabeth more like an eccentric professor than an evil warlock.

"I just wanted to come with you Daphers," he said pleadingly, "but SHE wouldn't let me," he pointed fiercely at Shiona his anger threatening again.

"Ok, OK George," Daphne said calming him, "but surely you had to know – deep down – that we couldn't bring you?"

"WHY?" He screamed startling all of the witches. "Because I'm not a WOMAN? So what? I am more powerful than any of the novices you brought to Branko. More powerful than HER," and once again he turned on Elizabeth, "more powerful than she will ever be!"

Daphne took a step away from George's hysterical outburst. "What happened to you?" she asked quietly.

"I was rejected Daphers! That's what happened to me. I wanted to live the life you lived. I wanted *you*! But you sided with your bitter, twisted sister. If you had just stood up for me things would be different now..."

"So it's Daphne's fault now is it?" Elizabeth asked stopping George mid-rant.

He turned towards Elizabeth. She was pleased to see that he was confused by the interruption, clearly wanting to get through his well-rehearsed speech.

"Oh, I'm just checking," Elizabeth said calmly walking towards him. "Because a minute ago it was all Shiona's doing now you've just tried to lay all the blame on Daphne. I suppose it won't be long before it's my fault. I'm looking forward to how you're going to explain that one!" she chuckled. "So what part did *you* play in all this George?"

George said nothing but stared menacingly at her. Elizabeth did not know why she felt so calm around this madman. Perhaps it was because of her encounter with Wilhelm or her bizarre connection to Victor but of all the men she had met since entering the borders of Branko – George was the least threatening.

"Because whatever is happening," Elizabeth continued, "make no mistake, it's because of *you*. *You* made these terrible decisions George, for whatever reasons. *You* are to blame for putting the entire world in danger. So.....," she paused for effect, "....what do you want to do now?"

"What do you mean?" he said eyeing Elizabeth suspiciously.

"Is there still enough humanity left in you to help, George?"

The other witches stood in confused silence trying to decipher Elizabeth's plan.

"What about it George," Elizabeth said, "are you part of the solution, or part of the problem."

The performance was rather overplayed and Elizabeth hoped that the witches would pick up on their cues. They did. As she finished speaking the three witches took up their rehearsed positions. Shiona moved to the tip of the triangle, Elizabeth made her way to Shiona's left and even Daphne stepped into formation. All three ready for battle.

For a moment George looked shocked, staring wildly from one witch to another and Elizabeth could perceive a naivety in the man. She saw innocence in him and understood why he must have been so appealing to Daphne. Then, like a vision, she saw Daphne and George laughing together. The laughter in her mind's eye was genuine and joy-filled but then it turned into something more menacing and cruel. Suddenly, she snapped back to reality and heard the malicious laughter right next to her.

It was George. "Do you really think you can frighten me? You are a *powerless* child."

If George was expecting this to intimidate Elizabeth he was sadly mistaken. She was sick of hearing how useless she was. Before she could stop herself she flicked her wrist and sent a bolt of power flying towards George, knocking him off his feet.

"Betty!" Daphne chastised.

"What?" Elizabeth said defensively.

George got to his knees and pointed at Elizabeth, "you'll be the first to go". As he stood he began mumbling inaudibly under his breath.

Suddenly Elizabeth heard a low grumble resonate through the forest. Shiona heard it too. "What's that?" she asked.

"Those are my animals Shiona," George said. "The creatures I created to help Lord Darius stop you. And *you* too are now as powerless as your student. Your ancient spells are useless against them."

"What have you done George?" Daphne asked again.

"I have given Lord Darius the knowledge. He now knows how to defeat you!" He gesticulated wildly at the witches. "You creatures who are governed by the laws of the planet and the people you protect. You are great only because of the universal life force of the planet. Even the great and powerful Lord Darius is useless against you because he has some kind of soul left, a consciousness that keeps him human. And your control makes him safe to the villagers and their safety calms their fears and with no fear or greed or unkindness Darius cannot become strong. But I've created fear now," he said as the growling grew louder. "The villagers are frightened and Darius is stronger and soon you will be his prisoners because you will look in the eye of my creations and their soullessness will terrify you. You cannot stop them. You lost Shiona. You lost!"

"He's gone nuts!" Daphne hissed at the other two witches.

From behind them shapes started to appear in the forest. The soulless creatures that George had created from the terrified young villagers were flocking towards Elizabeth and her aunties from every direction. The witches cautiously stepped towards one another back to back, every corner of the threat seen by one of them.

The beasts moved slowly into the makeshift camp. Staring from George to the witches and back again – waiting for an order from their master. Elizabeth was desperate to look away, to close her eyes and hope this was all a dream. The creatures were like images from a nightmare. They were mostly human in form but they walked on all fours, growling and snarling. Nipping at each another if they got too close. When Elizabeth caught a glimpse of their eyes in the floundering firelight she could see nothing but hatred and death.

"Oh no," Shiona said. "Look at them."

And in that moment, Elizabeth felt the pain and horror coming from the other two witches. She suddenly understood how hard it must be for them. What a crushing sight for Daphne and Shiona to see their friends, the people they spent decades protecting; people they had come to know, respect and love. These people, at the mercy of George and his fragile ego, had become nothing but monsters and Darius's slaves.

The growling grew louder as they approached. A low guttural rumble

– unnatural and terrifying. As they came closer Elizabeth could see that their hair was matted and any exposed skin was filthy. Their clothes were torn just as Gretchen's had been; their bodies were full of scratches and bruises and, unprepared for the animalistic nature they were now adopting, their feet bled onto the forest floor.

George saw Elizabeth looking at their bleeding limbs.

"Innocent blood spilt on Branko once again," he said in a daze, "and I made it happen."

"George you're an idiot!" The outburst came from Daphne.

"Daphers?" was all George could say.

"What the hell do you think is going to happen when this is all over?" She cried. "Do you think Darius is going to welcome you into his family? Do you actually think he will let you sit alongside him in the *real* world? Will you be his right hand man, George? Hermann Göring to his Hitler? Do you honestly think he's going to let you rule with him? Do you? DO YOU?" Daphne stepped away from the witches and drawing herself up to her full height, she loomed over the tiny little man. "If you do then you're a bloody idiot. There are more corruptible, vile, greedy souls in our world than *you* George. He only has to find the nearest merchant banker!"

"That's enough Daphne," George said stepping away from her, "I will not let you confuse me. Lord Darius said you would try to use our past connection to weaken my resolve. You will not speak anymore."

He murmured something once again and the creatures leapt forward stopping just inches from the alarmed witches.

"Stop acting like a child George," it was Shiona's turn. "If they're going to attack then let them do it. I'm not prepared to play this game of cat and mouse with you!"

"Oh Shiona," George scoffed, "I don't want them to attack you. I want them to catch you. I told Darius I would bring you back alive, that you would be my captives. *Then* he could see what a majestic warlock I really am."

Shiona snorted a derisive laugh and started arguing with George but Elizabeth had stopped listening. She realised quickly that George was never going to listen to reason and hoped the witches had another plan.

"What are we going to do?" Elizabeth whispered to Daphne, her question hidden beneath the noise of Shiona's shouts.

197

"I don't really know Betty," Daphne said looking at the snarling beasts clearly in shock. It suddenly dawned on Elizabeth how torn the witches would be at this moment. They had the power to fight the threat but would be reluctant to harm these creatures, these pawns in Darius' game. After all, these beasts had once been their friends.

As Shiona carried on jibing and insulting George, hoping that there was still a reasonable conscience inside him to see sense, Elizabeth struck on an idea. She looked wildly around the forest floor for the one thing she *knew* she was good at.

She bent low to the ground a couple of times, grabbing at twigs, discarding any that were not suitable.

"What are you doing Betty," Daphne hissed.

Elizabeth looked up, Daphne was not the only one to notice that she was up to something, the villager-animals around her were also getting jittery. Luckily for Elizabeth though, George was still distracted. His old rivalry with Shiona had surfaced and he wanted his moment of triumph.

On her third search of the forest floor Elizabeth's attempt finally bore fruit. She picked up a small branch from under her feet. It was warm and alive and Elizabeth knew that it had only recently fallen from its original source, knocked off in the fray.

Holding it firmly at one end she shoved it towards Daphne. The beasts surrounding them were suddenly alert to her change of mood, and Elizabeth did not know how long she would have before the creatures acted of their own accord instead of waiting for orders from George. They were animals after all and their instincts were telling them, they might be losing their prey.

"Hold onto this and grab Shiona," Elizabeth hissed at Daphne.

It all happened in an instant. Daphne seized Shiona tightly around the waist, just as Elizabeth said her growing spell and the branch she held burst into life, growing just enough to lift the three witches into the air.

George watched in stunned silence but the creatures were ready, had already sensed Elizabeth was up to something. But Shiona and Daphne were unprepared for what Elizabeth was planning and merely hung in the air leaving Elizabeth to concentrate on the flying spell. She had only ever used the spell for herself, she was struggling with the extra weight.

The beasts were jumping and grabbing at the witches. One of the taller boys managed to hit Daphne's dangling feet, knocking the three witches into a spin.

Elizabeth was desperately trying to control the broom *and* get them skywards, but she was in trouble.

"HELP ME!" She screamed at the other two witches.

Her shout had the desired effect. The moment the witches realised what was happening – everything changed. They summoned all their flying abilities and poured their spells into Elizabeth's makeshift broomstick, suddenly the witches zoomed high into the air for a moment. But the punch of power was too much for the broom. It vibrated worryingly under their grip. The witches looked at one another wide-eyed when suddenly the broom exploded into pieces sending the witches spinning in all directions. No sooner had they escaped from the leaping beasts and George's livid screams, that they had another force to contend with – gravity.

Elizabeth groaned as she realised she was about to spend another agonising few minutes falling through the trees but then she remembered, *things are different this time.* The witches were close. Summoning up everything she learned and holding out her hands she cleared her mind as much as she could. Her spell was strong, she left nothing to chance, and within moments branches from all of the nearby trees grew skyward to meet her, stopping her fall and cushioning her landing.

She lay still for a moment. Sticks, pine cones and leaves poked her, but she did not care about the discomfort, she was just grateful to be alive and powerful again. She listened intently to the noises in the forest. She could hear George shouting orders at his league of brutes and she could hear the beasts growling and chasing wildly about the forest in utter confusion. They created such a din that Elizabeth struggled to hear anything else. She strained to find any sight or sound of the witches.

Elizabeth. She heard the voice whisper her name. It was quiet, eerily quiet. She span around quickly in her bed of branches to see if one of the witches were near.

Where are you Elizabeth? The whispering voice said again. Elizabeth still could not tell where or who it was coming from.

"Where are *you*?" Elizabeth said loudly.

Shh! Not so loud Betty! The voice said again, and this time Elizabeth knew exactly who it was. *Try to think your words.*

"Oh, OK." Elizabeth said. Then added, *is this better?*

Yes! Now where are you Betty?

Up a tree!

Can you be more specific? Shiona's voice joined the party in Elizabeth's head.

Not really Aunty Shiona, Elizabeth thought and was impressed that she could even make her thoughts sarcastic. *I wasn't using a compass when I was trying not to die!*

There's no need for that/Come on Betty we're just trying to/forgive me if I only want to make sure you're/find you so we can ......

Stop it! Elizabeth sent the desperate thought to the two sisters. *One at a time please! You're giving me a migraine!*

Go on then/No, you go/You found her first/Yes but you're the better......

Oh for goodness sake, thought Elizabeth, *where are you?*

We're not together Betty.

Oh?

We got blown apart when the broomstick exploded Shiona thought.

Elizabeth was starting to find the conversation in her head rather disconcerting and it was particularly uncomfortable having Shiona's voice running through her consciousness.

I heard that Shiona's thought snapped.

I didn't say anything, Elizabeth thought defensively.

You didn't say anything but you definitely thought it was uncomfortable having my voice.........

This isn't getting us anywhere Shiona, Daphne's consciousness interjected, *let's all just get to the forest floor and try to meet up. And for goodness sake KEEP QUIET.*

Daphne's last thought sent a white flash stabbing through Elizabeth's head unbalancing her and nearly toppling her from her nest at the top of the tree.

STOP SHOUTING, she retorted back, secretly hoping she might have done some damage of her own.

Not funny, Shiona said quietly and Elizabeth could sense that she was nursing a headache.

Smirking to herself, Elizabeth instructed the trees to recede slightly and they carefully lowered her to the ground.

Elizabeth could sense that the witches were quite close. After searching for them when she left Victor she knew exactly what sensations to follow. She was getting much better at tuning into her instincts especially where the power of the witches was concerned. She knew they were near because she could feel the use of their power at her fingertips. But as she searched for them she felt stretched in two different directions. Elizabeth realised that although they were close to her, they were far away from one another.

Elizabeth closed her eyes, and tried to sense the women. To her right Elizabeth felt the usual purity of power but this time it was tinged with a slight redness and pulled at that place of power just below her navel. On her left was the same distinct feeling of clarity but with a velvety green hue and it surrounded her chest. The second feeling was getting stronger, moving closer to Elizabeth. Quickly Elizabeth turned left hoping to meet with the green witch.

After treading carefully through the forest for a few moments, Elizabeth found Daphne tiptoeing towards her, finding it impossible to stay quiet with her huge feet and a larger than life frame.

"I knew it was you!" Elizabeth whispered excitedly.

"Yes Betty, it's me. No prizes for guessing that. I'm pretty hard to miss!"

"No! I don't mean that. I *sensed* different powers from you and Shiona. One was slightly green and getting closer to me so I followed it. I knew it would be you, and it was!"

"Oh! I see," Daphne said. "You're getting very clever Betty old girl. I'm a bit green, Shiona's a bit red – no surprise! And you are a bit purple."

"Am I?" Elizabeth said excitedly.

"Yes Betty. So is Gladys. Now as fun as this is, perhaps we should find Shiona and try to stop Darius taking over the world?"

"Oh yeah." Elizabeth said, "she's this way somewhere."

Within minutes two witches became three as Shiona joined the pair.

"Seen anything?" Shiona asked the others quietly.

"Nothing," Daphne answered. "You?"

"Just George's monsters," Shiona replied, "they've been instructed to separate the weak one from the pack." Shiona nodded towards

Elizabeth.

"Once again, thanks!" Elizabeth was tiring of the label.

"There's no time for ego boosting now Elizabeth we have to face facts. Darius knows you have no powers unless you're near us. He also knows we can't fight soulless creatures and George has helped him create an army of them. The villagers are frightened of him, which is making him stronger and stronger and unless we come up with a magnificent strategy, to use your youthful vernacular – we're stuffed!"

"Well we can't stay here can we?" Elizabeth offered. "As long as we're in this forest they've got the upper hand."

"She's right Shiona," Daphne said. "They've got local knowledge. Whether the soul is there or not, it doesn't matter, they've probably got some kind of muscle memory and if that's the case they know these woods a damn sight better than we do."

"Ok. Let's get back to the pub if we can." Shiona agreed. "We'll find Greta and Yorik and make them rally the rest of the villagers. We'll blast that fear out of them with a show of strength of our own, eh?"

For the first time since knowing them Elizabeth suddenly felt like part of the team. These women had kept things from her, supposedly for her own good, but now she knew everything and their attitudes had changed towards her, even Shiona's. She was part of this trio of witches and she felt an overwhelming sense of allegiance.

"'All for one and one for all' eh Betty!" Daphne said, clearly still reading Elizabeth's thoughts.

"Stop listening to my........" Elizabeth stopped abruptly.

All three witches sensed the danger at once but it was too late. The beasts were upon them before they knew it. Shiona was quick enough to set off a bright, light show from her wand which managed to confuse them but did not stop them.

"Run!" She shouted at the others and unwittingly falling in with George's plan, they separated.

Each witch had at least a dozen beasts tailing them. Elizabeth's heart sank as she watched Shiona and Daphne disappear into the woods. If she did not stay near them, she would be of no use to them. Without them she was a mere mortal, able to generate enough fear of her own to feed Darius for a lifetime! She desperately tried to tune into their energy fields and although the red and green vibrations were clear, they were getting weaker and weaker.

STAY CLose... Shiona's shout became a whisper in Elizabeth's head. The witches were gone.

Elizabeth was powerless again and the vicious animals were snarling at her heals. What could she do now that she was devoid of power?

Trust your instincts. Victor's words flashed in her mind. But listening to her instincts was a relatively new skill for Elizabeth and she racked her brains to try to find something, anything that could help her now. All at once she remembered her confrontation with Wilhelm. In her own way, she had confused Wilhelm by refusing to be intimidated by him and by playing a little game of her own.

Elizabeth's magical powers had gone and her physical strength was starting to wane. The pack of human animals were getting closer and closer. She would not be able to stay ahead of them for much longer. She had no choice. The only option open to her was to try and confuse the beasts. Grabbing handfuls of stones as she ran she made her way to higher ground. Her resolve gave her the energy to carry on.

Just a little bit further. Not far now. She told herself as she clambered up the hill. The beasts were snapping and snarling at her heals, but she still managed to make headway as a rush of adrenaline hit her. She knew what she was about to do was crazy but it was all she could think of. She only hoped it would work. She reached an overhanging of rock, a vantage point. She jumped onto the higher ground and stopped, turned to face the beasts and roared at the top of her voice.

The noise stopped them dead in their tracks. Suddenly it was their turn to feel threatened and disorientated.

Elizabeth knew this was only a minor victory. The confusion of the pack animals was paramount to the plan working, but what next? *Play to your strengths* this time it was her mother's voice in her head. Unfortunately, without the witches, Elizabeth did not know what her strengths were but she knew she was getting very good at bluffing.

She stood on top of the outcropping of rock not daring to move. The beasts were still and silent, their soulless eyes staring at her. Elizabeth played with the stones she had grabbed, hoping she could use them as weapons. They felt like pebbles in her hand, no more able to do damage to these vile beasts than a sponge. She was out of ideas and nearly out of time. She knew it would not be long before the creatures realised she was no threat.

One by one, the beasts started to sniff the air, getting restless. One sat down on the ground and started to lick his wounded feet. Elizabeth could not understand it. From the moment she screamed the creatures had stopped their attack, and now it looked as though they were getting thoroughly bored with her. Elizabeth stayed as still as possible. She watched and waited and after a few minutes two of the creatures turned and made their way down the hill walking away from her. Those that remained, milled around aimlessly looking bizarrely like teenagers, awkward and inexperienced not really knowing what to do.

Suddenly, a bloodcurdling scream bellowed from the forest floor. The beasts' ears pricked up and they sped quickly towards the sound. Unable to stop herself, Elizabeth started to follow but what she saw froze her to the spot. Below her in the forest, illuminated by a hideous green glow were Daphne and Shiona. They lay on their backs seemingly frozen, being carried aloft by George's beasts, their eyes staring fixedly above them.

"No, no!" Elizabeth cried. "This is all wrong!"

She knew there was no way that Daphne and Shiona could have been out-manoeuvred by those dumb animals or George. The women were far too clever and powerful for that.

"They must be planning *something*," she said to herself and started to climb down to see if she could help.

When all at once Elizabeth saw Lord Darius striding through the trees, hands held towards the witches encasing them in a muddy green spell. She sagged. There *was* no way that George and his beasts could have defeated the witches, Elizabeth was right about that much. But George was not alone. He brought Lord Darius back from the brink through the fear of the villagers and the certain knowledge he could not fail. Darius was the reason for the witches' helplessness. And Elizabeth was powerless to stop him.

Chapter Twenty-Three

Elizabeth stood rooted to the spot. The sight of the witches, these phenomenal women, useless under Darius's spell was sickening. She stared at the unearthly mob manhandling her friends through the forest. She could hear the voice of Darius rising up towards her, bellowing orders and laughing cruelly. He was in control again and was relishing every moment. Elizabeth could not tear her eyes away from the hideous sight. They were frozen solid in a block of Darius's power. Motionless and helpless, they were Darius' prizes. His spoils of war.

Agreeing to visit Branko all those months ago, Elizabeth was under no illusion that she would be a great asset. She was new to everything magical and every day that passed in the witches company was like a new day at school. And like school she always felt out of her depth, slightly bullied with much to learn. That was *before* she found out how utterly powerless she was without the witches. How on earth could she be of any help now?

From the safety of her vantage point Elizabeth could just about see the castle. She watched the terrifying entourage until every last one of them had disappeared through its gates. She was numb. Unable to move. Elizabeth was lost and lonely and without the two women at her side, she could not summon one inspiring thought about how to help. The sun was beginning to rise, illuminating Castle Von Diederich. It looked harmless enough, like ancient ruins, there was no hint of the evil that was taking place inside.

The forest was quiet. All evidence of the previous night's commotion gone. Elizabeth could only hear the sound of her own breath, even and deep, each inhalation her only sustenance. She could see the plumes of steam rising from her mouth in the cold morning air. She shivered and in that small action she suddenly became aware of her body. Stiff and aching, scratched and bruised, every muscle felt the aftermath of the battle. She wanted to stop. To lie down and sleep. To close her eyes and hope it would all be over soon. But she could not stay where she was. Not only was she exposed to the elements as the damp night turned into a frosty morning but she was also visible from the castle. She had to move.

She crouched down slowly and her whole body screamed. She stood and stretched again, trying to bring life back into her limbs before climbing down from the overhanging rock. Satisfied that her injuries were superficial she jumped and landed with a thud. She looked around cautiously hoping the dull noise had not given away her hiding place.

She looked around cautiously, checking for signs of Darius' mutant family or the soulless villagers. When she was sure she was alone she carefully crept down the hill trying not to over-exert her battered and bruised body. Each step brought a loosening of muscles and an easing of aches. She reached the bottom of the hill and considered going back to Greta and Yorik. Maybe she could try to find some unaffected villagers and come back to the castle mob handed. This was probably her best and only course of action, but Elizabeth could not shake the sight of Shiona and Daphne being carried like cadavers by the beasts. Before she could do anything else, she had to know if they were alive. She wandered slowly and silently through the forest and made her way to the castle.

She approached cautiously. It was not hard to find a way in. Castle Von Diederich was mostly in ruins. Elizabeth kept low as she picked her way through the fallen stones of the once magnificent fortress. She stopped suddenly as she heard a noise. Two of George's villager-creatures were crossing the courtyard ahead of her. Elizabeth watched them as they passed. After Gretchen, Elizabeth's next sight of the creatures was at the masquerade ball where their dancing skills were better than her own. Then, once they had been ordered to chase, they were nothing but beasts, searching out their next kill. Now, in the cold light of day, they once again looked like normal people. Standing on two legs instead of bent down on all fours. They were merely men. They looked like a couple of security guards checking the perimeter.

"What has George done to you?" Elizabeth said under her breath and secretly hoped that one day she would have the chance to interrogate the vile little man herself.

The castle was bustling and alive. There was no denying the excitement. Lord Darius and his people were closer to invading Elizabeth's world than they had ever been. Nothing could stop them now.

A door opened at the other end of the courtyard opposite Elizabeth and the man in question stepped out. Darius looked every inch the triumphant conqueror. He looked taller and younger than Elizabeth remembered and she could see for herself that his powers were returning. Out-witting the witches was his coup d'etat. He raised his face skywards as he stepped into the sun, drinking in his success. Behind him Elizabeth could see the rest of his family appear in the doorway. Ingrid and Diana were chatting and giggling like schoolgirls; Victor had his usual expression of fearful dismay but Wilhelm looked agitated.

"What about the other one?" Wilhelm asked pulling at his father's sleeve like a petulant schoolboy and all at once Victor became more animated, listening intently to his father's reply.

"What about her Wilhelm?" Darius asked. "She is useless without her *friends*. She is the least of our worries."

"But father she.........."

"WILHELM!" Darius screamed, "I will not have you chasing around the countryside for a helpless animal because she embarrassed you. You should not have been so stupid in the first place! Now you will come with me and we will ready ourselves for the witches' final encounter."

"What else can you do to them father?" Victor asked timidly, "they are powerless now."

"Oh Victor," Darius laughed cruelly, "they can be of so much more use to us. We still have not yet taken *all* of the villagers, yes? Imagine their terror when they see the defenders of their realm burnt at the stake, *after* we have separated them from their souls," he laughed maniacally. "Then – I will defy them not to fear me!"

Darius swept away unaware of Victor's horrified expression. Wilhelm, however, did notice.

"I am watching you Victor," Wilhelm said menacingly, "I do not know how but I am sure you helped that little bitch last night." He pushed Victor to one side and followed his father.

Ingrid and Diana witnessed the exchange between Wilhelm and his little brother and they flanked Victor as they walked away from the courtyard. From a distance their embrace might have looked genuine, a mother and sister comforting him after a distasteful encounter with his sibling, but this was not a normal family. Elizabeth could tell that Diana and Ingrid were intrigued by Wilhelm's comments and wanted to know more.

Elizabeth's heart went out to Victor. She could not believe that he had lasted so long with that horrific family. The family who were convinced they had won. Against all the odds they had finally beaten the witches and were preparing to take over Elizabeth's world. But they had one more opponent to face – Elizabeth. She may be useless, but if nothing else, she would carry on fighting to save the witches – or die trying.

She waited until the vile family were out of sight. She was determined to find Daphne and Shiona and she had an inkling where they might be. Now she was close to them she could feel the strength of their powers once again inside her mortal body. She eyed the door at the other end of the courtyard, the door Darius had just walked through. It was not hard to imagine the scene. The witches captured and the evil Lord Darius crowing over them forcing them to cower before him. *It's a safe bet they're in there,* she thought.

She edged around the walls of the courtyard making her way carefully to the door. She jumped at every noise, sure she would be discovered at any moment; convinced that every breath she took was her last. Inch by inch, moment by moment Elizabeth felt herself get closer to the witches. She could feel their energy and her power getting stronger and stronger until finally she reached the door. Carefully she opened it and gazed into the unknown. It was dark and damp inside and there was a stairway spiralling downwards. She listened for a noise – nothing. She ventured inside and closed the door slowly behind her as quietly as possible.

She was immediately plunged into darkness. She waited as long as she dared for her eyes to grow accustomed to the dark. There was no light to navigate the winding steps. She leant heavily on the wall next to her, using it as her only guide in the pitch black. Further and further she spiralled down the unending staircase blind to anything around her. She slipped on moss half way down, lost her footing and fell hard. Downwards she tumbled, hitting every stone step as she fell. Finally she jammed her foot into one of the steps and somehow she managed to stop herself from falling all the way to the bottom. Carefully she stood up wondering if her body could take any more knocks.

After what seemed like an eternity she finally saw a hint of green light at the end of the staircase. She quickened her pace. Within minutes she had reached the bottom and a damp and dreary dungeon faced her. The cells stood in rows either side of the long corridor. The flagstone floor was covered in straw. There would have been no light if not for a sickening green glow at the end of the corridor of cells. Elizabeth recognised it immediately. It was the same green that trapped the witches when they were dragged like fugitives from the forest. This was Darius' legacy.

Elizabeth ran towards the light slipping and sliding on the damp stone floor. She imagined she would find the witches frozen in horror like the chilling statues she saw in the forest. She wondered if they were dead or alive. And if they *were* alive, she wondered how on earth she was going to free them?

What she was not prepared for was the sight that awaited her when she finally reached the cell. The green light filled the chamber, hurting her eyes after the dark of the dungeon. As she squinted through the discomfort she saw Shiona. Not wracked with agony or frozen like a statue but pacing up and down, grumbling and moaning. Behind her sitting on a long bench against the wall, shoes off, rubbing her feet was the undeniable, gigantic form of Daphne.

"H...Hello?" said Elizabeth bemused.

"Betty!"

"What on earth are you doing here Elizabeth?" Shiona raced to the bars to greet her.

"What do you think?" Elizabeth said. "I've come to rescue you."

"And just how do you think you're going to do that?" Shiona asked.

"Uh, well....I hadn't really got that far."

"That's my Betty!" Daphne said from the back of the cell, still rubbing her enormous feet.

Shiona sighed, "I really wish there was something you could do

Elizabeth, but I'm afraid we're fresh out of luck."

"No we're not!" Elizabeth said. "I've got my powers back now, look."

With that Elizabeth grabbed the door of the cell opposite the witches and within seconds the hinges had melted and the door collapsed to the floor.

"Brilliant Betty!" Daphne said rising from her seat. "Now try that over here."

Pleased with herself Elizabeth grabbed the door of the glowing green cell. She performed the same spell.

Nothing happened.

"Hang on a minute," she said concentrating harder.

Doubling her efforts she put all she had into blasting the door from its hinges, straining in the attempt.

"Careful Betty, you might hurt yourself."

Nothing happened.

"What's going on?" Elizabeth asked.

"That wasn't funny Daphne," Shiona said. "We're all useless under Darius's spell. He's stronger than ever thanks to George. Everything he lost in the battle with Baron Von Diederich is back. He's reborn. We can't do anything whilst we're under his spell Elizabeth, and neither can you."

Elizabeth stared at the light that encased the witches, "there must be something......"

A noise at the end of the corridor startled Elizabeth.

"Quickly, hide!" Shiona hissed at her.

Elizabeth climbed over the cell door that she had practiced her magic on. She scrambled to the back of the cell as she heard footsteps approaching. She backed herself into the darkest corner and attempted a disappearing spell. She had never tried it before and she was not even sure it was possible. But she believed that if she could blend into the background she would be safe. The witches were watching her, their concern was clear. But once she applied her improvised spell Shiona nodded. *Wow!* Elizabeth thought, *it must have worked!*

And not before time, seconds after she nodded to Elizabeth, Shiona was face to face with Darius, Diana and George.

"How are you liking your new home." Darius asked smugly.

"Loving it actually Dario," Daphne said getting up from the bench and approaching the bars brazenly, "how are you enjoying your last moment of power?"

Darius only laughed. "That is what I have always loved about you Daphne, your sense of humour."

"Oh this is no joke Darius," Shiona said grasping the cell bars, looking Darius directly in the eye, "do you honestly think your spell can hold us forever."

Shiona's bravado amused Darius. "Well it seems to be doing a good job so far does it not? After all, I have been given insider knowledge by one of your *friends*."

Darius pushed George towards the cell. The witches just stared at him.

"Is there nothing you want to say to your – betrayer?" Darius asked.

"No Darius," Shiona said, "we have nothing to say to this person."

"Well there is something *I* have to say to *you*," George fumed, "Lord Darius is my *friend* now. He has offered me a friendship that goes beyond your comprehension Shiona AND," he said turning his attention to Daphne, "he is a *loyal* friend!"

"Father?" Diana said sidling up to Darius regarding him with puppy dog eyes.

"Yes, yes my dear, I have not forgotten. Sorry George, my *friend*."

This time it was George's turn to look confused, "My Lord?"

"My daughter tells me you have an obsessive interest in her," Darius said coolly, "that you pay her too much attention. She does not like it George."

"I'm sorry," George said to Darius, then he turned his attention to Diana, "I'm sorry. I just thought we could be friends, that's all."

"What makes you think I would want to be friends with you," Diana said haughtily. "You are a hideous little man and I was only being kind to you because of my father."

"My LORD!" George said.

"Enough *friend*," Darius said oozing coldness and cruelty. "You have served your purpose well, now you will die along with those you betrayed."

His magical powers returned to him, Darius effortlessly lifted George into the air as Diana opened the door of the cell right next to the witches'. Darius flung him inside and George crashed to the ground.

Elizabeth heard a sickening crack as he landed followed by an ear-splitting scream.

"Please, my Lord I think I've broken........"

"ENOUGH!" Darius cried and held his hands towards the cell door which slammed shut violently. George cowered beneath his withering stare. Darius composed himself and walked towards the witches.

"Monster though I am," Darius said conspiratorially, "I cannot abide a traitor. Although he has helped me, he has betrayed you. *That* I cannot forgive."

"You're a lunatic," Shiona said quietly.

"Perhaps," Darius replied, "but what ruler throughout history has ever been completely in their right mind? Do not worry if you cannot sleep well tonight dear ladies, tomorrow you shall sleep for eternity."

Turning on his heal, his malicious daughter dripping off his arm, the evil Lord Darius walked away from the prisoners and out of the dungeon.

The witches waited in silence as the footsteps of father and daughter receded into the distance. George groaned pitifully in the stillness. Then they heard the soft thud of the door at the top of the staircase being closed. Elizabeth waited and watched for a few moments more. When she was sure Darius had gone, she stepped out of the corner of the cell.

George gasped. "You! What are you doing here?"

"What do you think?" Elizabeth said impatiently. She stumbled over the door, out of the cell and walked quietly to the witches. "What can I do?"

"Darius will know you're here," George said before the witches had a chance to answer her question, "If *I* tell him that you're here then I will once again be in favour. MY L....."

George's shout was cut short by Elizabeth's spell that held his lips tightly together. The power of the witches was undeniably strong in Elizabeth's hands.

"What do you think George?" Elizabeth hissed. "Do you think he's going to embrace you and take you back into the fold? Wake up! He hates you, his daughter hates you and I'm pretty damn sure the rest of the family hate you too."

"Let it go Georgie," Daphne said softly.

George whimpered unable to speak and clearly in pain from Darius's attack.

"Help him Betty," Daphne asked.

Elizabeth looked at her bemused, "After everything he's done!?"

"Please Betty, for my sake. I know he's not a bad person. I know it."

Sighing Elizabeth walked over to George. He was huddled on the floor of the cell. Reaching through the bars she took hold of his injured leg and began to heal it. As the bone knitted together it was clear that George was in agony. His muffled cries of pain through Elizabeth's gagging spell were testimony to that. After a few minutes, George lay back breathing heavily and sweating. The bone was healed and Elizabeth removed her gagging spell.

"Thank you," he said quietly.

"Thank you Betty," Daphne said holding out her hand through the bars to Elizabeth.

Elizabeth rushed over to take it. Suddenly Elizabeth's emotions overwhelmed her, she wept softly into her auntie's hand. Daphne stroked her hair.

"You're an emotional one aren't you Betty," Daphne said trying to hold back her own tears. "It's good to see you too. We thought you were a gonner for sure."

"That's right!" Shiona said moving closer to her niece, "how on earth did you get away Elizabeth?"

"I've no idea," Elizabeth said composing herself. "They were on me, so close I could smell their breath. I knew I had nothing to fight them with, so I thought I would try to brazen it out. Stupid eh?" she said looking at the disapproving faces of her aunties. "And then when I turned to face them, they suddenly got bored of me, like I was no longer worth the effort. Then there was a scream and they just ran away."

"That was probably me Betty," Daphne said quietly. "It got a little bit hairy down there."

"I'm so sorry I wasn't with you." Elizabeth said as a new wave of emotion hit her.

"I'm glad you weren't Elizabeth, then you would be in here too and what good would that do us?"

Suddenly they heard a noise from above them as the door from the courtyard opened once again.

"You have to go," George said weakly. "They know you're here."

"How could they know that?" Elizabeth hissed and rounded on him, "*Who* could have told them? Do you have a psychic link with them George is that what you've done? I've just healed you and you repay me by giving me up to Darius!?" Elizabeth crouched down next to him on the other side of his cell, her anger rising. "I can always break the other leg myself George, then you really will have to go crawling back."

"It's not Darius." George said. "It's the animals."

"What?" Elizabeth said standing up and looking towards the staircase.

"They've probably sensed you are here by now."

"Oh no!" Elizabeth said. "What do I do? Shiona what can I do? Last night was a fluke. Please Shiona, tell me what to do!"

Shiona looked towards the staircase in a panic. "I just don't know... ...I don't..." she began.

"Last night wasn't a fluke," George interrupted.

For a moment Elizabeth stared at George, still not knowing what to make of this odious little man.

"What are you playing at now?" she hissed.

"They've been trained to seek out the witches' power. When you ran further away from the sisters you actually *saved* yourself. They're like dogs chasing after a ball. They get no reward if they bring back the wrong one. Even if there are hundreds of balls for them to choose from, they still need to bring the right one home. As soon as you were far enough away from the witches you were only a distraction."

The creatures were coming down the stairs, getting closer.

"And now?" Elizabeth asked George backing away from the noise.

"Now you're powerful once again. They've smelt your magic and they're hunting you. Clever eh?" George said, impressed with himself. "There's no point them wasting their energy if you're no threat."

"What can we do Georgie?" Daphne asked in a soft tone, as though she were speaking to a child. "There's got to be something."

"There's nothing," George said distractedly. "You were clever enough to make sure she was powerful when she was with you and now that's going to destroy her. Nothing personal," he said looking at Elizabeth, "it would have been the same for any witch they brought with them."

Elizabeth had backed all the way to the end of the corridor of cells. She stretched out her arms and looked down at them.

"Take it away!" she said.

"I can't...." George began.

"Not you!" Elizabeth hissed and turned towards the witches. "Take it away. Take your power away from me."

"But Elizabeth you've got a chance....." Shiona said.

"A chance to blast them into dust, destroying the bodies of your friends, whilst letting Darius know I'm here. Just take you're powers away from me. I'm gonna lose them eventually anyway. Just take them away!"

"Betty, we're useless in here in case you haven't notice, we couldn't take power even if we wanted to."

"*I'm* not useless." Elizabeth said simply. "Tell me what to do."

The creatures were getting closer, soon they would be at the bottom of the stairs.

"Elizabeth really, I don't think........."

"She's right," George said, "it's her only chance."

"Please Shiona!" Elizabeth said her fear rising.

"Ok, ok, but if you get out of here you have to try to get word to your Mum," Shiona said.

"Of course," Elizabeth said. "Now what do I do?"

"Just give it back Betty."

"That's right Elizabeth. You're the one taking it from us, you just have to send it back to us."

"How?" Elizabeth said staring wildly towards the door at the bottom of the stairs. Suddenly she saw one of the creatures emerge from the gloom.

"You have to figure that out for yourself Elizabeth," Shiona said. "Somehow you've taught yourself a way to use the power that's available to you. Now you have to un-learn."

Elizabeth could not keep her eyes from the staircase. The creatures were pouring through, growling as they came, alert to their prize.

"Whatever you do, do it quickly," George said flatly.

Suddenly the beasts at the edge of the group caught a glimpse of Elizabeth.

"Try something Betty! Anything!"

A boy-beast at the front of the pack growled softly, he had Elizabeth in his sights. He crouched low, edging towards her.

215

"Any minute now," George said gleefully.

"Elizabeth! Give it back or use it!" Shiona said.

Elizabeth heard the low growl of the beast deepen as he sensed his prey, she could feel the rumble of it reverberate through the dungeon. She was starting to panic. She knew she had to try something but as with every spell she had to calm her mind. *That* was proving to be the hardest part. She took a few deep, shaky breaths and closed her eyes trying to ignore the imminent danger.

As the seconds ticked by one beast after another became alerted to Elizabeth's presence. Even with her eyes closed Elizabeth could sense the awakening within them. They were no longer hunting their prey, they had found it.

"BETTY!" Daphne screamed as the beast-boy jumped towards Elizabeth. Elizabeth summoned all the power she had and sent it zooming towards the witches. Like pushing out the last of her breath she tried to lose every last molecule of magic. She did it. It flew towards the witches in a brilliant burst of white light. Yelping in the blinding light the beasts jumped back. Elizabeth sighed in relief as she watched the power circle around the dungeon. Suddenly it honed in on its target and zipped towards Daphne and Shiona. But it bounced off Darius's spell. Needing somewhere to go it searched out another target and finding Elizabeth it poured straight back into her.

"Shit!" Elizabeth said as she felt the power within.

"Elizabeth! There's no need for that language!"

"Shiona! We've got other things to worry about than Betty's potty-mouth!"

"What am I going to do now?" Elizabeth asked. She had failed to give the magic back but she had succeeded in momentarily confusing the beasts. They were trained to follow the witches' magic but did not know where it was going. Once the power had settled back in Elizabeth the pack refocused on her and resumed the hunt. But Elizabeth had noted the effect of displacing the magic on them and she tried again. Once again the blinding light confused the creatures but once again the power bounced off Darius's spell and sought out an alternate home.

"What's gonna happen, what's gonnna happen?" George sang, enjoying the spectacle.

"Just use it against them, Elizabeth," Shiona hissed, "you've got enough power to destroy them."

"NO!" Elizabeth said as the blast of magic hit her again. "They're your friends!"

She forced the magic back towards the witches, praying that this time the strength of it would penetrate Darius's force field but it only sprang back, flew around the dungeon for a moment and settled into Elizabeth once more.

The coursing power was sparkling through the air like fireworks. The threat of attack was gone each time she cast the magic away. Most of the creatures were confused by the sight, but the beast-boy at the front of the pack was staring directly at Elizabeth. Even in his animalistic state he knew that she was the source of the danger.

"Remember, remember the 5th of November......." George began reciting as he watched the dungeon light up with magic.

Suddenly Elizabeth hit on idea, "use it wisely Georgie porgie," she said and with all her might she threw the magic at the unsuspecting George.

The effect was immediate. George was thrown backwards from the blast of the spell. Opposite him Elizabeth collapsed in a heap exhausted from the effort. The beast-boy was upon her, growling, only inches away, set for his final attack. He was so close to Elizabeth that she could smell his foul breath. She looked at her aunties and saw them staring horrified at the beast that was about to take their niece's life. Elizabeth squeezed her eyes shut. When suddenly everything changed.

The next few agonising seconds felt like an eternity to Elizabeth. The growl from the beast changed slowly and he began to sniff the air between her and George. He knew something was different but he went back to Elizabeth, his nose rustling her hair.

"Come on, come on!" Daphne said, willing the beast to find his next victim.

Behind him the other villager-creatures had already refocused their attention. All eyes were on George as he lay unconscious at the back of his cell, their snarls intensified as they found their target. They became agitated and one or two of them started to bark. This set a chain reaction in place as each creature one after the other barked at their newly acquired victim.

Finally, Elizabeth's hunter shifted his attention. Giving Elizabeth one last snort he reluctantly joined his pack and added his own voice to the yapping cacophony.

"Quickly," Shiona shouted barely audible over the din, "you've got to go. Darius will be here any minute. Try to get word to Gladys."

Elizabeth took a step towards the exit when a sickening thought struck her. If she could not find a way to save them, then this could be the last time she would see her aunties. She rushed over to them, and grabbed hold of Shiona through the bars. Daphne joined the embrace and all three women sobbed quietly.

"Go," Shiona said pushing Elizabeth away.

Elizabeth took one last look at the women who trained her, inspired her and sometimes bullied her, and turned away quickly, before it was too late.

The villager-beasts blocked her way as they stood en masse crowded around George's cell. Frustrated that they were unable to reach him through the bars they carried on growling and yapping. Elizabeth had no choice but to pick her way through them. Breathing heavily she inched forward towards the staircase, stepping carefully through the assembled creatures. For the most part they ignored Elizabeth, once or twice she attracted a curious sniff but when they decided she was no threat, they let her pass.

Within minutes she reached the end of the corridor of cells. She chanced a quick look back but she could not see her aunties, the creatures blocked her view. Beneath the growls she could hear George stirring, he was regaining consciousness and panicking as he was faced with the horrifying sight of his own creations turning on him. Elizabeth smirked at the irony but she could not help question the wisdom of giving the witches' incredible power to this madman. But it was too late to change things now.

As fast as she could she raced up the slippery, spiral staircase. There was nowhere to hide once she was on it so she had to keep going. The noise of the yapping, growling creatures was deafening. Darius and his family were sure to have heard. Elizabeth needed to make her escape before Darius reached the entrance of the dungeons or it was all for nothing.

Once she was at the top, she listened intently at the door. She could definitely hear raised voices but they were far away. She opened the door an inch and peeped through. The courtyard looked deserted so she stepped out into the sunlight, carefully shutting the door behind her, leaving it as she found it.

She ran back to the pile of rubble that had hidden her when she first saw Darius emerge from the doorway. As she crouched down behind the rocks Darius and his family rounded the corner, alerted by the commotion in the cells. *That was close*, Elizabeth thought, seconds later and Darius would have caught her mid-flight.

She waited as the family disappeared down the stairs then rested heavily, her back against the pile of rocks. She closed her eyes and took a few deep breaths waiting for the right time to make her escape. As before her thoughts turned to Yorik and Greta.

Suddenly, she sensed someone close to her, she opened her eyes and standing in front of her, staring down at her with a malicious grin, was Wilhelm.

Elizabeth raised her eyes to the skies, "Oh, give me a break!"

Chapter Twenty-Four

The sun blazed overhead and Elizabeth squinted at the figure of Wilhelm towering over her.

"Hello little witch," Wilhelm said menacingly.

Elizabeth sighed. "Hello Wilhelm," she said.

She had found various cunning ways out of one terrible situation after another, but now she was stumped. What on earth was she supposed to do about Wilhelm and his bruised ego?

"Are you not scared little witch?" Wilhelm said bristling under her indifference.

"No," she said honestly.

"WHY NOT!" He bellowed and grabbed her by the shoulders lifting her off the ground.

She hung in the air as Wilhelm held her firmly, his nails digging into her skin. His face was so close to hers she could see the pit marks of his open pores.

"WHY ARE YOU NOT AFRAID?"

He spat the words at Elizabeth and she turned away from the moist blast.

"Because......" she said, wondering how the hell she was going to get out of this one, "because........" and then she hit upon an idea, "I'm glad I've found you!"

"What?" He said suspiciously.

"I've been looking for you," she said looking earnestly into his eyes. "I needed to tell you – you were right!"

"What was I right about?" he said and roughly lowered her to the ground careful to keep hold of her with his firm and painful grasp.

Elizabeth marvelled at how easy it was to fool him. It was obvious all his years of supernatural existence he had rarely encountered a dishonest foe. Any treachery in Branko came from one source only – Wilhelm's family.

"You were right about me," she continued, "I have absolutely NO powers! The witches told me last night."

"You mean..... you did not know?"

"NO! They fooled me and humiliated me." Elizabeth was enjoying this lie and his gullibility. "They gave me that ridiculous twig...."

"This one?" Wilhelm produced Sonny from inside his coat.

Elizabeth's heart sank at the sight of Sonny. It looked as though it had been trampled half to death and was losing any spark of life. The bark had peeled back exposing dry flesh underneath. No longer able to perform her nightly growing spell Elizabeth's broom was clearly suffering.

"Yes! That one," she said grabbing it from him careful not to let her concern show. "They told me it was a magic wand. A *magic wand* for goodness sake! They made a fool out of me Wilhelm." She faked a sob. "You were the only one who told me the truth. They've been lying to me for months but *you* were honest with me. Thank you." She dissolved into a fit of mock misery.

Wilhelm was utterly perplexed. Once again his confrontation with Elizabeth was not playing out as he had imagined.

"Do you think I am going to fall for this nonsense," he said seizing her again.

"Why else do you think I'm here?" She said looking him straight in the eye. "To save the other witches? And how am I supposed to do that with *no* powers? Think about it Wilhelm, what other reason would I have come here for? You offered me a life, a magical life that I could share with you. Is that offer still open?"

Wilhelm's stare bore into Elizabeth for any sign of dishonestly but she knew he would not be able to see through her act, her life depended on it.

Suddenly they heard a noise from behind them as George was dragged kicking and screaming from the dungeons, followed closely by his yelping creations.

"Get down!" Elizabeth said and forced Wilhelm to duck down behind her rocky hiding place. In his confusion, Wilhelm dutifully obeyed.

They watched as George protested his innocence.

"Please my Lord," he said, "this is not my fault."

"What is wrong with these beasts then George my *friend*?" Darius sneered. "They have been trained to find the ones with power. Are you trying to tell me that your training was wrong?"

"No! No, I did everything I said I would," George said, "this has nothing to do with me it was......."

Suddenly George spied Elizabeth behind the rocks. She looked pleadingly at him. She knew she was taking a risk giving him her power, but she prayed Daphne was right about him.

"Please George, please." She said quietly. She closed her eyes and hoped he could hear her thoughts. Wilhelm looked at her suspiciously.

"....your fault!" George said finally.

Elizabeth did not dare look, she was sure that George was pointing towards her hiding place and any moment now she would be discovered.

"What was my fault?" Darius asked and from the tone in his voice he was clearly perplexed.

Elizabeth looked up. George was not pointing at Elizabeth at all, he was directing his accusations at Darius.

"The pack has turned on me, because their leader turned on me first," George continued. "You! You are the alpha male, my Lord. You have no further use for me, so neither do they."

Now it was Darius's turn to look bemused.

"Bring him," he said to the yapping beasts, "and stop that infernal noise!"

The group of beasts quietened as much as they could in their animal state and followed obediently behind Darius dragging George with them.

"Thank you George," Elizabeth said with relief when all at once she remembered her companion. She turned to face Wilhelm. He was no longer crouching with her but had risen to his full height, a smug smile on his face, his sickening green eyes piercing into her.

"What a clever little witch you are," he said menacingly. "You almost had me fooled - again."

Elizabeth got to her feet and backed away from him hoping her luck had not just run out.

"You did something to that foul little man and he is protecting you is he not? What did you do?" Wilhelm said circling her. "Tell me and maybe I will spare your life."

"I gave him my powers," Elizabeth said simply and another idea struck her.

"*Gave* him your powers?" Wilhelm scoffed. "How is that even possible if you have no powers to give?"

"But I do actually. Let me see if I can show you."

Wilhelm smiled at his helpless victim, amused by her audacity. Elizabeth, however, had one last trick up her sleeve. She closed her eyes and sought out George's power, the power that lurked within the witches, the same power that now coursed through George's veins. She found it quickly, and retrieved it easily. It sat uncomfortably with George and it gave no resistance when Elizabeth summoned it back to her. The familiar feeling washed over her like a wave.

She acted quickly. All of a sudden Sonny jumped back to life, the useless brown stick now became an efficient flying machine. Elizabeth hopped onto it and soared away from Wilhelm's grasp. But Wilhelm's reactions were also quick. He leapt into the air behind her, quickly changing into the vicious winged-creature, and gave chase.

Elizabeth knew she could not go far. She had to stay close to the witches otherwise she would fall like a stone from the sky and end up a useless lump on the ground. She circled around the castle careful to stay as close as she could to the dungeon but her assailant was agile and clever. Her few months of training were nothing compared to his decades of supernatural power. Wilhelm flew closer and closer grabbing at the witch, his claws skimming her and Sonny and at anything they could reach. He swiped at Sonny's bristles and Elizabeth momentarily lost control of the broom. She regained her balance quickly but she knew this game of cat and mouse couldn't last for long, she had to think fast. The wall on the far side of the castle was getting closer, and Elizabeth knew exactly what to do. Adapting the same stunt that she had perfected in the aircraft hangar months ago, she sped up and headed for the boundary wall with Wilhelm hot on her heels.

Aiming straight for the wall she flew closer and closer, until only inches away, she let go of the broom and dropped from the sky. She plummeted downwards as Sonny rocketed skywards. Unable to manoeuvre away, Wilhelm screamed just as he smashed straight into the side of the castle.

He was knocked unconscious and fell quickly past Elizabeth his weight a much heavier force for gravity. But Elizabeth was still not out of trouble. She summoned Sonny and he looped away from the castle and flew quickly underneath her taking her weight. She pulled up just before she hit the ground.

She dismounted clumsily. She hurried over to the unconscious Wilhelm and kicked him to make sure he was no longer a threat. She smiled. "That's the way to do it Betty," she said quietly to herself.

Suddenly she heard a growling noise behind her, followed by yelping then an almighty howl. The beasts were once again alerted to her presence.

"Of course they're coming," she said knocking her hands against her head in frustration, "I've got my powers back!"

Elizabeth stared at the motionless Wilhelm and listened to the yapping of George's creatures getting closer and closer. She knew that if she were to give up her powers she would never defeat Wilhelm now that he was wise to her schemes. However, if she kept the power, she would be set upon by George's rampaging beasts. Elizabeth had no choice, for now the unconscious Wilhelm was the lesser threat, so she closed her eyes and hunted for George.

She searched with the same telepathic intuition that came with the witches' magic. But she could not find him. She heard the creatures getting closer, sickeningly close. She tried hard to quiet her mind. She did not want to risk another near miss like the one in the dungeon. She tried to retrace his steps. She focussed on the courtyard but Darius had moved him. It did not take long, however, before she sensed George's nervous erratic, energy. She started to telepathically follow the energy back to its source, like following a river back to the stream it sprang from. Up the steps of the castle her mind went, into the great hall, through the door at the back that she herself had gone through with Wilhelm and up the spiralling staircase. And there he was, tied up in the room she had seen her *perfection reflection*. Elizabeth sent her powers racing back to him.

She opened her eyes, once again listening for the monsters. They stopped dead in their tracks as soon as they sensed the witches' magic flying through the sky over their heads. After a moment the sound of the hoard slowly receded and Elizabeth was left alone with Wilhelm who was beginning to stir.

Elizabeth groaned and started to run from the slumped figure but she was not quick enough. Wilhelm grabbed her by the foot and she fell awkwardly to the ground, twisting her ankle. She tried to scramble away from him as he struggled to gain consciousness, but the pain in her ankle was excruciating and without the witches' magic there was no way she could heal herself. She crawled away.

Her attempt at escape was ridiculously laboured. Her ankle seared with pain, her body was scratched and bruised and she was exhausted from lack of sleep. Wilhelm was now awake and alert. He got up and walked menacingly towards Elizabeth.

Elizabeth could tell by the look on his face that playtime was over. He was not about to engage in another baffling conversation, he was merely going to end this grudge match quickly and he was going to make it painful. Out of luck and out of ideas, Elizabeth covered her head and waited for the onslaught to begin.

"What are you doing Wilhelm?"

It was Victor and Elizabeth had never been more relieved to hear his voice.

"This is none of your concern Victor. Leave us alone. NOW!"

"I will not let you hurt Elizabeth Wilhelm, I think you already know that."

"Oh, I am not going to hurt her Victor," Wilhelm said simply, "I am just going to kill her."

"No you are not," Victor said nervously, "I will not allow it."

Wilhelm laughed. "And just how do you think you are going to stop me, baby brother?"

"I do not want to hurt you Wilhelm, please just let her go, let *me* have her. She is harmless without the witches you know that."

"This one is cunning," Wilhelm said looking at Elizabeth and eyeing her suspiciously, "she may not have magical powers but she may yet be a danger to Father."

"Pah!" Victor snorted. "How could she possibly threaten Father now? He is more powerful than he has been for centuries. Please Wilhelm you know she interests me, just let me have her."

225

"I am sorry baby brother," Wilhelm said and he dragged Elizabeth to her feet, "I want her dead."

Elizabeth looked pleadingly at Victor.

Victor stared at the helpless woman and then seemed to reach a decision.

"I am sorry to have to do this Wilhelm," Victor said and began whispering in Wilhelm's ear.

Elizabeth could not understand what Victor was saying. He was speaking German, a language Elizabeth did not understand, but it was clearly affecting Wilhelm. He stared blankly at Elizabeth as though he were being hypnotised and he began to loosen his grip. Elizabeth squirmed away as Victor continued to whisper. Slowly Wilhelm's expression changed, his mouth started to curl down at the corners, his lip started to wobble and his eyes started to droop. As soon as Victor stopped Wilhelm slumped to the floor and howled in anguish.

"Come on," Victor said holding out his hand to Elizabeth, "I do not know how long we have got."

"My ankle," Elizabeth said. Victor picked her up in his arms and ran out of the castle grounds towards the village.

He kept on running until he felt sure they were a safe distance away. Then he carefully lowered Elizabeth to the ground.

"What did you say to him?" Elizabeth asked.

"I am not proud of what I have just done," Victor said quietly, "if the same was done to me, I am not sure I would survive it."

"What?" Elizabeth asked.

"I told you before Elizabeth that we all lived very different lives. We had families and friends, mothers and fathers, people who loved us, before Darius decided to use us to gain respectability. He needed a family of his own and we were the unfortunate ones that he chose. I still remember a little of my own family but Ingrid, Diana and Wilhelm have blocked it all out. I just reminded him that he was once human. I only pray he forgives me."

"*Forgives* you?" Elizabeth said. "Surely it's a blessing to know where you came from."

"Of course not Elizabeth! We are much better off not knowing, it is too agonising to remember."

"I'm sorry," she said quietly. "But surely if you have the memory of your human selves, then you have a little bit of your soul left."

"Yes, I believe that we are different from the poor villagers who have lost everything."

"I'm not so sure they have," Elizabeth said and suddenly an idea struck her.

"What are you thinking Elizabeth?"

"We found Gretchen, the *creature* Gretchen, in the village. Why was she there?" Elizabeth asked. "If Darius was planning a big reveal of his monstrous creations, why did Gretchen come to the village?"

"I do not know."

"I've got a theory," Elizabeth said lowering herself cautiously onto a nearby boulder. Victor sat on the ground next to her as she continued. "Soulless though they are, I think those poor bodies know there's something missing, especially Gretchen. If she was as lovely as everyone says she was then there must be some residual goodness in her."

"She was lovely," Victor said quietly.

"Did you know her?"

"I knew them all. And they were all wonderful people."

"You knew them *all*?" Elizabeth repeated.

Victor nodded silently and hugged his knees to his chest staring at his feet. He was every inch a gangly schoolboy and Elizabeth wondered how his mind had survived the immortal existence.

"Who did you know Victor?"

"I cannot say Elizabeth, please do not make me. It is too painful." He buried his face in his knees.

Elizabeth pulled him into an embrace.

"You don't have to tell me Victor if you don't want to. But if it's important, if it could help me save them and my aunties, then I really hope you can be brave."

Victor breathed heavily as Elizabeth comforted him.

"If I tell you, you will hate me, and I will have no one left."

"Look Victor," Elizabeth said, "Shiona has been trying to make me hate you ever since we came here. Even after your brother and sister destroyed the tavern and you stood by and let it happen, I still liked you. I know there's something good in you, I'm convinced of it. The same way that Daphne is convinced that George isn't all bad."

"They were my friends," Victor said raising his head, "I was so careful

227

to keep it a secret, but Darius found out about them somehow."

"Your *friends*?"

"Branko has been hidden for so many years Elizabeth," Victor said as he got up. "More years than I can even bear to remember. Life has been monotonous and dull. My family were cruel and the villagers hated me, I was so lonely."

Victor pulled away from her, got up and wandered into the forest.

"Victor!" She called after him, but he carried on walking slowly away. She tried putting weight on her swollen ankle. The worst of the pain had gone, all that was left was a dull ache. She hobbled after him.

"The young people in the village must have started to feel the boredom too," he continued when she caught up with him, "for every once in a while I would catch a glimpse of them near the castle. One day I went into the forest and I found a group of them. They panicked when they saw me and ran, but one of the boys fell and I helped him to his feet. I could tell he was curious about me. I told him not to fear me and he did not run away again. The conversation I had with that boy reminded me of home, of who I was. As we spoke I suddenly realised that I had made a friend.

"Word must have spread to the other young people in the village that one of Darius's family was not to be feared, and I acquired friend after friend after friend. Gretchen was very wary of me to begin with. She did not think I could be trusted at all but I did not mind. She was such a beautiful soul, I was happy just to be near her. But like the rest of them Elizabeth she finally came to trust me."

Victor was clearly remembering a happier time and Elizabeth listened silently.

"Life passed in a daydream for us for many years," he continued, "until the witches started to visit and then suddenly there was something to look forward to. The villagers would put on wonderful parties for the ladies and sometimes my young friends would try to sneak me in, disguised of course, so that I could enjoy the festivities.

"Then, a year ago, George came." Victor's face darkened with the memory. "He was a strange little man, but I honestly think if my father had not taken him from the tavern that first night, he might have been happy just to live out his life with the villagers, waiting to see the witches, to prove to them he was resourceful. But Darius is an animal.

And he could smell the stranger the moment he stepped through the shield. He knew there was someone different in Branko. He sought him out and kidnapped him from the tavern. He confused and brainwashed the man and used the information George had about the witches for his own gain.

"Then one day, Darius turned on me." Victor stopped suddenly and Elizabeth walked into him. Victor turned to her and carried on. "He announced that he had known about my friends for many years. He had not said a word because he was waiting for the time when he could use them. Use my relationship with them. That day came when George revealed he knew a way to separate a person's soul from its body. Father needed people to experiment on. So he used my friends."

"Oh Victor! I'm so sorry." Elizabeth and Victor were standing so close and she had to fight the urge to embrace him. He was lost in the memory and the revelation horrified Elizabeth.

"What did he do?" she asked. "Did he follow you when you were meeting them? Is that when he caught them and gave them to George?"

Victor looked away from Elizabeth.

"I'm so sorry Victor. I can't imagine what it must have been like for you. To see him hurt your friends like that. How can you bear to be up at the castle knowing you were betrayed so vilely?"

"It was not my father that did the betraying Elizabeth." Victor said quietly.

"What do you mean?" Elizabeth asked when a thought struck her. "It was Wilhelm wasn't it? He's such a little grunt. He would quite happily turn on you in favour of his father."

"No Elizabeth please, please listen."

"Greta and Yorik said they disappeared one by one," Elizabeth continued ignoring Victor. "They must have got it wrong. You would have warned the other villagers if you knew what was going to happen to them."

Victor sighed heavily and hung his head. "Greta and Yorik were right Elizabeth. The young people did disappear one by one."

"But......."

"Because one by one they came to see me, and one by one I led them to my father."

"I don't......."

"They trusted me, but I was too frightened of Darius, too scared of what he would do to me or what he would take from me to resist."

He walked slowly away from Elizabeth and stopped at the edge of the forest, the boundary of the village, and gazed at the picture perfect houses.

"He promised me that if I gave him my friends, then they would never leave me again. They would never have to go home, they would be my constant companions. And I believed him. I took him at his word, like the fool I am. But I was so lonely Elizabeth," he stepped pleadingly towards a horrified Elizabeth. "When I was with my friends I felt alive again, like the hideous existence I was living was only a dream and I was normal. I was like them. Gretchen was the last, and she was the hardest, she never really trusted me and part of me wanted her to run away, screaming. Tell the villagers what I was doing but she wanted to find her friends, to bring them home, so I told her the only way to do that was to join them. She did so willingly."

Elizabeth backed away from Victor, appalled by his revelation.

"*You* gave them to your father," she hissed as she backed into a tree that barred any further retreat, "because you were lonely?"

"You do not understand Elizabeth," Victor said holding her by the arms.

"You're right," she said shrugging him off, "I don't understand. I don't understand how you can stand there feeling sorry for yourself all the time knowing *you* destroyed those poor people. That *you* subjected them to evil experiments and helped tear their souls from their bodies. And I thought Wilhelm was evil! How could you Victor? How could you?!"

Elizabeth turned away from him and started limping towards the village.

"Please Elizabeth, do not leave me."

"Why?" She shouted over her shoulder. "So you can give me to your father too?"

"No! There is more that I have to tell you."

Victor jumped high in the sky and flew over Elizabeth's head landing in front of her blocking her path.

Elizabeth sneered, "I should have trusted Shiona, *you* are as much of a monster as the rest of them."

230

"Do not say that," Victor said grabbing her, "I want to help."

"How Victor? Just exactly how are you going to do that?"

"You talked of their souls, the lost souls of the villagers and you were right. They are not gone for ever."

"What do you mean?" Elizabeth asked suspiciously.

"When I set in motion this hideous chain of events even I, in my naivety, knew there was something horribly wrong. I made sure I was at every extraction that George made. And every time I rescued the soul of my friend by giving them a body, my body, until I could get them to safety."

Victor looked behind him at the village of Branko.

"Elizabeth, I took them home."

Elizabeth edged around Victor as he stared fixedly at the village. There was nothing left to say to him. She walked away carefully, not knowing what to believe anymore. After a few moments she heard a whoosh from behind her, she looked around and Victor was gone. She looked to the sky, he was airborne again, but this time he was heading back towards the castle.

Elizabeth carried on limping towards the deserted village. When she reached the safety of the houses she collapsed onto the ground, all strength gone from her exhausted body. She knew she could not make it to the tavern on the other side of the village. She also knew that it would not be long before Wilhelm would continue his pursuit. But before he did he was sure to warn Darius that Elizabeth might still be a problem. The alleyway she was hiding in would have to do until she could catch her breath and make a final dash for the tavern. Physically she was in a terrible state. Her body was exhausted from lack of sleep; her stomach was empty and nauseous; her wounds throbbed and her muscles ached and all she wanted to do was rest. But she was careful not to close her eyes. She knew that sleep would come quickly rendering her useless and exposed.

She looked around the alleyway, desperate to find something, anything to keep her alert. Suddenly she realised where she was, it was the same alleyway she had first encountered Gretchen. In her weakened state Elizabeth struggled to stay focussed on reality, images of her first alleyway attack in London swam in and out of view. She rubbed her eyes, she felt she had come a long way since that day, but not far enough.

She had no plan, no idea of how to help the witches and no clue how to get in touch with her mother.

Mum, what am I going to do? How on earth was she supposed to contact her mother? They were in a land lost in time and space. For the protection of the human race, hundreds of years ago, three witches hid this place in an alternative reality. How on earth was Gladys meant to get to them? The border was stronger again now and without the power of all three witches, there was no way she could get through.

Elizabeth recalled the dream she had about her mother. They had spoken so vividly, she remembered believing that her mother was really there, and she held on to her so tightly and did not want to let her go. But she had to, she had to wake up. Greta's soft voice had revived her and she woke in her little room at the tavern. She remembered feeling shamed by Greta's resilience. She remembered following Greta out of the room to help clear up what was left of the destroyed tavern. And she remembered something else. Just before she left the room she noticed something, something important.

"The amulet!" she said aloud.

It had been glowing in the room, just after the dream.

"The amulet! Is that how I contact her?"

The question was aimed at no one in particular but as the words left her mouth an earthenware pot came crashing out of a window opposite her and landed at her feet. Elizabeth stood up quickly ready to run. But everything went silent again and Elizabeth's curiosity was aroused. She looked up at the window on the first floor of the building on the opposite side of the alleyway to see who had thrown the pot. No one was there. Elizabeth craned her neck to see through the broken window for any sign of life but there was nothing. She could just about see inside the room and her eyes fell on a painting, a portrait of a woman. The woman was young and pretty and there was kindness in her eyes. As Elizabeth stared at the picture a sense of familiarity niggled at her. She had seen this girl before.

Suddenly it dawned on her, "Gretchen!" she said. And summoning the last of her strength she got up and hobbled towards the entrance of the little house. "Victor *did* bring you home."

Chapter Twenty-Five

The entrance to the little house was higher than street level and Elizabeth shuffled up the stairs nursing her swollen ankle. When she got to the front door she noticed a marked drop in temperature. Excited anticipation drained from her. A drop in temperature was sometimes a sign that a supernatural presence was near. If Gretchen's spirit was in there, Elizabeth suddenly feared the worst. She tried to convince herself that coming face to face with a ghost would be different here, in Branko. *Everything's different here*, she thought.

Nevertheless she breathed deeply, trying to calm herself, and was shocked to see smoky breath rising from her mouth. She stole herself to be brave once again. *This is almost over*, she said to herself, *one way or another*. If Darius was true to his word then tomorrow the witches would be separated from their souls before being burnt at the stake. Elizabeth hoped that Gretchen's misplaced spirit held the key to their survival.

"I have to try," she said quietly to herself.

She knocked gingerly on the old wooden door. Silence. Nothing but the sound of her own nervous breath. She knocked again, a little louder this time - again nothing. She was about to knock for a third time when suddenly the door swung open with such ferocity that it nearly came off its hinges. Elizabeth backed away instinctively and momentarily lost her footing. She grabbed at the handrail almost falling backwards down the steps.

Holding firmly onto the banister Elizabeth looked into the dwelling. The open door led into a deserted room. There was no light and there was no sign of life. Steadying herself she walked towards the open door.

Once again she could feel the drop in temperature and could see her hot breath swirl in the icy cold air.

"Hello," she called from the safety of the porch.

She waited a few moments and when there was no reply she reluctantly stepped over the threshold of the home haunted by Gretchen. Once inside she did not know what to expect. The space was innocuous and quiet. She took another step into the house and the door slammed shut behind her. She swung around quickly and grabbed the handle trying to pull the door towards her. It was stuck. She looked cautiously into the room when all of a sudden supernatural chaos broke out.

The pictures on the wall started spinning. The doors opposite her that must have led to other rooms kept opening and shutting, opening and shutting, with spine-chilling speed. The candles and fireplace in the room lit up fiercely and were blown out again by an unseen force and the smashed window that led to the alleyway started to sickeningly mend itself.

"Stop!" Elizabeth shouted over the melee. "Please Gretchen – STOP!"

But the bombardment did not stop, it only increased. This time objects were hurled through the air, aimed at Elizabeth. Another earthenware pot narrowly missed her head. Then, from one of the doors on the other side of the room, Elizabeth stared in horror as knives flew towards her and hovered in the air just inches away. She turned quickly and tried the front door again. But it was no use. The door was stuck tight as though someone on the outside was pulling with more force than Elizabeth. Suddenly one of the butter knives clattered against the door and landed at her feet. Elizabeth stared at it in dumb disbelief. She slowly turned back to where the knives had been hovering just as they started to fly towards her face one by one. She ran away from the front door and into the room, but the knives followed her. Elizabeth had no choice but to crouch down in a corner of the room and cower against the onslaught.

"Why are you doing this to me?" She cried, "I only want to help! Victor told me what he did to you and I'm trying to find a way to help you *and* the others *and* my aunties!"

Elizabeth sobbed under the barrage of flung objects. She heard yet another door open and imagined Gretchen's spirit was collecting more implements, using everything to rid herself of Elizabeth. All of a sudden Elizabeth heard a voice she recognised.

"What are you doing Gretchen?"

In an instant peace and normality returned to the little home and Elizabeth noticed that the door she had just desperately tried to escape through had been flung open and Greta walked easily through it.

"Greta!" Elizabeth cried and scrambled to her feet. She flung herself at Greta and sobbed. Her sobbing turned into laboured breathing and Elizabeth grew light-headed. Unable to stop herself, Elizabeth lost consciousness and fainted in Greta's arms.

Images of burning witches and wolves swam through Elizabeth's head in her half-sleeping, semiconscious state. She heard screaming and crying, smelt putrid flesh as she stepped over mountains of bodies.

She woke with a start, pouring with sweat. She shook her head trying to dislodge the visions from her mind. She looked around. She did not know where she was. Then the memory of the attack came flooding back. She groaned. *I'm still in Gretchen's home*, she thought. She scanned the room but could see no sign of Greta. She started to panic, appalled at being left alone with Gretchen's spirit. She got up from the small sofa she was lying on and her head started to spin. She sat down with a thump willing herself to stay conscious. Her head spinning, her body tired, her ankle aching and her stomach empty Elizabeth threw up stomach bile on Gretchen's clean floor.

Tut

The sound startled Elizabeth who looked up quickly, too quickly. Once again her sudden movements were too much for her body and she vomited again.

TUT

The sound came again but louder. This time Elizabeth was careful not to move too quickly. Slowly she raised her head and looked around the dark little room. It was the kitchen. There was a dresser and a large table both of which were covered in a fine layer of dust. Scanning the room Elizabeth saw a stool next to the table. The stool was normal enough until Elizabeth glanced away from it. As she did, in the corner of her vision, she saw a figure sitting on it. She looked back quickly but the figure had gone. She looked away again slowly and she could see a smoky outline of a person in her peripheral vision. If she looked back the figure was gone but if she looked just to the left of where the figure should be there was undeniably an ethereal being sitting there.

"Gretchen?" she whispered.

Why are you here?

It was the same voice that Elizabeth had just heard tutting her disapproval. The sound was like a sigh. The words were barely audible, quieter than a whisper.

"I want to help you."

Elizabeth could instantly feel the warmth in the room plummet. Once again she had angered Gretchen's spirit who was about to deliver another wave of aggression.

"Please," Elizabeth said putting her hand to her mouth to stop herself being sick again. "I can't...if you....." she said between gags, "no more, please no more." She said and led back down on the makeshift bed.

She did not know if it was Gretchen's pity that made her stop, or if she was too house proud to see anymore of Elizabeth's vomit on her floor, but the attack did not come.

Elizabeth realised that she would have to use the right words to reassure Gretchen but she did not know why. From the stories she had been told about the girl, Gretchen was a beautiful soul. Elizabeth did not understand this change. She was also in no fit state to reason with Gretchen. Like a travel sick flyer that cannot engage in conversation for fear of throwing up their mediocre in-flight meal, Elizabeth did not dare open her mouth to speak.

After a few minutes in the angry spirit's company Elizabeth was relieved to hear the door of the little house open and the sound of familiar voices travelling towards her. Greta was back and this time Yorik was with her.

They hurried into the kitchen. Yorik nearly slipped in the pile of sick in his rush to embrace Elizabeth, but he was so glad to see her that he did not seem to mind. Greta cleared the mess up quickly as Yorik prepared Elizabeth some food.

"Eat, eat." He said forcing the plate on a reluctant Elizabeth, "you have to eat something."

Let her starve

As wonderful as it was to see her two friends the atmosphere was charged with Gretchen's anger and Elizabeth found it stifling.

"What is the matter with you?" Greta asked, "Elizabeth is our friend."

How could she be a friend if she was cavorting with that creature?

"What creature?" Elizabeth asked fearing the answer.

You know who I mean

"Do you mean Victor?"

DO NOT DARE SAY HIS NAME HERE

Once again Gretchen threatened Elizabeth with her uncontrollable rage.

"STOP IT!" Elizabeth screamed and to everyone's surprise, Gretchen's hate-charged atmosphere calmed.

"I'm sorry Greta, I'm sorry Yorik," Elizabeth said rising to her feet, "I can't do this anymore. I don't know which way is up and which way is down. Everyone told me what a wonderful person Gretchen was, and Victor told me he had brought her home. I just thought if I could get her spirit back to her body, we might find a way of saving my aunties. But I have to get out of here. She's scaring the shit out of me and she's making me feel as sick as a dog!"

Elizabeth wandered to the little window in the kitchen hoping to find some fresher air. Her heart sank as she noticed the setting sun.

"It's nearly night-time," she said quietly, "they die tomorrow if I can't help them. And I can't waste time here with this malignant spirit. I just can't. I've got to find a way to save them."

For the first time in a very long time, Elizabeth felt like a child. Here she stood with these immortal souls who knew Darius inside out. The people she felt sure would have a solution, but all they could offer was another problem, Gretchen. She knew she was all alone with absolutely no clue how to prevent the execution. Her body was beaten, her mind was weak but somehow she had to find a way to save the sisters. She was all they had left.

"I understand, truly I do." Yorik said soothingly. "But you must eat little witch or you will not have the strength to do anything."

"And sleep," Greta added.

"That, I can't do." Elizabeth said accepting the plate of food from Yorik. "I have to get back to the tavern. I left something there and it could be important."

"That is impossible," Yorik said gravely, "there is nothing of the tavern left."

"What?"

"Wilhelm came looking for you last night and destroyed what was left of it," Greta said. "You will not find anything there. I am so sorry."

"You don't understand," Elizabeth said feeling hysteria rising, "it was the one thing, the one thing I had left to try. If it's gone....then........ then..."

Once again Elizabeth could feel her legs begin to weaken, she was close to fainting but Yorik was at her side quickly, catching her as she fell. He sat her on the seat and stood over her while she ate fresh bread and drank tepid milk. He made sure she ate every last morsel before he spoke again.

"Do you honestly believe you can reunite Gretchen with her body?" he asked.

Once again the energy in the little kitchen changed as Elizabeth sensed Gretchen's curiosity. It was a strange sensation being near a soul without a body. The moods were not contained to the immediate area of the physical being but were everywhere, permeating the whole room.

"I don't know." Elizabeth said. "But when I was being chased by the beasts...."

Elizabeth flinched as the air around her quickly darkened with Gretchen's mood.

"By the *young villagers*," Elizabeth corrected herself "I knew that I didn't want to hurt them. I was trapped in the dungeons with the other witches and one of my choices was to destroy them, but I couldn't. Something told me, some inner knowing – I don't know what. But I knew that those bodies were going to be needed by their rightful owners one day, and I couldn't harm them. That's why I thought the souls must be somewhere. Then Victor...,"

Elizabeth sensed Gretchen's anger but she ploughed on regardless.

"...*Victor* told me what he had done and it was horrific, but I thought, if he had taken every soul home, then they could be found. And here you are. All we need to do now is get the souls to their bodies and find a way of joining them."

How?

"Yeah," Elizabeth sagged, "that's where I ran out of ideas."

"It is a good theory little witch, but how is it possible?" Yorik asked.

"I don't know. But my Moth…" she paused not wanting to reveal too much to the couple, "…I mean, the witches, taught me that every spell can be reversed. Maybe if I can convince George to work with us rather than against us, then it could be done.....in theory."

George did not have the power to cast the spell. Darius did. George merely had the idea.

"Yeah." Elizabeth said with a sigh, "I thought that was probably how it happened, but George *has* got powers now. If I could just find a way to convince him.....*"

George does not have any power.

"He *didn't*," Elizabeth argued, "but he does now."

What power?

"*My* power. Well, not technically my power, actually the witches' power. Anyway, he's got it but Darius has turned on him."

"Poor deluded soul," Yorik said. "If only he had talked to us first, we would have told him not to trust Darius."

How dare you show him sympathy Father!

"Father?" Elizabeth said, "I didn't know....."

"I know little witch. It is not because we did not want to tell you, we just did not have the heart, especially after the attack." Yorik said.

"Oh yeah," Elizabeth said and remembered that this supernatural attack was not the first she had suffered at Gretchen's hands. "It doesn't matter now," she said "I'm so sorry for all of this."

It is not your fault. You are merely a pathetic child desperate for adventure who…

"Why are you so bloody horrible?" Elizabeth said cutting Gretchen off mid insult. "You were supposed to be this pure incorruptible soul. But as far as I can tell you're just a brat who can't control her temper!"

The atmosphere began to fizz with Gretchen's outrage at Elizabeth's remarks.

"Please Gretchen calm down," Greta said. "Do not blame her Elizabeth. She was torn prematurely from her body. Both aspects are incomplete without one another. Death is the natural way for a soul to be parted from its body and those souls can pass in peace. Gretchen is not meant to be this way. The Angel of Death has not come for her. This is not meant to be."

Elizabeth could tell that Gretchen's spirit was becoming melancholy listening to her mother's words.

I apologise little witch. If you find a way to bring me back to my body I will try to make it right with you.

"That's OK." Elizabeth said. "I'm the one that should say sorry. I didn't think. And I'm prone to the occasional outburst myself," suddenly she remembered the constant battle of wills between her and Shiona and her throat grew thick with emotion. "I would love to get you back to your body Gretchen I truly would. But there's one thing none of us have thought about. How on earth are we supposed to get dozens of lost souls up to the castle? Victor is a supernatural beast, but even he could only take one soul at a time."

"We are all supernatural in Branko in our own way," Greta said.

"Oh, I know that. I didn't mean to imply......."

"Did you say that Victor took *all* of the souls home?" Greta asked deep in thought.

"That's what he told me. I suppose he could have been lying but he had no reason to. I already knew the worst of what he'd done."

"So we have not seen our neighbours for the same reason they have not seen us," Yorik said. "They have all been at home with the lost souls of their loved ones."

Suddenly they heard a sound outside and Yorik signalled for Greta and Elizabeth to get down. Crouching low Yorik sidled over to the window.

"It is Darius's children," he said, "they must be looking for Elizabeth."

"I have to go," Elizabeth said. "I've got to get back to the tavern before it's too late."

"It is already dark little witch," Yorik said, "believe me when I say that you will not find what you are looking for."

"I have to try Yorik." Elizabeth got up. "I have to try."

"Yes. We all have to try something, or the world is destroyed forever is it not?" Greta asked.

Elizabeth nodded gravely.

"Go," Greta said and Elizabeth made her way to the door. "But go safely! Do not worry about the lost souls. I might have a trick or two up my sleeve. Go and find your amulet Elizabeth."

Elizabeth stopped mid-stride, "How did you......"

"I saw it glowing in your room when you healed me. I knew it was

240

significant but I had no time to find it when Wilhelm returned. I am sorry."

"That's OK. I should have been more careful with it. My Dad'll be livid when he finds out."

"Your Father?" Yorik asked.

"Yeah. Why?"

"I felt sure a lucky amulet would be from your mother. She was the witch after all."

"You know about that as well?"

"Yes," Greta said. "Your aunts like to think they were very secretive but it was quite obvious you were different from the rest."

"You have your mother's eyes for a start," Yorik laughed. "Does your father have magical powers too?"

"No!" It was Elizabeth's turn to giggle. "It was just his lucky amulet, given to him by 'Buddy', his Grandfather."

"Buddy?" Yorik asked.

"Yes." Elizabeth said warmed by the nostalgic memory. "It's got Bud engraved on the back of it in old English so it looks a little bit like b-v-d."

"B-V-D?" Yorik asked distractedly. "A little like Baron Von Diederich. Oh, how we could do with him here now."

"Oh yeah," Elizabeth said, "I never thought......."

All at once Elizabeth perceived a seed of a memory. She tried to grab hold of it, but it slipped away from her like grains of sand through her fingertips.

"What is it?" Yorik asked.

"I don't know," Elizabeth said, "it's nothing - or something. I don't know. But I have to go. I have to find Dad's pendant."

She embraced Yorik and Greta tightly. As with the witches she did not know if she would ever see them again.

"Whether I find the amulet or not, I'm heading straight back to the castle. If you can find a way to transport the souls Greta, I'll see you up there. Otherwise – pray for me."

She turned and walked away from Yorik, Greta and Gretchen's confused spirit. She walked easily out of the kitchen to the front door her ankle was almost back to normal. She took a deep breath and cautiously opened the door. She tiptoed down the stairs to street level, checked the sky for any sign of Wilhelm or Diana and Elizabeth ran into the night.

241

Chapter Twenty-Six

The chill in the night air almost took Elizabeth's breath away, but it was welcoming and refreshing. In the little house Elizabeth had grown accustomed to the oppression of Gretchen's spirit. Now she was no longer in her company Elizabeth felt her mood lift, she felt like she could breathe again. Now that the heavy weight of Gretchen's supernatural mood swings no longer sat on her brow, clarity had returned.

Suddenly Elizabeth heard a noise from high above her. It was Diana and Wilhelm scanning the village in their desperate hunt for Elizabeth. She wondered if Victor was with them. When they were out of sight, she ran. It was slow going at first because of her injured ankle, but the exercise did it some good and the pain eased as she raced through the village.

The siblings circled overhead. Every time they got close to her, she ducked out of the way. Hiding in doorways, underneath buildings and sometimes venturing inside the little homes. With every mad dash she was getting closer and closer to the tavern. The strange memory that scratched around in the periphery of her mind was still there, tantalisingly close but agonisingly untouchable.

In the gloom of the late night Elizabeth saw the undeniable shadow of Wilhelm above her and heard a ripple of movement from the trees. The siblings were circling close again and Elizabeth hid beside one of the houses. She crouched low, breathing heavily, allowing the coolness of the fresh night air to wash over her. She cast her mind back to her first night in Branko and remembered enjoying the prickling sensation of the Branko breeze on her skin. She could not believe how much had happened in the past two days. She stared down at her raggedy clothes, tarnished and torn from her adventures. The dress she had customised now looked like rags falling from her body, her tights were ripped and her exposed flesh was scratched and bruised. She could easily be mistaken for one of George's creatures.

She stared up at the bristling trees, the fresh breeze was turning into a squall and Elizabeth took comfort in it. Whatever or whoever else it was controlled by, Branko was still subject to the elements. The natural law of the environment was still at work even in this magical place.

Watching the treetops being moved by an invisible breeze somehow made the memory Elizabeth had been hunting for reveal itself a little more. It was daytime and she was looking up at trees taller than mountains. A fierce wind was blowing through them. She saw objects flying through the sky, a car wheel, a rope, a wheelbarrow, but somehow she knew she was safe. She ran through an avenue of trees on her way back to a house. A pristine, luxurious house that, in her daydream, was owned by her grandmother. Once inside she knew there was a presence in the house, but she was still not afraid. Elizabeth lost herself in this childhood dream.

All at once the sound of Wilhelm's cruel laugh snapped her out of the daydream. The memory would have to wait. She suddenly realised how exposed she was sitting next to the cottage with only the darkness to hide her. Her head bowed low Elizabeth dashed towards the edge of the village to try to find what was left of the tavern.

The little village of Branko was a mishmash of wooden shacks, Tudor dwellings, terraced miners cottages, and Victorian wharf houses. It was as though the villagers were trying to reinvent their little village with the idea of what modern life should be. But whatever the size or shape of the street, all roads led to the tavern.

Elizabeth ran as fast as she could to where the tavern once stood. As she neared the end of the street she stopped suddenly. Yorik was right, Wilhelm had been in a destructive mood. Not only was the tavern in ruins but so were the houses nearest to it. The ones she had gazed at on her first morning in Branko.

Elizabeth's heart sank, she felt responsible. The humiliation that Wilhelm suffered at her hands meant that someone had to pay. Whether it was Elizabeth or not was probably irrelevant to Wilhelm's fragile ego. What a year it had been for Branko's villagers. This year, more than any other, they needed the witches to be on top of their game. So far Shiona and Daphne had only succeeded in getting themselves captured and Elizabeth had caused the destruction of their homes by a maniacal egomaniac.

"What great saviours we've turned out to be," Elizabeth said and flinched at the loudness of her voice in the otherwise silent night. Her outburst suddenly alerted Darius's children to her presence. She had no option but to try to take refuge in one of the deserted houses. She ran inside the nearest cottage. It stood alone and exposed amongst the devastation, but Elizabeth had no other choice.

She closed the door quietly behind her and crouched low in the gloom. She hid beneath a window chancing a look outside whenever she dared. Suddenly a figure appeared on the street. She ducked back down seconds before the monster looked towards the little cottage. It was Wilhelm.

She tried to breathe as evenly and quietly as she could, but every time she focused on quieting her breath it became more laboured. The very act of concentrating on exhaling soundlessly was inducing hyperventilation. Her panic escalated as she realised Wilhelm was getting closer. His senses were alive, every sense. Elizabeth knew that Darius and his monstrous family could hear and smell and see better than any other animal. And any minute now Wilhelm would discover her hiding place.

Suddenly Elizabeth felt another energy from within the little cottage. It surrounded her with a wave of confused anticipation. She gulped hard as a familiar feeling of stifling oppression took hold of her. She had entered a deserted cottage but she was not alone.

Wilhelm was closer now. She looked up at the window she was cowering under, hidden by the window ledge, and she saw his hot breath steaming up the cold pane. He knew she was there. But he was only one of her problems. The presence of the spirits was becoming unbearable. She was faced with a dilemma, if she left the little stone cottage Wilhelm would be on to her at once, but if she stayed she was risking the wrath of its bodiless inhabitant. She could feel the air thicken around her.

I remember you.

The same breathless voice as Gretchen's, but this time the soul was clearly male. Elizabeth did not know what to say in reply, everything she said to Gretchen enraged her. She decided to remain quiet. Behind her Wilhelm was trying the door.

Stay down.

Elizabeth jumped at the closeness of the voice, the spirit was right next to her. But the voice in her ear sounded different from the first, still male, but more youthful. She looked wildly around but could not see a thing. The cottage was pitch black and was occupied by more than one spirit.

As with Gretchen, the heaviness in the atmosphere increased as the mood of the spirits intensified. She could tell she was not welcome, that the spirits wanted her gone. There was a chill in the room, a powerful feeling of hostility and it was nearly suffocating her. As with Gretchen she started to feel nauseous. She knew she should stay hidden but the instinct to run from these supernatural souls was overwhelming. She tried to move but suddenly she realised she could not leave the house even if she wanted to. Elizabeth was forced backwards by an unseen force. She could feel her skin tighten, she was unable to move, she was fuzzy headed and was about to lose consciousness. There was nothing she could do, she was at the mercy of the spirits.

All of a sudden she realised that Wilhelm was not rattling the door handle anymore. She could hear his grunts as he stood next to the cottage, then finally he snorted his derision and walked away. With one final *whoosh* Wilhelm was airborne and Elizabeth was left with her bodiless captives.

Almost as soon as Wilhelm was out of sight the weight of the atmosphere surrounding her started to ease. The cool hostility turned to warm curiosity and Elizabeth realised that the spirits were not trying to harm her, they were trying to protect her. The intense aggression was meant for Wilhelm, not for her, and his animal instincts told him to stay away.

Suddenly at the back of the cottage a door opened.

"I am so sorry we could not warn you," it was a man and he was definitely flesh and blood.

"We could not be in the room when the boys were trying to hide you," a lady said appearing from behind him, "it makes us very ill."

"I can understand that!" Elizabeth said. Grateful to be able to move once again, she got up and stretched her aching body.

245

They all stood in silence for a while. Elizabeth could tell that every person in the room, both with and without a body, was watching her with keen interest.

"Do you need to sit down," the man said, he was plump and kindly looking. A little like Yorik but he was shorter and had more hair.

"That would probably be wise," Elizabeth said knowing she would not get far in her weakened state.

"My name is Hannah," the lady said, who was small and round like her husband. "This is Friedrich," she said pointing to the man. "And the two curious boys are Daniel and Lukas."

I have seen you before.

Said one of the curious boys.

"That one is Lukas, he is the elder of the two," said Hannah and then she corrected herself, "*was*. He *was* the elder of the two. You must forgive me, I find it very difficult to believe they will not be returned to us one day."

*But we **are** here Mamma.*

The second voice pitched in.

"You must be Daniel?" Elizabeth asked. Not only did he sound younger than his brother but he also sounded much less serious. His voice seemed to move across the room as though he were talking in flight. He was clearly enjoying the chance to be free of his physical body. His joy was contagious, as were most of the feelings projected by these spirits and Elizabeth could not stop herself from laughing.

This is not funny.

"No, I'm sorry..." Elizabeth started to apologise to Lukas.

I did not mean you I meant my silly little brother.

"Do not be too hard on him Lukas," Hannah said, "it must be very strange for him."

It is strange for all of us.

"Of course, it must be," Elizabeth said, "I can't even imagine."

"Lukas believes he has seen you before young lady," Freidrich said.

I have.

"I'm sorry Lukas," Elizabeth replied, "I don't know. Maybe if I could see a picture...."

You have met my body little witch but I was not in it.

"I don't understand," Elizabeth said.

246

In the dungeon, when you were trying to save your aunts. You were set upon by the pack of animals.

"Yes I remember that, but......."

I was the one at the front of the pack, the one who saw you first. The one you could not kill.

"I don't understand, I thought those bodies were soulless."

Sometimes we can see through their eyes. It was Daniel's turn to offer an explanation. *I do not know how it happens. I choose not to see because it is very strange, but Lukas likes to know where his body is and what it is doing.*

"Why would you do that?" Elizabeth asked.

That body is me, it is who I am on this planet, I cannot bear to lose connection with it. I saw you in that dungeon, saw you could not harm our bodies – why?

"I suppose I feel the same way as you Hannah," Elizabeth replied, "I can't quite shift the feeling that body and soul could be reunited one day."

I hope you are right. Thank you little witch for not harming me.

The atmosphere created by the two boys was decidedly more convivial than Gretchen's antagonism but Elizabeth's strength was returning and she knew she could not stay there forever.

"Greta might try to find you," Elizabeth said to Hannah and Friedrich. "She thinks she may know a way of transporting the lost souls back to the castle. If I can get the bodies and souls together, in the same place, I might be able to force George to reunite them. Be ready."

"What about the other witches," Friedrich asked as Elizabeth opened the door.

"I'm sorry," Elizabeth said sadly, "I'm afraid I'm all you've got left."

Elizabeth took a step into the night just as she heard a sound above her. She looked up just in time to see a shadow pass over head. Suddenly a figure landed heavily in front of her. It was Diana grinning with the same malicious cruelty as her brother.

"Wilhelm struggled to find you," Diana said advancing on Elizabeth, "I told him he was pathetic, that I would find you in a moment. And I have."

Bring her inside.

Elizabeth heard Lukas whisper behind her.

As Diana stepped towards Elizabeth, Elizabeth stepped back into the house. Luckily Diana was as arrogant as her brother and did not sense the danger. Elizabeth backed all the way into the little room.

"I do not know where you think you are going," Diana said smugly, "do not resist child and I will not harm you." With that Diana stepped into the cottage.

As soon as she did the door slammed shut behind her plunging the room into darkness.

"You cannot harm me," Diana said dismissively, "you mere mortals are no match for the power bestowed on me by my father."

WE ARE NOT MERE MORTALS!

The air grew heavy quickly.

"Go!" Shouted Friedrich from behind Elizabeth and pushed her through the door at the back of the room. "The boys will deal with Diana." He followed her out and shut the door behind him.

Elizabeth once again found herself in a kitchen of one of the little cottages. Even with the door closed Elizabeth new that the boys were upping their game. The density of the air was bleeding through the walls. She backed quickly away and bumped into Hannah who directed her to the back door.

"We will see you again little witch," Hannah said as she ushered her out of the house. "Do not look back, this will not be pretty. Lukas has waited a long time for his revenge."

Elizabeth ran quickly away from the cottage towards the remnants of the tavern. She heard Diana's blood-curdling scream turn into a deep growl and then silence. Elizabeth shook the scene from her mind. As vicious as Diana was, Elizabeth could not bear to imagine what horrors Lukas and Daniel were subjecting her to.

She ran as quickly as she could. Wilhelm with his exaggerated senses would have heard Diana's howl. He would be here in minutes and Elizabeth still had a mammoth task ahead of her. She had to find the amulet. Something deep inside her knew it was important. Not just because it was from her father and not just because it had glowed so brightly in her room. It was more than that. And it was linked to a memory of her childhood, a memory that was triggered when Yorik pointed out the coincidence of the engraving.

She could hear the undeniable *flap-flap* of Wilhelm's wings overhead.

248

He was trying to find his sister. Elizabeth knew he was getting closer every passing second but she did not know which direction he was coming from. She scanned the skies as she carried on running flat out to get to the tavern as quickly as she could.

Suddenly, before she could take cover Elizabeth saw Wilhelm ahead, whizzing towards her from the forest behind the tavern. All she could do was drop down. Hoping he would not see her in the dark. He zoomed over her as she lay flat on the ground. Luckily for Elizabeth he only had one destination on his mind, the cottage where his sister was being held.

She turned to watch. From a safe distance she could see Wilhelm blow the cottage door off its hinges. She watched as Hannah and Friedrich scuttled out of the back door and towards the village. Elizabeth was relieved to see them quickly take cover in the streets of houses but she could not watch any longer. She doubled her speed and finally made it to the tavern. She was living on borrowed time. It would not take long for Wilhelm to figure out where Elizabeth was going. She had to act quickly.

Stepping cautiously over the rubble in the dark Elizabeth tried to work out the layout of the pub. She recognised the bar area that Wilhelm and Diana destroyed the first day, now all she had to do was find the bedrooms. That would not be easy. The roof was the last thing to collapse and remnants of it covered the entire site. She climbed over the shattered pieces of wood hungrily tearing at timber and stones to try to find something she recognised – anything. Even if it was one of the other bedrooms at least that would give her a starting point.

Elizabeth listened to the battle at Lukas' cottage. It was still raging on. Wilhelm was not easily going to rescue his sister from these vengeful spirits and Elizabeth hoped that he would be distracted long enough for her to finish the search. She moved rock after rock, brick after brick, tile after tile but she was still no closer to finding the amulet.

"Come on, come on!" She said in frustration. All at once she heard a scuffle on the street behind her. She looked around and in the distance she could see Wilhelm extricate himself from the cottage dragging an unconscious Diana with him. He fell on the floor panting. After a few moments he got to his knees and crawled over to Diana trying to revive her.

"Where are you?" Elizabeth hissed knowing how quick Wilhelm's recovery was.

"Where are you?" She sobbed and closed her eyes. Immediately she saw a glowing green object and her eyes snapped open again. As soon as she did the light went out, the object was lost again in the devastation.

Suddenly a thought occurred to her, "where are you?" she said once again, looking wildly around but she could see nothing in the darkness.

She tried again, "where are you?" This time she closed her eyes. The soft glowing green hue was back. She opened her eyes again and again she saw nothing but when she closed them, the light from the amulet was unmistakable. The source of the light was four feet away from her just to the left of where she was standing. She scrambled gingerly towards it, trying to stay silent in her temporary blindness.

She reached the site of the amulet quickly but her search was not going to be easy. With her eyes closed she could tell she was practically on top of the amulet, but it was still far away, buried deep beneath the rubble. She opened her eyes again and saw that massive job ahead of her. She had a lot of digging to do. Glancing fearfully behind she saw that Diana was beginning to regain consciousness. Wilhelm had revived her. It would not be long before they would resume their search. Elizabeth started digging. She moved pieces of timber and stone, earthenware and china, rocks and rugs. She closed her eyes and saw that the amulet was getting closer.

She heard Wilhelm and Diana talking animatedly behind her, both of them almost completely recovered. But Elizabeth was still not close enough to the amulet.

"Come on, come on!" she said in frustration and the amulet came flying out of the rubble and leapt into her hand.

Amazed to have the prize in her grasp, Elizabeth sat in shocked silence for a moment, until the angry voices of Darius's children grew louder behind her. She knew she had to move. She scrabbled to her feet and staying low she crawled, tumbled and slipped to the edge of the tavern ruins. When she finally reached even ground she chanced a look back. Diana was still having some trouble moving so Wilhelm was carrying her and trying to fly at the same time. The pair looked ridiculous with Diana anchoring a relentless Wilhelm to the ground.

Even in this laboured state the siblings were still gaining ground. Elizabeth knew it was useless to try to outrun them, her only option was to hide. The tavern was at the far edge of the village. There were no more houses with conveniently placed spirit guardians for her to take refuge in; she would have to find a hiding place in the forest. Just as she was about to run into the woods the amulet flew out of her hand and hit the nearest tree. She lost sight of it in the dark and found herself having to use the same sightless search as before. When she did she saw that it had imbedded itself into the trunk of an old oak tree. She desperately tried to prise it out of the bark but it was not budging. She panicked as Wilhelm and Diana got closer and closer. Elizabeth started to climb the tree. As soon as she did the amulet dislodged itself and popped obligingly into her hand.

"You want me to go this way I take it," she said and as quickly as she could she scrambled up the tree.

She was an efficient tree climber. It was a skill that her Dad taught her when she was little. Jessie was much more feminine, people would call her a "girly girl" but Elizabeth was something of a tomboy. She climbed the tree with ease and once at the top it dawned on her that it was the same tree she had seen Victor in on her first night in Branko. She was still close to the tavern, and very close to Victor's siblings. But she was hidden by the tree branches and invisible from the ground. Of course, that would not necessarily stop these creatures. They could use all their senses, like animals. Elizabeth was not convinced that her father's talisman had found her the ideal hiding place. *Surely they'll find me here*, she thought.

She chanced a look below her and there at the bottom of the tree were Wilhelm and Diana staring up. She quickly pulled her head out of view. What was she thinking? Wilhelm was already starting to sniff the air, any moment now he would smell her, fly up and capture her. She had followed the advice of an inanimate object. She only hoped the amulet knew what it was doing.

"Stop sulking," Wilhelm called. "We know you are there."

Wilhelm's comment startled Elizabeth. She was doing many things, panicking, squatting, aching but she was certainly not sulking.

"Come down now!" Diana said.

Elizabeth wondered what Diana was expecting, what self-respecting prey would walk into the arms of its predator just because it was told to?

"You wait until father finds out," Wilhelm shouted, "he will be very

251

angry."

Elizabeth certainly did not want to incur the wrath of Darius but she was surprised that Wilhelm would pass the challenge of defeating her to his father.

"Come down now," Diana repeated. "Victor!"

Elizabeth held her breath and suddenly understood the bizarre tone of the conversation. *Why do they think Victor is up here?* She thought. Was there a residual essence of him in the tree from the night they first met? Just then Elizabeth sensed a tiny movement behind her, like a soft breeze. She turned quickly, and almost lost her footing. She raised her hand to her mouth to stifle a scream. There magically extricating himself from the bark of the tree was Victor. He opened his eyes and Elizabeth saw the familiar green glow.

"That was a trick I learned from you Elizabeth," Victor whispered, "close my eyes and I am invisible."

Elizabeth stared at him and backed away as much as she dared. She was getting very close to the edge of the branch, if she took one more step she would fall.

Victor looked at her and smiled mirthlessly, "goodbye *friend*," he said and jumped straight out of the tree landing next to his siblings.

"Did you find anything?" Wilhelm asked.

Elizabeth could feel her heart beating heavily in her chest, it was so loud she was sure that Darius's children could hear it from the ground. She waited for Victor's reply. Was he really the friend he pretended to be? He seemed so different, so much more confident than the gawky schoolboy.

"Nothing," he said quietly and leaping into the sky he flew home leaving Wilhelm to deal with the weighty Diana.

"Wait, wait," Wilhelm called after him. "I need some help."

Wilhelm and Diana disappeared into the forest, calling after Victor as they went.

Elizabeth stared after them. She did not dare to move, barely even drew breath until they were out of sight. When she was sure they would not return she sat heavily on the thick tree branch she had just shared with Victor. She knew she needed to rest, she knew she needed to have some physical strength if she was going to stop the witches from being murdered, but she had never felt weaker or more useless in her life.

She leant against the gnarled tree trunk, resting her head and closed her eyes. She saw the warm comforting glow of the talisman in her hand. She opened her eyes and looked carefully at the amulet. She turned it this way and that, wondering if it were some kind of communicative device to contact her mother. But even though she held the amulet in her hand Elizabeth was no closer to knowing how to use it. She clasped it tightly and rested her head on her clenched fists.

"What am I supposed to do?" She asked and instantly she was transported into a memory and the visions she thought were childhood dreams replayed themselves in vivid detail.

Chapter Twenty-Seven

Elizabeth woke with a start, almost toppling out of the tree. The memory was buzzing in her mind like an angry wasp. It was not a dream. It had never been a dream. Finally, she knew why she had come to Branko, why she was destined to come. Gazing skyward she felt the warmth of the morning sun on her face. She had slept for a long time, too long. She had to move quickly or she would be too late to save the witches from execution.

She got to her feet and her muscles screamed. She had slept in the same position all night not daring to budge for fear of falling. As she moved her body groaned its disapproval but she could not heed the discomfort. She could not afford to pay attention to the pain searing through every fibre of her body. She had to move and move fast. It was a long walk back to the castle and she had no magical powers to aid her journey.

She climbed down the tree slowly, breathing heavily, her stiff body easing as she descended. She was pushing herself to the limit of her endurance but she had to keep going. She had to put the old complaining, *can't do it* Elizabeth to one side, just for now, and accomplish the task that her great-grandfather set for her all those years ago.

At the bottom of the tree she paused. Now was the moment for her to finish what the Baron and the witches had started all those years ago. Salvation rested with her. She was solely responsible for the protection of Branko and the human race. *No pressure then,* she thought. But now was not the time to wonder if she was up to the task. She took one last long deep breath, exhaled evenly, turned away from the tree in the tavern ruins and ran.

She made her way quickly northwards towards the castle, remembering the words her great-grandfather had said to her, 'one day you will take me home'. She quickened her pace.

For years she had visions of larger than life trees and an unseen force in her grandmother's house, but she had always believed that it was just a recurring dream. But last night, perched precariously in the old oak tree next to Yorik's tavern, the amulet had shown her it was not a dream, it was a memory.

Elizabeth looked up at the Branko sky, the wind was picking up. It looked as though a storm was approaching. Elizabeth remembered the blustery day at her Grandmother's house all those years ago. She had gone to visit with her family and as was their usual routine, Elizabeth, Jessie and their parents were taking a walk in the nearby countryside. Elizabeth was about six years old, Jessie was nine and as with all their rambles, Jessie was being taught how to cast spells. She was the 'princess' the one that would inherit her mother's skill and Gladys spent a lot of time coaching her. Elizabeth and her father were left alone to spend their own time together, climbing trees, making up stories, wrestling, playing games. And in all this time Elizabeth was never jealous of the attention and power being lavished on her sister. She couldn't be. She had her father and they were having a great time. On the day of the memory they were up a tree, playing pirates and laughing like best friends. But Bertie was being summoned.

"Quick Bertie, quick," Gladys called, "come and see what Jessie can do."

Elizabeth remembered her father rolling his eyes, but he dutifully climbed down the tree to witness yet another of his eldest daughter's achievements. Elizabeth waited for him as she always did when Jessie was performing. After only a few minutes, that felt like hours to the six-year-old Elizabeth, she got thoroughly bored of waiting. She climbed down the tree to find the others, when suddenly she heard a loud *CREAK* coming from above her. The trees were not monstrously big as they had appeared in her dreams, they just seemed that way to the tiny Elizabeth. The wind rustled through the canopy and Elizabeth was sure the leaves were calling her name.

ELIZABETH

They said, and Elizabeth whirled around.

ELIZABETH

She heard the voice once more and her curiosity eclipsed her fear. The sound was coming from one particular direction and Elizabeth followed it. The voice was leading her back to her grandmother's house. She followed the breath of the voice in the trees as they rippled. Sometimes it would play a game with her and creep up behind her blowing through her hair. Elizabeth giggled – to her it was a brilliant game. She galloped along the avenue of trees back to the house, pretending to ride on a horse like a knight. That was her favourite game to play when she visited her grandmother.

She followed the beckoning voice into the house. She walked inside her grandmother's immaculately kept kitchen remembering to take off her shoes. Through the kitchen was the grand hallway that led upstairs. Elizabeth was alone inside the house with the playful spirit, but she was not afraid. She had not yet reached the age when life experiences had taught her to fear unexplained phenomena. Elizabeth was merely curious. The entity was ushering her upstairs. She felt a tiny push from behind her as if she was still being moved by an invisible breeze even inside the house.

At the top of the stairs, the air became cold and Elizabeth shivered. She knew that her new friend wanted her to follow but Elizabeth also knew enough of her mother's rules to put on a jumper if she was starting to get cold. She went to her own room first, picked out her favourite pink sweatshirt from her small case and clumsily dressed herself. The spirit waited patiently and even then Elizabeth could sense its amusement.

When she was clothed and warmed she followed her new friend. It wanted her to go to her father's old bedroom. She knocked on the door, always good mannered at Grandmother's house, but there was no answer. She didn't knock again. She just walked in. At the end of the bed sat an outline of an old man. His appearance was fuzzy, as though he were a projection of old film footage. He was tall and regal with a thick grey moustache over his top lip. Elizabeth giggled at him, he smiled kindly back at her.

"Hello little one," he said.

"What you doing?" Elizabeth asked.

"I am waiting for you?"

"Why?" She said screwing up her face in curiosity.

"I have a message for you."

"Who from?"

The spirit smiled at Elizabeth's youthful curiosity.

"From myself."

"Oh," she said and stared at the figure.

"Do you want to hear it?"

"I 'spose."

"It is a simple message Little One, are you ready?"

"Yeah," Elizabeth said, not really knowing what she was agreeing to.

"You have a very important job to do Elizabeth. One day you will have to take me home."

"Where's that?"

But before she got an answer from the spirit the door burst open behind her.

"Buddy!" It was Bertie and he was angry. "What are you doing?" The spirit looked at Bertie and smiled, then the image of Buddy started to disperse. He transformed into deep green smoke and disappeared into the pendant sitting on Bertie's old chest of drawers. Even in her dream, Elizabeth recognised the amulet.

The six-year-old Elizabeth remembered very little after that. There was a heated argument between her mother and father. She remembered Gladys shouting about witches and something Shiona and Daphne had discovered and Elizabeth remembered her mother saying "why didn't you tell me?" – a lot.

And Elizabeth remembered her aunties. Remembered sitting on their knees and getting kisses cuddles from both Daphne *and* Shiona – much to her surprise. But her childhood memory was becoming confused with her adult memory because the women she had shared that affection with as a child had not aged at all.

"That can't be right," Elizabeth said and shook the idea from her mind.

As she ran through the forest in Branko, Elizabeth put the pieces of the puzzle together. Shiona and Daphne must have already noticed the leaks in reality and found out about Darius before Elizabeth's encounter with her great-grandfather. Gladys clearly had never kept anything from Bertie. Elizabeth's memory was testament to that. Bertie knew Gladys was a witch and was even happy to encourage Jessie to follow in her footsteps. But Bertie had kept his very significant ancestry a secret. Bertie was Baron Von Deiderich's grandson.

Elizabeth remembered her father saying, "I never wanted you to be part of this."

She remembered her mother retorting, "I AM a part of this! And you've put us in danger by trying to protect us."

Then a decision was made by Gladys and Bertie to keep the past a secret from the girls, including the fact that their mother was a witch. There were lots of tears that night, mostly from Jessie who looked at Elizabeth as though she had ruined her life forever. And the adult Elizabeth had to admit that their relationship had been strained ever since. That night, all those years ago, Bertie watched as Gladys cast a spell over each of the girls, "it's time to forget Princess," she said to Jessie and touched her gently on the forehead. "It's time to forget Little One," she said to Elizabeth and touched her in the same place. Bertie picked up a sleepy Jessie and carried her to bed. Gladys picked up Elizabeth, and when she was sure that Bertie was out of earshot, she whispered softly in Elizabeth's ear, "until it's time to remember."

And *now* it was definitely the time to remember. Elizabeth put the amulet, containing the spirit of her great-grandfather, around her neck and rushed towards his old home – Castle Von Deiderich.

The sky crackled with the oncoming thunderstorm and Elizabeth remembered that first night in the alleyway. She honestly believed that that fateful encounter was the catalyst for setting this chain of events in motion, but she was wrong. The catalyst happened many, many years before that. This was her destiny even before she was born.

Elizabeth found herself in the woods surrounding the village of Branko – again. And once again she was running as though her life depended on it. But this time she was not trying to escape and save herself, this time she was trying to save her aunties.

"And the rest of the world I suppose!" she said aloud.

She only hoped she knew how to do it. Her great-grandfather wanted her to bring him home. He knew, even back then that it would be Elizabeth who would be the One, and apparently so did Gladys. It was to Elizabeth she had muttered her counter-spell, not Jessie. It was Elizabeth who had been summoned by the Baron, not Jessie; and it was Elizabeth who was running for her life through the woods of Branko –

NOT Jessie. This was *her* destiny. And the thought of finally stepping out of her sister's shadow drove her onwards.

It was no coincidence that this was the year Gladys had sent Elizabeth, that this was the year George had given Darius his power back, and this was the year Elizabeth *had* to be in Branko with her father's amulet. For some reason, that Elizabeth hoped would soon become clear, Elizabeth was the only one for the job. She scratched around in her head to see if she could remember any other clues given to her by her great-grandfather but there was nothing other than the memory of him sitting on the bed. All she knew was that she had to take him home, and she was very nearly there.

She slowed down as she reached the outskirts of the castle that her great-grandfather had once called home. She knew very little of the layout but she did know her way through the courtyard, so she made her way there. She scaled a pile of bricks that once must have been part of the grand outer wall protecting the inhabitants from invasion. Only a section of the wall was still standing, that was where Wilhelm had crashed the previous day. She smiled at the memory. She *could* do this. She had done so much already.

Elizabeth picked her way through the ruins with caution. Massive drops of rain were beginning to fall moistening the bricks. *Not good*, she thought to herself. It would not be easy to scale the unstable stones especially if they were wet from the rain. If she placed her foot badly, she might slip and the whole lot would collapse under her, alerting everyone to her presence. The element of surprise would certainly be lost then.

She climbed up cautiously but it was agonisingly slow. There were times when she slid backwards and had to start again. She had to fight every instinct to rush her ascent. She placed her feet and hands cautiously within the rocks climbing as carefully and as soundlessly as possible.

She finally reached the top of the pile and looked into the courtyard. She could not believe her eyes. She ducked down again quickly, clasping her hand to her mouth stifling any involuntary outburst. She waited, her heart thumping wildly in her chest, not daring to look. After a few moments she forced herself to view the spectacle. Her heart sank at the sight.

In the courtyard were two huge timber stakes piled high with sticks and kindling. Clearly these were the bonfires where the witches would burn. There were boxes piled up next to the stakes forming makeshift steps. At the back of the courtyard Shiona and Daphne were being dragged from the dungeon by the creatures. They were no longer encased in Darius's spell because there was no need for it. They were surrounded by the villager-creatures and they could not escape George's beasts even if they tried. And they were trying. Daphne's hands were tied behind her back but Elizabeth could still see a sizzle of magic bursting from her fingers but it stopped inches from her body. Nothing could make it through the soulless guard. Shiona had managed to free her hands and was doing the same. She was casting spells wildly, but again they were falling short, hitting an invisible force field.

Slowly, inexorably, the creatures were forcing the witches to take their final journey to the funeral pyres.

As sickening as it was to see her aunties fight with every last atom of strength and power they could find, it was nothing compared to the rest of the scene. There assembled as an audience to witness the execution were the villagers. Not just George's creatures, but Elizabeth's friends. She easily spotted Yorik, with his larger than life frame and stood next to him was Greta. Opposite them were Hannah and Freiderich. Elizabeth recognised other faces too, the curious villagers that quizzed them that first day at the tavern. And behind them all, making sure they could not flee, were their beast-like children.

The villagers were poised to witness the horrific execution of the witches held captive by their own children. Elizabeth could see some of the women sobbing in their husband's arms. Elizabeth had no idea if Greta had been true to her word and managed to transport the souls to the castle.

She scanned the scene looking for George, as far as Darius knew George was still harmless but Elizabeth hoped he could still be of some use. Shiona and Daphne were now being forced up the makeshift steps towards the stakes. Above them was a balcony. The same balcony that Elizabeth fought with Wilhelm on, and there sat on a gilded throne was Darius. Elizabeth scoffed at his tasteless arrogance. Behind him stood Diana and Ingrid and next to them were Wilhelm and Victor. Tucked further away, to the far right of the balcony, was George. It was his turn to look battered and bruised. His clothes were torn and he looked thoroughly exhausted, but Elizabeth did not feel any pity for him. He was the reason they were all in this mess and it was clear to Elizabeth that he was not in a state to help. Witches powers or not, he was useless to Elizabeth, he was encased in Darius's muddy green spell. Darius was taking no chances with him.

Elizabeth seized the amulet from her neck. Her only hope now was her great-grandfather. Baron Von Deiderich himself. The same man that had beaten Darius all those years ago and had imprisoned him in this land lost in time and space.

"Come on then gramps," Elizabeth said shaking the amulet, "out you come."

Nothing. Elizabeth closed her eyes. But in the cold light of day this trick did not work. She could not see the glow of the amulet even with her eyes squeezed shut. She racked her brains trying to remember the words she used when it had flown into her hands.

"Come on, come on!" She remembered. Nothing.

"What am I supposed to do?" She hissed, recalling this phrase as the trigger for her memory, but again there was nothing. The amulet did not jump to life and the smoky green figure of Baron Von Deiderich did not burst forth from it.

Elizabeth sat back on the stones and raised her head to the skies. She saw a flash of forked lightening in the air and after a few moments she heard a distant rumble of thunder. The storm was coming. Elizabeth's only hope now was the falling rain. She prayed it would be monsoonal, at least then it might extinguish the fires.

The sky began to darken quickly. In this eerie half-light, like the grey of a solar eclipse, nothing looked real to Elizabeth. The villagers looked superimposed onto a background of forests and castles.

Suddenly she saw Darius appear in the courtyard. He was no longer sitting on the balcony but had joined the villagers, both friends and foes, and was carrying a burning torch.

"Oh no," Elizabeth said as she watched him approach the witches.

"This is your last chance Dario," Daphne blustered, "walk away now and we promise to spare your life!"

Darius stopped for a moment and then roared with laughter. "You are so funny Daphne, I will be sad to say goodbye."

"Oh let's not say goodbye," Shiona sneered, "let's just say *au reviour*."

Elizabeth was amazed to see her aunties' bare faced bravado. They were moments away from an agonising death but they were still not about to beg for mercy. They were either unbelievably courageous or just plain crazy.

"Very well Shiona dear," Darius said coolly, "*au reviour*."

Darius leant low to light the fire at Daphne's feet.

"Hang on," she said, "what about separating us from our souls, hm?"

Elizabeth could tell she was playing for time and it seemed to work. Darius got up slowly.

"Well I'm afraid to say, your little Georgie is not going to be of any use to us now." He gestured towards the balcony. "He was foolish enough to try to fight me with magic and I had to make him suffer."

Elizabeth looked closer at the figure of George encased in the spell. He did indeed look inches from death. Another time Elizabeth would have felt sorry for him but her attention was sharply focussed elsewhere.

"So you see, I decided to go straight for burning," and with that he lit the fire at Daphne's feet. "I thought you would like to watch your sister die first," he said staring at Shiona.

"STOP!"

The noise echoed through the scene and Elizabeth was amazed to hear the scream coming from her own mouth. She realised then that crazy must run in the family.

The effect was instant. Darius whirled around to see where the voice was coming from; Ingrid, Diana, Wilhelm and Victor flew down to the courtyard and landed next to Darius; the villager-creatures became agitated and started howling and yapping.

Finally Darius set his eyes on Elizabeth, and was not pleased to see her.

"What do you think you are going to do," he said and rose into the air. "You think you can hurt me, you useless, powerless child!"

With that he sent a bolt of magic towards Elizabeth knocking her off her perch and sending her tumbling to the bottom of the rocks. She tried to embrace her fall as much as she could, giving control to her body, rolling the way it wanted to go. She knew it was useless and probably fatal to try to stop herself from falling down the slippery rocks. She landed in a heap at the bottom of the rubble.

"Anytime you want to make an appearance," she hissed at the amulet in her hand as she lay crumpled on the floor.

But she had no time to wait for a reply. Darius raised her into the air with another of his spells and was drawing her to him. She floated past the creature-villagers and their captives, she caught a glimpse of Yorik as she neared him and was surprised at how relaxed he looked. Suddenly she was face to face with Darius.

"I have heard a lot about you child." Darius said, and now Elizabeth was close to him she could see the evil in his eyes, smell the putrid arrogance in his breath and feel cruelty ooze from every pore. "You have been a bother to my children."

Elizabeth looked across at her aunties' and followed their example, "Well, I try," she said brazenly.

He scoffed and threw her to the floor. "You are nothing, I will let my animals have you." He waved at the creatures and one by one they advanced on Elizabeth.

"I have a friend of yours with me," she said desperate to keep Darius's attention.

"Do not listen to her father, she has a very convincing tongue," Wilhelm warned.

Darius laughed dismissively, "you are a fool Wilhelm, you let her deceive you but she cannot fool me."

"You're right," she shouted over the growing noise of the creatures, "I'm not the one who is going to beat you. I'll leave that to my great-grandfather."

"Whatever you're doing Betty, it's not working," Daphne said and Elizabeth was horrified to see that the flames were getting closer and closer to Daphne.

"I think you know him as BARON VON DIEDRICH!" She shouted as the beasts were almost upon her.

Darius raised his hands quickly and the creatures stopped in their tracks.

"Maybe I am wrong to give you to my pets," Darius said staring at her with his cool eyes. "You do have a very clever mind."

Elizabeth knew that if she could engage Darius in conversation then maybe she could buy some time for the witches, *and* find out how to summon her infuriatingly absent Great-Grandfather.

"I give you to my son," he said and turned his back on her, "he seems to be very taken with you."

Darius walked away from Elizabeth and nodded at Wilhelm as he passed. Wilhelm looked from his father to Elizabeth, a cruel grin spread across his face. He advanced on her.

"Do you recognise this?" She said and raised the amulet aloft. "This is what's left of the Baron, your old adversary."

"ENOUGH," Darius said and hovered towards Elizabeth with sickening speed. "You will not say his name here! He is gone and he will not return."

"That's not what he said to me," Elizabeth said trying hard not to cower under Darius's wrath. "He told me he wanted to come home."

She raised the amulet once again and looked at her aunts for encouragement, hoping they too would recognise it and help her release the Baron's spirit. To Elizabeth's dismay they looked utterly mystified.

Daphne mouthed *what are you doing Betty?* just as Darius snatched the amulet out of her hand.

"What is this?" he said. "Costume jewellery? Are you still putting on a show child, like your aunties? Look," he said and he held up the pendant for his family to see, "see what she threatens me with."

His back was turned long enough for Elizabeth to make her move, she ran towards Daphne. But she was not quick enough, Wilhelm flew over her head and landed in front of her, blocking her way.

"You are becoming a bore little witch," Wilhelm said, "I think I will just kill you quickly."

"DO SOMETHING," Elizabeth shouted, "ANYTHING!"

"I will," said Wilhelm, shocked by her outburst.

"Not you!" she said and she could feel her anger start to grow. She was livid with her great-grandfather for not making an appearance. She was sick of feeling at the edge of control and she just wanted someone, anyone, to clarify what the hell she was meant to do. She hated the perpetual feeling of helplessness.

The sky cracked above her as lightening hit the forest behind the castle, and Elizabeth empathised with the elements. She felt her mood fuse with the electricity in the air when suddenly it dawned on her.

"Give me some power," she shouted, "anything!"

Wilhelm was baffled once again by her words. "I will not give you my power!"

"NOT YOU!" Elizabeth shouted in his face.

"You have to take it Betty," Daphne called over the crackling air.

"You know how to Elizabeth," Shiona added, "just do it!"

And Elizabeth reached out with every last ounce of strength and hunted for the witches' power, she even extended the hunt to George imprisoned in the balcony.

Everything happened in an instant. Wilhelm, taking no chances, grabbed her, just as she summoned the witches' power. Once she was powerful again, the pack of beasts turned on her but she ignored them. Wilhelm was holding her by the throat, the creatures were biting and pawing at her, but all she could think about was the alleyway in London. She found the power spot below her navel, reached out for the lightening and with all her might she threw the electricity at the little pendant that Darius held in his hands.

Suddenly the amulet exploded into dazzling hues of emerald green. The light was blinding throwing everything in the courtyard into chaos. There were screams and yelps, groans and howls. Wilhelm dropped Elizabeth and she watched the scene unfold as if in slow-motion from the ground. Elizabeth looked around for her aunties, for Greta, even Victor – anyone she could recognise but it was useless. The courtyard was covered in a sea-green dust, dulling the barrage of noise and making it impossible to see a thing. Suddenly Elizabeth heard a voice in the carnage.

"Hello old friend," it said

Chapter Twenty-Eight

The vibrant dust was beginning to settle and Elizabeth could see that chaos had descended on the courtyard. Bodies were strewn across the ground, forced backwards by the blast. George's creatures were running for cover, their only instinct now was to preserve their lives. With their soulless gaolers gone Shiona and Daphne were once again powerful. Elizabeth could feel their energy just as she could feel the same power coursing through her own veins. Elizabeth hunted through the falling dust and debris for them. As she scrabbled around in the dirt she heard a rasping cough.

"Shiona? Daphne?" She called.

Suddenly a figure blasted skyward and landed next to her with a thump. It was Darius.

"Oh bollocks," she said as she watched him rise through the gloom. Quickly she tried to crawl away but he was on her in seconds, like a wild animal, dragging her to her feet and lifting her by the throat.

"WHAT DID YOU DO?" He screamed at her, "I know you have no powers! I know you cannot harm me! WHO DID YOU SUMMON?"

Face to face with the evil monster Elizabeth could see that he was starting to lose his air of respectability. Underneath the thin human veneer, the real Darius was beginning to show. The skin on his face was cracking exposing a burning red flesh below. One eye was still human but the other was yellow and cat like and enraged. Elizabeth was struck dumb by the sight when suddenly she heard the same rasping cough.

"Put...her down...Darius." The voice was weak, elderly, and spoke between splutters.

"Who is that?" Darius said. He dropped Elizabeth and looked

around wildly.

"It........is me........old friend." The same voice, the same splutters.

The dust was settling quickly now, and as it dispersed Elizabeth could see an old man with long, white hair and a long, white handlebar moustache dressed in a dented and battered suit of golden armour.

"Who are you?" Darius asked the same question that was on Elizabeth's lips.

"Do you not remember me, Ryder? After the days, weeks and years we spent together?"

"Buddy?" Elizabeth asked.

"Oh, oh yes," the figure laughed at first then coughed so badly he almost choked. Recovering he said, "some people did call me Buddy, when I left this place. I quite liked it."

Meanwhile, Darius was sizing up the frail old man, watching him carefully as he spoke to Elizabeth.

"This is impossible. You cannot be the Baron." Darius said.

"Why not?" The little old man asked simply.

"Because he was great, he was magnificent. When he left here, he was the most powerful creature in the universe."

"Oh, tosh!" Buddy said. "I beat you so I must have been omnipotent, is that what you're saying? What arrogance! But then again, I'm sure I felt the same way at the time. But the arrogance of youth has left me now, and I am not quite the boy I used to be."

"I do not believe it," Darius said getting angry, "I will not believe it." He pushed Elizabeth to one side and threw a bolt of power towards Buddy knocking him off his feet.

Elizabeth gasped as the little old man hit the ground hard. She was about to rush over to him when he started to get up, giggling in his own raspy way.

"Just like old times eh Ryder?" He said chuckling.

"Do not call me that!" Darius said and once again sent a bolt of magic flying towards the old man.

This time Buddy somersaulted in the air before landing hard on his face. But the knock only managed to amuse Buddy all the more.

"Oh, I've not done this for ages," he said brushing off his tarnished armour as he stood. "Got anymore?"

Elizabeth looked back at Darius and saw the flicker of a decision

267

ripple across his face. The time for playing games had come to an end. Any minute now Darius was going to release the full force of his powers. She did not want to watch but found it impossible to tear her gaze away.

Suddenly, Darius let loose his power and Elizabeth watched it fly through the air towards Buddy. But Buddy's reflexes were quick. His hands flew up and grabbed the magic in mid-air.

"That's more like it," Buddy said grinning at his old foe, and he cupped the powerful spell in his hands, dispersing it in an instant.

"What is this?" Darius said lowering his hands. "Where have you come from? You are NOT the Baron. I will not believe it."

"You don't have to," Buddy said and Elizabeth noticed that he seemed a little younger.

"It is time for you to give up this fight, Darius," Buddy continued. "Time for you to leave this village and its people alone. It is time for you, for both of us, to go home."

"What are you talking about you ridiculous old man, this has always been my home. But you are right, I will be going soon. I will be entering a world that has been kept from me for centuries." With that Darius threw another spell at the old man but Buddy was ready. His own spell was sublime. His energy burst outwards into a huge protective sphere and started to form a shape. The energy shaped and moulded itself into the figure of a man, a gigantic echo of the little old man that stood in its centre. The giant grew taller and taller, wider and wider until a huge entity stood towering over Darius, his head taller than the tallest tree, his body wider than the castle itself, and in the middle was little old Buddy. His arms were stretched up high, his eyes had clouded over, and he was performing exquisite magic.

The little bolt of power sent by Darius to harm Buddy dissolved even before it reached the giant.

"Why didn't you do that before?" Elizabeth shouted at Buddy. "I was trying to get you out of that amulet for ages!"

"This was not just about me Elizabeth," gone was the raspy wheezing of the old man, now the voice was ethereal and hypnotic, "*you* had to bring me back, only *you*. You had to find a way to do it properly, powerfully."

"Why?" Elizabeth asked. But she did not hear the answer, she was knocked to the floor by a heavy monster. Groaning under the weight she

268

looked up and was surprised to see Daphne grinning in her face.

"Sorry Betty," Daphne said, "but if you had gone on flapping your gums you might have been hit by much worse than me."

Daphne pointed towards Darius who was looking at the crumpled pair on the ground with pure hatred. Daphne then gestured towards a tree opposite that had exploded into bits. That spell was meant for Elizabeth. If Daphne had not saved her, *she* would be the one in pieces.

"Thanks," she said weakly.

"Come on you two," Shiona said dragging Daphne and Elizabeth to their feet. "I don't think he's finished with you yet."

The three witches turned towards Darius who was summoning another spell. They leapt out of the way just in time.

"DO NOT HARM THEM!" Buddy screamed at Darius and knocking him off his feet he forced him into a magical sphere that levitated off the ground.

Elizabeth, Daphne and Shiona watched as Darius was hoisted writhing and screaming into the air.

"Oh – wow!" Elizabeth said watching the scene like a child marvelling at fireworks. "You can do that Shiona!"

Shiona just raised her eyes to the skies.

"This is it," Elizabeth continued watching the warring men, "now he'll get what's coming to him."

"Let's hope so Betty," Daphne said.

Shiona said nothing but carried on watching Darius suspiciously.

"It's OK now Shiona," Elizabeth said, "the Baron's back. He'll sort Darius out once and for all."

"Oh really," Shiona said pointing towards Darius.

Daphne and Elizabeth followed her gaze. Elizabeth's heart leapt into her mouth. Darius was mimicking Buddy's power play. He was creating an energy giant of his own.

"He's never been this powerful before," Shiona said, "not in my memory."

"It's that bloody George," Elizabeth said. "He's told Darius how to be a better wizard, I know it."

"Betty," Daphne said, "don't be horrible. He's my friend."

"Some friend he turned out to be Daphne," Elizabeth said, "he's the reason you nearly died."

"I don't think so Elizabeth," Shiona said.

"What?"

"What!" Daphne and Elizabeth said in unison.

"Well there's no doubt, he's to blame for a lot of what's happened, of course, but not all of it. There's something else, and I think I know what. Come on." With that Shiona took off towards the castle.

Daphne and Elizabeth stood and watched the departing witch run with an efficiency that belied her age.

"What's she talking about?" Elizabeth asked.

"I don't know." Suddenly they heard a crackle behind them and they looked towards the battle. "But I think we'd better go soon Betty!" Daphne added.

Elizabeth watched Buddy's and Darius's energy giants locked in fierce battle. At first glance neither one seemed to be gaining ground, but Daphne was not looking at the giants she was looking at the men. Darius, the younger of the men, was relishing the competition but Buddy, the frail old warrior, was clearly suffering. His magical confidence had gone, he was on his knees and his face had contorted from the agonising effort of fighting his foe.

"Buddy!" Elizabeth called and started toward him but Daphne held her back.

"Come on Betty," she said firmly, "let's find Shiona. Maybe she's onto something."

"Ok," Elizabeth said and reluctantly tore herself away.

Daphne and Elizabeth sprinted towards the castle leaving the battle behind them.

When they found Shiona she was back in the courtyard trying to revive her fallen friends. "Come on you two!" She shouted at Daphne and Elizabeth. They obediently started healing the injured villagers.

"AAAH!" Daphne screamed as she touched one of the villagers, making Shiona and Elizabeth jump.

"What's the matter with you Daphne?" Shiona chastised.

"She's not alone," Daphne said staring horrified at Shiona.

"What do you mean?" Shiona said.

"There's someone else in there."

"I don't believe it," Elizabeth said crawling across to the woman Daphne was helping, "they've done it."

270

"Done what Betty?"

"They've found a way to get the lost souls up here."

"Um........?" Shiona began.

"Long story," Elizabeth interrupted and crawled back to her own villager, "no time to explain now, let's just get them revived."

While Daphne and Shiona set about healing the fallen villagers Elizabeth scanned the debris for Greta. Greta had been planning something and Elizabeth had to know what it was. In a far corner of the courtyard underneath a high stone walkway Elizabeth thought she could see a larger than life figure.

"Yorik," she called and ran towards him.

When she reached him, he was crouching over Greta, blood streaming from his temple.

"Oh little witch!" He said pleased to see her. "Can you help my Greta?"

Elizabeth looked at his fallen wife, she was completely still and her skin was deathly pale. Yorik saw the concern in Elizabeth's face.

"She is not dead little witch," he pleaded, "she cannot be."

"It's OK," Elizabeth said, "I can help."

She took hold of Greta's cool hand. She closed her eyes and searched for a spark of life. She could tell – Greta was broken. In her mind's eye Elizabeth could see Greta's last moments. As the amulet exploded Greta was catapulted into the air. Elizabeth could see Greta's body being flung backwards hitting a column; her body was practically bent in two on impact and Elizabeth heard a sickening crack.

"Oh no," Elizabeth's heart sank.

She knew she was too inexperienced to help this kind of wound. Wordlessly she called for her aunts. She tried the same telepathy she had in the forest and prayed they would hear her.

Within seconds they were at her side, both of them looking in shock at Greta's broken body.

"Please," Yorik said seeing their reactions, "it is not too late."

"I'm sorry Yorik......." Shiona began.

"NO!" Elizabeth shouted. "There's still something here Shiona I can feel it. We have to try!"

"Betty....."

"I mean it Daphne," Elizabeth said angrily fighting back the tears,

271

"you get down on your bloody knees and you help me heal her!"

Shiona and Daphne looked doubtfully at one another but dutifully obliged. The three witches took up positions around Greta, even Yorik took hold of his wife's hand, hoping that he too could help. Daphne and Shiona did not believe that Greta could recover so Elizabeth knew it was up to her to start the healing. She closed her eyes and held onto Greta's feet. She allowed her consciousness to slip through her arms and start searching Greta's body for a sign of life. She was becoming quite proficient at improvising spells. Whenever the witches were close she knew anything was possible, the only limit to her powers was her own imagination. And since being in Branko, Elizabeth's imagination had flourished.

As she hunted through Greta's body Elizabeth could tell a crowd was gathering behind her. The villagers who had been revived came over to watch them resuscitate Greta. Elizabeth could sense their hope. She knew that they wanted their friend back as much as Elizabeth did, more so. As she carried on her desperate search she perceived something else residing in Greta's body. Something that was not meant to be there – a displaced soul. It was Gretchen.

Gretchen, can you help? Elizabeth thought.

Shiona and Daphne were shocked to hear the question.

I can try.

Came the answer that only the three witches could hear.

I know she has not gone yet. I know the Angel has not taken her.

That's something, Elizabeth thought in reply and struck on another idea.

She turned to the assembled crowd, "hold on to one another," she said and held the ankle of the woman nearest her.

With one hand on the foot of her lifeless friend and the other on the leg of a stranger, Elizabeth pulled all the hope she found in the crowd and poured it into Greta. It did not take long for the villagers to realised what she was trying to do and they all crowded around joining hands, clasping arms and trying to maintain contact with one another. Daphne and Shiona started sending their own healing into Greta. All the time they were working, Elizabeth was searching for a glimmer of life.

All at once she perceived a flicker, like the spark of a cigarette lighter that cannot quite fire up. As soon as she sensed it she aimed for it. She summoned everything and poured it towards the little ray of light. The surrounding villagers took a shocked breath as Elizabeth took all of what they were happy to give and forced that source of life to ignite. The spark was there, trying to fire up. It sparked once, twice, and suddenly dulled completely.

Elizabeth opened her eyes in shock. "No, NO!" she screamed.

Daphne put her hand on Elizabeth's shoulder, "It's no use..."

"NO!" She shouted shaking Daphne off. "AGAIN!"

She looked at the surrounding crowd and defied them not to obey her. They all resumed positions as before. But this time they struggled to find hope.

GRETCHEN? Elizabeth called.

I'm here.

Is she there? Elizabeth asked.

I don't know. I don't see her.

Elizabeth closed her eyes and held on tight to Greta's feet. A lady behind Elizabeth knelt down and put her hands on Elizabeth's shoulders. The rest of the villagers dutifully made a physical connection with one another.

"Don't give up," Elizabeth whispered, "don't you dare give up! I know you Greta. I have seen your resilience." *DON'T YOU DARE GIVE UP!* She blasted her thought into Greta's lifeless body.

I see something! Gretchen cried.

The spark was back and Elizabeth saw it too. Elizabeth drew all of the energy from the villagers once again and in her head she heard Shiona say, *I've got an idea Elizabeth.* Suddenly Shiona seized all the energy in the atmosphere, as soon as she realised what was happening Daphne joined her sister in the search, Elizabeth used the power of the villagers, Gretchen softly coaxed her mother, Shiona took charge, *Ready?* she thought, *One – two – three!* and the three witches blasted the spark with everything they had.

WHOOSH! The flame took hold and the life-giving energy from all her friends and family and from the atmosphere itself coursed through Greta's body. She sucked in a deep breath and the crowd cheered but Elizabeth and the witches knew their work was not yet done.

Greta had crashed with her back against one of the stone columns and she was going to be in agony or paralysed when she fully recovered if the witches did not work fast. Elizabeth left this complex healing to her experienced aunts whilst she healed Greta's lesser breaks and bruises. Elizabeth felt the white hot power of the witches as they took no chances and bombarded Greta's broken back with their growing and healing powers. Somehow they were stronger and more focused in Branko. Their healing powers were miraculous.

All at once they stopped. The white energy they were injecting into Greta was gone and in its place was the soft warm golden glow of Greta's soul. Elizabeth opened her eyes as she felt a strong hand on her shoulders.

"You can stop now little witch," Yorik said and as Elizabeth looked up at him she saw clean tears streaking his dirty face. She realised her own cheeks were moist. The effort and the hope had brought tears to all their eyes including, Elizabeth was surprised to see, Shiona's.

"Thank you," Elizabeth heard a weakened voice say. It was Greta. She was alive.

"You're welcome," Elizabeth said quietly and managed a soft smile of reassurance.

Yorik landed heavily on the ground in front of Elizabeth and scooped his wife into his arms. Elizabeth watched the couple embrace. It was a heart-warming and heart-breaking sight. Moments before Greta could have been lost forever. Tears filled Elizabeth's eyes, blurring her vision.

"Well done Betty," Daphne said softly. "You didn't give up hope."

"That's my girl," Shiona said and patted Elizabeth on the back. "Now are you going to explain about the *lost souls*?"

"I can do that," Yorik interrupted, "we have brought the souls with us, just as you said Elizabeth. Now all we have to do is find a way of connecting them to their bodies."

"Betty! Did you tell them we could do that?"

"I said I thought it might be possible," Elizabeth said defensively.

"How on earth......?" Shiona started.

"George," Elizabeth interrupted. "He separated them, all he has to do is reattach them. Surely it's as simple as reversing the spell."

"Of course it isn't Elizabeth." Shiona said.

"How do you know?" Elizabeth asked.

Shiona was quiet, she had no answer.

"You see!" Elizabeth continued. "You can't know for sure. It's worth a try."

"But what good will it do Betty?"

"Elizabeth's right," to Elizabeth's surprise it was Shiona agreeing with her. "We have to try. We need the people to be fighting fit. That's why Darius is so powerful now. He's no longer weakened by the purity of the people."

"But how are we supposed to.........?" Daphne started.

"Yorik," Elizabeth said ignoring her, "round up all of the villagers who are hosting a spirit and keep them together."

"And how are they 'hosting a spirit' Betty?"

"We'll have to try to find George," Shiona said to Yorik ignoring Daphne, "and for goodness sake, stay away from Darius's family."

"But...but," spluttered Daphne.

"That shouldn't be much of a problem," Elizabeth added, "they've got no idea about the spirits so they won't think you're a threat. It's the witches they'll be after."

"Will you two......" Daphne tried once again.

"It will be OK," Yorik said, "I will do as you ask, please just find George."

With that Shiona and Elizabeth ran towards the castle.

"He was on the balcony the last time I saw him," Elizabeth said.

"I know!" Shiona said.

"Oh I give up!" Daphne cried and sprinted after them.

"I don't suppose you want to tell us about the amulet and the Baron, Elizabeth?" Shiona asked as they made their way up the front steps to the castle.

"Mum was training Jessie, did you know that?" Elizabeth said bounding up the steps two at a time.

"Yes," Shiona answered, "until your father found out she was a witch and put a stop to it."

"No! That's not what happened," Elizabeth said. "It was the other way around! Mum found out that Dad was related to the Baron and she nearly killed him for not telling her. They *both* decided to keep their past lives from us. *That's* why she stopped training Jessie."

"Why didn't she tell us?" Daphne asked.

"I don't know. But I do know she knew something different was going to happen this year. That's why she sent me and that's why she gave me Dad's amulet."

"She's always had a frighteningly accurate sixth sense," Daphne said breathlessly as she ran up the stairs. "We made her stop using it after a while, it was too weird."

"*Too weird*?" Elizabeth scoffed. "You've got supernatural powers but Mum's sixth sense was *too weird*."

"You know what I mean Betty!"

"I wish she'd warned us it was all going to be different this year," Shiona said as they reached the top of the stairs.

"Tell me about it," Elizabeth said and they pushed open the huge wooden doors.

Inside they saw the same threadbare curtains that stood between them and the dance floor on the night of the masquerade.

"Head's up ladies," Daphne said, "I don't suppose Darius's family are going to take this lying down."

They threw open the curtains and sure enough assembled in the great hall were Ingrid, Diana, Wilhelm and Victor.

"What an interesting turn of events this has been," Ingrid drawled, "well Darius might be a little bit preoccupied but I assure you WE are still ready for you."

"I bet you are," Shiona said under her breath. "Elizabeth you find George. Daphne and I have got this."

Elizabeth could see that Shiona was pleased to have the playing field even once again. Now that Darius and his unusually powerful magic were otherwise engaged normality had resumed.

Elizabeth, Shiona and Daphne walked slowly down the stairs to the dance floor in the great hall. Elizabeth was ready to split off as soon as she dared, but she had to bide her time. They reached the bottom of the stairs and stared defiantly at Darius's family. The air began to sizzle as each faction readied themselves for battle. Elizabeth had her orders but by the look on Wilhelm's face, he was not about to let her get away easily.

"Don't you worry about him," Shiona whispered to her, sensing the problem, "Wilhelm and I have got a little bit of unfinished business."

"*Hell hath no fury* and all that," Daphne called across to Elizabeth.

"Subtle *Aunty* Daphne," Elizabeth said, "very subtle."

With that Wilhelm, unable to take the anticipation a moment longer, launched himself at Elizabeth. But he was swiftly knocked sideways by

Shiona's spell.

"Go!" Shiona shouted and Elizabeth ran to the same door she had gone through at the masquerade ball.

Once at the door she chanced a look back. Battle had commenced and spells and bodies were flying everywhere. For a moment she considered helping her aunties, she could not bear to be parted from them again. Then she saw Shiona's scornful face in her mind's eye and thought she would better serve them by doing the job she had been charged with. She hurried through the door.

Elizabeth ran up the spiral stone staircase as fast as she could, opened the door at the top and entered the bedroom. It looked different in the cold light of day. It was dusty and dingy, a lot less romantic than it had been under Wilhelm's intoxicating spell. She shuddered at the thought of letting that monster get so close to her. She found her way easily onto the balcony and there was the pitiful sight of George, sat on the floor in the corner still encased in the Baron's muddy green spell.

"What do you think you are going to do?" A voice said from behind her.

Elizabeth spun around and saw a familiar figure extricate himself from the gloom.

"I knew you'd follow me," she said.

Chapter Twenty-Nine

Elizabeth drew herself up to her full height and summoned all the power of the witches to her. They were close, so close to seeing an end to Darius's evil reign. Elizabeth was not about to let this boy stand in her way.

"How did you get away from the witches?" she asked.

"They do not think I am much of a threat," Victor replied. "It was easy to sneak away when they thought I was injured."

Elizabeth could feel the sizzle of supernatural power within. Victor had confused her from day one and now he stood before her, the creature she thought might be an ally, and she felt nothing but anger towards him.

"Be careful Victor," she said slowly, "I'm powerful now and you are not going to stand in my way."

"I do not want to stop you Elizabeth," he said taking a step closer to her. "I want to help."

"Really?! Just like you *helped* the rest of your friends?"

From behind her George was suddenly alerted to their conversation.

"Don't let him near me Elizabeth," George pleaded from the balcony. "He is the worst, the very worst of them. He was the one who brought those poor unsuspecting children to me."

"I know," Elizabeth said through gritted teeth keeping a cautious eye on Victor.

"Please Elizabeth," Victor said. "You know me, we are friends. You know I would not harm you. I have never tried to harm you. I have only wanted to keep you safe."

"Why?" Elizabeth asked.

"Because I want an end to all of this, I want it over. And," he added, "because you remind me of Gladys."

"What do you know about my mother?" Elizabeth said, shocked at the mention of her name.

"Don't listen to him," George called from behind her, "he's just trying to bamboozle you. If you let him in he'll destroy you just like he did those poor children."

"Be quiet George!" Elizabeth snapped. "What do you know about my mother?"

"I thought she was my only hope." Victor replied, "I thought she could help me. She knows so much about the life force that resides within people. She did not believe that any soul could be completely evil, even my father. She knew the last time I saw her would be her last visit because Darius looked deep within her and found her weakness – you."

Elizabeth knew the truth of these words, had heard them from her mother's own lips but was amazed to hear them coming from Victor.

"She was such a kind soul." Victor continued still edging towards Elizabeth. "If Darius is everything evil about mankind, then your mother is everything good. I had such a feeling of peace when she was near, almost as though she could make everything better."

The things Victor knew about her mother stung at Elizabeth.

"How dare you speak about her!" She cried.

"Because she was my friend!" Victor said earnestly and took another step towards Elizabeth. "And if anyone were to ask me about you I will say the same thing. You have been a friend to me Elizabeth and I have tried to be a friend to you."

"I don't think I like your idea of *friendship*," Elizabeth railed, "look what happened to the last people you called *friend*!"

Victor sighed and walked towards the balcony. "I had my reasons for turning on my friends."

"Oh, I know your *reasons* Victor," Elizabeth said, "fear and selfishness were your *reasons*. You knew that your father would hurt you or worse, you were more interested in preserving your own pitiful life than saving the villagers. That was your reason."

"I have spent so many years living in fear of Darius," Victor said staring vacantly towards the captured George, "fear is not a new experience for me. But when I started making friends, I started to feel emotions I thought were long lost to me. Then the witches came, and I suddenly felt alive again.

"On her last visit your mother took me to one side. It was the day they were due to leave. My family were back at the castle, licking their wounds. The witches were preparing for their journey. Your mother summoned me and we walked in the woods. She told me something that day that filled me with hope – and dread."

"What?" Elizabeth asked suspiciously.

"She had a premonition that our interminable existence would one day come to an end but before it did I would have to betray my friends and put my faith in a stranger. I thought that stranger was George, that is why I did what he asked, but now I believe Elizabeth," Victor said and turned towards her, "the stranger your mother was talking about is you."

"Well that's convenient," Elizabeth said, "as she's not here and there's no way I can check with her so you can pretty much say anything you like, can't you?"

"Surely you know enough of your mother to know there must be some truth in my words?"

"I do," Elizabeth said, "in fact I'm learning more and more about her every day, but that still doesn't mean I trust you."

"Let me help you Elizabeth," Victor said, "that's all I ask."

"How can you possibly help me?"

"Watch," Victor said.

With that he puts his hands above the spell holding George and starting stripping it away. It was a laborious process. Victor's powers were not as strong as his father's but he knew exactly what he was doing. Bit by bit he tore away Darius's spell.

Elizabeth watched in amazement as Victor pulled layer after layer away from George, grunting and groaning with the exertion. All the while George complained and tried to convince Elizabeth that Victor was not to be trusted. All Elizabeth knew was that she needed George to help her reverse the spell on the soulless villagers and Victor was managing to free him.

As Victor got down to the last layer of the spell, a silence had fallen over George and Elizabeth watched him suspiciously. The two men in front of her had been both friend and foe to the witches and she did not know which one to trust, if any.

By the time he was completely free George acted quickly. Using the power of the witches he cast a spell on Victor spinning him around and clamping his arms tightly to his side. Instantly Victor tried to cast a counter-spell, but it was no use, George was more devious with his gifts than Victor. Victor remained stuck tight.

"Let go of him George!" Elizabeth shouted.

"I don't think so Elizabeth," he said concentrating his spell on a squirming Victor. "He's a bargaining point for Darius and for you. Darius would love to be informed that his son is a traitor and you will not dare harm me whilst I'm holding your *friend*."

"George, are you stupid?" Elizabeth said. "Don't you remember what Darius said to you in the dungeon? If he was angry that you betrayed the witches he's gonna be twice as mad that you've betrayed his own son."

A flicker of doubt flashed across George's face.

"Come on George," Elizabeth said attempting to reason with him, "what kind of a man do you want to be? You've got a chance to help now, to make a difference. We can save Branko and go home as heroes. But if you keep running back to Darius all you'll ever do is spread evil throughout the world. Surely you don't want that? My Aunty Daphne believes in you, the question is George, do you believe in yourself?"

George seemed to consider this for a moment but then he looked up slowly with a sly grin.

"That was pretty cheesy Elizabeth," he said, "but it nearly worked. Unfortunately for you, I'm not stupid. I know I won't be given a hero's welcome when I go home. I will be punished. But here, in Branko, here I can be great. I can have great power and I can achieve great things hand in hand with Lord Darius."

George moved towards the door using Victor as a shield between him and Elizabeth. But Elizabeth raced to the door with lightning speed, enhanced by the power of the witches, and blocked his retreat.

"Think very carefully," she said to a shocked George, "I'm giving you one more chance. Are you going to make the right decision?"

"I already have Elizabeth," he said, "now OUT OF MY WAY!"

He strengthened his hold over Victor crushing him, warning Elizabeth he was not to be messed with. Victor let out a yelp.

"You are such an idiot," Elizabeth said and with that she reversed her own spell with ease. All the power she had given George in the dungeon, she took back, every last drop, leaving him with nothing. By the time she had finished the position of strength had swapped between George and Victor. The captor now became the captive. Victor had George in a head lock with one arm forced behind his back.

Elizabeth rounded on him, "now you will tell me how to get those souls back to their bodies or so help me George I will unleash the wrath of Shiona on your sorry arse!"

From Victor's chokehold George let out a stifled laugh. "If you think I'm going to help you, you've got another thing coming."

Elizabeth leaned close to him, "we'll see," she whispered threateningly in his ear. "Bring him this way," she said to Victor and he dutifully obliged dragging the pitiful George behind him. Victor and Elizabeth were once again allies but Elizabeth was not sure how long the truce would last.

At the bottom of the winding stairway Elizabeth looked cautiously through the door wondering if the battle was still in full swing. She searched the room for any sign of Darius's family, but an eerie silence had descended over the hall. Elizabeth walked in. The room was devastated and Shiona and Daphne were picking through the ruins. They turned sharply around when they heard Elizabeth preparing for another onslaught.

"At ease soldiers," Elizabeth said raising her hands, "it's only me."

But Shiona and Daphne did not lower their defences.

"Elizabeth move away slowly," Shiona said, "we've got him."

Elizabeth followed Shiona's gaze and saw she was pointing her wand at Victor.

"You might want to just hear him out." Elizabeth said blocking Shiona's aim.

"Haven't you learned anything yet Betty," Daphne said, "you can't trust these buggers."

"I'm not the only one who has put their trust in the enemy Daphne," Elizabeth said and moved to one side revealing Victor's captive.

"Daphne, help me," George pleaded. "They're both mad! I only want to help and they've trapped me. She's in league with that beast you know. You can't trust this girl."

"Betty," Daphne said, "what's he talking about?"

"Oh come on Daphne," Elizabeth said, "are you seriously going to take his word over mine?"

"I wouldn't trust him as far as I could throw him Elizabeth," Shiona said, "but what I want to know is why are *you* trusting Victor?"

"I know you have no reason to believe me ladies," Victor interjected from behind Elizabeth, "but I only want an end to this miserable existence. I have no interest in living this half-life as Darius's *child*. It is not who I am, I only want to go home."

Shiona looked at Victor suspiciously and Elizabeth could tell she was deciding whether to trust him or not.

"Alright," Shiona said finally, "you can come with us but if he makes one wrong move Elizabeth I expect you to deal with him. If you want him to come, then you better watch your back my girl."

Elizabeth nodded.

"What about George?" Daphne asked.

"I've never trusted that man Daphne you know I haven't. He stays with Elizabeth and Victor until we know what to do with him."

"Just don't hurt him Victor," Daphne said, "or I promise you won't know what hit you."

"Oh Aunty Daphne," Elizabeth said patting her on the shoulder, "love really is blind isn't it!"

"That's enough you two, we've got to get back to the Baron," Shiona said.

"Where are my family?" Victor asked.

"They fled when it was all too much for them. I suppose they're so used to hiding behind Darius that they don't know how to fight alone, the cowards," Shiona said.

"Please Shiona," Victor said, "they might be fools, they might have lost sight of who they truly are, but they are not cowards."

"Er.. shall we discuss the merits of malevolent creatures another time children," Daphne said looking out of the window, "I think Betty's great-grandfather is in a bit of trouble."

Shiona and Elizabeth rushed over to the window and were stunned by what they saw. There, cowering under the wrath of Darius's giant monster, was Buddy. His own giant, nothing but a faint aura, was all that was standing between him and utter devastation.

"Come on," Shiona said grabbing a long stick she found in the mess of the great hall. Suddenly Shiona flew out of the window using the stick as a makeshift broom leaving Elizabeth and Daphne wide-eyed in astonishment.

"Well we could all do that!" Daphne shouted at her departing sister. "Come on Betty, we'll be here all day trying to find another suitable branch. Let's go the conventional way."

Daphne and Elizabeth ran back up the steps of the great hall and out of the main doors with Victor hot on their heels half dragging, half carrying, a reluctant George behind him. As they got to the bottom of the stairs they were met by some of the recovered villagers.

"What is happening Elizabeth?" It was Yorik.

"Buddy's losing and we've got to try to help him," she said.

"Who is this 'Buddy'?" Yorik asked.

"Elizabeth," Greta interrupted, "who did you release from that amulet?"

"An old friend of yours Greta, and yours Yorik, and all of yours," she said, addressing the crowd, "and he needs our help if we're ever going to live through this."

"Alright Elizabeth," Yorik said, "what do you need us to do?"

"I have absolutely no idea to be honest," she said, "just follow us and keep those lost souls with you."

Elizabeth and the others ran through the crowd and one by one the villagers followed eyeing Victor and George suspiciously.

"I don't suppose my Mum gave you any hints about how to stop Darius," Elizabeth said to Victor as they ran.

"I am afraid not," Victor said struggling to keep up dragging his prisoner behind him. "That was where everything got a bit vague for her."

"Well that's handy," Elizabeth said.

"But she did say the stranger would help or die trying."

"Well that's not very comforting Victor, especially as you think *I'm* the stranger," Elizabeth said. "I'm kind of hoping you were right the first time, and George is the stranger in question!"

As they rounded the corner at the edge of the forest they could see the battle between Darius and the Baron taking place and Shiona was right in the thick of it.

"What the hell are you doing Shiona," Daphne shouted, "you mad

284

witch!"

Shiona was adding her power and strength to the Baron's giant and he was starting to grow.

"I can't keep this up for much longer," wheezed Buddy.

"Come on you two," Shiona shouted, "I need your help."

Daphne and Elizabeth stared at each other for a moment, shocked by this admission of weakness from their formidable relative.

"NOW!" Shiona barked. Daphne ran to her side and Elizabeth took up position opposite them. They added their own power to the melee.

Buddy's giant grew bigger and bigger and as the witches magic merged with the Baron's the air around them sizzled. Concentrating on her energy blast Elizabeth could sense the villager-creatures just beyond the castles boundary. They were becoming more and more agitated. Their instinct to run and hide when Buddy first appeared was being replaced by their training. The witches were powerful again and the beasts were on the prowl.

"Oh bugger," Elizabeth said quietly.

"What's the matter Betty," Daphne asked.

"If we don't finish this soon, we're in a lot of trouble." Elizabeth said, "George's creatures are coming back."

"Victor," Shiona shouted behind her, hearing the conversation, "get that bugger to tell you how to reverse his spell!"

"I have been trying Shiona," Victor shouted back and then more quietly to George, "tell me now or I will destroy you."

"You can't destroy me Sonny Jim," George said, "or you will never get those villagers back to their bodies. Looks like I'm the one with the power now!"

"Please Georgie," Daphne called, "we need your help."

"It's a shame you didn't think about that before Daphers. I would have helped you, would have been more than happy to come on one of your trips but you rejected me and I........"

"Oh SHUT UP George!" Elizabeth interrupted, "I've heard that story before and it was dull the first time. Don't destroy him Victor, just hurt him – a lot!"

"You may not have to worry about the creatures little one," it was the Baron. Elizabeth looked across at him, shocked to hear the strength in his voice. There standing where the wheezing, cowering figure of

Buddy had been was Baron Von Deiderich. Even the villagers gasped at the sight. He was young and he was strong and his energy giant was magnificent.

"It *is* the Baron!" Yorik said from behind the witches and a murmur of recognition rumbled through the crowd.

The Baron winked knowingly at Elizabeth and started to expand. Breathing deeply he grew and grew until his whole body matched the size of Darius's magical giant. But the Baron was flesh, blood and bones. The gigantic creature was no longer a projected vision, it was now an enormous man. The saviour of Branko had returned. The Baron grew until he was the size of Darius's spell and stared at Darius's creation in its evil eye. All at once the Baron started to grow even bigger and bigger until, within seconds, he towered over the evil creature.

Darius was no match for him. The blast of power he was using to create his giant paled into insignificance as the Baron, a huge warlock made of flesh and blood, joined the battle. The witches' magic made the Baron formidable. His ancient power merged with the power of the witches just as it had centuries ago. Even though they were different witches the effect was still the same.

The Baron watched as Darius weakened under his force but he was taking no chances with his old foe. Raising his gigantic arms to the sky he cast a spell to suck all of the power from Darius's projection until all that was standing between the evil Lord Darius and the colossal Baron was nothing but thin air.

"Please old friend, please," Darius cried. "It does not have to end like this. We were once such great friends. I could change. We can be great again – together!"

"I WISH I COULD BELIEVE YOU," the Baron's voice boomed through the ruins, "BUT I KNOW YOU TOO WELL FOR THAT OLD FRIEND. YOUR TIME RULING BRANKO IS OVER *LORD DARIUS* IT IS TIME TO SAY GOODBYE."

"NO!" A voice from behind Elizabeth screamed, "do not hurt him." It was Ingrid, "please Baron, I am begging you!"

"No mother," Victor cried and rushed towards her holding her back from the battle, "stay away."

"Do not touch me," Ingrid said and she pushed Victor violently to the floor, "you are a coward and a traitor, you will never speak to me again!"

"I AM SORRY INGRID, THIS WAS NEVER YOUR FAULT BUT YOU KNOW I CANNOT SPARE HIM."

Elizabeth could see that Ingrid was about to plead with the Baron again, but it was too late. The Baron picked up the protesting and writhing figure of Darius in his enormous hand. He took one last deep breath, Elizabeth could feel the air around her being sucked into the gigantic form, and blew a toxic spell at Darius. As Darius breathed in the poison expelled by the Baron, the enormous warlock crushed the evil creature in his colossal hand.

The villagers and witches collectively held their breath as they witnessed the last moments of Lord Darius. As soon as the giant Baron released Darius from his grasp, he began to shrink. He shrank back to the man that the villagers once new as Baron Von Deiderick but his transformation did not stop there. In front of their eyes the Baron aged and Buddy, the little old man appeared coughing and spluttering.

"That's it," Buddy said as he sat heavily on the ground. "That's all I've got."

"That's all it took," Elizabeth said sitting next to her great-grandfather and putting her head on his shoulder. "What happens now?"

"I'll wait for him," Buddy said quietly, "and we'll go home together."

"You murderer!" Ingrid screamed and rushed over to the Darius's fallen body. "You've killed him!"

"That's a bit rich isn't it Ingrid," Daphne said indignantly, "considering how many people your old man there has killed, or would have killed given half the chance."

Ingrid said nothing but sobbed into the lifeless form of her husband.

"It's over," Victor said dropping on his knees next to Ingrid, "it's really over."

"Not quite," Elizabeth said, "there's the small problem of George's creatures."

At these words everyone looked up. The villager-creatures were approaching, snarling and yapping as they circled the crowd. Their master was dead and they were ready to take revenge.

Shiona marched over to where George was cowering like a useless lump on the floor.

"What the hell do we do with them George!" She said lifting him bodily to his feet.

"I'm not going to tell you," George said but there was uncertainty in his face as he was confronted by the magnitude of Shiona's anger.

"Ok Georgie Porgie," Shiona said cruelly, "what's it gonna be, searing agony in the knees, the chest or the groin? I'm partial to the groin area myself, but you choose."

"Shiona!" Daphne said.

"Not now Daphne! I can't bear to hear another of your sob stories of how 'he really is nice deep down'!" Shiona barked as the villager-creatures inched closer and closer to the crowd. "I tell you what Daphne, why don't we open him up and see what a softy he really is on the inside."

"Shiona!" Elizabeth shouted.

"It's OK Elizabeth," Shiona continued, "we won't kill him we'll just peel his skin back and look at what's underneath!"

Shiona was fixing George with a sadistic stare but Elizabeth knew that at this moment in time, George was the least of their worries. Staring over Shiona's shoulder George could also see the devastating change of events and he started to laugh maniacally.

"Oh you think this is funny, do you?" Shiona continued. "Well you won't be laughing when......."

"SHIONA!"

"SHIONA!" Daphne and Elizabeth screamed.

"What!" She said and spun quickly around.

There in front of them rising from the fallen body of Darius like a phoenix from the ashes was Darius's twisted, malignant soul.

It groaned and screamed as it extricated itself from its defeated physical form. It grew in size until it was at least as big as the Baron had just been. It was a fusion of animal and man with horns growing from its head, a tail growing from its spine and cloven hooves where its feet should have been and its skin was alive with a raging inferno of flames.

"Come on," Elizabeth whispered to Buddy and tried to raise him to his feet. "We have to move."

She raised Buddy to his feet. The man had no strength left in him so he leant his frail body on Elizabeth. She turned to run but came face to face with the villager-creatures who were blocking their escape. There was no way out and Buddy had nothing left to fight with.

Suddenly Darius's evil soul spied Elizabeth and the Baron.

"*HA-HA, HA-HA, HA!*" He boomed his voice deeper and crueller than Buddy's had been. "*NOW WE ARE EQUALS ONCE AGAIN, EH OLD FRIEND?*"

Chapter Thirty

"You are no friend of mine," Buddy rasped, "you are nothing but a monster..."

The cruel soul of Darius rose above them, infused with swirling scarlet clouds, alive with hatred and anger, contained within his grotesque form. It howled in humourless mirth at the Baron.

"..but I have been waiting a long time to meet you," Buddy wheezed.

Elizabeth looked incredulously at her great-grandfather, and so did the gathered crowd. Even the devilish soul was momentarily intrigued.

"What do you mean Buddy?" Elizabeth asked.

"Ryder was naïve and ignorant but he was not evil. I recognised his face as soon as he walked back into Branko all those years ago. He had adopted the persona of Lord Darius but the body was still the same. It didn't take me long to realise that the man I knew was lost forever. The Ryder that I knew was curious about supernatural powers, he even dabbled with darker elements. But he would never, ever have subjected the world to such cruelty."

"*CLEVER, VERY CLEVER. NOT THAT IT DOES YOU ANY GOOD NOW. I WILL DESTROY YOU EVEN WITH THE KNOWLEDGE THAT RYDER HAS GONE.*"

"NO!" A voice screamed from behind them, "I will not believe it!" It was Ingrid, tears streaming down her face.

"Mother," Victor said leaving George and rushing to her side, "he has turned you into a monster, no mere mortal can do that. He is not the person you thought he was."

Ingrid fell into Victor's arms and sobbed.

Elizabeth watched Darius's family huddle together in shock and disbelief and suddenly an idea struck her.

"I don't know Victor," Elizabeth said, "maybe there is something of Ryder left."

"What do you mean Little One?" Buddy asked.

"If he was nothing but evil," she said, "why would he need a family around him?"

"*I NEEDED MINIONS YOU RIDICULOUS CHILD!*"

"Go on Elizabeth," Buddy said encouragingly.

"But you didn't use them as minions did you," she continued. "Mostly they were just your family."

"*ENOUGH!*" The monster screamed at Elizabeth and the whirling clouds within him deepened and darkened. "*WE HAVE PLAYED FOR LONG ENOUGH. IT IS TIME TO END THIS.*"

With that the creature slowly started to spin. Turn after turn grew quicker and quicker. Faster and faster he span and started to create a suction of air around him. He span on and on until he was a crimson tornado, swirling violently amongst the devastation. The crowd scattered and ran in all directions as Darius's spinning soul sucked earth, branches and smashed castle remnants towards him. But they could not run far, George's creatures were still faithful to their master no matter what form he took and they snapped and snarled at the villagers stopping their escape.

"Elizabeth you have to make a choice," Buddy said as Elizabeth dragged him to his feet keeping him as far away from Darius as possible. "What shall we do?"

"How on earth should I know Buddy?!" Elizabeth said. "You're the wizard in the family – you tell me!"

"I can't Little One, it has to be you!" Buddy said as Elizabeth tried to drag him away.

"Why?" She said when suddenly she bumped into Yorik and some of the villagers who were backing away from their soulless children.

"It has to be you Elizabeth because you have to know," Buddy said. "You have to finally know what it is to make a life changing decision and not just for yourself but for the greater good."

"Why me?" Elizabeth shouted over the growing noise. "Surely we can talk about my selfishness when Darius is defeated!"

"Oh Elizabeth," Buddy said and held her face in his hands, "it's not just about letting go of who you *don't* want to be – it's about embracing who you *are*."

The villagers were shouting and screaming; the creatures were growling and yelping; and Darius's soul was creating a vortex, trying to suck every last one of them in.

"*SOON I WILL HAVE YOU ALL. EACH AND EVERY TERRIFIED SOUL AT MY DISPOSAL AND I WILL BE INVINCIBLE.*"

"That's it!" Elizabeth said suddenly. "The souls! He has still got a soul no matter how evil it is, he was contained by the purity of the villagers."

"So what do we have to do Little One?"

"SHIONA," Elizabeth screamed above the noise, "find a way to release those souls!"

"Good girl!" Buddy said and using the last of his strength he pushed himself away from her and took up position in front of the swirling monster.

Shiona quickly took out her wand, aimed it at George who was cowering next to Victor and his inconsolable mother, and sent a spell flying towards him. It sparkled all around him and encased him in a bubble of light that brought him flying speedily towards Shiona. As soon as he was near she grabbed him by the neck.

"Do it now!" She spat in his face. But George did nothing but weep and gibber in her grip.

"I don't know if he can help!" Shiona called, "he's totally lost it."

"Buddy," Elizabeth screamed, "what do I do now?"

"Do not worry little witch." The voice came from within the crowd. Elizabeth was surprised to see Greta emerge with a smile on her face. "Letting go of these souls will be easy. It has been very difficult holding onto them for so long."

With that the villagers hosting the souls of their loved ones stepped forward and Elizabeth was amazed to see that they were all women, and they were all mothers. Elizabeth marvelled at the miracle of motherhood. All these women had at one time experienced another life within them, an unborn soul on the precipice of birth. Now, when they needed them most, these incredible women were once again playing host to their children.

"Daphne, Shiona," Elizabeth shouted, "try to make sure they don't float away!"

The village mothers all held onto one another for support and quickly, easily breathed their loved ones into the air. Once the souls were airborne George's creatures stopped in their tracks. The witches rushed behind the villagers and created a force field in the sky above the spirits so they would not disappear into the ether. Then Buddy began to levitate above the ground to join them. Once he was level with the souls they poured their lightness and goodness into him.

The squally, dark sky began to transform. The eerie greyness slowly became more light and bright. Brighter and lighter the air around them grew until the sky crackled with the dazzling golden light of the purest of souls. The rays from the semi-circle of bodiless spirits aimed at Buddy. And the golden light around Buddy grew into a sparkling sphere gaining strength and greatness from the bodiless souls of the lost villagers. From the ground Elizabeth could see that Buddy looked like a child's drawing of the sun. He was at the centre of a perfect golden circle of light and his connection to the souls looked like rays of sunshine.

Elizabeth watched as Buddy once again became strong, young and handsome. He was face to face with the incredible evil power of Darius, and was biding his time. Darius, however, was sucking everything he could into the swirling tornado, using every last atom of power. Bricks, debris, branches, trees, vegetation were all careering towards him.

The villagers on the ground were coaxing the bodies of their soulless children away from the devastation. They were faced with no resistance. The souls, now free, had halted all control over the bodies. Like balloons being pushed in the air by small children, the creatures were allowing themselves to be moved to safety.

The witches, however, were not out of danger. Elizabeth could feel the force of Darius's spell and suddenly her feet started to slide involuntarily across the ground.

"SHIONA!" She screamed. "I can't hold on for much longer!"

She was trying to resist the pull but also trying to hold the souls in place with the other two witches.

"Give it everything you've got my girl!" Shiona shouted across at her. "Everything you've got!"

"AARGH!" Elizabeth screamed and tried to dig her feet harder into

293

the ground.

"You can do it Betty," Daphne called, trying to reassure her. Elizabeth chanced a look over at her aunty and was horrified to see that she was having the same problem. Even this Amazonian warrior of a woman was being drawn inexorably towards the swirling tornado.

"SHIONA!" Elizabeth called again.

"I know, I know!" Shiona cried at her distressed niece. "Whatever you're doing, Baron von Buddy, please do it quickly!"

As if on cue the Baron seemed to have gathered every last ounce of goodness he needed and suddenly he created a massive, solid, golden column of light and shot it directly at the middle of the spinning vortex of evil.

As soon as Darius's soul was hit he let out a bloodcurdling scream and the tornado stopped immediately. The witches felt the instant release and with nothing to resist they fell over backwards.

"Get up, get up!" Shiona shouted across at Daphne and Elizabeth as the fall had broken the spell containing the bodiless souls. Shiona cast her containment spell first quickly followed by the others and thankfully not a soul was lost.

They all looked to see what Buddy would do next. Now that he had stopped the sickening tornado he sent the evil soul of Darius spinning quickly in the opposite direction. The monster became disorientated and once again took on its devil-like form. It writhed, collapsed, grew again and slumped under the force of the blow.

At times it looked as though the monster was about to fight back. He was cowering under the might of the spell one minute, then would suddenly jump towards Buddy lashing out with his hideous claws. But he was no match for the purity of the spell being cast by the magnificent wizard. And slowly, very slowly Buddy was beginning to take control. His spell was working. By separating the souls from their bodies George had inadvertently found a way to defeat the evil within Darius once and for all. The souls were not bound by the egos of their physical form. There were no limits to what they could achieve and they were not imprisoned by the fear that Darius thrived on.

As the connection between the souls and Buddy grew stronger and stronger the witches stepped away. He was their anchor now. They were attached to Buddy by solid rays of goodness like umbilical cords.

Elizabeth stepped back breathing heavily, the relief from the exertion was welcome. She bent over putting her hands on her knees for support, trying to catch her breath when suddenly she noticed movement in her peripheral vision. She turned to see what it was. Behind the huddle of villagers who were staring in amazement at the scene, George's villager-creatures were collapsing.

She wandered cautiously through the crowd towards them. One by one they were sinking to their knees. In their animal state there was some kind of awareness in their eyes but as they fell their faces were vacant. As though a light were being switched off and a power source was going out.

"Shiona! Daphne!" Elizabeth called the witches over.

"What's the matter Bet........" but Daphne did not need to finish. It was clear what the problem was.

"What's happening to them?" Elizabeth asked kneeling beside one of the creatures.

"I don't know," Shiona responded. "They've been without souls for so long, I can't understand why this would be happening now."

"Oh no," Elizabeth said as she felt the neck of the nearest creature. "The pulse is getting weaker. They're dying."

"Why now?" Daphne asked.

"It doesn't matter why Daphne," Shiona said, "just try to help them."

Daphne, Shiona and Elizabeth each knelt next to a creature searching for signs of life.

"It's no use," Shiona said finally. "They have no will to live. Without a consciousness the bodies are just shutting down, like robots."

"We need to get their souls back to them," Elizabeth said.

"How are we going to do that Betty? Your great-grandpa needs them."

Elizabeth watched the battle taking place between Buddy and Darius. Buddy was definitely gaining ground but slowly, very slowly. The power of the disembodied souls was constant, it was not waning but whilst they were concentrating on the fight with Darius they could not get back to their bodies.

"Even if they could get back," Shiona said as if she was reading Elizabeth's mind, "we have no idea how to keep them in there."

"I know," a small voice said from behind them.

"Georgie!" Daphne said jumping to her feet and picking the small man up in a big bear hug. "Can you help us?"

"I found an ancient Egyptian spell," George said in a daze, "the Pharaohs weren't as cruel as we think."

"Go on," Shiona said as she gently laid her hand on Daphne's arm encouraging her to put the man down.

"They would release the souls of the servants who were to be buried alive in the pyramids with their masters," George continued. "They felt it was the kindest way. Elizabeth was right, I might be able to reverse that spell."

"That's all very well," Shiona said, "but the Baron needs those souls and meanwhile these bodies are dying."

At these words Elizabeth ran back through the crowd towards her great-grandfather.

"Be careful!" Shiona shouted but Elizabeth ignored her.

Buddy was just about keeping Darius from regaining strength but it was taking everything he, and the spirits, could throw at the monster.

"Buddy!" Elizabeth screamed, "the bodies are dying. We need the souls back. You need to end this now!"

Even in his warring trance, acting as a conduit for the purity of the villagers Buddy was shocked at Elizabeth's words. Elizabeth could tell he was struggling with a difficult decision, he did not dare look back at the collapsed bodies.

I'm doing all I can little one, he sent the thought to Elizabeth and she could hear him clearly in her head. *I need them. We all need them. We cannot let this evil enter the world.*

From behind the distorted devil they once called 'father' Elizabeth could see Wilhelm, Diana, Ingrid and Victor. They were staring at the demon writhing and screaming in stunned, horrified silence. They were separated by the villagers and the witches by his monstrous form. From the huddle Victor looked up at Elizabeth who motioned towards the fallen villager-creatures. Victor was shocked, his friends were dying and it was clear that he felt he was to blame.

"They need our help," Elizabeth heard Victor plead with his family. "They cannot defeat Darius alone."

"What is he?" Was Wilhelm's only response.

Victor grabbed Wilhelm and shook him by the shoulders.

"Why are you so surprised brother?" Victor said. "You always knew he was evil, how else could he have turned us into monsters? Why else would he have subjected us all to this unnatural existence?"

"He was our *father*," Diana said staring at Darius, revolted by what he had become.

"Do not be a fool Diana," Victor said, "he was nothing of the sort. Our real mothers and fathers are long gone and he stole us from them. We have a chance to be free now, to go home, but we need to help the witches."

Elizabeth did not have time to hear the outcome of Victor's argument. Daphne was beckoning her back to the fallen creatures.

"We can't help them Betty," she said as Elizabeth approached her. "We're losing them."

The rest of the villagers were gathered around the members of their family who were collapsed in lifeless heaps. Bodies were strewn across the ground, the light of their life had been extinguished. The elder relatives were approaching them carefully. These bodies that once had been so dear to them, had been nothing but soulless enemies for months and now they were dying. The vehicles that had housed the consciousness of their loved ones would be lost to them forever if Elizabeth could not think of a way to save them.

"I don't know what to do," she said desperately to Shiona. "What should I do?"

"I don't know Elizabeth," Shiona replied quietly, "I just don't know."

"This one's nearly gone," Daphne said as she checked the heartbeat of a teenage boy and Elizabeth saw a mother crouch over him, it was Hannah. Elizabeth crawled over to take a closer look.

"It is Daniel," Hannah said quietly, "*was* Daniel."

The youthful, vacant body of Daniel was taking shallow erratic breaths, and Elizabeth knew it would not be long before he stopped breathing altogether. She could not bear the sight a moment longer, she got to her feet and rushed towards the fray.

"Buddy please, PLEASE!" She screamed. "We need those souls!"

Chapter Thirty-One

It was an impossible situation for Buddy. He was fighting with all he had, with all the purity from the souls but what ground he had been making against Darius was fast disappearing. Once again Darius's evil spirit was gaining strength and the fear from Elizabeth and all the elder relatives, as they desperately watched their young ones dying all around them, was helping him. If Buddy were to release the souls then the fight would be over. Darius would win and evil would be unleashed on the world.

Elizabeth felt a strong hand on her shoulder, "can we help little witch?" It was Yorik.

"I just don't know," Elizabeth said in a daze as Shiona came to join them.

"We *all* have souls Shiona," Yorik said, "surely the Baron can use our souls to help?"

"It's not as simple as that Yorik," Shiona replied. "The purity comes from being released from their bodies. They aren't tainted by the negativity of their egos."

"Then make George release our souls too Shiona," Yorik said. "We can help."

"NO!" Elizabeth shouted. "We won't lose the rest of you!"

Elizabeth shouted to her great grand-father as he hovered in the air. "Buddy!" she screamed, "tell me what to do. I can't figure this out by myself. Just tell me!"

"Not...this...time," Buddy said as he struggled with the exertion of the fight, "there are....no secrets. I have no more plans up my sleeve. I'm out of ideas Little One."

298

Elizabeth stared in amazement at this admission by her great-grandfather. She looked across at the form that Darius's cruelty had taken and could see he was resisting the goodness from the souls of the villagers with every ounce of his being. Collectively the purity of the souls was strong, but this ancient evil that Ryder had unleashed was stronger. Century after century it had waited for a curious, unsuspecting, naivety to find it and Ryder had wandering into its midst. Ryder was hungry for power and status, unable to keep up with his prominent best friend. He was desperate to find a way to not only equal the Baron's supremacy but to surpass it.

Elizabeth had no idea where he had found the evil that now thrashed and screamed in front of her, but she knew even though Ryder had started the search, the creature had ended it. Ryder was exactly what this evil being was looking for and now he was free he was not about to relinquish control easily.

The creature was digging his feet deep into the earth, creating a trench beneath him and even the earth was screaming in pain. It was a devastating power and nothing would be safe once he was free and by the way his strength was returning, Elizabeth knew that moment of freedom was not far away.

"Elizabeth, what can I do?" Victor shouted from behind the writhing monster.

Elizabeth just shook her head, lost for words.

Wilhelm approached Victor and Elizabeth could see his shock at the tender touch of his brother as he placed a hand on Victor's shoulder.

"You are the best of us," Elizabeth heard Wilhelm say, "what shall we do?"

Victor hung his head. Elizabeth knew that the battle was all but lost and from where she was standing it looked as though Victor knew it too. Then suddenly his head shot up and Elizabeth could tell that he was searching his memory. She recognised that expression anywhere. It was the same one she was wearing when she was trying to recall her dream about Buddy.

"What is it?" she shouted across at Victor.

"Father!" Victor shouted at the evil being, ignoring Elizabeth.

"*I WAS NEVER YOUR FATHER IDIOT BOY! RYDER NEEDED A FAMILY AND I NEEDED PEOPLE TO DO MY BIDDING.*"

"Whoever you are," Victor continued, "I have to know one thing."

"*I AM NOT ANSWERABLE TO YOU!*"

"Who turned us into monsters?" Victor said ploughing on regardless. "You or Ryder?"

"*AS IF THAT MERE MORTAL COULD HAVE GIVEN YOU WHAT I HAVE GIVEN YOU! HE WAS NOTHING BUT A VESSEL FOR MY INCREDIBLE POWER.*"

"So each of us," Victor said gesturing towards his family, "is imbued with your evil?"

"Victor what are you doing?" Wilhelm hissed.

Before waiting for an answer Victor approached his family once again. His voice was barely audible over the roar of the monster and Elizabeth strained to hear him.

"If he is kept at bay by the purity of these souls, the souls that have always been good, that were born to goodness, imagine what we could do to him," Victor said, "those of us that have been inhabited by evil but still *choose* to be pure."

"What can we do in the face of such a devil," Diana said, "we have always been loyal to father, perhaps we should be loyal to the creature that was living within him."

"NO!" Elizabeth was surprised to hear this answer come from Wilhelm. "I am not prepared to join forces with this monster. We were stupid and deluded Diana. All the time we thought we were imprisoned in Branko because the people were afraid of our power. But we were wrong. There will be nothing of the world left to live in if we allow this creature to be set free. We have to help. Victor what shall we do?"

"Elizabeth!" Shiona shouted behind her. "They're almost gone!"

Elizabeth turned to see the villager-creatures taking their dying breaths. She looked over at Buddy and the souls. They were using the last of their strength to contain the creature whose power was increasing by the second. It would not be long before even they had nothing left to fight him with.

"VICTOR!" Elizabeth screamed. "Whatever you're doing, do it quickly! We're running out of time!"

Victor looked at his brother. "Where you lead, we will follow," Wilhelm reassured him.

"Father!" Victor shouted.

"I TOLD YOU......."

But before the evil soul could speak another word Victor stood up to his full height and summoned all of his magic to him. He walked towards the creature and sent out a surge of power above him, joining with the souls of the bodiless villagers. Darius was now surrounded by a circle of brilliant white light. It was just a thin arc coming from Victor but Wilhelm quickly realised what his brother was trying to do. He put his hand on his brother's shoulder and the blast of bright light thickened.

Through her tears even Ingrid understood the sense of Victor's words. Standing opposite Wilhelm she placed her hand on Victor's other shoulder. The burst of power coming from Ingrid equalled and surpassed that of her sons. Encased in a circle of brilliant white light, Darius's soul wailed.

"AAAARRGGHH! YOU CANNOT BEAT ME! I MADE YOU!"

"And we have chosen to stand up to you," Victor shouted, "even with your evil coursing through our veins. What does that mean to you?"

In its hideous, monstrous form Darius's soul looked incredulously at Victor.

"It means that even with the control you have exerted over us," Victor continued, "we still choose the side of goodness. After centuries of poisoning us with your evil, we still remain loyal to the Baron. We choose to fight against you, and we use your own power to do it!"

"Fire with fire," Elizabeth heard a voice say from behind her, "it just might work Betty."

"It's more than that Daphne," Elizabeth said, "they have all the power they could ever need but they still choose to be good. It's a sign that wherever there is a spark of a soul, there is goodness. Mum always knew that."

"BUT NOT ALL OF YOU HAVE CHOSEN THE GOOD PATH."

Elizabeth followed the creature's gaze, he was looking at Diana.

"Come sister," Wilhelm said quietly, "you know what you must do."

It was clear to Elizabeth that Diana was warring with an internal demon of her own. She looked up at the creature, searching for answers. Then her eyes settled on her brother. She smiled at him with a tenderness that surprised Elizabeth. Diana came to a decision and walked towards her family. She took hold of Wilhelm's outstretched hand and as she reached him, her mother grasped her other hand.

The family was united with the Baron and the villagers and their powers were stronger than ever. The ring of brilliant light started to climb skywards. Slowly it formed a dome encasing Darius's monstrous soul beneath it.

"*AAAARRGGHH!*" Darius howled as the weight of the power hit him.

Shiona joined Daphne and Elizabeth as they stood in amazement watching the scene.

"Don't just stand there," she said, "they need our help."

"They seem to have it in hand now Shiona," Daphne said.

"What can we do?" Elizabeth asked.

"They're not going to be able to keep up that level of power forever," Shiona said. "That evil needs a prison."

"And how on earth are we supposed to imprison it Shiona?" Daphne asked.

"Exactly!" Shiona replied and raced towards the creature.

"Er, Shiona," Elizabeth said struggling to be heard over the crackling of spells in the air and the ear-splitting roar coming from the monster. "Did you hear what Daphne said?"

"Yes," Shiona replied stopping at the trench being dug by Darius's enormous feet. "And the *earth* is exactly what we're going to use."

With that Shiona directed a spell beneath the feet of the monster and the shallow trench started to get deeper.

"Take a position and start digging," Shiona said.

"I hope you don't mean literally!" Daphne shouted as she and Elizabeth separated and ran.

Daphne managed to run beneath the Baron and took up position opposite Shiona almost in the woods. Elizabeth ran around behind Victor and his family and carefully aimed beyond them at Darius's feet.

"Dig!" Shiona shouted and the witches sent their spell downwards.

Elizabeth did not know how exactly to command the earth. She had only ever concentrated on one little thing at a time. It was another skill entirely to convince the planet to bend to her will. She started her spell by clearing her mind as usual and she made a quiet promise to the earth.

"This is for the good of the whole planet. If you take this evil and keep him imprisoned then I promise we will do everything within our power to make sure he is never found again."

Elizabeth could sense the planet acquiesce to her request. There was not exactly a consciousness there, just an idea. And the idea was a simple one, life. The earth wanted one thing and one thing only, what was best for the planet and all her inhabitants.

Elizabeth's spell worked instantly and a chasm opened up beneath the monster. He started to fall.

There was no escape for him. He could not penetrate the dome of purity and light above him and the earth was beginning to swallow him. He was beaten.

"Come on, come on," Elizabeth murmured under her breath, the fallen bodies of the soulless villagers never far from her mind.

But she had nothing to fear, the fight was almost over. As the cruel soul was pulled down into the earth Elizabeth could tell that he knew it was the end. Inch by inch he was consumed by the earth until only his head and one arm remained.

As his face reached the level of the earth Elizabeth could see an evil grin spread across it. He was almost beaten, his battle was all but lost but Elizabeth could tell he had one last trick up his sleeve.

As his head slowly dissolved into the earth, his left hand was all that remained. Before he was swallowed entirely to be a prisoner of the planet, he decided to take something with him.

With the last of his power he grabbed up at the Baron, but the Baron was too far away. Darius missed his target and in frustration his bodiless hand hunted around for someone at ground height and found Elizabeth.

He knocked her off her feet and the colossal hand was about to grab her and drag her into the chasm Elizabeth.

When suddenly, "NO!" Victor cried as he leapt to save Elizabeth, knocking her from the monster's path.

She was safe from his reach but Victor was not. He lay on the ground that Elizabeth had occupied moments before and the giant hand fell onto the body of the fallen boy.

Chapter Thirty-Two

Victor was being dragged into the earth. He grabbed at the ground all around him trying to get a hold of something, anything to stop his inexorable descent. Elizabeth watched frozen in horror. Victor's fight was futile, he was being dragged into the earth. Disappearing in the same way as Darius's evil soul, with only his head and one arm exposed above the ground.

Ingrid, Wilhelm and Diana had been thrown backwards. The strength of their spell was no longer needed once Darius was imprisoned in the earth. Elizabeth ran, bounded and leapt over their crumpled bodies as she tried to get to Victor.

As Elizabeth reached him his terrified face was being consumed by the ground. Victor was coughing and spitting out dirt as he descended. Elizabeth threw herself towards him and grabbed hold of his outstretched arm.

"Help me!" She cried as she fought against the strength of the monster. "I can't hold him!"

Wilhelm was the first by her side, quickly followed by Ingrid. Wilhelm grabbed hold of his brother's arm and pushed Elizabeth away.

"DIG!" He shouted at her.

Already on her hands and knees Elizabeth started scratching away at the ground trying to release Victor.

"What kind of a witch are you?" Wilhelm shouted. "Cast a spell!"

Elizabeth shook her head at her own stupidity. *Please, let him go!* She pleaded with the earth, sending out her intention and using what she hoped was telepathy.

Ingrid was digging at the earth as Diana approached. Diana tried to use a spell to help Elizabeth but nothing happened.

"Darius is gone," Wilhelm said, "with all of his powers, including ours. He is welcome to them."

All that was left of Victor was a hand and Wilhelm was straining to keep hold of him.

"Please!" Elizabeth said out loud. "LET HIM GO!"

This time the spell worked and the earth opened up for a split second, but it was long enough. Wilhelm acted quickly, he pulled Victor out as if he were popping a cork. The boys fell to the ground together in a heap and the earth shut the evil of Lord Darius inside for all eternity.

"I thought I had lost you little brother," Wilhelm said as Victor lay on top of him.

"Not yet," Victor replied, "but soon."

"What?" Wilhelm said and gently laid Victor to the ground.

Now they could all see the extent of his injuries. He had been sucked into the earth by a malevolent power and the scorch marks on his skin were evidence. The whole of his body was covered in vicious burns like the slash marks of a giant tiger. He was bleeding and suffering and he was right. He did not have long to live.

"No," Elizabeth said as she slumped to her knees next to him, tears rolling down her cheeks.

"Elizabeth, look!" Shiona shouted and gestured skyward.

Elizabeth looked to where Shiona was pointing. Buddy was hovering in mid-air. His power was no longer needed, neither were the bodiless souls. Buddy was trying to plunge the spirits back into their bodies. But as he released them from his magical grasp the spirits floated away unable to connect with the bodies they were born to. As each soul flew into the ether Buddy quickly sent an energy tendril towards them, holding them in place, but he was losing his strength.

"Elizabeth!" Shiona shouted again, "we need you."

Elizabeth was torn. She looked down at the dying figure of her friend and wanted to heal him. But she knew she had to help Buddy who was struggling to keep the souls from drifting away.

"Go," Victor said raising a hand to her face, "I promise I will wait."

Elizabeth looked at Wilhelm who nodded. She knew he would try to keep Victor alive as long as possible. She got up and with one final look at the heart-breaking sight of a family finally united but destined to be torn apart she walked away.

As she approached the fallen villagers she could see more clearly the desperate battle the spirits were having as they tried to catch hold of their bodies. Their struggles were to no avail. The bodies lying on the ground were no longer the physical homes of these ethereal beings. They had been separated for so long Elizabeth could not conceive how they were ever to be reunited.

"They must not go," Yorik said desperately to Elizabeth, "if we cannot return them to their bodies they will not find peace in the afterlife. They will be doomed to roam the planet. They have not been taken by the angel."

"What angel?" Elizabeth asked.

"Not really relevant Betty," Daphne said. "The main aim now is to reattach these souls like you promised!"

"Get on it then *Aunty* Daphne," Elizabeth said in frustration, "it's your boyfriend who can help!"

The two witches exchanged angry looks until Daphne turned her attention to George.

"Alright then Georgie," Daphne said. "What do we do now? Tell us and tell us quickly because I've just about had enough of you."

In the face of Daphne's rage, which equalled Shiona's, George knew he was beaten. He did not dare argue with her.

Straining to remember George finally said, "The original spell translated to something like this, 'you who have been so loyal in life, are now free from the pain of an agonising death, I release you from your earthbound form and set your spirit free'. But Darius was the key, it was his power that made the spell work. I could never have done it without him."

"Well we're here now *Georgie*," Elizabeth said sarcastically, "and we've got more than just a little power of our own."

"Alright then," Shiona said, "let's try something."

She walked over to Daniel's body. Hannah's youngest child was moments from death. Shiona knelt next to him and cradled his head in her hands. Suddenly a deep golden glow radiated from her palms and spread down the length of his body. Shiona leant low, closed her eyes, and whispered in his ear.

"You who have been so loyal in spirit are now free from the pain of

306

an agonising existence. I return you to your earthbound form and bring your soul home."

For a moment the crowd did not dare to breathe, they just stared at the fallen child and the witch desperate to save him. In the air around her, Elizabeth could tell Daniel's spirit was smiling. He had enjoyed so much the freedom of being without a body that he did not really mind if he was returned or not.

Suddenly Elizabeth could no longer perceive Daniel's spirit, it was gone. Just as she started to panic, wondering where the soul could be, the lifeless boy in Shiona's arms took a long, deep breath. The assembled crowd watched in amazement. Daniel exhaled slowly then took a few shorter breaths. Slowly the boy opened his eyes.

"Daniel!" Hannah cried as she embraced him. "Oh, my child!"

Shiona looked up at Elizabeth and Daphne her face moist with tears. "Go!" she said choking on the words. "Help the others!"

The witches got to work as quickly as they could and did not stop until they had reunited each and every soul with their wayward bodies. Cradling the heads of the broken bodies in their hands they sent the soft golden light through the body.

"You who have been so loyal in spirit," Elizabeth would start;

"Are now free from the pain of an agonising existence," Daphne would continue;

"I return you to your earthbound form and bring your soul home," Shiona finished.

The same spell was said to all of the bodies. The witches moved swiftly between the fallen villagers trying to reunite body and soul before the body lost all hope of life. As each teenager was brought to life the witches had no time to celebrate. They jumped straight to the next body and started again.

After what seemed like a lifetime, they finally came to the last body.

"You who have been so loyal in spirit," Shiona said. "Are now free from the pain of an agonising existence." This was the strongest body of all and had the most life left in it. "I return you to your earthbound form and bring your soul home." Shiona whispered into Gretchen's ear and the body and soul, that Elizabeth had had two terrifying encounters with, were finally reunited.

When the last spell was said Buddy relinquished his hold on the spirit and dropped to the ground.

"Buddy," Elizabeth said as she embraced her great-grandfather, "you did it."

"Oh child," he said and he took Elizabeth's face in his hand, "we all did it. Could one of us really have succeeded without the other?"

"No," Elizabeth said quietly.

"Never be afraid to admit you need help Little One, it may save your life one day."

"Erich," a soft voice said from behind them and Buddy was clearly startled to hear the name.

"Help me," Buddy said to Elizabeth and she supported him as he got to his feet.

"It is so dark now Erich, it has been dark for so long." The voice said.

"I know old friend, I know," Buddy said as he hobbled towards the sound aided by Elizabeth, "but it's nearly over, we're nearly home."

As they stepped over the mound of earth that encased Darius's soul, Elizabeth could see the body of a young man lying naked on the ground. For a moment she thought it was one of the villager-creatures who had lost his way until it suddenly dawned on her who it was.

"Erich old friend," the young man said, "is that you."

"It is me Ryder," Buddy said and gestured Elizabeth to stay further back as he approached his fallen friend. Gingerly Buddy lowered himself to the floor and drew his old friend towards him.

"I have been lost, for so long." Ryder said, "I thought nobody would find me, but here you are. I knew you would not give up on me. It is you isn't it Erich? I cannot see. I have been blinded by evil."

"It is me old friend. You're safe now."

Elizabeth watched as the frail old man cuddled the youth to him. Darius was gone and the figure now lying on the ground was how the boy must have looked when the evil found him. He was beautiful. He had dark, swarthy skin and shoulder length black hair. His features were strong and warm and his eyes, now useless from gazing at the darkness within, were a mesmerising, ocean blue.

"I have fought for so long, to keep that monster at bay," Ryder said.

"And you did well old friend, you gave him a weakness and he didn't even know you were doing it."

"Ah!" Ryder said, "my family!"

"That's right old friend. You chose them well. In the end they were the ones who saved you, who saved us all."

"Where are they?"

"Here I am my love," it was Ingrid. She had left the side of her dying son to be by the side of her dying husband. She covered him tenderly with her cloak.

"You were the strongest of all my love," he said as he blindly held out his hand to her, "I knew you would triumph."

"Oh my love," Ingrid said weeping into his hand, "I did not understand."

"Please, do not cry child," Ryder said, "we have been punished enough."

Suddenly Ryder began to choke and struggled for breath.

"Old friend!" He said panicking, "are you there?"

"I'm here," Buddy said, "I'm not going anywhere without you."

"I am so frightened, where do I go from here? I am dying but I have been so evil, where does my soul belong."

"Dear friend," Buddy said gently, "you have never been evil. Your only crime was to be young. You have been punished enough. You will suffer no more – I promise. It is time to let go."

Elizabeth watched as Ryder listened to the wise words of his oldest friend. She saw him close his eyes and allow death to release him from his miserable existence.

Ingrid wept as her husband's hand grew limp in her grasp. Elizabeth stood and stared at the three people, divided in their lives but united in their love.

Suddenly a call came out from behind her.

"Quickly Elizabeth." It was Wilhelm. "Victor cannot hold on much longer."

Shiona, Daphne, help me, she summoned her aunties telepathically and ran towards Victor.

She knelt close to him and could hear his breath shortening and becoming more laboured. He was looking towards the sky, staring upwards, trying to control his breath coming to the end of his life.

"It's OK," she said, "the others are coming. We can help."

"No," he said reaching out for her.

Daphne and Shiona were at her side, searching for a way to heal

Victor. Shiona looked up at Elizabeth and shook her head.

"It is alright... young... Elizabeth," Victor said losing strength, "I am ...ready now. I am ready ....to be with ...my family. They did not survive ...Darius's attack, and they wait for me. They ...call to me."

Victor was staring at the sky. The sun was shining, it was early morning. It was a dawning of a brand new life for the people of Branko.

With the last of his strength Victor turned towards Elizabeth. She felt his cool hand on her cheek, he wiped away her tears with his thumb.

"I have been a friend to you, yes?" He asked.

Elizabeth nodded, unable to speak.

"You are such a good soul Elizabeth, like your mother. Your dear mother. Nothing but a child when we first met, now here *you* are – her grown up daughter. She was right when she talked of putting trust in a stranger and that the stranger would risk his life. I just did not realise *I* would be the stranger, a stranger to you Elizabeth."

"Every good friend starts as a stranger Victor," Elizabeth said holding back the tears, "and you really are a good friend – the best. You're certainly the only friend that's ever known the real me, warts and all."

"Yes Elizabeth, *warts and all*." He smiled. "You are a wonderful person Elizabeth, warts and all. Always remember that."

He took one last deep breath and looked back towards the sky. Elizabeth could see him silently mouth a word and a small smile spread across his face. He closed his eyes and he was gone.

Elizabeth put her head to his forehead and wept. She could hear the sounds of his cobbled together family crying around her. Wilhelm's cries were the loudest.

"Goodbye Victor," Elizabeth said softly, "and thank-you."

She looked up slowly and gasped. Kneeling at Victor's head Elizabeth could see a figure. It was a beautiful warm golden outline of a man. It shone so vibrantly it was like watching the rising sun. She squinted at the vision and could see that there was a golden hand placed on Victor's forehead in exactly the same spot that her own hand had just been. Unable to stop herself, she reached out for the hand and touched it. Immediately she felt the warmth from the figure course through her body. It was like walking into the summer sun after spending too much time in the shade. Visions of thousands of lifetimes rushed through her mind each one of them ending in the presence of this amazing being. He was a magnificent power, he was omnipresent, he was purity, love and light all rolled into one, but there was another feeling amongst this omnipotence. It was a settling, happy, peaceful notion. The feeling was one she was so familiar with but could not immediately place. The figure looked at her as she was regarding him. She looked deeply into his ocean blue eyes and felt like at long last she was finally home.

"It's not really the done thing to go holding hands with the Angel of Death, Betty," Daphne said breaking the spell.

"*The Angel of Death?*" Elizabeth said pulling her hand away quickly.

The figure merely smiled lovingly at her. When Shiona appeared at his side.

"Don't worry Elizabeth," Shiona said looking directly at the Angel, "you've got plenty of time to meet him."

"You hope," Daphne said grinning and nudging Elizabeth.

"Funny," Elizabeth said and turned her attention back to Victor. He was gone, only his body remained and in the blink of an eye the Angel of Death disappeared too.

"It's time to go now Elizabeth," Buddy said from behind her still cradling Ryder's body.

Elizabeth gently lowered Victor's hand to his chest, kissed his cool forehead and got up. As she walked towards her great-grandfather there was a rumbling in the air, like the sound of distant thunder and the ground shuddered for a moment.

"We must say our goodbyes now Little One," Buddy said. "You will not see me again, the amulet is completely destroyed. Apologise to little Bertie for me."

"I will," Elizabeth said sadly.

"But I do have this," Buddy said producing a small piece of the bottle green stone from Bertie's pendant. "Keep this with you and you will always be powerful. You will not need to be near the witches you will have the combined power of your mother *and* father with you – always."

Elizabeth took the stone from Buddy it was now nothing but a small round disc, the size of a penny. Suddenly something in Buddy's words struck her.

"The power of my father?" she asked.

"Oh yes. He is more powerful than you think," Buddy replied, "more powerful than he cares to admit."

The rumbling through the forest grew louder and the ground beneath Elizabeth's feet began to shake. This time it did not stop.

"What's happening?" She asked.

"We are going home Little One and you do not belong here. Go and go quickly." With that Buddy waved her away.

"But..."

"Come on Betty," Daphne said and grabbed her around the waist pulling her up. "We've got to fly!" With that she thrust a sad looking stick into Elizabeth's hands.

"Sonny!" Elizabeth said, pleased to see her old flying companion.

Daphne and Shiona had found their own brooms and were edging away.

"There'll be plenty of time for reunions later Elizabeth," Shiona said, "grow him and let's get the hell out of here."

"I don't understand," Elizabeth said breaking away from the witches and confronting her great-grandfather. "What did you mean about my father? Why is he powerful?"

Another tremor rumbled through the ground nearly knocking her off her feet. Elizabeth looked at the landscape. It was changing right in front of her eyes. It shimmered and flashed and the figures of the villagers looked as though they were dissolving.

"What's happening to Branko? What..." But Elizabeth had no time to finish, everything around her was beginning to crumble.

"Come on Betty!" Daphne said dragging her away. "It's a long way to the shield from here."

"What about him?" Elizabeth said and pointed to where George was curled up in a ball on the floor. All the original inhabitants of Branko were disappearing along with the land itself, but George was as solid as the three witches. "He doesn't belong here."

"Just leave him," Shiona said.

"Shiona you know what will happen to him if he stays," Daphne said.

"What?" Elizabeth asked.

"His body will be ripped apart as space and time corrects itself. George is an anomaly that doesn't belong here." Shiona said coldly.

The fixing of reality was gaining momentum. The swirling vortex of Darius was nothing compared to the vacuum being created as Branko readied itself for its journey home.

"Oh come on Shiona!" Elizabeth said. "Nobody deserves that, and you know it. You have no right to be judge, jury and executioner."

"Just get him," Shiona said finally, "and hurry up!"

As she spoke her final words, Shiona mounted her broomstick and took off. Daphne ran across to George and easily manhandled him onto her own broom. As Elizabeth watched the witches float into the sky she noticed the villagers behind them. They were shouting something, trying to wave, trying to have one last moment with their saviours, their friends.

"We haven't even said goodbye," Elizabeth said.

But her words fell on practical ears. "If you stop to say goodbye Betty then 'goodbye' might be the last word you ever speak! Now COME ON!"

Shiona and Daphne, who still had a tight hold of George, swooped either side of Elizabeth and gripping her firmly under the arms scooped her into the air and flew away.

"Now get that thing to grow and FLY!" Shiona screamed at her.

Elizabeth was zooming through the air backwards being held by her aunts. She struggled to get her mind to focus on Sonny's growing spell as she watched reality implode all around her. Branko was vanishing a little bit at a time, it was disappearing into a vast void right in front of her eyes.

And it was catching up with the flight of the witches.

"Hurry up Betty," Daphne shouted, "I can't hold you for much longer."

Within seconds Sonny had burst to life and Daphne and Shiona let go of Elizabeth so that she could fly unaided. Elizabeth fell hard onto Sonny as they released her and stared straight into the mouth of the gaping void as it was swallowing Branko.

"This way!" Shiona shouted from behind her.

She had to manoeuvre quickly away from the advancing darkness. She shot straight up into the air, looped the loop and flipped over. Now she was flying in the same direction as the other two witches.

But the manoeuvre had cost her precious seconds. Her aunts, the more efficient flyers, had zoomed ahead of her and were nearly at the weak spot in the border. Shiona blasted a spell at it, it opened up easily. Now that it was no longer needed to protect Branko, it was weaker than ever.

"Come on Sonny, come on," Elizabeth said encouraging her broom, "we can do this."

But time and space were catching up with them. The void that was pulling Branko back into its own time had almost reached her. Elizabeth could feel the strong force behind her, pulling her backwards. But no matter how much it tried to suck her towards it, Elizabeth kept fighting, forcing Sonny onwards.

Closer and closer to the border she got as the expanding emptiness got closer and closer to her. She was nearly there. She could see her aunts standing a few hundred yards in front of her. They were through. They had reached the weakness at the edge of the village and they were clear of danger. Now they were watching Elizabeth. And Elizabeth could tell from the expression on their faces – they did not like what they saw.

"COME ON BETTY!" Daphne shouted.

Second after agonising second she grew closer to the edges of Branko. She was so close, she could almost reach out and touch the outstretched arms of her aunties when suddenly she stopped. Sonny had been grabbed by the void and was being dragged backwards. All around her she could see Branko being sucked into the black hole including her escape route. She could see clearly that it was stretching and thinning. Soon it would be gone altogether leaving Elizabeth to be destroyed by time and space.

"ELIZABETH!" Shiona shouted at her, tears streaming down her cheeks. Elizabeth could see her so clearly. She could see Daphne too, holding onto her own face in horror.

Elizabeth hopped up onto Sonny like a surfer trying to ride his board. She could feel the suction behind her, dragging Sonny in. She struggled with her balance but as soon as she was surefooted she leapt. She dove straight towards the thinning hole, casting a desperate spell for survival as she jumped.

Reality slowed for Elizabeth as she closed her eyes and prayed. Suddenly she felt herself hit something solid and then a softness wrapped itself tightly around her. She could barely breath, she thought she was going to suffocate when she heard a familiar voice.

"It's OK Daphne, you can let her go. She's safe now." Shiona's words were filled with relief.

Elizabeth looked up to see the giant figure of her Aunty Daphne cuddling her so closely that she was nearly squeezing the life out of her.

"Don't you ever frighten me like that again Betty!" Daphne said and promptly burst into tears.

"It's not over yet," George said and pointed towards the emptiness that was sucking Branko back home, "brace yourselves!"

The witches threw themselves to the ground. Daphne was not taking any more chances with Elizabeth's safety and dropped down hard on her unsuspecting niece knocking the wind out of her.

The blast was magnificent. It blew outwards from Branko's protective shield and covered the witches, George and the surrounding area in a great cloud of dust and ashes. Then just as they thought it was all over, Branko created another strong vacuum, sucking the dust and ashes back towards it. The witches had to hold onto the ground with all their strength to stop themselves from being pulled back in and just as quickly as it had started, with one final 'POP' it stopped.

Daphne, Shiona, Elizabeth and George all tentatively looked back to where they had just come from. Branko had gone.

"They've finally gone home." Shiona said softly.

"Where is *home*?" Elizabeth asked as she picked herself up off the ground.

"Back to where they came from Elizabeth," Shiona said. "Back to their own time and space. Probably back to the very day that the Baron and the witches left and cast their spell to protect and displace it. And now look at it." Shiona could not hide her contempt. The magnificent village of Branko with its eclectic houses, rustic tavern and majestic castle were gone. In the distance all they could see was a motorway and a shopping complex.

"Where are we?" Elizabeth asked.

"We've come home too Betty. We're back in our time and I think we're somewhere in Germany."

"What exactly is *our time*?" Shiona asked bitterly, surveying at the transformed landscape.

Elizabeth walked over to her aunty and saw that tears were creating clean grooves in her otherwise filthy face.

"What's the matter Shiona," she asked.

"They've gone Elizabeth," Shiona said simply. "The people that we've known, cared for, spent time with every year for decades. They've gone. And we didn't even get to say goodbye."

"Hello!" A voice said from behind them.

They jumped up quickly and turned to face the stranger. They immediately took up their three-pointed formation – ready for a fight.

"Please!" The stranger said raising her hands. "I am not an enemy."

The stranger walked towards them, viewing them with hungry interest. She was a middle-aged woman dressed in modern clothes.

"Is it really you?" She asked.

"Who are you?" Shiona barked at her.

"Oh I am so sorry," the woman said, "you do not know me, but I know so much about you. Let me guess, you are definitely Shiona," then she turned to Daphne, "you must be Daphne then that must make you little Elizabeth?" She walked slowly towards Elizabeth, her eyes filled with emotion.

"That's me," Elizabeth said cautiously.

"Oh! I am finally meeting you!" She said and with that she pulled Elizabeth into a deep embrace.

"Um?" Was all Elizabeth could say encased in the woman's rather ample breasts.

"Forgive me, forgive me." The stranger said finally releasing Elizabeth. "We have been waiting for this moment for so very long."

"We?" Shiona asked suspiciously.

The lady gestured to where she had come from and there, appearing from the surrounding landscape were dozens of strangers.

"What's this now," Shiona said raising her wand.

"Oh please do not be afraid," the lady said, "we are friends. I am Greta, named after my great-grandmother. My grandmother was Gretchen I believe you knew them?"

She looked at the three witches for an answer but they only stared back in stunned amazement and nodded wordlessly.

"And these," Greta said waving to the approaching strangers, "are all descendants of the Branko families.

Greta looked at the three witches and Elizabeth knew she was taking in the bedraggled sight of their somewhat post-apocalyptic look. The final battle had started on the night of the masquerade ball. Elizabeth and her aunts were all dressed in makeshift ball gowns that had been torn and slashed and were now covered in blood. They were battle-worn, dirty and in desperate need of a wash. They looked at each other, imagining what a bizarre trio they made for the descendants of Branko who were finally meeting their saviours. Shiona was mortified, Elizabeth was embarrassed and Daphne was heartily amused – as always.

"We have heard for many, many years," Greta continued, "how we all owe our lives to the three witches and we have waited so long to finally meet you. Now here you are. And it is our turn to help you."

Chapter Thirty-Three

Shiona, Daphne, Elizabeth and George were slowly coaxed away from the place they had known as Branko by its hospitable descendants. It was hard for the witches to leave, to believe that the battle was over – fought and won. Shiona and Daphne found it impossible to believe that they would never see their friends again.

A smart-looking car, large enough to carry 8 people, was put on for their journey back to civilization. It was driven by one of the grandchildren of a villager-creature, who told them in broken English, the story of how his grandfather coped after being reunited with his battered, bruised and broken body. How it had taken years of recuperation for him to walk properly again and how the emotional scars never really healed. Elizabeth, Shiona and Daphne looked accusingly at George as the young man told his story and George finally had the decency to look ashamed, confronted by the reality of his hideous actions.

They arrived at Greta's smart apartment an hour later and everything was a blur. They feigned politeness but after the long car journey they were feeling tired and hungry. Like her namesake Greta seemed to have a sixth sense and easily picked up on the witches' exhaustion so she ushered the relatives of the Branko villagers out of her home. Her husband was on hand to dish out as much food as they could eat. The witches and George had not eaten for days and felt bilious as they tried to reintroduce nourishment into their systems.

One by one they bathed, ate and changed into the clean clothes provided by Greta. They had many questions for Greta and her husband and Greta had questions of her own but as Shiona began quizzing her, Greta held up her hand.

"I think we will have answers for each other in the morning Shiona, yes?" Greta said. "You must get some rest. Any questions can wait."

With that she showed Elizabeth to a room with a single bed and a separate room with a double bed for the two sisters. George was made to sleep on the sofa. As magnanimous as she was, Greta could not bring herself to treat George like an honoured guest.

Elizabeth fell into a fitful sleep that first night away from Branko. Her body was exhausted but her mind relived incident after incident. On one occasion she woke up covered in sweat as she remembered watching her aunts being carried through the forest by Darius's soulless minions. Her emotions, that she had been in absolute control of since the battle, suddenly began to overwhelm her. She wept like a baby and could not stop. Her cries were hysterical and she had to put on every light in the room to make sure she was definitely back in her own time, her own reality.

She heard a knock at the door and tried to compose herself.

"Come.....in," she just about managed through her tears.

"Hello Betty," a familiar and welcome voice said, "you alright?"

"Oh Daphne," she sobbed and ran across to her aunty who was waiting to embrace her.

"It's alright Little One," Daphne said choking back her own tears, "it's all over now. Come on."

With that she dragged Elizabeth's duvet from her bed and guided her into the room she was sharing with Shiona. Shiona was also awake. She was pacing up and down in the room and rushed to help Daphne with Elizabeth as soon as she saw them.

The two older witches made Elizabeth a bed on a small sofa in their bedroom and comforted her until her cries turned to sighs and her sighs turned to snores. Elizabeth cried herself to sleep that night and for many nights after.

When they woke the next morning Shiona was allowed to ask her questions. She was eager to hear news of the friends she made during her visits to Branko.

Greta told them that once Ryder was finally gone the earthquake hit. That earthquake was the shuddering that Elizabeth and the others had felt, their signal to get going. To the villagers it was Elizabeth and her aunties who were disappearing. They were desperate to say their goodbyes, to show their appreciation, but Branko had other ideas. When the earthquake finally stopped Branko had been devastated. All the buildings including the castle were levelled and nothing of the village remained.

It took the villagers a while to re-orientate themselves and when they finally did they suddenly noticed people appearing from the forest. They were the same friends and family who had left them centuries ago, they had not aged and not grown one day older, they were exactly the same as they remembered them. Then all at once a magnificent man strode into the devastation. It was someone they all remembered. It was the Baron. He nearly collapsed at the sight of his dead friend in the arms of an older version of himself. But Buddy calmed him and whispered something in his ear. They talked for a while and when they had finished Buddy closed his eyes and joined Ryder on his journey to the afterlife.

Greta explained that after the younger Baron had made his peace with his friend, he got up and made his way to the youngest of the three witches who had helped him cast the spell to displace Branko. He looked rather sheepishly at the young woman and whispered something in her ear, turned red and walked away. Apparently Buddy had explained to him that he would marry the young witch one day and that their descendants would be the ones to save Branko. It seemed as if the Baron had already harboured a secret crush on the lady and the confirmation of a future relationship excited and embarrassed the young man.

"And he was young," Greta said, "as were all the villagers who had left behind loved ones in Branko. It was not hard for them to readjust to lives with the family they had seen only moments before. The ones who struggled with their normal existence were the villagers who had stayed with Darius. They had not seen their people for centuries. Had mourned them, had come to terms with an unnaturally long existence and suddenly they were back in the arms of their youthful relations. Sometimes too youthful. There were such clashes between young and old souls, but they survived. And lived on to have families of their own. My grandmother married Lukas, who I believe you also knew Elizabeth? And they went on to have three children. Gretchen would tell me stories when I was little of the young witch who wanted to save her when she was nothing but a bodiless soul. She would always end the tale in tears as she remembered how cruel she had been and how frightened, and sick, she had made the young woman."

Greta walked over to Elizabeth and crouched next to her on the floor. "When Grandmamma told her stories of the young witch and how she wanted to say thank-you and apologise to her for the discomfort she caused her, I knew one day I would be the one to pass on the message. So thank-you little witch," Greta said holding Elizabeth's hands tightly, "thank-you for all of my family, for all of Branko. Thank you for not giving up on us."

Greta dropped her head into Elizabeth's hands and wept softly.

"It's OK," Elizabeth said nervously, feeling thoroughly undeserving of such gratitude. "Anyway, it's like Buddy said, none of us could have done it without everyone else. We all played our part in saving Branko, including your Grandmother."

The next few days passed in a haze for the witches and George. George barely said a word to the villagers. The impact of his actions was slowly dawning on him and he was unable to look any of them in the eye. Their collective politeness meant that they were never rude to George but his presence was never welcome. As best as they could the four adventurers rested and recuperated so they had strength enough to attempt the journey home.

On the fourth morning of their stay Shiona announced they were fit enough to travel and they would be making their way home that very night. Elizabeth was relieved. As kind as the people were, the whole Branko experience had been life-changing and she was finding it difficult to make small talk with the descendants of the people she had only really known in soulless form. She tried with difficulty to make the transition from fighting for her life to chit-chatting with people that were strangers to her but she just wanted to go home. She had a lot of questions for her mother *and* her father.

"I really wish you would stay, there are so many things left to ask you," Greta said sadly after Shiona's announcement.

"I'm sure you have," Daphne said putting an arm around Greta, "but there comes a time when you have to live your life. You have to move on now from ancient stories about witches and devils. We all do."

"I understand. You are right Daphne," Greta replied, "but please remember that our doors are always open if you want to return one day."

"I doubt that will happen," Shiona said bluntly, "but thank you anyway."

Shiona walked across to Greta's mantelpiece and looked at the painting of Gretchen hanging above it. It was the same picture that Elizabeth had seen in Gretchen's own home. "But I would like to see them one more time," Shiona continued.

"Who?" Greta asked.

"Your ancestors," Shiona replied, "the villagers of Branko. Our friends. Where are they now?"

"Shiona? Are you alright?" Daphne said cautiously approaching her sister. "You do know they probably died a long time ago."

"Of course I know that Daphne I'm not an imbecile! I just want to see their final resting place. I want to pay my respects before I leave. I want to see where they were buried."

"Oh, I see," Greta said, "of course. We can take you there this afternoon. The cemetery is not far from where we found you. The Baron owned the land and he made sure that it could not be sold or modernised in anyway. It is still a fitting memorial to them. All the Branko families that were devastated by Darius's actions are there – resting in peace."

The journey to the graveyard was a quiet one. Even Daphne, usually full of jokes and inappropriate humour, was uncharacteristically sombre. Elizabeth knew something of what her aunts must be feeling. She had only known the villagers for a few days but they had had an eternal impact on her. Their resilience and kindness in the face of such atrocity was humbling. Elizabeth considered the life she lived before meeting these people and coloured with embarrassment and shame at how much she belly-ached and bemoaned her lot. In comparison to the people of Branko she lived an idyllic existence, not living with the perpetual threat of evil hanging over her. The witches, in their annual quest, and the villagers of Branko made sure she stayed safe. Made sure everyone in the world stayed safe.

They stopped next to the cemetery and Shiona was the first to follow Greta out of the car. The graveyard had an unkempt looking façade with ivy climbing up the huge wrought iron gates that led to the graves. The gateway was the only way in, the rest of the graveyard was surrounded by a huge, stone wall that was easily 12 foot high.

Greta scrabbled around on the ground near the bottom of the left hand gate and produced an old iron key.

"Only the relatives of the Branko families know where to find this," Greta said. "It was the Baron's dying wish that these people who had lived through so much were not to be disturbed by any unwanted guests in their final resting place. We are the only ones who are allowed access."

Once inside Elizabeth noticed that the gardens and graves were well maintained and well loved. The appearance of the outside of the cemetery gave no clue as to how beautiful and peaceful the grounds were within.

Greta took Shiona by the arm. Elizabeth was amused to see Shiona jump at this unusual display of intimacy but Greta did not flinch. It was amazing to see how much Greta resembled her great-grandmother, her namesake. She was the same age as the woman that Elizabeth remembered and they both displayed a sincerity and kindness to strangers that Elizabeth had never known.

Shiona and Greta walked on ahead and Elizabeth could see Greta talking quietly to Shiona as they passed the graves. Daphne and Elizabeth walked a respectful distance behind and George began to follow them.

"I don't think so George," Daphne said, "you don't really deserve to be in here now do you?"

George did not dare argue with Daphne. He backed away sheepishly and waited at the gates.

Elizabeth and Daphne carried on and Elizabeth linked arms with her aunt.

"You OK?" She asked.

"Course Betty," Daphne said wiping away a tear as she read a name on one of the gravestones. "You know me."

"I think I do," Elizabeth said and patted her aunty on the arm.

They walked passed grave after grave. Some names Elizabeth recognised but others she did not. In front of them Elizabeth could hear Greta explaining to Shiona that some of the graves belonged to the families that were left behind when Branko first disappeared. These were the people that Shiona and Daphne never met.

"We heard a lot about them though," Shiona explained to Greta. "Over the years there was much said about the loved ones that were lost to them. How strange it must have been to see them again."

"Indeed," Greta said, "they certainly found it difficult to adjust."

Suddenly something caught Greta's eye. "There," she said, "these are the graves I wanted to show you."

Greta and Shiona made their way quickly to another part of the cemetery ahead of Elizabeth and Daphne. Once they were there Elizabeth saw Shiona's legs buckle under her. Greta grabbed her quickly to stop her from falling to the ground and Elizabeth and Daphne ran to her side.

"Alright old girl?" Daphne asked as she sat her sister gently on the ground.

Shiona grabbed hold of Daphne's arms and looked desperately up at her, "it's Greta," she said shakily, "and Yorik. They're here."

Daphne took a sharp breath and slowly got to her feet. She motioned for Elizabeth to look after Shiona and walked towards the graves. Elizabeth watched the giant of a woman crumble. She did not drop to the floor or wail in misery, but something of Daphne died that day.

"You have to excuse us," Daphne said as she choked back the tears. "It's difficult for us to understand that the people we fought desperately to save, less than a week ago, are now dead."

"Please," Greta said as she moved Daphne away from the grave, "I do understand and I think it is time for you to go now."

"But..." Shiona said.

"She's right Shiona," Daphne said, "there's no relief to be found here. We should just remember them how they were a few days ago. And we need to keep reminding ourselves that they lived out their lives in peace. Now let's go home."

Daphne helped Shiona off the ground and supported her as they made their way back towards the gates.

"Wait a minute," Elizabeth said stopping them in their tracks. "What's that?"

A small building caught her eye just behind Yorik and Greta's graves almost blocked from view by some overgrown bracken.

"Oh yes," Greta said, "I forgot. That is the Baron's tomb. He shares it with his wife. His children left Branko many, many years ago and only the Baron and his wife remained. The story goes that he sent them out into the world to find husbands and wives that were not related to the Branko inhabitants. Some of the villagers were angry, said that he thought the Branko families were not good enough for his precious children. They were insulted that he should feel this way after everything they did for him, the sacrifices they made. But the story goes that he calmed them by saying they would not have been saved if his children had not been forced to find their way in the wider world. He lived on long after my great-grandmother and grandmother died. I even remember sitting on his knee."

"You remember him?" Elizabeth asked incredulously.

"I do," he was a very funny old man. Nothing like you would expect him to be. The stories of him are full of his youthful prowess, but I knew him as a raspy old man with a long white moustache." Greta giggled at the memory, "he looked more like a wizard than a warrior."

Elizabeth tried to smile but a tear trickled down her face, "Greta?" she asked. "Did anyone ever call him Buddy?"

"Not that I recall," Greta said. "Why?"

"It doesn't matter." Elizabeth said and searched in her pocket for her last link with him, the penny sized green stone that contained her family's power. She walked away from her great-grandfather's grave knowing she would never return.

Shiona, Daphne and Elizabeth sombrely walked away from the graves to the entrance of the graveyard. Suddenly Shiona stopped abruptly and Daphne and Elizabeth collided with the older witch.

"Shiona!" Daphne chastised. "Be careful!"

"What's that?" Shiona asked and pointed towards a shimmering clearing deep within the cemetery.

"Ah," Greta said solemnly, "that is somewhere we do not dare to go. That is the final resting place of Darius's evil soul."

Shiona started marching towards it.

"I will not join you on this visit Shiona," Greta called after her.

Shiona just waved her hand impatiently and carried on. Elizabeth and Daphne followed quickly behind her.

"Is this wise, old girl?" Daphne said cautiously as they approached the spot.

In front of them was an area that had been paved over with an enormous concrete pentagon. The ground above the pentagon shimmered with all the dazzling colours of the rainbow. Each colour layered over the other finished off with a sparkling, white, translucent blanket. The beauty of the picture belied the evil within.

"I had to be sure," Shiona said. "I had to know he was gone, and gone forever." She nodded her approval. "Nothing's getting past those spells! It looks like they threw everything at him."

"Let's go home," Daphne said putting her arm on Shiona's shoulder and led her sister away.

The sun was setting as they waved goodbye to Greta and climbed back up the hill to the place where their journey had started. Greta had wanted to stay with them. Say her final farewells as she watched them soar into the sky on their brooms but Shiona insisted that she should not. She told Greta to think of them as another story told by one of her relatives, a fairy-tale, to be enjoyed but to be left where it belonged, in the imagination. Reluctantly Greta agreed and the witches were left alone, with George, waiting for darkness to conceal their journey home.

"How are we going to do this then?" Elizabeth asked.

"What's that Betty?"

"Well there are four of us and two brooms. Are we going to ride in tandem?"

"You're not jumping on with me my girl," Shiona said, "just pick up a twig and grow your own."

"I can't," Elizabeth said sulkily. "It's not the same without Sonny."

"That's where we've got a little surprise for you Betty." Daphne smirked.

"What? You've got Sonny?"

"No you donut! He got sucked back into Branko didn't he," Daphne said. "But there's always this."

Daphne walked over to an old tree that looked as though it had been there for centuries. It was gnarled and majestic and was covered in pine needles and cones.

"How the hell am I supposed to fly that home?" Elizabeth asked thinking that her aunty had finally snapped.

"Honestly Betty, you can be a bit thick. What do you think this is?"

"I'm guessing – pine tree, *Aunty* Daphne considering it's riddled with pine cones!"

"For goodness sake Betty. Alright then, let me ask this another way, *who* do you think this is?"

"Do you want to give me another clue here Daphne 'cos you're not making any sense.........oh... OH!"

"Give the girl a prize, she finally got it." Daphne said as Elizabeth ran over to the old tree.

"It's Sonny! Is this Sonny?"

"It is Little One," Shiona said with a smile, "now why don't you cast your growing spell and let's go home."

Elizabeth snapped off a branch and cast her growing spell. Sonny *Junior* sprang to life.

"Atta girl Betty."

"Daphne?"

"Yes Betty."

"You do know I HATE being called Betty don't you."

"Of course I do Betty." With that she climbed on her broom, grabbed George and zoomed into the sky.

"She's a pain in the a......."

"I know I know," Shiona said, "and she's cocky about flying too. Although she *is* carrying that extra weight." Shiona looked slyly at Elizabeth. "Shall we race her home?"

"Let's do it!" Elizabeth said.

And the eldest and youngest witch leapt onto their brooms and soared into the sky easily passing Daphne and laughing as they left her behind.

****

The flight back to Scotland was over before they knew it. Daphne tried to gain ground on the other two witches but as soon as they sensed her getting close they effortlessly zoomed ahead of her again.

"That's not fair!" she called.

"We could just talk," Elizabeth heard George say from behind Daphne after another failed attempt to overtake them.

"Oh shut up George!" Daphne said sulkily and they rode on in silence.

Eventually Shiona dropped Elizabeth outside her little cottage just on the outskirts of Edinburgh. Daphne and George hovered in the air next to them.

"Quickly Shiona," Daphne said. "We don't want to be caught flying

327

home when the sun rises."

"You go on," Shiona said impatiently. "Don't you worry about me."

"Bye-bye then Betty," Daphne said as she took to the sky once more. "See you at work tomorrow."

"Work?!" Elizabeth called after the departing figure.

"Oh aye Elizabeth." Shiona said with a wry smile. "You don't expect to get a sick day just because you saved the world do you? We need you in the shop."

Elizabeth smiled.

"But seriously, Elizabeth, what are you going to do now?"

"Oh I don't know," Elizabeth sighed. "Mum and Dad have got a lot of explaining to do for one thing. Especially about the two aunties I seem to have acquired!"

"Well don't give them too much of a hard time. I'm sure they thought they were protecting you."

"I know," Elizabeth said and produced Buddy's green disc from her pocket. "I've also got to give this back to Dad. It is his after all."

"Are you sure you want to do that?" Shiona asked. "If Buddy was right then it could give you your own power. You won't need to be around us to be magical."

"But it still amounts to the same thing doesn't it Shiona? Borrowing from you or borrowing from a stone. It's still not going to be me. If I'm meant to have powers then I'll have them – one day. Otherwise it just doesn't seem right."

Shiona looked sympathetically at her niece. "If you're sure?" she said.

"I am."

Suddenly Shiona pulled Elizabeth towards her.

"You did yourself proud back there Little One. Thank-you."

Elizabeth was startled by the affection and only managed to say "s'alright" in response to her auntie's sincerity.

Releasing Elizabeth from the awkward hug Shiona climbed onto her broom.

"I hate to admit that Daphne might be right, but the sun is coming up. I'd better go. You don't have to come to the shop tomorrow, but that's where we'll be if you need company."

"What about George?"

"We'll have to do something with him," Shiona said pondering the question. "We can't take him to the police and he won't survive in the world on his own after all the horrors he's seen."

"Will any of us," Elizabeth said quietly.

"You are stronger than you think you are Elizabeth Mary Livewell! Don't you forget it!"

"There's one thing I don't get Shiona. If Darius invaded Branko hundreds of years ago, how can Buddy be *my* great-grandfather? The timings just don't add up."

"Let's just say....," Shiona said considering how best to answer her, "that longevity runs in magical families Elizabeth."

"Longevity? Does that mean.....? Do you...........?" Elizabeth paused. "Do you know what – I don't even want to know."

"Best not to worry about it now Little One. These things will be explained in the fullness of time."

With that Shiona took to the sky and flew away.

Elizabeth watched her until she was nothing but a speck in the distance. When Shiona had all but disappeared Elizabeth turned to the front door of her little cottage. She reached for the key that she left under a plant pot on the doorstep when she noticed a piece of paper poking out underneath the front door.

At the top of the page, in blue ink, Elizabeth recognised her mother's undeniable scrawl. She had written: *I knew it was going to be OK when this changed.*

It was the parchment with the same story that had sparked Elizabeth's interest all those months ago. It was the account of the Baron and Ryder but this time it ended with an additional paragraph.

At the exact moment that the protective shield around Branko was created, that removed it from time and space, the village reappeared. The Baron and the witches walked cautiously into Branko and saw a sight that chilled them. Their home had been destroyed and amongst the devastation was a young man recognisable as Ryder. He was lying lifeless in the arms of an ancient soldier. The villagers of Branko told tales of the decades they spent trying to keep Darius from gaining powers and how he was finally defeated by witches from the future and an older version of the Baron himself. And all of this happened in a blink of an eye for those who escaped Darius's reign.

"*Witches from the future*," smirked Elizabeth. "Maybe I'm not magical," she said aloud to the early winter morning. "Maybe I was only ever meant to share someone else's powers. Who knows? All I know is – *this* is me. And I'm home."

THE END

Lightning Source UK Ltd.
Milton Keynes UK
UKOW04f0749180815

257099UK00001B/6/P